STARLIGHT'S ETERNITY SAGA

A FEAR OF KRONOS

BOOK 2 OF THE SARAH TRILOGY

COLTON HANING

Jaded Media LLC

A Fear of Kronos

Cover design by Indiana Maria Acosta Hernandez aka Indicreates
Paperback ISBN: 979-8-9908931-3-9
Hardcover ISBN: 979-8-9908931-4-6
Ebook ISBN: 979-8-9908931-5-3

JADED
MEDIA

CONTENTS

"Mastery over the mind comes at a cost — those who wield it too long forget which thoughts are theirs and which belong to the madness."

- Arkan Voss, Tales of the Butterfly's Crypt

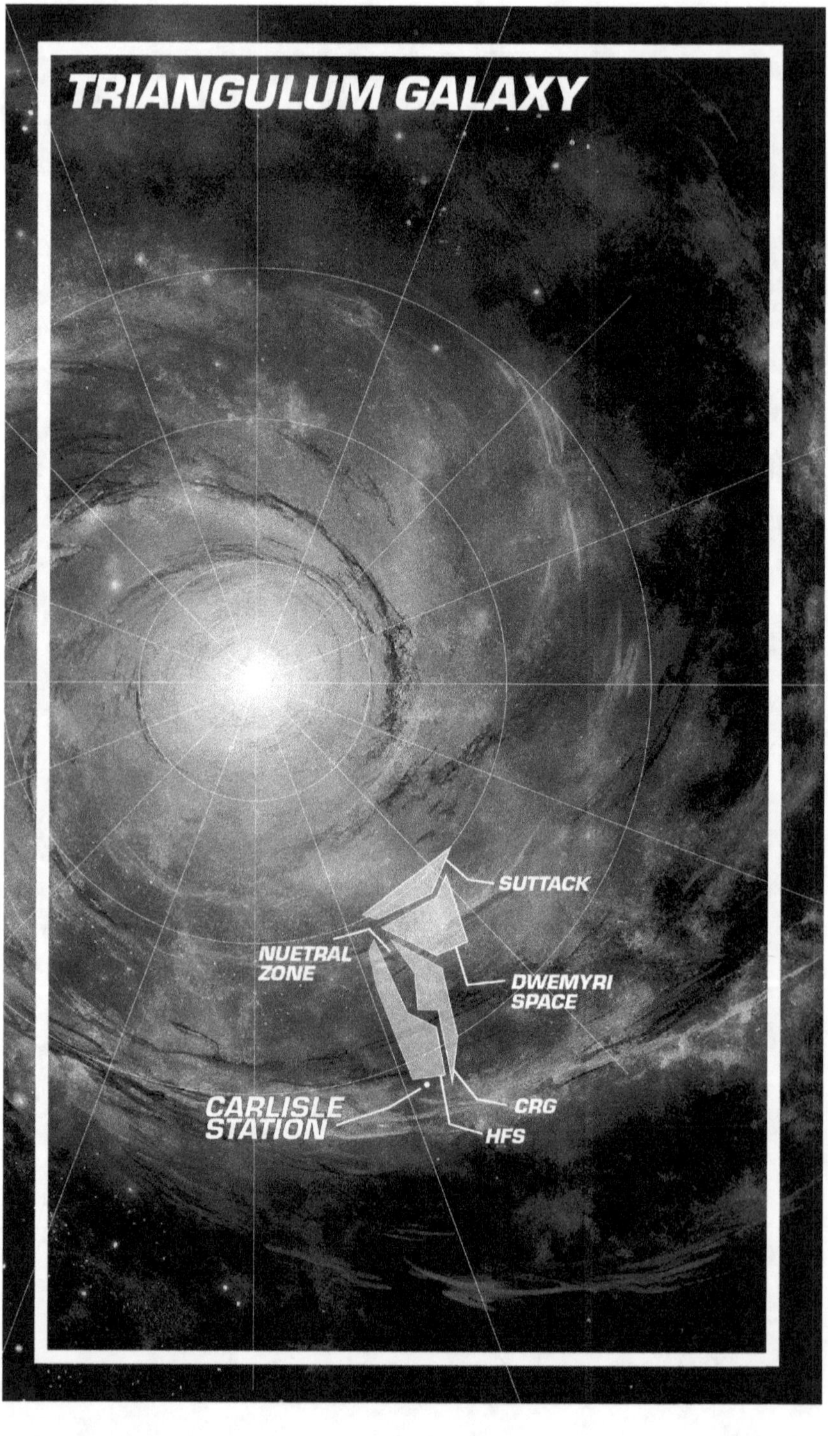
TRIANGULUM GALAXY
SUTTACK
NUETRAL ZONE
DWEMYRI SPACE
CARLISLE STATION
CRG
HFS

PART 1

PROLOGUE

1

The scritch-scritching and the scratch-scratching of a feather quill dragging ink across an aged parchment brought peace to William's otherwise tormented mind. Heights, especially at his age where bones cracked like dried twigs, were something to be feared. Taking notes in one of his thousands of ledgers was a way to create a momentary distraction from his current reality, a reality which William was doomed to repeat until the day he sucked in his last breath. For him, however, death may still be a distant dream. More augmentation than flesh, William had stopped counting his birthdays after the hundred and seventieth. Instead, he surrendered himself to his duties and homed in on his work. Glancing up from his notes to triple check the volume number of the book he had just returned; William did his best to not look down. With his anti-grav chair keeping him suspended hundreds of feet above the stone floor of the library, its lone engine sputtering and muttering, it proved to be a task too difficult. He glanced down, and his vision began to swirl in an instant. He focused on his hands, lumped and swollen as they were, and now clasped tight around the handholds of his chair with crooked fingers pointing in every direction save the correct one. His body was little more than clusters of unused flesh, pooled into a circular seat and held together by countless mechanical and cybernetic technologies.

"Master Ledger, indeed," he muttered to himself.

He pulled his eyes away from his mutilated hands to glare

up at the sky. Yellow light spilled in through the skylights of Xaranor's endless library. Rising story after story, and spanning across an endless distance, William was certain one could fit a small city within the library's confines. Instead, rows of bookshelves created an impenetrable labyrinth that not even he could navigate without the help of the navigation tools integrated into his dreaded, floating chair. Spawned from the tortuous sun of this backwater system to hammer away at the surface of this horrid desert planet, the light lingered for a hellish thirty-six hours a day before sinking back down across the horizon. The only thing saving William from melting away in the heat was the thick panels of thermal glass embedded in the ceiling which filtered out the heat and the harmful ultraviolet and converted them into energy for the library to utilize. There was a faint pink hue to the light shimmering through with the yellow which meant it was that time of year. Somewhere out in that desert groups of children would be slaughtering each other atop blood-soaked pyramids for their right to become morak'casai. A barbaric practice, but William could not argue its effectiveness.

He sighed, scribbled another note, and pushed another book back into its rightful place amongst its family. William loved the tactile feel of real books. It was a rare pleasantry in his life, getting to handle such delicate relics. He kept meticulous digital backlogs, of course, but here he saved the originals. He was, by far, the youngest thing in this library, and William liked to fantasize that some of these books may even be timeless works that survived their ancestors' travels across the great void. He laughed at himself for believing in such stories, but the idea of ancient humans once migrating to this galaxy from the Milky Way was a fable too exciting to ignore.

His brief moment of joy was shattered with the thunderous sound of a mallet slamming against a leather drum. Visitors were summoning him. He tilted his chin, thick flaps wobbling as he did so, and sniffed the air. Faint staleness lingered with enough motes of dust dancing about to help remind William of the last time he had any visitors come to the library. It had to have been at least six months ago, maybe seven. Loathsome things, guests were.

They always wanted something from him, and in most cases, it required the removal of one of his precious books. Grumbling, he punched the coordinates for the entrance into his chair. The engine whined, but soon enough he was buzzing through the labyrinth at an uncomfortable speed. Humming an old tune helped keep his mind away from the height. Before long, the view of towering bookshelves gave way to a monolithic gate of sandstone looming over a balcony held up by pillars of an impossible size. Their tan stone was carved to make the pillars look like the scholars of old holding up the balcony above their heads. The scene extended into the gate where an ornate depiction of the founding members of the library signing the first ledger was carved in intricate detail.

Though difficult to make out from this distance, William could see the figure of his assistant ledger standing near a drum a hundred times his size at the opposite end of the balcony from the gate. A mallet swung from a nearby chain as only a pulley system could be used to wield the mighty thing. He pushed his chair to go faster, wanting to be done with whatever business these new visitors might have. Drawing in close to hover a mere meter above the stone balcony, he inspected his assistant with an upturned nose. Everett looked as bad as William felt. Though the man had remained natural in both flesh and mind, a stark contrast to William, he looked to be on the constant edge of death. A simple brown robe clung to a frame withered away by more years than any natural born human had the right to live. Pale skin stretched tight over a bulbous and bald skull while wet, sunken eyes peered back up at William with a worried expression. Looking into those eyes reminded William of sunken craters on a planet with no atmosphere.

"Visitors, Master," Everett said while scrubbing one hand with the other. His voice sounded as dry as his skin. "They come seeking entrance to the library."

"What else would they be doing here?" William asked. He meant it as a rhetorical question more to himself, but Everett nodded in response as if the Master Ledger had made some scholarly discovery.

"Of course, Master," he said, and bobbed his head again.

"You are so very wise, Master."

"Who?" William croaked.

"The twins," Everett said, and William swore under his breath. "They've brought with them another guest as well. They did not give a name, but it appears to be a Suttack."

William spluttered a wet cough. "A Suttack? An actual Suttack? And with the twins? I'll be a thousand cycles dead before I let a creature like that step foot into a human library."

"Of course, Master," Everett bobbed his head, "but they've brought express permission from Zammon."

"So, Zammon thinks he has jurisdiction over Xaranor's sacred library?" William asked. "The Five will be hearing about this. Mark my words, Everett, and they'll be most displeased."

"Of course, Master, most displeased," Everett said with a final bob of his pale skull.

"Do they at least have Kade with them?" William asked. "He can keep those two in check."

"I'm afraid not, Master," Everett said. "Kade was sent on an urgent mission which he has yet to return from. However, Master, it is rumored the morak'casai newly assigned to them is of a higher prowess than even Kade."

William let out a pained sigh but waved a crooked hand. Everett nodded at the gesture and flicked his wrist at the gate. Deep rumbling echoed throughout the library as stone ground against stone, and the gargantuan doors began to separate. Four figures marched through the widening gap as if this library belonged to them, led by no one else but the twins. It was a rare occasion that a conduit was deemed so dangerous that a morak'casai was preemptively assigned to watch over them at all times. The usual method was to send the warriors out after the problem had presented itself. And here, marching through the gates of his library, were two such conduits. Clad in their black cloaks with their feathered collars, the two bore identical scarlet hair, shaved on one side, but flowing like a river down the other to sweep across the shoulder. Though one was male, the other female, it was impossible to tell the two apart. In William's mind, it didn't matter. They were both equally loathsome. Behind them, their lethal shadow followed in step. The white mask pointed forward as the warrior's dark robes swished about, but William knew every detail about the library was being analyzed regardless of how at ease the morak'casai appeared to be. To the warrior's left was the Suttack. The horrid alien stood head and shoulders taller than its companions making it hard to ignore. Violet silks swept across the Suttack's wiry frame and glints of gold shone at every opportunity. The Suttack reminded William of bipedal hairless cats that had grown too far along the evolutionary chain. The one exception being the narrow strip of carapace that ran from the top of their foreheads down to the tips of their thin tails to cover the entirety of their spinal columns.

"Honored guests," William called out to them as they approached. They walked past Everett as if he were not there and stopped in front of William. Only the Suttack bothered to bow. Perhaps the creature was not so horrid after all. At least it knew its manners. "I am loath to see Kade no longer in your company. What business could be so important as to draw away such a leader."

"Cracked conduit," the female twin said. Sri, William believed her name was. "Vincent destabilized at Sondra's hand, and Kade was sent to deal with them."

"Ah, a noble cause," William said. "He will bring them to justice."

"He's dead," the other twin said. Mudiwa was his name if memory served. "Along with his entire team. It's part of what brings us here, actually. Sondra and Vincent turned out to be separatists."

The knowledge of Kade's death was a blow that took William's breath away. He was one of the best, and to be felled by simple rebels felt like an insult to their entire institution. The first time the man had set foot in William's library, he was not but a boy. A lethal boy, but still only a child. William had taken a liking to him even then. There was a noble duty about Kade that was hard to find these days. Despite the brutish upbringing the morak'casai were subjected to, Kade still found a sense of honor in all he did. The universe felt a little emptier without him in it. To their credit, the twins let the information sink in, not pressing further until

William seemed ready.

"What is this business about, then?" William asked. He eyed the Suttack who seemed disinterested in his despair. "Why have you brought this stranger into my library?"

"We sent Cloudburst to investigate," Sri said. Behind her, the Suttack yawned. "What the crew found was an AI with some very interesting details."

"We believe the separatists have information about the Well," Mudiwa said. William attempted to look nonplussed at the mention of the Well, but the twins saw right through it. "You know of what I speak."

"A myth," William said, "a fable. The Eternity Well is nothing more than a legend told by treasure hunters and bards. To think separatists could find knowledge of such a thing is an insult."

"It is, of course, it is," the Suttack finally spoke up. William's translator chip had difficulty keeping up with its strange dialect, and he narrowed his eyes at the creature. "I have been confided in by your very own council to confirm if such knowledge holds any water. To my dismay, the information the AI managed to collect from the separatists is troubling, to say the least."

"Where is this AI?" William asked. "I would like to speak with it myself, if I could."

The twins exchanged a glance with one another, and Sri gave a nod before saying, "gone."

"The captain of Cloudburst attempted to bring back a partition of the AI they called Gayle," Mudiwa said, "but it vanished from their systems claiming it had unfinished business elsewhere."

William tapped a finger on the arm of his chair. The news these two brought him was growing more and more troubling with each word. *Business?* What *business* did any AI have? How did separatists of all people manage to find information about a relic Xaranor had only dreamt of? If the Starlight Eternity Well *did* exist, and the separatists *did* have information on it, no wonder the council was willing to bring in outside help. A Suttack, however, was not where William would expect to find that help. Their whole civilization held an isolationist policy due to their fear of outside influences on their culture. So much so, they went to war with any group that dare enter their territories. Religion was the primary cause. Not their religion, but the fear of religion in general. The practice of religious beliefs nearly wiped out their entire civilization which led the Suttack to ban its existence from their entire cultural identity. They filled the gap with lavish art and gratuitous amounts of luxury. The Suttack before him represented that ideal quite nicely with its many pieces of jewelry and silk robes. He was allowing himself to be distracted. William tapped a command on the arm of this chair, and a holo-feed projected above his armrest. It displayed a map of his entire library. He flicked a crooked finger to pan over it. The group before him watched with intense interest as he stopped on one particular shelf.

"I may have a book, or two," he said, and pointed at the shelf. "I have a condition if you wish to see them."

"Oh?" Sri asked. "And what might this condition be?"

"I'm in no shape to leave this library," William said. "I fear I am both blessed and cursed to forever remain within its walls. My assistant, however, is very capable of leaving on his own two legs. If you plan to investigate the Well, I insist you take him with you. If I can't go, at least someone can be there as my proxy. It would be a shame for such a discovery to go uncatalogued, or worse, cataloged by a group of uneducated savages like yourselves."

"Very well," Sri said, and all save the morak'casai nodded their agreement. Everett looked as if he were choking. His sunken eyes were wide and looked ready to fall out of his head. His mouth worked, but no words escaped his tongue. Holding up a long, narrow finger, Everett tried to call attention to his situation, but only succeeded in being further ignored. Giving up on speech, Everett dropped his hand and returned to dry washing them.

With that business being settled, William tapped the co-ordinates into his navigation, and allowed his chair to fly him off toward the indicated shelf. In his younger years, William would have leapt at any opportunity to run off chasing fables, his library be damned. Alas, those years were far behind him. He allowed himself to fantasize as he buzzed through bookshelf after book-shelf until his chair came to a stop. It lowered him all the way down to the ground floor and brought him before a tome nearly the size of his own body. Gold script was painted across its cracked, leather-bound spine, and William found himself running a ruined hand across its surface. Starlight's Eternity Saga was the title written in gold with no author mentioned. William removed the book carefully with both hands. Setting it in his lap, he felt the urge to crack it open and immediately read its contents from cover to cover. He refrained.

A butterfly, red wings with pale blue dots, flitted nearby to land on the book's corner. Shocked that such an insect could find its way into his sanctuary, William brushed it away only for it to land on the other corner. He could not kill the pest. Not only was violence against his nature, but it could damage his book. Instead, he let it be, hoping beyond hope the bug would fly away once he started moving. He took one final look at the cover before grumbling about having to give it up. Whatever storm was stirring up in the galaxy, William was afraid he was going to have to miss it. He patted the book and started back toward the balcony.

2

No one knew if Zammon was human. He appeared to be human in regards of shape and form, but his size belied his true origins. Pacing in front of Commander Malkus, the giant in golden armor made this large reading chamber look small. Glow orbs levitated around the walls of the cylindrical room, making up for the lack of windows. Their yellow light shone across rough, sandstone walls and ancient tapestries. The wooden desk at the room's center rattled with each new step Zammon took. His golden mask, one half depicting a weeping angel and the other a snarling devil, glinted with light as he passed in front of an orb. It was one of the few times Orian had met the leader of the morak'casai and, in all truth, he hoped it was his last. Compared to the leader of the conduits, this man seemed bellicose on a good day and downright murderous on a bad. However, Orian Malkus remained still in his black uniform with his hands clasped behind his back as to refrain from fiddling with his topknot.

"Kade, Eryn, and Zate are all dead," Zammon said, his voice thunder booming across a darkened sky. "Their trainees died with them."

"Yes, lord," Orian said.

"Sondra and Vincent turned out to be separatists, and are now dead," Zammon said, "so there'll be no bringing him in for questions, and no leads on Doctor Karaska's whereabouts. The AI named Gayle could have given us the information we needed, but disappeared into thin air on the basis that it had business to attend to. Not a single trace was left of it?"

"Not a single trace," Orian said, "but it did leave us with some useful information before it left. Some of which you might find interesting. The first piece of information it gave us was the name of a laboratory Sondra contacted before his death, Kronos Laboratory, followed by the coordinates the signal was sent to. The second, there were two survivors, a Vulture named Jax Vanlaere and an HFS prisoner turned Kara Corporation employee registered as Sarah Vermillion. Their whereabouts are also unknown."

"Find them," Zammon said, "bring them in, and find out more about what happened to Kade. I want to know what role they played."

"Here's the good news," Orian said, "we may be able to sweep up both the separatists, and the two survivors of Carlisle Station in one go."

"Oh?" Zammon asked. "And what makes you believe that?"

CHAPTER 1
- KALLIK -

1

Red was such an appealing color. The planet below glowed with it. As young Kallik looked out through the porthole, and gazed at the wonder of planet Hordred, he could not help but be reminded. Kallik had been born above a red planet, one not so dissimilar to this. That planet, however, had been bathed in fire, and doused in the bloodshed of innumerable people. Too young to recall the events himself, his father had told him all sorts of stories regarding the day of his birth. His people, or Groal as the humans called them, fought a war and lost. According to his father, the alien species known as the Suttack were not a merciful people. They hunted down and expunged every last pocket of resistance until the Groal had no planet left to call home. Kallik's birthplace was the last of these pockets. According to the accounts told by his father, Kallik's ship was attempting to flee, but his mother went into labor. Using the jump drives during the birthing process would have killed them both, so they held. For thirty grueling hours they held, hiding beneath the shadow of the moon while the rest of their kin were slaughtered on the planet below. Kallik shuddered at the fear his parents must have felt.

A hand grabbed his shoulder, and Kallik jumped. Twisting to see who interrupted his thought. His right antler scraped against the porthole causing an echoing screech to sound throughout his cabin, and Kallik winced. The laughing face of his eldest cousin, Amic, beamed at him. Amic's own antler, singular due to the left one being shorn off making his cousin appear lopsided and human-looking, was much larger than either of Kallik's. Several tips were tinted a deep black, marking Amic's adulthood. Kallik tried to put on an angry face, he hated being startled, but wherever his cousin went he brought enough joy with him to fill a room. Suppressing a grin, he batted away the hand which rattled as numerous gold bracelets and silver rings clacked against one another. His cousin wore his usual finery in the form of a red silk robe and more jewelry than Kallik could point out.

"They'll be growing much faster now," Amic said. He flicked the singular point of Kallik's left antler, still the pale color of bone. "Now that you're eleven they'll grow faster than you're used to, and you'll feel like a clumsy toddler. Not long now, and they'll even start to darken a bit, I'm sure."

"What do you want?" Kallik asked. "I'm too busy for your goading."

"*So* busy, I can tell," Amic said, sparing a glance through the porthole. "Believe it or not, I came to wish my favorite cousin a happy birthday."

"It was yesterday."

"I know," Amic said, "but yesterday was a bit complicated."

It was true. The day prior had been busy for Kallik's entire family. Running a trade ship in the middle of a neutral zone between two opposing human factions came with an insurmountable number of complications; complications which Kallik's father tried to teach him about daily. A swarm of facts regarding the relationships and standings between different groups of smugglers and Vultures swam through his head, and trying to keep them all straight yesterday was a pain. Members of high standing trade routes belonging to a Vulture colony ship visited his father with the promise of great opportunity. Kallik tried to do his part, but he was often dismissed with a smile as the real bargaining was for the adults. He spent the rest of his birthday sulking in his room, wishing he could have done anything but.

"I think we may have found a way to make it up to you," Amic said. He gestured to the door of Kallik's cabin which he had left open. Light from the corridor beyond spilled in, wrapping the small space with its artificial glow. Where Amic dressed in lavish attire, Kallik decorated his cabin with every gift his family had ever bestowed upon him. Silk pillows glinted gold, and sewn tapestries from the furthest reaches of the galaxy were draped on every wall. It was a safe space for him; a place where he could hide and feel comforted from his worries and woes. It was a place where he could use his data slate to read stories rather than lectures. It was a place where Kallik was free to be a kid without the looming expectations of his oncoming adulthood. He gave his room a final look before letting himself be ushered into the corridor.

Kallik's simple green tunic swished as he tried to keep pace with his cousin who hurried down the narrow passageway of dark metal adorned with a menagerie of fine art, and souvenirs traded for in distant places. Overhead lights beamed a golden-yellow, a color his father claimed added to the ambiance of their vessel. Kallik, however, thought it just made everything look old. The spices his father used to scent the ship only added to that sentiment. Amic looked over his shoulder with an excited grin. Whatever they planned must have been big, and the excitement started to spread to Kallik. His own face widened to a smile which widened even further when he heard a rumbling voice call his name from down the corridor. Stopping in his tracks, he turned to see a hulking figure leaning out of a doorway. Kallik's father was a mass of black beard, muscled shoulders, and enough gut to make any chef nervous. Beneath sprawling antlers, he bore a grin to rival that of Amic's and golden robes so ornate that his cousin looked a mere commoner in his presence. Coming the rest of the way out of the doorway, he strutted down the corridor toward the pair bellowing the whole way.

"You didn't think you were going to show him his birthday gift without me, did you?" He asked. "No way in all the universe I'd miss the look on my little trade prince's face when sees it. Hurry up, and let's get to the bridge."

Kallik's father waved one hand in a hurried motion toward the direction of the bridge while placing the other on Kallik's back to push him along. The trio wound their way through the ship in this manner until they reached the bridge that resided in the center. Fashioned in the style of a bazaar with hanging silks, shelves lined with trinkets, and golden bowls of odd gems and strange stones scattered about, the bridge's openness further defined by its domed ceiling stood in contrast with the narrow passageways of the rest of the ship. The lighting at least, Kallik had to admit, brought the entire ship together. At the bridge's center stood a large circular table of stone with numerous control displays lit up at each seat. Twinkling, and floating above the middle of the table was a holo-projected map. It displayed the layout of their current system with a red dot marking their ship.

Sitting next to each other at separate terminals was a pair of humans. The first, a bald-headed man wearing loose white silks, leaned over to the second, a stout woman in violet robes with gray hair piled atop her head, and pointed at something displayed on her terminal. Harold and Tilda were their names. Such human names, short and lacking punch. Kallik had few interactions with the pair, and he preferred it that way. Both of them were stuffy, and old, and both of them held opinions to match. Tilda started to mumble something in argument to whatever Harold had pointed out, but the two of them fell silent when Kallik's father led him over to the table. They both gave Kallik's father a pointed look. Harold looked as if he wanted to speak but didn't.

"Pull up the map," his father said, "you know, the one we discussed earlier."

"Yessir," Harold said, his voice as smooth as his scalp.

He straightened in his seat, punched a few commands into the terminal, and the map shifted and swirled to show a different system. A single planet expanded until it was the only thing floating above the table. The blue light of the rotating planet contrasted against the yellow of the overhead lights, creating a vibrant atmosphere in the bazaar. His father pointed a thick finger at the glowing orb, a stupid grin on both his and Amic's face, and Harold expanded the view of what his father pointed to. The map zoomed, panned, and rotated until a city came into view. Animated hovercraft buzzed through the artificial skyline of the rendered city's replica. Kallik was confused. It looked like any other planetary city, but neither his father nor Amic clarified further.

"What it is?" Kallik asked.

"What is it?" Kallik's father roared. His expression turned to incredulity. "That's Teir's Port. Don't you remember Teir's Port? They have dogs there, Kallik, dogs!"

Kallik remembered the dogs, but not the city. The furry bundles of joy were human's largest blessing to the galaxy, and he remembered fighting tooth and antler trying to convince his father to let him keep one. Teir had been the only city to actually have them in large enough quantities for individuals to purchase. He had never cried more than when his father had told him no. Kallik even remembered the exact one he wanted. It was an adorable pup, a brindled mix of browns and blacks, that when fully grown would have big floppy ears and a slender frame.

"You're getting me a dog?" Kallik asked. He couldn't keep the hesitation from his voice, as if it may yet be some trick. "A real-life dog?"

"Only if I can help pick it out," Amic said. "I missed the last time we stopped there."

"Yes," his father said, "we're getting you a dog."

"See?" Harold interrupted and pointed at Tilda's display. "I told you there's something there. There's something cruising between us and the planet."

"It's just debris," Tilda said.

"We've cataloged all the debris."

"Then you've missed one."

"I haven't missed anything," Harold said, "I'm telling you there's something else there."

"Then send a drone," Kallik's father boomed. His deep voice rumbled, cutting through the pair's argument like a knife through butter. He fixed each with a pointed look. "Figure it out instead of interrupting my family. Where's Hector? Where's that scoundrel gotten off to? Have him send out one of his scanner-drones, and be done with it."

"Of course," Harold nodded, and punched in a few commands while Tilda did the same.

"I heard my name," a smooth voice called out from the

corridor. A human, one of four aboard their ship, walked toward the table with an inappropriate amount of confidence given his station. How his father had been convinced to allow such a person to work under him was beyond Kallik. His long brown hair bobbed as he swaggered to his place at the table, black leather coat extending below his knees. The man named Hector sat down on the opposite side of the stone table, face obscured by the map and grabbed a bundle of his hair in one hand to tie it back with the other.

"If you heard that, you heard the rest," his father said, "hurry up and get to it. You're ruining the moment."

Hector set to work. The map vanished, and in its place a camera feed displayed as the drone was launched toward the planet. Blue light gave way to red as the planet enlarged on the holo-feed, and soon the drone slowed to a stop once its target came into view. Silhouetted by the planet's light, the object was difficult to make out until the drone started to send back images in different spectrums. It was a ship. It looked like a human ship at first, the kind the Federation always touted as being the best modern technology had to offer, but something was off about it. It was a long rectangle interrupted at various points with docking stations, viewing ports, and cylindrical engines. The ship did not have the clean edges, or the proud emblems that would usually adorn an HFS vessel. Instead, it was retrofitted with strange sponsons and patched up with scrap metal. The work wasn't sloppy, or haphazard, but every bit of the ship felt repurposed.

"Skren," his father muttered. "We need to leave. Now. Pack up, power up, and prep for jump."

Tilda sent the orders to the cockpit and opened all communications channels across the ship. Harold, however, sat back in his chair, face turning pale. Amic grabbed the bald man's shoulder and patted him on the back, telling him everything would be fine. Kallik had difficulty keeping the confusion from wrinkling his expression. His father had never mentioned the Skren or who they were in any of his numerous talks on trade. Everyone seemed scared, and now the whole ship was buzzing with ship workers scrambling to their posts. His father's personal security team came marching down one of the corridors to meet them on the bridge. Their golden robes shone proud over the red plates of armor beneath. Each of the five guards held a spear at the ready, and they stood waiting for his father's orders. Kallik tried to get his attention, but he had already gone to his position at the table and was too busy handing out commands. Amic took notice and grabbed Kallik.

"What's happening?" Kallik asked. "What's a Skren?"

"A subspecies of Dwemyri," Amic said. His usual carefree expression had been replaced with one of concern. "They aren't the nice ones, though. In fact, they selectively breed for war. We'll be out of here before they notice us, and well on our way into more secure space. Let's get you back to your room, so the crew can do its work."

"What happens if they catch us?" Kallik asked. Amic only gave him a sad smile and ushered him away from the bridge.

2

Kallik's room felt far more cramped now that he wanted to be elsewhere. What's worse, was their ship had turned away from the planet leaving Kallik with nothing for a view but the black void of space. He could hear the rumbling of the ship's cruising engines as the jump drives warmed up and flinched at a sharp pain in his hand. He hadn't realized he had been picking at a nail and managed to rip away a bit that was still attached to his flesh. Crimson blood welled up, and Kallik sucked on his finger, but his saliva just made the pain worse. Wrapping the finger in the corner of his tunic, he clamped down. He could still hear others bustling about in the corridors outside of his room which made being stuck here all the worse.

A flash of light pulsed outside of the porthole, and the ship lurched with a horrifying groan of bending metal. Kallik was thrown from his bed. He lashed out in an attempt to grab onto something for support but grabbed a tapestry which ripped free of the wall as he tumbled. Crumpled into a heap, Kallik untangled himself from both his blanket and the tapestry. Shouting sounded from somewhere deeper in the ship followed by a sharp crack. Scrambling to his feet, Kallik put an ear to the door and listened. More shouting echoed, and this time a bang. Kallik wanted to open the door but froze. There was no way of telling what could be waiting for him out there, and Amic told him to stay here until after they jumped. Kallik checked the time. The jump was supposed to have happened already. Something was wrong. Torn between fear and curiosity, Kallik's hand hovered near the door's control panel. Another shout compounded the emotions, yet his hand hovered, petrified with indecision. Had the roles been reversed, would his father or Amic have hesitated? Kallik slapped his hand to the panel, and watched it slide open.

Thin, white smoke covered the floor of the corridor beyond while the rest of the air contained a haze. It reacted to the opening of the door, and tendrils spread into his cabin covering Kallik's ankles. A scream of pain drew Kallik's attention. He was unsure if he should head that direction or toward the bridge, but he needed to decide fast. If his father was okay, he would be on the bridge giving out orders. Kallik turned that direction, away from the screaming, and ran down the corridor.

The smoke grew thicker the closer Kallik drew to the bridge, but he kept himself from slowing down. The corridors were quiet, empty, and Kallik could hear his heart pounding in his chest as he ran. He reached the bridge only to find it abandoned. A few of the terminals flickered, but the holo-feed which usually hovered above the table was dead. He glanced around for someone, anyone, but the place was barren. Maybe they all left for the cockpit. Something could have happened to the engines, and the pilots needed help resolving whatever it was. With all the smoke and loud noises, it sounded like a reasonable explanation to him. A shape out of the corner of his eye caught his attention, and a distinct smell wafted across his nose. It was a large heap little more than a dark shadow at the other end of the bridge. Acrid to the nose, there was no mistaking for anything other than a corpse. Kallik took several slow steps toward the shape, but hesitated. If it was someone he knew, he was not sure he would be able to handle it. What if it was his father? Amic? If it had to be anyone, he hoped it was Harold.

Guilt flared through him at the admittance, but he couldn't keep the thought away. Better the bald old man than anyone else.

Kallik needed to know. A few more steps brought him close enough to see the corpse, and a whirlwind of relief and fear swirled through him all at once. The body did not belong to anyone native to this ship. It was neither human nor Groal, but a mass of dark fur and pale skin. A bestial head with long, ribbed ears and a fang filled snout was curled into a final snarl of death. Padded leather armor covered its torso and arms, and long clawed fingers wrapped around the broken shaft of a spear still protruding from its belly. Kallik recognized the spear belonged to one of his father's guards. He hoped that meant his father was safe. He had difficulty pulling his eyes away from the corpse. It was the first one Kallik had ever seen. The smell was worse than the sight of it, and Kallik had to hold a hand up to his nose. He wanted to move on, but his curiosity kept him fixated on it. What was this thing? Was this one of the Skren Amic had told him about?

A hand grabbed Kallik's shoulder, and his heart stopped. One of these creatures was going to kill him, and there was nothing anyone could do about it. He would have screamed if it weren't for the other hand that clamped down over his mouth. Flailing did little good as powerful arms drew him close, and a deep voice attempted to calm him.

"Be still, little trade prince," Kallik recognized the man's voice, but he couldn't pinpoint from where. "I am not going to harm you."

The man drew his hand away from Kallik's mouth and turned him around so they were facing each other. It was one of his father's guards. One of his antlers was cracked, and there was a dark bruise on the side of his cheek. Blood stained the gold of his robes, and Kallik hoped it belonged to the creature and not the guard. Sarrak, he believed his name was. With his glittering eyes, and strong jaw, Kallik remembered this guard to be the one all of the girls were fond of. His usual appeal was worn thin, and worry lined his once smooth face. His dark eyes bored into Kallik's.

"Your father sent me to find you," he said, "but here you are, free of your cabin."

"What happened?" Kallik asked.

"They caught up," Sarrak said. "They sent a boarding party. We dealt with the advance team, but there'll be more. Come on, we need to get you out of here, and to the escape pods."

"Father?"

"Is there waiting for you."

Kallik was pushed toward the other corridor heading toward the cockpit. Waiting along that corridor would be a row of escape pods ready for immediate use. He wandered through the thickening smoke, and felt to make sure his father's guard was close behind. Sarrak tapped his shoulder in a reassuring gesture, and Kallik pressed on. The smoke made it difficult to breathe, and Kallik pulled his tunic up to cover his face. It did not help the stinging of his eyes, however. He found the next corridor and heard several voices. One in particular filled him with relief. The booming voice of his father could be heard billowing out orders in his usual fashion as Amic's voice tried to slip in a word here or there with little success. Emergency ventilation kicked in at last as Kallik hurried down the passageway. Smoke dissipated at a rapid pace. The broad figures of his two loved ones came into view surrounded by a group of other crewmembers and guards. His father was guiding each of them into escape pods with a calm demeanor despite the situation which the others responded to well. It was something father had always lectured Kallik about. When there is chaos, react with peace. The other guards looked little better than Sarrak. Kallik ran to them, and his father swept him up in a grand hug. Over his father's shoulder, Kallik noticed the human Hector trying to cut in line for the escape pods. He should have said something, but at the moment he was content with being in his father's arms.

"There you are!" Kallik's father said. "You were supposed to grab your things, but it's too late for that. Once we get out of here, we can contact the right authorities and have them hunt these bandits down. For now, we -"

His words were cut short as the ship lurched, and a deafening boom blasted through the corridor. Kallik was thrown from his feet and slammed into Sarrak who managed to stay upright.

Everywhere he looked people tumbled, and Kallik held on to Sarrak's arms as if his life depended on it. The ship stilled, and a quiet fell upon the group. Only the guards remained standing, one holding up his father who was halfway to his knees. Several others worked up enough confidence to push themselves back up to their feet, but most remained on the floor waiting for his father's direction. His father, in turn, looked mortified. His lips moved, but no words came out. Something was very wrong. Hissing sounded from one of the escape pod doors, and a bright light flared at the seam. Sarrak let go of Kallik and moved to block the path between the door and the crowd. With his spear gone, Sarrak drew a short blade from beneath his cloak, and took up a readied stance. Other guards followed suit, and Kallik's father slumped to the floor. A look of growing despair spread across his bearded face, and wide eyes rolled over to Kallik. He had never seen his father like this.

"We're too late," he said. "Kallik, my little trade prince, it's time for you to run."

The doors exploded into the corridor, one smashing into a guard flattening him against the far wall. Dark shapes poured from the entrance and assaulted the golden robes. It was more of the creatures Kallik had seen on the bridge. They swung cruel blades with muscle-laden arms, and snarled with delight as several of the guards were felled. Sarrak fought with an expertise unmatched by the others, and for a moment as Kallik watched the man cut down two of the beasts, he thought they might be safe. Then another figure emerged from the dark. It was a tall figure, but this one looked human. Dark robes covered everything but stopped short at the ankles, and a peculiar mask covered the figure's face. It was white, featureless like that of a porcelain doll. However, a black gash ran down one side as if someone had tried to gouge out one of the eyes. The figure stepped forward, a glint of steel flashed, and before Kallik knew what had happened, Sarrak fell over dead with a scarlet slash spread across his throat.

"Find Hector, collect any children you find" the figure said. Its gravelly voice was hardly above a whisper, but it carried, "do what you will with the others, but save a few for the viper pits."

"Run Kallik!" His father screamed, and Kallik ran.

3

No one gave chase when he ran, but the sounds of fighting followed him. Hiding was his first choice, but the where of it proved to be a challenge. He had no way of telling if these creatures had an enhanced sense of smell, but their snouts made Kallik think they might. His cabin would have to do. It was far enough away from the bridge that it would give him time to think. He rushed there, ducked inside, and closed the door. Engaging the door's lock, Kallik took a deep breath and looked around his cabin. Small as it may be, if he scattered enough clutter around, he could still make it next to impossible to find someone. He set to work pulling down tapestries, upending sheets, and making a general mess. An object on the corner of his shelf caught his eye, and he stopped. It was a small figurine made of brass. It depicted the ancient groal hero whom Kallik was named after. It was supposed to be a gift from his mother for his tenth birthday, but his father had given it to him early so he would have something to remember her by. The little brass hero held up a sword in one hand, and a shield in the other.

Kallik snatched it from the shelf, stuffed it in his pocket, and crawled beneath his bed. Had his antlers been any longer, he would not have been able to fit. There were still benefits to his youth. He pulled the sheets down to cover the gap between the floor and the bed, and took a deep breath. It was dark beneath the bed, and only then did he realize he had left the cabin light on when he entered. It was too late. He could hear the clambering of clawed feet rushing past his door. Kallik whispered a silent prayer that the beasts ignored his door. If they did, he could make his way back to his father. He would know what to do. Other escape pod bays were available, but Kallik refused to go on his own. He'd find his father and Amic, and they would all escape this nightmare together.

Something tried to open his door. The panel beeped to indicate access had been attempted but denied. It beeped again, and Kallik held his breath. The creature tapped on the door and mumbled something before a mechanical whirring noise started up. Kallik flinched as he heard a tool grind against the metal panel. The door chimed again, but this time slid open. Kallik's heart tried to beat out of his chest. He could hear the scratching of clawed feet moving closer, and he tensed. Loud sniffing noises were followed by another grumble, and a second creature entered. One slip, one muffled cry, and Kallik would be discovered. He tried not to breathe, but his lungs ached, and his heart betrayed him by pumping even faster. When he was much younger, he would make sure to keep his feet tucked in at night for fear of a monster grabbing one and dragging him beneath the bed. This fear was not so dissimilar to those nights, only this fear was real.

Kallik suppressed a flinch as his sheets were rifled through, and his belongings were tossed around. The sheet he had pulled down to cover the gap rustled, and a tear welled up at the corner of Kallik's eye. The monsters were going to get him. No amount of tucking his feet would save him. He bit back a sob, and the rustling stopped. One of the creatures grunted, slapped something, and the pair stomped out at the same pace they had come in. Kallik let out a sigh, and wiped his eyes. He lingered a few moments longer to be sure the beasts had left, and pulled the sheet aside to check. The cabin was empty. They had thrown around the few things Kallik had left untouched, making his cabin appear even more ransacked. The important thing, however, was he remained undiscovered. He clutched the brass figurine still in his pocket. At least one possession passed by unscathed.

He pulled himself out from under the bed as silently as he could and stole to the door. Peeking his head out revealed an empty corridor, so Kallik made a snap decision. Grabbing a sack, he packed a few of his favorite belongings as rapidly as he could, slung the pack over his shoulder, and headed back down the corridor toward where his father had been. His father was strong, and larger than life itself. He would have survived the scary man in the ugly mask. At least that's what he repeated to himself over and over again as he snuck down the narrow passageways of the ship. At an intersection, Kallik had to duck into a doorway as three more of the creatures stormed past. He gave them a four count and moved on. The entirety of the ship reeked of death, and even though the smoke had cleared, Kallik's eyes stung and his nose burned. He tried to blink away the sting and covered his nose with his free hand. Not long, and Kallik would reach the bridge. Someone started to scream, but the voice was cut off abruptly. He didn't want to think about the who or the what of that scream and forced himself to press on.

4

The bridge was empty once more. It seemed all the beasts had delved deeper into the ship to seek out the survivors. Kallik adjusted the pack over his shoulder which had grown progressively heavier along the way. Its single strap dug in and chaffed. He admitted to himself that not all the things he grabbed were worth dragging out of harm's way, but he liked his possessions. Many of them were gifts, and the thought of losing them made him sad. He patted the bronze figurine in his pocket and twisted it around so the miniature sword would not poke his leg.

The bridge was far too open for Kallik to linger, but he was afraid of what he'd find once he moved on. The next corridor was where he had left his father. He wanted to believe his father had managed to flee, or somehow went unnoticed by the invaders. A sinking pit in his stomach warned him against such hopes, however, and Kallik could not convince his feet to move forward. A red blinking light on one of the terminals caught his attention. It flashed on the far side of the bridge on the opposite side of the table from where he stood. He looked around to reassure himself the bridge was empty, found it was, and made his way over to the terminal. What he found was Tilda. The human woman was curled up on the floor with one hand outstretched toward the terminal. A pool of dark liquid surrounded her, and it took Kallik's mind several moments to register it as blood. It stained her clothes and was spattered across nearby surfaces. It was the first time Kallik had seen a human corpse. It didn't feel real. It was like he was viewing something out of a movie rather than his own life. He hated Tilda, but she never deserved this.

The red light flashed again, and this time Kallik saw what it was. A message ran across the terminal, and a yes or no prompt flashed underneath of it. The message read "Emergency signal blocked. Run diagnostic?" This seemed important, so Kallik set his pack to the side and did the best he could to get to the terminal without stepping through Tilda's blood. It had an overpowering metallic scent, and the sight of it was making him lightheaded. He found the best path was to climb from chair to chair to avoid stepping through the blood while being careful not to stick his hand on a spot that had been hit by the splatter. Reaching the terminal, Kallik hit the blinking "yes." Another message appeared, this time reading "Running bypass diagnostic, analyzing."

It remained this way for several long moments, and Kallik's nerves almost got the better of him. If he stayed here for too long, one of those beasts would find him. He thought he could hear the thumping of clawed feet marching down one of the corridors, but then the message changed. The new readout gave a recommended course of action. It read "Signal blocked by outside data inhibitor. Recommended action to launch drones with identical signals which will activate once outside the inhibited zone. Execute?" Another yes or no prompt flashed. Kallik tapped yes, and watched as the system conducted the procedure, and the drones were launched. With that finished, he could move on to find his father. Careful to follow the same path back to avoid the blood, he picked up his pack and spared the poor human a final glance. He wished he could do something for her, but it was too late.

"I'm sorry," he whispered. He turned to go and found the masked man standing at the entrance to the corridor. The scarred porcelain was staring right at him. Kallik spun on his heel to flee but was blocked by a Skren. It shoved him with a thick fist and sent him sprawling. Kallik fell flat on his back into Tilda's blood. He wanted to be sick. The stench overpowered him, and he could feel the sticky wet soaking into his tunic. Kallik groaned and wanted to retch. The beast loomed over him, smiled through a fang filled maw, and grunted something that his translator-implant did not recognize. It grabbed Kallik by the neck and lifted him from the ground. His feet hung in the air, and Kallik could hear the soft pit-ter-patter of blood dripping from his clothes. The creature pulled a long needle from a leather pouch with its free hand and smiled again. It spoke in a harsh tongue, but this time Kallik's translator picked it up.

"Nighty-night," it said. It jabbed the needle into Kallik's arm, and the effects were immediate. His head swam, his vision faded, and soon Kallik's world sank into nothingness.

CHAPTER 2
- SARAH -

1

Sican IV was just how Sarah remembered it. The arid wind swept over her scalp and through her cloak as she held onto the railing of the balcony. Black feathers rippled with each gust, and Sarah couldn't help but lean out further over the balcony. Far below was the endless wasteland of cracked soil and pale red sand. Unchanged and uncaring despite the immense skyline behind her where megastructures competed in a race to see which of them could climb to the stars. All these cycles and yet nothing was different. The sounds of the city were still deafening with the engines of hovercrafts, cars, and space shuttles all buzzing to and from while being sure to scream of their importance. Sarah never thought she'd be back here in the exact spot that started it all, but here she was.

Eleven months had come and gone since the events on Carlisle Station. The entire ordeal had happened over a span of less than three days, but it left her with a lifetime's worth of horrifying experiences. She had spent every day since then remotely discussing with a therapist – an AI as she couldn't trust a living being with the truth of her situation given that she was technically a prisoner now on the run – as well as using neuroblockers, stims, and net-soothers. All these things had varying degrees of effectiveness, but some memories stuck with her. Sarah absently used a finger to trace the long scar running across her belly. Some things would never fade.

"So, this is the origin of the Great Sarah Vermillion?" Jax's voice broke through Sarah's chain of thoughts and brought her back to the present. "Nice and broody I see."

"I was having a moment," Sarah said, "and the Great Sarah Vermillion? A bit of a stretch, no? Maybe the Adequate Sarah Vermillion, or the Just Enough to Get By Sarah Vermillion."

"I think you're pretty great," Jax said. She winked with a smile as a strand of frizzing hair pulled free of her messy bun and swept across her face with the onset of the wind. Bundled in her black shawl, a streak of teal running through her black curls, and her black-painted lips quirked into a mischievous grin, Jax was a dream. Sometimes Sarah wondered if it wasn't; that the truth of it was that she was still back on the station trapped in once of Vincent's mind games. Jax reached up and rubbed a thumb against Sarah's ear.

"You're making the face again," she said. "You're thinking what I think you're thinking, aren't you?"

"Maybe," Sarah said. It was her turn to smile which turned into a wince as Jax dug a teal fingernail into her earlobe.

"See," Jax said, "nothing but painful reality here."

There was an open door to go down a long winding pathway of conversation regarding existentialism, and the basis of what reality even was, but Sarah decided not to step through it. Those weren't the kinds of conversations Jax liked to partake in. No, Jax preferred the simple, the lewd, or the comical things sometimes all wrapped into one. While there were times she wished she could have deeper conversations, it was part of the reason she liked Jax's company so much. It gave her a respite from her own thoughts, and often times brought a simplicity to her reasoning she would have otherwise missed. She had a way of recognizing Sarah's overthinking and taking it by the hand to politely show it the door.

"This is where you and your brother used to hang out?" Jax asked.

"All of us," Sarah said. "We used to call ourselves the Gutter Rats. We had either no parents, or bad ones, so we skipped out on the schooling system to become petty thieves."

Sarah pulled aside her cloak to show Jax the rat silhouette

tattooed on her inner wrist. Jax merely glanced at it before looking away. She leaned on the railing to take in the view for herself.

"You're a Vulture now," Jax said. "We still have to swap out your ID-chip, file the paperwork, and do a fair share of shady dealings, but you're a Vulture in spirit at least, and that's all that matters. Speaking of, I found a guy here in the city who said he's willing. It'll cost us half of our last haul, but I think he's our best bet. You never told me this place was a hive of underground businesses."

"I thought it was implied by the whole orphan backstory," Sarah said, and Jax laughed.

"Are you ready?"

"No," Sarah said, "but I think it's time."

2

Neon lights saturated the waiting area in blue and pink. Red brick walls and exposed pipes were accented with numerous signs and images of motivational quotes and scantily clad women. The seat Sarah and Jax waited in was a cracked leather couch which they sank into. When Jax had said underground business, Sarah had not realized the statement was literal. They had to walk down a back alley and down a flight of stairs to find the place. The door was little more than an iron gate with a padlock. This so-called doctor, a man named Myrddin, was supposed to perform brain surgery on her, and the place looked like this? She wondered how sanitary the operation table would be. She curled up in the cloak and started to rub the tattoo on her wrist. The cloak – black with a collar of black feathers – was a gift from Modiri's old intruders. It belonged to one of the conduits, and now it belonged to Sarah.

Jax noticed Sarah messing with her wrist and asked, "still thinking about your brother?"

"I don't remember the last time I saw him," Sarah said, "four, maybe five cycles? It all blends together at this point."

"We'll find him," Jax said and grabbed Sarah's wrist with both of her hands. "It just takes time. The galaxy is a big place, you know? I've got a few connections that can make some inquiries, and I've been scanning every database we come across. It might not be tomorrow, but eventually something will turn up."

Finding Hector had been lingering in the back of her mind ever since the destruction of Carlisle Station. It was the only thing she knew she wanted. All her other goals, her desires, her wants, felt ambiguous and open ended. She was free to go where she wanted and do as she pleased as long as she didn't attract the wrong attention. There was a strange lack of direction to it all. She had spent so long doing what she was told and living by the means of others that there was no sense of purpose. Finding her brother, however, felt solid. Hector's whereabouts was something to strive for. Sure, Jax had guided her through salvage and recovery missions. It was how they had made all their credits over the last eleven months, but it wasn't what she wanted to spend the rest of her life doing.

"You must be my five o'clock," a voice interrupted them, and Jax pulled her hands back to herself. "Sarah Vermillion?"

Walking out of a door on the far end of the room was a man with two mechanical legs. Both his pant legs were rolled up to show them off as though he was proud of them. A shawl was draped over his shoulders, but he wore nothing beneath. Metal studs glittered and protruded from his skin on several areas of his bare chest. Thin gray hair hung to his shoulders to frame a face lined with glowing cybernetic implants. They traced from his jaw to his temple and ran across his forehead in bright streaks.

"Nice cloak," Myrddin said, "I feel like I've seen it somewhere before. As for you, Jax, I'll expect payment by the end of the week. Now, if you'll follow me, we'll get this taken care of so you can be on to your new life. If you sit nicely, I won't even leave a scar behind. Isn't that nice?"

Jax wished her good luck as Sarah was led through the far door of Myrddin's shop. The next room was identical in aesthetic, but instead of a leather couch pushed up against the wall, a series of terminals, rolling counters, and medical equipment was scattered throughout. At the room's center was a steel operating table. Myrddin gestured to the table and took a seat on a small stool with wheels.

"You can leave your clothes anywhere you'd like," he said, "but unless you want them to be ruined, you'll need to remove them. There's a gown under the table for you. Let me know when you're finished."

Myrddin pushed off with one foot to go rolling across the room toward a set of terminals. He busied himself with pulling up a holo-feed and inputting a bunch of data. Seeing as she had no desire to let her clothes get ruined, Sarah got undressed and changed into the designated gown. She sat on the table, the cold metal sending a shiver through her body as her skin made contact with it. Taking a deep breath to try and calm her nerves, she let the doctor know she was ready. She had to be. By swapping out her ID-chip, Sarah would no longer be registered as a prisoner, though after Carlisle Station she was more than likely registered as dead. Either way, she needed the new identity to get by. Myrddin wheeled back over to the table bringing a tray of tools and a large stand with a holo-monitor fixed to the top.

"Lie down for me," he said, "good, good. I'm going to cover your face with this mask and count down from four. You'll be asleep by the time I hit one. I'll warn you, the process of swapping out the chip will cause some strange dreams. Very strange. You'll need plenty of time to recover once we're done, so no rushing out of here either. Okay? Okay. Four. Three. Two-"

3

Sarah stood in an endless field of golden wheat. The golden sea swayed with every gust of wind and brushed against her white robe. A sun of deep orange and red kissed the horizon and sent its rays across a blue sky. White clouds, thick and lazy, looked as if their edges were afire in the sun's setting light. The sounds of chirping birds intermingled with that of the rustling wheat, and Sarah closed her eyes to absorb its peace. When she opened them again, a man stood before her. His black robes were half concealed by the golden stalks, and the man wore her brother's face though Sarah knew it could not be him. His sudden appearance did not disturb her sense of peace. In fact, she felt as though he were just another part of the field. He was supposed to be here in the same sense that she was. He took a step closer, and his face shifted to that of Kade's. Another step, and the face belonged to Jax. By the time he reached Sarah, he was no longer a man but a boy. The top of his head only reached her shoulder, but the small antlers protruding from his skin added a few centimeters. The boy looked at his hands and nodded. He looked up, blue eyes boring into Sarah's. He reached under his robes and pulled a spherical object from his pocket. Holding it up to Sarah, he showed her the apple. Plump and red with small streaks of yellow running across its surface, it looked perfect to eat.

She took the fruit from the boy and rolled it over in her hand. Something felt strange about the apple, but she couldn't pinpoint what it was. Sarah took another look at the boy, but he was no longer looking at her. His attention had been drawn to a young girl. Standing a few paces to Sarah's left, this girl too bore antlers and black robes. A good deal smaller than the boy, she was staring at him with a hurt look. A small spider crawled up the girl's arm and stopped on her shoulder. She turned her head and whispered to it before the arachnid leapt into her mouth. The little girl then looked at both of them as more spiders began to crawl up her person. So many that it grew difficult to see the girl through the swarm.

Still, Sarah felt at peace. Nothing about the scene before her caused alarm, and nothing could. They all belonged here in their own way. Sarah lifted the apple to her mouth and took a bite. Instead of the crunch she was expecting, there was a soft pop like biting into a balloon filled with water. Blood splattered her mouth and coursed down her hand. Sarah jolted, and the apple continued to pump blood like a beating heart. Sarah looked up, finding the wheat field was on fire. Flames and smoke billowed from the outer edges of the field, and the little girl howled with laughter. The little boy, however, stood silent and watched Sarah's reaction. He nodded at the apple. Sarah didn't want to, the thought of it made her sick, but she took another bite. Another pop, and more blood rushed through her fingers and down her hand. She kept eating until the apple was gone, the little girl howling her laughter all the while.

Sarah's white robes were stained a deep crimson and stank of copper. The little boy smiled and held out his hand for Sarah to take. She took it with her blood-soaked hand, holding back the urge to vomit. The boy didn't seem to mind the blood that now covered his own hand. He embraced her grasp and led her through the field away from the laughing little girl. Sarah knew if they left the girl there, they would never see her again. The pitiful thing would laugh through her pain, but forever be in torment. They didn't stop, instead continuing through the field and into the fire. Where she expected to be burned there was a flash of bright light, and Sarah found herself somewhere else.

She stood at the bottom of a large crater. Far above at the crater's rim, trees poked over the edge to watch her from up high. Within the crater, ruined trees and charred stumps were scattered throughout large hunks of metal and the wreckage of a ship. At least, Sarah thought it was a ship. If it was, it was a large one to say the least. Motion caught her eye, and Sarah squinted to see two figures walking amongst the wreckage on the far side of the crater. One of the figures was unmistakably human. With short, brown hair and a suit of strange black armor, the figure carried a long rifle with them. The second figure looked to be Dwemyri, but something was off about it. It walked with a limp and most of its limbs appeared to be artificial. They were searching for something. The Dwemyri pulled aside pieces of wreckage and dug through piles of scrap metal while the human held up the rifle as if something they uncovered might jump out at them. The light flashed again, and Sarah was somewhere else.

She was surrounded by a crowd of people, all shouting in the stands of an arena. They were all dressed for the desert with cowls and light scarves of dull colors. Each of them was screaming down into the pit of the arena, and Sarah had to crane her neck to see why. Below was a monster and man. The man was shirtless with black trousers and leather sandals. His hair was impossibly black and sweat glistened from his lithe muscles. Crouched low in a readied stance, he gripped the short blade of a morak'casai in one hand. The monster was a gargantuan shelled beast with a spiked carapace of dark tan and pinching claws that could crush a vehicle. The crowd chanted a name, and the man smiled.

"Adimus!" They chanted, "Adimus!"

White light flashed again, and Sara was in an illustrious bed chamber. Pillars of a white bone-like material stretched from a marbled floor to reach a vaulted ceiling. More of the bone material was embedded in colorful walls, branching off to create sculptures of trees. A young woman sat on the edge of a canopied bed. She wasn't human, but Sarah wasn't sure what she could be. Gray skin with a purplish hue, the woman's nose was ribbed with an eccentric swoop toward the tip. The ends of her ears were elongated into sharp points, and silver and gold rings looped through the length of each. She wore a beautiful silk dress of misty gray, and it shimmered with each small movement the woman made. One delicate hand fiddled with the red silk of the bed's canopy, while the other flipped through the pages of a leatherbound book. Sarah noticed another woman standing near the corner. She stood before a large mirror framed by the bone material. The woman's black hair was tied in a thick braid and pulled over one shoulder. She was glaring at herself clad in a suit of shining silver armor with ornate filigree worked over every centimeter. A cloak of the purest white Sarah had ever seen was pinned to the woman's pauldrons.

"Relax," the woman on the bed said, "you're going to do perfectly."

"I'm the first human to hold this position," the woman before the mirror said, "most are going to hate me for it."

"My uncle Tychan picked you for a reason," the sitting woman said, "any person worth their weight will see that too."

Sarah glanced toward the other side of the room where it opened to a wide balcony. Outside rose a city of white stone and golden domes with a hulking statue of a four-armed woman erected at its center.

Light flashed, and Sarah's world shifted once more. She was in a temple. Sandstone pillars formed a circle within a dark chamber, and yellow sand covered the tiled floor. Small drones hovered around with dim bulbs of light giving the place an eerie sense of dread. Massive statues of sandstone faces floated between each pillar and looked down at the chamber's center. A person covered head to toe in golden plates of armor stood there looking back up at the statues. The figure turned toward Sarah's direction. Piercing eyes gleamed through a golden mask. Half was shaped like a weeping angel while the other half was carved into the shape of a snarling devil. At first, Sarah thought the armor-clad figure was staring at her, but another individual emerged from the dark. The newcomer wore the white mask of a morak'casai, but instead of the black robes, they wore a cloak of deep crimson. The red-cloaked figure paused as they strode past Sarah, white mask looking her up and down.

"You shouldn't be here, little specter," their voice was deep and pleasant, "this is not your timeline, nor is this for your eyes to see."

The figure reached a black-gloved hand up toward Sarah, and another flash of white light fired sharp pain through head. Sarah's eyes snapped open to a bare ceiling with several white lights dangling above her. She was laying on a cushion atop an operating table beneath a thin blanket, and several monitors loomed over her like macabre watchers. Each beep signified whether she'd live or die. An IV was sticking out of her left arm, and Sarah felt a bandage wrapped around her head. Memories started to flood back, and she remembered where she was. She touched her head with her free hand and felt the spot at the back where the spine meets the skull. There was no pain, but through bandages it was hard to tell what kind of damage had been done. She ran a diagnostic of each body part to be certain she still had feeling throughout. Satisfied with the results, Sarah took a deep breath and relaxed.

"Welcome back to the world of the living," Myrddin said, "have a pleasant trip?"

"Can't say it was the most exciting vacation," Sarah said, "you were right about the dreams. How long was I out?"

"Three days," Myrddin said, "I kept you under to speed up the healing process. Nasty business replacing an ID chip. It is. Much sleep is needed, and we can't have you bouncing around the city with an open sore on the back of your skull. My work has a reputation to uphold."

Taking a few moments to collect herself, Sarah rested her head against the cushion. The dreams had felt too real, too visceral. She felt like she had been watching other people's lives play out before her. She held a hand up toward the ceiling and wiggled her fingers in the light. This was real. She was real. Those other people were dreams. Sarah rubbed sleep from her eyes, tasted her own breath, and winced. An hour with some hot water and a gallon of mouthwash was all she wanted at the moment. She asked, "Where's Jax? You can unhook me from all of this?"

Myrddin nodded to the corner, and Sarah saw Jax sleeping in a makeshift cot. Myrddin cleared his throat and said, "hasn't left your side once. It was up to me to feed her too. Troublesome that was. Felt like a caretaker for both of you. As for your second question, yes, you're free to go. Before you do, however, you need to be aware of your new information. I've sent a detailed report to your ship, but I'll give you a summary. Your name is still Sarah, but now it's Sarah Renza. Don't ask me about the name, it was the simplest to get registered. You grew up on Pletaa VII, a moon deep in CRG mining territory. I've added details about that region to your report. Your father worked in the mines, your mother a waitress at a local cantina. Both agreed to move to a Vulture colony once they got married. They had you on the way, and you became adjusted to living from outpost to outpost, colony to colony while your parents moved from place to place trying to collect enough credits to make the trip. They never made it. They perished in a shipwreck before they got the chance. You used the opportunity to create a new life and snuck aboard a freighter traveling to Sican IV. Which brings us here. The gritty details have been sent to your ship to review when you have time. I recommend vague answers should anyone ever ask about you. Keeps things easier to maintain."

Sarah tried to keep track of everything Myrddin said, but her head was groggy, and the information made her head spin. Myrddin rolled over to the table on a wheeled stool. His gray hair was tied into a ponytail, and his tongue was stuck between his lips as he removed the IV and monitoring equipment. He took the bandages off next and scooted away. Sarah heard him stand and get ready to leave.

"Your clothes are on the stand next to you," he said, "I'll leave you to it. Exit isn't hard to find. I've left a bottle of munmos for you as well. It's for the nightmares but use it sparingly. Addictive stuff it is. I'm not one to judge, but that's a dangerous hill to slide down if you ask me. Better to dream of nightmares than live them."

"Isn't everything a dream?" Sarah asked. She meant it more for herself and hadn't realized she'd spoken aloud. "We just keep dreaming until one day we wake up. Then the whole thing is over."

"Asverit'ansibilis," Myrddin said.

"What's that?" Sarah asked.

"A Dwemyri term," Myrddin said, "or as close to it as I can get. The actual pronunciation is too difficult for a human tongue. It's a word in their old language to refer to reality. It literally translates to *inconceivable* as reality is a concept too incomprehensible for a mortal mind to put language to."

"I suppose they're right," Sarah said.

"Whatever events took place to lead you to my doorstep," Myrddin said, "separate yourself from it. Find peace, Sarah Renza, as I sense monsters lurking in the shadows of your past."

With that, Myrddin left her alone in the operating room. She took her time climbing off the table, every joint creaking and cracking like dried wood. Her muscles were stiff as she pulled her clothes on. Sarah threw on the cloak, a sharp twinge shooting through her shoulders, and she went over to her sleeping partner. Gently shaking her, Jax awoke bleary eyed and confused. Her eyes widened when she realized it was Sarah and a wide smile spread across her face.

"I'm clear to go," Sarah said.

"Perfect," Jax said, "because while you were under, I got news about your brother."

4

From atop the landing platform which docked smaller ships and shuttles that would carry people to the larger ships in orbit, Sican IV didn't look nearly as large. The megastructures still towered above one another, but being above them, Sarah realized the city's footprint wasn't all it was chalked up to be. It looked like a narrow gray hexagon in the center of an empty desert. Behind her, the landing pad of the docking port buzzed with activity. Jax was busy having the Modiri's latest cargo offloaded as payment for Sarah's treatment. Seeing as she would just be in the way, Sarah waited and watched the city below.

The news of her brother came as a surprise, but not an entirely pleasant one. Jax had managed to catch word of Hector, but that word placed him on a ship that had been reported missing. Over the days Sarah slept, Jax followed a trail of reports leading back to a Vulture colony ship named the Ifrit and a man named Ziven Diluca, a small-time smuggler running operations out of the Ifrit's Kyonai District. Given the ship's connection to smugglers, the local authorities wrote the ship off as having succumbed to the risks of the business. Afterall, the lawless neutral zone could be a dangerous place. Ziven, on the other hand, was not content with that answer. He was collecting mercenaries where he could in order to form a search and rescue operation. Sarah needed to find a way into that operation, so Jax had arranged a call with Ziven once they reached orbit. Unsure of what to expect from this smuggler, Sarah could only hope she would be allowed a spot on the mission, free of any strings or red tape, but she knew better than to expect otherwise. She tried to come up with a list of skills and talents she could contribute to a band of mercenaries but came up short. What kind of special talents set her apart from someone else? Other than the mechanical skills she had learned through Kara Corps, Sarah felt as though she had nothing to offer. Jax was clever, she'd help spin a way for Sarah's work to sound more appealing.

"Sarah?" A man's voice said from behind her. "Sarah Vermillion?"

Confused, Sarah turned around to see a tall man with a slender frame. Red hair and a red beard framed a narrow face with blue eyes. Dressed in the garb of a dock mechanic - thick padded leathers with patches of armor covering the knees, elbows, and shoulders - the man wiped a spot of grease from his cheek with a glove. Instead of cleaning it, the glove smeared the grease across his face. It took Sarah a moment to register, but then it hit her like a freighter.

"Zeke?" She asked.

"It is you," the man said and he cracked a wide smile, "how long's it been? I could have sworn you were gone for good."

"Too long," Sarah said. She smiled back, but it was a hesitant one. Part of her was overjoyed to see her old friend still alive and in good health. The other part was dismayed at his timing. She was no longer supposed to be Sarah Vermillion. Sarah Vermillion was dead. Now, there was a person who knew otherwise and could point someone in the right direction should they come looking for her. It wasn't like Zeke wouldn't have reason to give her up either. The trouble she and Hector had gotten poor Zeke into as a boy would be enough for anyone to hold a grudge.

"What brings you back?" Zeke asked. "I heard you got locked up."

"I got out. Doing a reunion tour before I head out for good," Sarah said. She played it vague and tried to change the subject. "Looks like you got cleaned up. Dock worker now, huh?"

"Not a glamorous life," he said, "but it's an honest one. I get off in a few hours if you want to grab a drink and talk about it?"

Sarah glanced over his shoulder in search of the words to get her out of this situation. That was when she noticed the two of them were being watched. A woman in similar garb to Zeke stared at her from beside the landing ramp of another ship. She had black hair and a pale complexion. It took Sarah a moment to notice the woman was an android. It was unnerving how far the technology for androids had gotten. The only features that gave her away was the lack of pupils and the thin line running down the center of her face. Each of these things were a mandate put in place upon manufacturers to make it apparent the individual was an android. Why this android was so interested in her was another question.

"Is this guy bothering you?" Jax asked. She sauntered toward the pair with an extra edge of attitude using her hood as a shield against the wind.

"No, no," Sarah said and gave Zeke an apologetic look,

"he's an old friend. But it looks like everything is ready to go. Another time perhaps."

"Of course," he said, but his expression said he knew she wasn't coming back.

Sarah glanced over to where the android had been, but it was gone. Other dock workers were busy carrying crates up and down the ship's landing ramp, but there was no sign of the dark-haired android. She wrote it off as nothing more than coincidence, but something about the way it was watching her made Sarah uneasy. Jax took her by the elbow, and the two of them hurried off toward the Modiri. Sarah tried to not let her thoughts spiral out of control. She needed to be ready for her interaction with Ziven. As it stood, he was her only ticket to finding Hector.

5

Sarah nestled into the copilot's seat. The holo-feed displaying the view behind them showed Sican IV becoming a small glowing marble. The holo-feed displayed between her and Jax showed a connection trying to be made between the Modiri and another ship. Sarah started to pick at her scalp, realized what she was doing, and stopped. Instead, she contented herself with peeling the dead skin off a callus on her hand. The callus was determined to stay in one piece and attached to her hand which only further spiked her anxiety. Sarah forced her hands into her lap and took a deep breath.

"It's going to be fine," Jax said. Sarah hadn't noticed her watching. "If he says no, then we track his ship and follow him anyway. Either way, we're finding your brother. Though if I can speak my mind, I'm not sure why you want to find him. From what I've heard about him the dude's an ass. He's the reason you ended up in all your troubles to begin with. It should be your turn to leave him."

"It should be," Sarah said, "but I can't. He's still my brother, and he was all I had growing up. Besides, maybe he's changed since then."

"Maybe," Jax said, "but I wouldn't hang my life up on it."

The holo-feed between them lit up green to confirm the connection had been accomplished. An audio wavelength appeared to show the connection was voice only which was fine with Sarah. At least she didn't have to visibly keep her calm and she could give Jax all the nervous glances her heart desired. A gruff baritone echoed through the cockpit's speakers.

"Jax of the Modiri," it said, "Ziven speaking. We have business?"

"We do," Jax said.

"Then let's cut to it," Ziven said, "I'm running short on time. You have someone who wants in on my mission. Trouble is, I don't have a lot of room for amateurs and I've never heard of this Sarah Renza. Why would I want her aboard? My background checks prove she's a nobody. Not even a Vulture, just a nobody with no home."

"My brother was aboard the ship that went missing," Sarah said, "a feeling I'm sure you can sympathize with."

"Funny, your records don't say anything about a brother," Ziven said.

"Adoptive," Sarah said, "family doesn't always mean blood relatives."

"That I can understand," Ziven said. "Okay, let's say this hypothetical brother was on this ship. While you have my sympathies, what qualifications put you on board any rescue mission?"

Sarah hesitated, but Jax gave her a reassuring nod. She pointed to a tool bag left on the floor and made a motion with her hand like she was using a wrench. Sarah nodded and started to explain her skills and history as a mechanic, adding as much flare and fluff as she could to pad her experience. It was difficult to remember everything Myrddin had put in her report, but she did her best not to stray from what he'd written. The slip up of her brother was bad enough. After she was done, Ziven let out a long sigh before speaking again.

"Listen," he said, "you want part of this mission, I want to find out what happened to my own family, and right now I'm taking whatever gift presents itself. So, here's the deal. I might need weapons for this mission. Lots of them. I was tipped off about an abandoned CRG military base within three jumps of your current location. I send you the coordinates, you bring me the weapons, I give you a spot on my team. Deal?"

"Deal," Jax blurted and ended the communications line. When Sarah raised a brow, Jax laughed and said, "never give a guy like that a chance to second guess himself. Never ends well."

Laughing, Sarah opened the navigation feeds to await the new coordinates. It sounded simple enough, and if they played it right the two of them could skim a bit of the cargo off the top and make a quick credit or two. She laughed again realizing just how much like Jax she was starting to become.

CHAPTER 3
- KALLIK -

1

Kallik faded in and out of consciousness. Catching only snippets of his surroundings, a bright lamp here, a bulkhead there, he had no way of knowing what was happening to him. Just when he thought he might be waking, a brutish hand would jab him with another needle, or he'd be thrown into a cryotube. Back into the void he'd slip with little hope of ever coming back, but he always did. Teetering on the edge of sleep, he'd gain a few precious moments of reality before falling back to sleep. He was someplace hot, someplace cold, someplace with humid air, and someplace where the air tasted sterile.

Kallik blinked, realizing he was starting to come to. A bright orb of light hovered above his head, making it impossible to discern his surroundings. It was all he could see except for a shape which tormented him from the corner of his eye. He tried to turn his head to look only to find he was strapped down, incapable of moving a muscle. It dawned on him that Kallik could not feel the straps tying him down. Kallik could not feel anything. He tried to squirm, but it was pointless. There was a faint ringing in his ears accompanied by the sound of an air recycler. The thing in the corner of his eye moved, and he thought he could start to make out voices. One sounded familiar. It was the horrible voice made of grinding stones belonging to the man who hid behind the white mask. The other was higher pitched, more feminine. That one was closer. Close enough, in fact, that Kallik thought the speaker might be sitting next to him.

"About the other thing," the feminine voice said. "You took care of it?"

"I did," the voice of stone answered.

"She'll find out?" The feminine voice asked. "You made sure she'll find us?"

"If the woman was capable of killing Vincent," the masked man said, "she's capable of following a trail of breadcrumbs."

"Perfect," the feminine voice said, "I'd very much like to find her. Such an elusive creature, she is, and to be able to take out both Sondra and our conduit is a thing worth studying. Her brother is who you managed to find?"

"Correct," The stone voice said. "Nothing like family to lure someone in."

"Patient J047X is what I'll call her," the feminine voice said, "a fitting label for a fitting subject. Pity we're running out of psycholith. Why not make a trip to Xaranor and raid their stores."

"Funny joke," the stone voice said, "I'll wipe out the five while I'm at it and kill Zammon in his sleep."

"We should be the real Xaranor," the feminine voice said, "what we're doing here is progress. Not listening to a council of statues. They hide behind archaic morals implanted in their minds by old men who knew no better."

"As you say," the stone voice said.

Kallik's head was swimming. Xaranor? Psycholith? Patient something or other? What were these people talking about; what did it have to do with him? Why did they attack his father's ship? His father. He wanted to see his father. Did he make it off the ship? Was he captured by these people as well? Kallik's vision was beginning to adjust and he could make out the silhouette of a person on his right. The individual was sitting in a chair with their back to him. And, if he weren't mistaken, they reminded him of a tall feline. Furless, with pointed ears atop its head, the figure looked like a hairless cat. They matched the description his father had given him of the Suttack.

"I suppose we have other things we should be more concerned with," the Suttack said with a heavy sigh. "You did good with this catch, Vigamere, but I'm afraid it might be one of our last."

"You're getting sloppy doc," the stone voice said, "the boy is awake."

Kallik flinched as the Suttack spun around. Its face only solidified the cat imagery in his mind with its short snout and large, slitted eyes. Sensation was starting to come back, and Kallik found he could move the tips of his fingers. He was pressed against something, lying on his back. Realizing he was strapped to a table made him panic, and the Suttack grumbled something as it pushed a needle into his neck. Kallik stopped his struggle and allowed the drugs to overwhelm his body. Darkness pulled him into its cold embrace.

2

When Kallik next awoke, he was in a bed. It wasn't *his* bed, but it was a bed nonetheless. He could feel it with its plastic, sterilized sheets and its paper pillow. He stared up at a white ceiling, its white, fluorescent bulb glowing dimly. It was a purposeful light and little more. Used for seeing the bare minimum one should need, the light offered no comfort nor aesthetic beauty. It was nothing like home. He turned his head and winced. Sharp pain spiked through his cranium, starting at the soft spot behind his left ear. Raising a hand to touch the spot, he found it to be wrapped in thick, cotton bandages. Using a finger to trace the bandages, he discovered they wrapped around his full head only leaving room for his antlers to poke through. What had they done to him?

He sat up, another mistake which made his head spin, and nearly fell out of bed. This room was even smaller than his cabin on his father's ship. It reminded him of a prison cell they used in all the video productions and stories. White walls surrounded him, and beside the bed was a toilet within arm's reach. It protruded from the wall like a strange decoration. Past that was the opposite wall. Kallik supposed that was all anyone truly needed, a toilet and a bed, but it still sank his heart into his stomach. A thought occurred to him, and he shot a panicked hand to his pocket. They had changed him. These simple cotton pants had no pockets, and no pockets meant no bronze figure. They had taken it along with his other possessions. Kallik wanted to weep. He pushed himself out of bed and walked over to the room's only door. It was a plane panel of cold metal with a small, circular window carved through the middle. Kallik had to stand on his toes to peek through.

The hallway on the other side was just as stark as his room. White walls stood close together to create a narrow corridor, and a dark floor of a rough texture stretched between them. More doors like Kallik's own patterned the length of the hallway, and he wondered how many other children were trapped here. Maybe his father was here too. He tapped on the glass with his finger.

"Dad?" He called. "Dad, are you there?"

Hearing himself call out only escalated his longing to see his father, and panic began to set in. The tapping grew to pounding, and he slammed his fist against the glass. Sharp pain rattled the bones of his hand, but he didn't care. The calling turned into screaming. His own voice tore his throat raw, but he carried on anyway. Tears streamed down his cheeks, and he kept on pounding, and screaming, and pounding some more, until finally a voice answered. A holo-feed bloomed over the window. A man's face appeared, fat, bald, and sweating profusely. Deep wrinkles creased his forehead, and beady eyes sat deep within dark sockets. His head looked tiny sitting atop such wide shoulders. His white uniform stretched to compensate for his girth.

"Ah, guess who's awake," he said, "looks like we got ourselves a squealer. Listen here little squealer, if you want to make it for long in this place, you better shut that yapper of yours."

Kallik closed his mouth and gave the fat man a dirty look. Stepping away from the door, he wiped his eyes and cheeks with the sleeve of his cotton shirt. He stuck up his chin and narrowed his eyes.

"Good," the fat man said, "so the squealer can listen. Take off that bandage. Been asleep long enough, you should be good and healed by now."

Kallik hesitated with one hand on the edge of the bandage. The fat man glared at him, one pudgy finger scratching the tip of his nose. His nail was short, almost non-existent making it appear as if the rest of his finger were trying to swallow it. Black dirt showed beneath what little there was, and Kallik frowned. He held a firm belief that the quality of a person's nails could be used as a good indicator toward the quality of the person. His father used to make fun of him for thinking this way, but it was an opinion he was never able to shake. He made up his mind about the fat man and decided to do as he was told for the time being. There was no telling what this stranger was capable of. Unwrapping the bandages, Kallik winced with each turn of his head. Whatever they had done to him did not feel healed regardless of what this man told him. Once the bandages were off, he dropped them to the floor. Feeling at the soft tissue behind his ear, he could tell there was a small scar. It felt like a bumpy line across the bone.

"Great, now approach the door," the fat man said. "At the bottom is a slot you can open. Put your hand through, and you'll find a small device. I want you to pick it up."

Kallik walked over to the door keeping a cautious eye on the window. He had to take a few seconds to look over the door before he noticed what the man was talking about. Kneeling down, he pulled open the slot, and saw what he was supposed to grab. Sitting on the floor in front of his door was a small, flat device no larger than the tip of his thumb. Disc shaped; it looked like a white coin. Kallik picked it up, closed the slot, and stepped away so he could present the object to the holo-feed.

"What are you showing it to me for?" He asked. "Stupid squealer, stick the thing behind your ear on the same spot you felt the scar. It should stick like a magnet. You know what a magnet is, don't you?"

The command gave him pause. The harshness in the fat man's voice meant nothing good could come from listening to him, but it also meant he could get hurt for not doing what he was told. Kallik turned the disk over in his hand to get an unobstructed view of both sides. It looked harmless enough. There was nothing to indicate what it was. No writing or logos marked its surface, and not even a scratch marred the edges.

"What is it?" Kallik asked. "Why should I do what you

say?"

"It's your only ticket out of that room," the fat man said, "so you better damn well use it, squealer."

Kallik was growing tired of the name calling, so he did as he was told. He placed the disk over the scar, and sure enough, it snapped to his head like a magnet. It pinched his skin, and Kallik had to grit his teeth to keep from yelping. He would not cry in front of this man again. Without another word, the holo-feed died, and a soft click sounded from the door. Kallik hurried over to it and pulled. The door slid open. Before him waited the long, empty hallway of monochrome. He touched a bare foot to the textured floor to find it grated against his toe like sandpaper. Putting his full weight on it, he found the sensation not to be uncomfortable, but not enjoyable either.

"It's so you don't slip," a pleasant voice said from his right. Kallik gave a start and twisted to face the newcomer. He had not realized there was another hallway reaching down that direction. A woman stood there in the same white cotton clothes as himself and the bald man. She was a human, tall as most humans seemed to be, with short blonde hair, smooth skin and a warm smile. Her eyes were pretty, hazel with a knowing twinkle in them. Kallik tried not to blush, failed, and looked at his feet instead.

"This facility is mostly underwater," she said. "Old as it is, sometimes it can spring a leak or two. Not great for walking, that. Anyway, I was just on my way to get you, but it would seem Sabastian has already told you what to do?"

"Sort of," Kallik said and pointed to his ear. "He didn't say anything about what's next."

"Oh, perfect," she said, and her warm smile grew. Kallik liked this woman much more than Sabastian. Her nails were long and painted a deep blue. In one hand, he noticed she was carrying a pair of black slippers. "I'll show you where you need to be."

3

The woman said little along the way, but Kallik didn't mind. Her presence felt a strange comfort in this alien place, and he clung to it like a drowning man did a raft. He was led through similar hallways, however, not all of the doors had windows. Some had signs pinned to the wall next to them, though Kallik no idea what they meant. They passed through a large open area. It looked like a gymnasium with a sprawling jungle gym on one side and an array of shelves on the other. Books and toys littered their surfaces. The walls lacked the white paint her, instead opting for a light blue. Kallik saw other children, a few weaving in and out of the jungle gym, a few standing in a huddled group in the far corner. A lone girl sat by the bookshelves reading a book that was entirely too big for her. At least, it was too big from Kallik's perspective. Chapter books were fine, but no one other than an adult had business reading a tome of that size. Every one of them stopped what they were doing to observe him as he was led by.

The reading girl smiled at him and waved. Long golden hair bounced about her shoulders as she did. The huddled group measured him up, but not in an unkind way. The first, a taller boy with chestnut hair and slender cheeks, gave him a nod. It felt like a final salute before a soldier marched to their death. A little girl next to him caused Kallik to do a double take. He did not recognize her, but she was Groal like himself. Her antlers were shorter than his, marking her as younger, and her wiry brown hair hung in a jumbled mess around her face. She stuck out her tongue when he looked at her. The third was a freckled red-headed boy. He looked small for a human child, more Kallik's size than the others. Groal did eventually grow to be similar in height to their human counterparts, but it took them much longer. Perhaps that meant this boy was the youngest of the lot. He did not have time to catch a glimpse of those in the jungle gym, but he could feel their eyes on his back.

Kallik felt the walls shrink in around him as he was guided out of the open area and down another white hall. Eventually they stopped in front of a door, indistinguishable from any of the others. His guide knocked on it twice and turned to face him. Taking a device from her pocket, a small rectangle roughly the length of her finger, she waved near his ear. The disk he had put on earlier popped off, and she caught it before it hit the ground. Confused,

Kallik asked, "why did you need to use that? If you wanted it, I could have just given it to you." Her expression darkened, and Kallik felt taken aback by the sudden change.

"Sabastian didn't tell you, did he?" She asked. Kallik shook his head. "Once it's on, it's on. If anyone tries to take it off without this," she waved the device in front of his face, "it triggers the kill switch, and a charge of high voltage energy is released to fry your brain. Never touch it, okay?"

Kallik nodded, dumbfounded. Her smile returned and she opened the door. She waved him through with a muttered "good luck," and the door slid shut behind him. He found himself in a large room with next to nothing in it. At the far end stood a table. Several small objects - a metal ball, a wooden cube, and a feather - were lined up on top of it. He started to walk toward them when several panels of the right wall rose into the ceiling. Behind them were thick panes of glass separating this room from the next. Several individuals stood on the other side, observing his every move. One was the woman that led him here. Gone was the smile, and instead she wore an expression of concern as if Kallik might be in some sort of trouble. Next to her, taller than any creature had the right to be, stood the Suttack Kallik thought he had dreamed up. The Suttack was adorned in elegant robes of crimson streaked with blue. A golden sash was slung over one shoulder, and cords of gold were tied around its waist like a belt. Numerous rings were looped through its feline ears, and it narrowed its cat-eyes as it noticed Kallik observing it. Next to it waited the masked man. He looked like a demon with his black robes, and scarred, white mask. A motionless sentinel, he looked to be waiting for one wrong step.

"Good morning," the Suttack said, "you can call me Doctor Karaska. Your ident-chip marks you as Kallik Hikkarsan, is this correct?"

Kallik looked at the blonde woman. She smiled, but her aura of ease was gone. It was more a nervous grin than a comforting expression. Kallik nodded at Karaska. He could not help but notice the doctor's eyes were gauging his every twitch. It felt like a predator watching its next meal.

"Anna here treated you well?" Karaska asked and ran a

long-fingered hand through the woman's hair. Kallik nodded again. "We are supposed to be joined by another, but he seems to be running late as usual. In the meantime, I'll lay down some rules for you while you'll be staying with us. We are going to run a few tests, but after that you are free to go. You are free to move about the facility as you please as long as you are wearing your inhibitor. I'll explain more about it after we are done. You must stay on this level, however, if you are awarded enough marks for good behavior, you will be allowed visitation hours up on the garden level. Misbehave, and you'll be confined to your room. Understand?"

Kallik did not. He had no idea what was happening, or what was about to happen, but Karaska seemed to only want compliance. Kallik nodded. The doctor smiled. It was a fanged grin that did more to unsettle him than comfort. They were interrupted by the door opening, and a man strolled through. Rubbing sleep from his eyes, he was a slender man with shockingly red-dyed hair, worn messy as if he'd just gotten out of bed. Kallik wondered how much dye he had to use to get it to that tone. He was dressed in a form fitting black uniform, with a collar that rose to cover most of his neck. Trimmed with silver, the uniform was wrinkled like the man had slept in it. A black feather was tucked behind his ear, and Kallik found his entire presence to be quite dominating despite his sleepy aesthetic.

"Sorry I'm late," he said, "lost track of the time. Easy to do when there's no sun."

"You're lucky I can't afford to punish you, Aillon," Karaska said. The doctor waved a hand in a dismissive motion. "Whatever, be on with it."

Aillon strode over to Kallik and held up his hand. "Master Aillon," he said.

Kallik stood there, unmoving, and glared at the red-haired man's outstretched palm. Several awkward seconds crept by until Master Aillon cleared his throat.

"Ah, a human thing, of course," he said, and dropped his hand. It wasn't. Kallik understood the meaning of a handshake. His father had taught him all kinds of courtesies. His father had also taught him that the shake of a hand indicated trust. Kallik did not trust this man, and so he kept his hand to himself.

"What am I doing here?" He asked.

"Praying you aren't a viper," Master Aillon said.

4

Kallik was positioned in front of the table with Master Aillon hovering close behind. The three on the other side of the glass watched with interest as Aillon circled around to stand in front of Kallik. He placed himself between Kallik and the table while still leaving a full view of the three objects placed across its smooth surface. He gestured toward the feather with a slender hand.

"Before you is a feather. You see it, I see it, and we can both agree it's stationary, no?" He asked, and Kallik nodded. "Good. Now, I want you to picture it in your mind. Solidify the image of that feather in your vision. Can you do that?"

Aillon acted with a general attitude of disinterest, but there was an edge to his voice. His outward appearance spoke of a day-in, day-out nonchalance, but a nervous energy lurked behind the curtain. This Master Aillon almost seemed afraid for Kallik. Kallik glanced at Karaska who, in turn, was watching him with hungry eyes. Fixating on the feather, he tried to do as Aillon urged. He imprinted the image of the feather, and held it in his mind. The room's fluorescent light pounded at his eyes. The power running through it made an aggravating hum, but he kept his attention on the feather.

"Picture the feather to be floating," Aillon said. "Picture it like it is your reality. You aren't imagining it to happen, it is happening."

It was easy for Kallik to imagine a feather floating up to the ceiling, and he pictured it doing just that. However, reason still told him the feather was resting on the table. His father had always lectured him about letting his head float in the clouds. Because of this, Kallik had tried to temper his imagination at every step. He hesitated, broke his concentration, and blinked at Master Aillon. The red-haired man smiled at him. It was a tired smile, but an honest one. Placing a hand on Kallik's shoulder, Aillon stepped between him and the table to block his view of the objects.

"We can try again," he said. "I know what I'm telling you is difficult. No one ever gets it on their first try. This time, I want you to close your eyes."

Kallik did so. He was beginning to move Aillon into the same category as Anna. It's not that he trusted either of the two, but when compared to his surroundings, Kallik did not exactly distrust them. With the whereabouts of both his father and cousin still unknown, it was the only thing he had to rely on. His awareness of the light's humming grew more acute now that his vision was gone.

"Recollect the image of the table," Aillon said. "Picture the feather once more. It is floating. No longer is it sitting on the table. Up, up, up it floats until it touches the light."

Kallik imagined the feather floating, told himself it was the truth, and his scalp grew warm. A tingling sensation prickled his skin, and his palms grew sweaty. He felt the strong urge to scratch his head, his hair being all too warm. Aillon let out a long sigh of relief, and patted Kallik's arm.

"Open your eyes," he said. Kallik's eyelids snapped open, and in an instant the heat was gone. Aillon was turned away from him, watching a feather descending from the ceiling. It spun and swayed through the air before nestling back into its original position. Aillon turned to him, face beaming. It wasn't a smile someone could fake. Had he truly caused the feather to fly with his mind like this Master Aillon seemed to believe? Kallik looked past him to the feather. Keeping his eyes open, he tried it again. He pictured the feather floating, told himself it was. The heat returned, sharp pinpricks on his scalp. The feather began to lift just as he imagined it; like a gust of air had scooped it up and carried it off. Aillon laughed and clapped him on the shoulder.

"You're a natural," he said. "Just a few more tests, and we can get you out of here."

"Test his strength," Karaska snapped, "now, Aillon, or I'll rip the stone from his pointy head and cut our losses."

Kallik could not explain why he had the thought, only

that he did. The sheen of the metal caught his eye, and the idea simply clicked. His imagination ran wild with the thought of that shiny, metal ball whizzing through the air to smash through the glass and bury itself in the Suttack's head. His newfound powers put his thoughts into action. Nettles scraped and dug against his skin as the ball exploded from the table and slammed into the glass. It buried itself several centimeters deep, and stuck. The Suttack didn't flinch as the ball was suspended in glass not a hand's width away from its face. Karaska sized Kallik up, and grinned.

"I think I've seen enough."

It wasn't enough for Kallik. He wanted the doctor to feel his fear, his pain, for what they were doing to him. He tried to warp the glass, break it, to will the ball to fly through it. The glass began to vibrate and warp inward. Sharp pain stabbed at his head, and pressure built up in his chest. He couldn't breathe, but he didn't care. He pushed harder on the glass with his will until cracks began to spread from the ball. He gritted his teeth, and imagined the glass shattering into a million pieces. Aillon grabbed his shoulder, and spun Kallik around to face him. He screamed Kallik's name, and shoved him. Kallik stumbled, losing the image, and sagged to the floor. Everything stopped, and a deathly quiet clung to the air. Kallik looked over his shoulder and saw Karaska with a single hand raised to stop the masked man. His short blade was drawn, and he was ready to strike.

"I believe you have a bright future with us," Karaska said, the grin nowhere in sight. "I will call upon you again, but for now you are dismissed."

5

Kallik was ushered back to the play area and left there to stand by himself. Little was said to him after he was dismissed, and Anna simply dropped him off and left. There he stood in the center of this open space with a jungle gym on one side and bookshelves on the other. He felt vulnerable. Many of the other kids stopped what they were doing to watch his every move, and Kallik was unsure of what to do or where to go. Was he supposed to stay here or go back to his room? Perhaps if he returned to his room, he could find some solace in sleep. He didn't know his way back, however, and would get lost if he tried. He settled for examining the bookshelves. If he lingered long enough, he'd find something interesting to pass the time with or otherwise be told what to do.

The selves were a simple construction of white plastic, lined with several diverse kinds of objects ranging from pre-programmed data-slates to actual books. A collection of children's toys and occasional pieces of sports gear were dispersed throughout. Kallik walked down the length of a bookshelf, running his hand along the plastic, and skimmed over the items for something interesting. He tried to peek at the upper shelves, but he was too short. The top shelves were just out of his reach, so he kept to the lower ones. Getting caught up in scanning the different titles, he forgot to keep track of his surroundings. He set a data-slate back on the shelf, stepped away, and bumped into someone behind him. Kallik turned to apologize, but the words fled as soon as he saw who it was. The reading girl from before stood with the large tome clutched to her chest. She gave him an inviting smile, her narrow features framed by her golden hair.

"Hey there," she said, "I'm Xoriah."

"Kallik," Kallik said, unsure of what else to say. He was painfully aware of how he must look, startled and caught out like prey. He shuffled his feet trying to find new ground, but all he found was nervous energy. He noticed from the corner of his eye that some of the others were getting closer. There was a large, brooding kid with broad shoulders and a round belly making little effort to hide the fact that he was eavesdropping. An ugly girl of similar size lingered close to the boy's shoulder, giving Kallik a judgmental glare. On the other side, Kallik noticed the trio with the taller boy, the red-head, and the other Groal was starting to walk over.

"Do you mind if I ask you what your results were?" She asked. Kallik hesitated, and the trio stopped just behind Xoriah to wait for an answer as well. "Were you a viper or a bull?"

Stammering, Kallik tried to figure out what she was asking. Master Aillon had told him to pray he wasn't a viper and seemed relieved with his test results. "I think I'm a bull."

"You think?" The red-headed boy asked, and the taller one with chestnut hair smacked his chest. The red head gave the taller boy an incredulous look, and rubbed where he'd been struck.

"You're being rude," the taller boy said to the red head. "Toby wants to know if you made things move, or if you made people see things that weren't there."

By now, most of the kids in the area had congregated around him. Xoriah looked apologetic about the sudden gathering, but the other children all repeated her question. The large boy with his ugly shadow remained silent but watched him with deep intent. He clenched and unclenched meaty fists while he waited for Kallik to answer. As shrinking into the bookshelf behind him was not an option, Kallik attempted to find his voice.

"I made a ball fly into the glass," he said. He picked that detail over the feather as to him, it sounded more impressive. "Then I tried to break the glass to make it go through."

"A bull then," the taller boy said, and shot him a grin. Some of the other children made noises of appreciation, and a bald kid in the back even gave him a thumbs up. "I'm Leo, also a bull. You've just met Xoriah, another bull, and this here is-"

Kallik hadn't seen him coming. He turned away to see everyone Leo was introducing, and the next thing he knew, he was on the ground. On his back, and staring up at a white ceiling, a hulking figure loomed over him. It was the large boy. He had short, dark hair, and his brown eyes boiled with hatred. The ugly girl showed up next to him, pointed a finger, and laughed at his dismay. The boy smacked a thick hand against his broad chest, and grunted.

"Know your place, squealer," he said. "Sabastian told me all about you calling out for daddy. You're weak. Know that I'm the strongest bull this place has ever seen, and you better remember it."

Leo darted between the two of them, and threw his shoulder into the larger boy. The ugly girl shouted something in return, as the pair stumbled apart. Kallik pushed himself up to his knees, but did not dare stand all the way when someone else could easily knock him down again. A circle of kids formed around them, and the two boys were poised to go at each other's throats. Just when Kallik thought one of them would strike, Sabastian bulldozed his way through the crowd wielding a thick baton. He waved it around, children shrinking away at the sight of it. He reached the center of the makeshift arena and slammed the weapon into Leo's side. The boy cried out and fell to the ground, clutching his ribs.

"Starting fights again, are we?" Sabastian said. He grabbed Leo by the back of his neck and hauled him to his feet. Leo gritted his teeth and spat. "I'll see to it you'll have an extra session with the ol' misses for that. Now go on, break it up. Break it up."

Sabastian let go of Leo, and waved his baton around some more until the circle dispersed. Once satisfied, the bald man stomped over to a corner to continue watching over the kids. Still trying to catch his breath, Kallik watched the other kids scatter. All except the trio and Xoriah left to their separate areas. Setting down her book, Xoriah took his hand and helped Kallik to his feet. This close, he couldn't help but notice how pretty she truly was. Her green eyes were a particular draw. He blushed at the sudden contact and cleared his throat to distract himself. Leo wiped his mouth, and his two friends flanked him to see if he was alright.

"That was Morkus," Leo said, "and the girl with him was Mauricia. They think they run the place, but don't let them get to you."

Leo held out his hand. This time, Kallik took it. Leo's grip was tight, and Kallik remembered something else his father told him about the ritual. His father told him that many humans were dumb, and believed a firm handshake indicated a dependable person. In truth, a firm handshake meant nothing more than an animalistic grip strength, but his father told him to play along with it should the situation ever arise. Kallik wanted to wince, but instead tightened his hand right back. He was awarded with another of Leo's grins. Kallik tried to smile back but couldn't find it in him, not after the display he just put on. They finished introductions, each of them telling him their name and conduit type which was a term Kallik had never heard before. Everyone except for the little Groal girl was a bull like himself. It meant they were able to manipulate physical objects with their mind. Kallik learned the only other Groal, Rekkeh, was a viper. She was able to dig into people's thoughts, and change their perception of the reality around them.

They took turns telling him about the experiments. What Kallik had endured was just a placement procedure to find out what category he fell under. After, there would be an endless number of trials that he'd be forced to run through until he burnt out. The small discs they put on behind their ears was to prevent them from using their abilities outside of these experiments and potentially burning themselves out early. When Kallik pressed them on what happened if someone burned out, all he got in response was a shrug and that it was different for everyone. The only commonality was that "The Butcher" took them away. The Butcher was their name for the masked man.

"And what about this trial?" Kallik asked. "Why is it so important?"

"Dunno," Leo said, "but it's different for bulls and vipers. For us, they take you out of the facility to this underwater ship. Some kind of alien tech no one has seen before."

"Inside is a spooky naked alien woman," Toby cut in, "with four arms!" Kallik thought it was a joke, but the others nodded. Toby made a rude gesture in front of his chest, and Leo slapped him upside the head. Rekkeh giggled while Xoriah blushed.

"They hook you up to a bunch of brain wires," Leo said, and put his hands around his head to make it look like a helmet. "Then you get zapped into a different reality where this alien woman hunts you. The longer you survive, the happier all the scientists are with you."

"The strongest don't have to go in as often," Xoriah added. "They want to keep us preserved."

Xoriah's comment made something about Morkus make sense. If being stronger meant being tested less, then maybe his attitude was a way of survival. "What about vipers? How are they tested?"

Rekkeh shied away from his question, and the others seemed to find the floor rather interesting. Kallik looked from one to the other until someone answered his question. Clearly, he had asked something wrong, but not one of them was correcting him.

At last, Xoraih spoke up.

"They won't talk about it," she said. "There's only a few left including Rekkeh and Mauricia, and none of them will say what they do."

Kallik let it go, and worked up the courage for his last question. "And what about our parents? What did they do with my dad?"

CHAPTER 4
- KALLIK -

1

Kallik cried himself to sleep that night, or what he thought was night. There was no way of telling what time it was in this place. There were no clocks or automated light sequences to help determine what time of day it was, only the bright, fluorescent lights throughout the facility. His new friends avoided giving him a direct answer to his last question, but their faces told him enough. His worst fear was coming to light. The Butcher and his horrible crew of Skren had killed them and everyone else he knew. Kallik had voiced the thought aloud, and only Rekkeh started to protest, but she fell silent before a single word left her lips. Perhaps she thought to console Kallik then decided against it. Whatever the reason, they permitted him to believe those words. If the truth was worse, he didn't want to know.

He sat up in the corner of his bed using the wall as a backrest. He rotated a book around and around in his hands but never opened it. Xoriah had given it to him before he separated from the group to mourn in solitude. He had fallen asleep with it on his chest and he handled it as if it were his last possession in the galaxy. Maybe it was. The book was real, with pages and ink, but it was a simple picture book without words. Not even a title adorned its cover. It depicted strange creatures, twisted humanoids that looked half human and half avian, and cloaked figures with floating swords. Xoriah had told him it was a favorite of hers, but Kallik suspected it was just something more in line with what she thought he'd like. He appreciated it all the same. He opened the front cover and something fell out onto his lap. A flower, red petaled and flat from being stowed within the book, lay across his thigh. He remembered there being mention of a garden on the upper floor, and remembered that only well-behaved children were permitted to visit. If one had to adhere to the will of these monsters in order to see the greenery, Kallik had no intention of ever going there. He picked up the flower, twirling it between his index finger and thumb, and brought it to his nose. Breathing in deep, he let its faint aroma fill his senses. Pleasant, but not overpowering, the floral scent was similar to how he remembered Xoriah smelling when she helped him to his feet. Was she the one that placed the flower in this book? He liked to think she had, and he liked to think she had intentionally done it for his benefit. He touched the end of a delicate petal with the tip of his finger, cautious not break it off. Looking around his tiny coffin of a room, Kallik wondered if this single flower would be the last time he saw such greenery.

A knock sounded at his door, and Kallik was quick to stow both the book and flower beneath the plastic sheet. He would need to find a better place to keep them safe later. Crawling out of bed and opening the door, he found Master Aillon waiting in the hallway. He had on the same uniform as the day prior. A bit cleaner this time, Kallik also noticed his hair was not as disheveled. The black feather tucked behind his ear seemed a permanent feature. Aillon inclined his head when Kallik opened the door.

"I don't mean to intrude," he said, "but your first test is rapidly approaching, and I'd like to give a bit of preparation before you're thrown to the wolves, so to speak."

"You mean the alien that hunts me?" Kallik asked. "You are going to prepare me for that?"

"Ah, so you've spoken to the other children," Aillon said. He ran a narrow hand through his shock of red hair, and Kallik noticed his nails were particularly well kept. "Yes, I'm going to do my best to prepare you for the witch of the woods who gobbles up little children for breakfast."

"Help, or no help, I die anyway, right?" Kallik asked. Master Aillon was taken aback by his question, face twitching as if he'd been struck. His hand scrubbed his hair again, and he shrugged.

"It's true," he said after a long moment, "all of us here are doomed to the same fate. However, if my teaching may serve to prolong such times, I feel it is still in your best interest."

"Fine," Kallik said. He looked back at his bed, and double checked no one could see the book there. Stepping out in the hall, Aillon moving aside to give him room, Kallik closed the door behind him. He had no idea if anyone checked the rooms while the kids weren't in them, but he hoped it would be his one place of privacy.

Master Aillon gave Kallik a sad smile and gestured for him to follow. He was once again led through the maze of white hallways and identical doors until he was shown into what closely resembled a classroom. Someday, if he had the chance, Kallik would have to try and memorize the layout of this place. He was sure if he lived long enough, it would prove to be useful. The classroom was small, but at least it offered more space than his bedroom. A large teacher's desk sat at one end with several smaller student's desks lined up in front of it. Aillon gave the place a strange look as if it brought back some sort of memory. Kallik could not tell if said memory was a good one or a bad one, but Master Aillon steeped in his rumination for several moments before realizing Kallik was watching him.

"My apologies," he said, "this was never meant to be mine. An old colleague used to teach the bulls, and his sibling the vipers. Both are gone, and now you bulls are stuck with me. As for the vipers, well, let's not get into that. Please, take a seat."

Master Aillon waved a hand at one of the desks, and Kallik chose to sit at a different desk. The small act of rebellion gave him only a slight pang of satisfaction, but he would take what he could. Aillon appeared not to notice, or not to care. Either way, he took his place at the teacher's desk pulling out the larger wheeled chair, and slumping into it. Kallik's own chair was stiff backed and uncomfortable. He supposed it was what real schools were like had he ever been to one. His life had been a nomadic one with his father and cousin tutoring him on the go. They seemed to like it better that way claiming he would only learn the necessary skills, the real skills, he needed to know to thrive.

"Right, let's get started," Master Aillon said. "Now that you know about your powers, I am to teach you how to use them. You got a feel for how they work, but here are some important things you need to know both to improve your skills, and to keep yourself as safe as possible."

"This place cares about my safety?" Kallik asked. It was a mean question, a rude question, but Kallik let it slip out. Master Aillon looked genuinely hurt by his words, and Kallik wished he could have taken them back.

"This place?" Aillon asked. He leaned back in his chair, and stared up at the ceiling. He seemed to be searching for his thoughts up there. "No. No, it does not. Neither do its scientists, or many of its orderlies. These walls have seen hundreds of kids like yourself enter to never leave again, and they shrug off the guilt, unbothered, and uncaring claiming it all to be in the great name of progress. Do not, however, make the mistake of believing everyone who works here does so by their own free will. Not everyone was given that choice."

"I'm sorry," Kallik said, and he found that he meant it. Tears started to well up at the corners of his eyes, and he wanted to cry. Not because of this situation in particular, but the emotions were compounding like water behind a struggling dam, and Kallik was on the constant edge of sobbing. He wiped his eyes with his sleeve, still having enough pride to not want a complete stranger witnessing his moment of weakness. Acknowledging the tears were there just added to his urge to let them loose, and soon they were free flowing down his cheek. He heard a deep sigh come from Aillon, and the Master walked over to sit on the desk next to him.

"Xek was much better at this," Aillon said more to himself than to Kallik. "Allow me to let you in on a little secret."

He ran a hand back and forth along the top of Kallik's back in a soothing motion. He did not hush Kallik, nor tell him to stop crying. Instead, Aillon simply comforted him and talked about a different subject entirely. Kallik found the result far more consoling than he expected, and wondered if Aillon was one of the only good people in this facility.

"This place is dying," Master Aillon said. "The shitty kitty Karaska doesn't want to admit it, but this place is on its last leg." Kallik could not help but giggle through his tears at Aillon's insult toward the doctor. "He loses more resources every day, and soon he will no longer have the means to produce young conduits such as yourself. Now, all he does is bide time and hope he figures out the riddle to this alien ship he's found. This is good news for both of us." Aillon leaned back on the desk and craned his neck to check the hallway. Finding it empty he continued on. "There's an advantage here we can pounce on, but absolute care must be taken. You understand?"

He was dodging around a point, but Kallik could see what Master Aillon was implying. He was just as much a prisoner as Kallik. Sniffing, and wiping his nose, Kallik nodded. To his disappointment, Master Aillon stopped rubbing his back, and returned to his teacher's desk. He propped his elbows up on the desk surface, and rested his chin between his fists. It squished his cheeks together like some sort of rodent, and Kallik almost laughed again. He kept quiet, however, as the gesture did not seem to be an intended joke.

"I won't say more right now," Master Aillon said. "For the time being, we have to play their little game. So please Kallik, let me teach you what I can."

Kallik agreed this time, giving Master Aillon a tear-stained smile. Aillon had given him something Kallik had not realized he had lost. Hope. It was handed to him in a ribbon-tied box with a feather tucked beneath its fabric, just waiting to be opened.

2

Aillon started by reviewing what he had already told Kallik during his placement testing. His imagination was the key, but not the only factor. Conduits needed to work themselves into a state of mind where they genuinely believed what they envisioned, and the stone would do the rest. The stone, which Aillon called psycholith, altered reality to suit the conduit's thoughts. How it did this, Master Aillon was unsure of. He waved his hands about in a wide arc.

"Magic," he said, "for all we know about it, the stone's effects might as well be magic. The material isn't native to this galaxy, and as far as studies go it might not even be native to this dimension. What I can tell you is Xaranor founded its entire existence from the discovery of its use."

"This facility is Xaranor?" Kallik asked. It was a piece of information he could use later should the chance for escape arise.

"No," Master Aillon said. "Karaska and Xaranor go way back, but there was a bit of a moral quandary, and Karaska split off. Now he steals from Xaranor where he can in order to conduct his own work."

Kallik raised his eyebrow at this. "Which one had the moral high ground?"

"Good question," Aillon snorted. "Xaranor has plenty of blood on their hands, but abduction isn't their style. Every member of Xaranor is there because they want to be, and conduits become so voluntarily. Karaska, on the other hand, loves his experiments too much to let a silly thing like morality get in the way."

"So, it's nice there?" Kallik asked. "Wherever Xaranor is?"

Master Aillon got a faraway look and took a moment. "It's hot, dry, and some would call it a tomb, but if it is a tomb, it is quite the beautiful one. The planet is mostly desert with sand dunes as high as skyscrapers and canyons deep enough to conceal mountains. The capitol is nestled within the planet's only oasis. It's new tech built into ancient architecture. Makes for a remarkable sight. Old temples and palaces stand next to a modern spaceport, and I get the feeling you would love the library there. Maybe not its caretaker, but definitely the library itself."

"What's wrong with the librarian?" Kallik asked. He was growing invested in Aillon's description and wanted to know about the place. "Are they mean or something?"

"Or something," Aillon said, "but you're veering me off course. I actually have things I need to teach you. Unfortunately, we don't have much time today, so I'll cut to the important bit. There's a difference between you and me. Xaranor gave me my powers. The difference lies in that Xaranor discovered a way to put limits on a conduit's powers without inhibiting them. It's a preventative measure to keep us from going overboard with our abilities and causing our brains to snap. Karaska provides no such luxury to you kids. He wants all of you functioning at the highest performance you can provide, consequences be damned."

"What happens when we snap?" Kallik asked.

"It's different between bulls and vipers," Master Aillon said, "but that's a different lesson for a different time. Just be careful with how much you exercise your abilities, yeah?"

Kallik agreed, and Master Aillon started to move on to a different subject. He said something about weight ratios when he was interrupted by an orderly. Anna cleared her throat from the doorway to get both of their attention, and asked if Kallik could be dismissed. With a wave of a hand Master Aillon gave his approval, but muttered something about not having a choice.

"Come then," Anna said, "it's time for your first test."

3

Kallik waited before a door which resembled an airlock. A thick "X" pattern was painted onto the front of a double door, and a narrow line at the center marked where it opened. Beside him, Anna waited patiently and watched a small countdown above the door. It was a countdown, but for what, Kallik had not been told. Instead of asking, Kallik waited in silence. Anna had a comforting presence, but he was not sure if he trusted it yet. She could be a device of Karaska's meant to lull him into a false sense of compliance. The thought occurred to him that Master Aillon could be as well, but the red-haired man seemed too genuine to Kallik for that to be the case. He watched Anna out of the corner of his eye, trying to look for some kind of tell.

Little information was garnered before the countdown hit zero. Kallik could hear loud mechanical clicking followed by a whooshing noise from the other side of the door. What were they stepping into? The answer came soon after as the door split apart to reveal the interior of a small transport pod. Spherical in shape, the transport pod resembled a steel bubble with large glass windows. Through the windows Kallik could see water. Lots of water. When he had first met Anna, she had told him most of the facility resided underwater. Until now, Kallik had not contemplated what that might look like. Seeing the pod and knowing he was meant to step into it caused terror to creep into the crevices of his chest. Its cold grasp weaved through his organs and wrapped around the base of his heart. Nausea came next. He could feel the blood draining from his face and the saliva building up in the back of his mouth. Swallowing helped little, wiping his palms on his pants helped less. Anna stepped into the pod without hesitation and gave Kallik a confused look.

"Why put a building underwater?" Kallik asked. "What's the point?"

"This whole planet is an ocean beneath a thick sheet of ice," she said as if that answered his question. "Come now, Kallik, the scientists tend to be impatient."

"I don't want to," Kallik said. "I don't like deep water."

Anna eyed the windows with a thoughtful expression. She took a few moments to search the pod's walls before she lit up as if she'd found something. Pushing a button next to a window, metal panels slid downward to cover the glass. Once they were down, the windows were completely blocked. She held out her hand for Kallik while making a grabbing motion. Double checking to be sure he could not see the water, Kallik wiped the sweat from his hand and took Anna's. She gently pulled him into the pod, and the door closed.

"Better?" She asked. Kallik nodded but hung his head in shame. He was embarrassed for having such an adverse reaction and wished he had done better to hide it. Anna placed a finger beneath his chin and tilted his head up to face hers. She was smiling her usual warm smile.

"It's okay," she said. "I'm deathly afraid of spiders. One time when I was younger, maybe a cycle or two older than yourself, my sister pulled a rather mean prank on me. I was sitting beneath a tree next to a pond, and it was getting close to evening hours. This was at the very edge of an oasis, so I could watch the sunset over the desert while I read. Well, where I'm from has some very nasty spiders. Some can grow as large as cats. I was enjoying some reading time to myself, as I liked to back then, when I felt a strange tickle on the back of my shoulder. When I turned to check, I saw the largest spider I've ever seen climbing down from the tree. It was almost as big as you, little Kallik. I screamed bloody murder and fell backward into the pond. When I got up, I found it was my sister and her friends using a projector to play a trick on me. I was so embarrassed that I cried in front of all of them."

"I'm sorry," Kallik said, "that must have been awful."

"It was," Anna said, "but it goes to show that all of us have our fears, and they are nothing to be ashamed of."

"You're more like Aillon than the others," Kallik said. He meant to say it to himself alone, but the words escaped him and were loud enough for Anna to hear. She started to cackle with laughter, and Kallik turned beet red. "I meant it as a compliment, what's so funny about that?"

"Maybe I'll tell you one day," she said, "but I'm afraid we've lingered long enough."

Anna tapped on a display and a holo-feed sprang up at the front of the pod. There were few commands available, with most of those grayed out. Anna pushed the start command, and the pod lurched into motion. She kept hold of Kallik's hand, however, both of them still had to grab onto a rail to keep from falling over. Focusing his mind on today's events rather than being underwater helped his mood a great deal. Both Aillon and Anna seemed to be good people in the wrong place, and many of the other kids were alright as well. If he really worked hard at it, he may be able to come up with a plan to save all of them. Just maybe.

The pod slowed to a stop, and Kallik could feel it turning in the water to face a different direction. The noises he heard before started with their mechanical whirring and the whooshing of water as it was expelled from the chamber between the pod and the facility. Anna let go of his hand, and the pod door opened. She ran her hand across the back of his head and gave Kallik a sad smile.

"I need you to do your best, okay?" She said, "at least this one time."

4

Anna stayed inside the pod while a pair of rough hands reached in to pull him out. The hands belonged to a creature from his nightmare. It was one of the Skren Dwemyri, a hulking bat-like creature with patched fur and clawed hands. Dragging Kallik into the airlock, it opened the second set of doors to reveal a dark corridor beyond. Without so much as a word, the Skren forced Kallik down the passageway. The place had an organic feel to it with each passageway having a ribbed structure to it as if they were inside some massive organ. The bulkhead itself seemed made less of a metal and more like it was made from stone or carapace. Kallik wanted to feel the material, but at the same time was disgusted by its appearance. Everything was dark red, and even the small bulbs protruding from the ceiling gave off a light that resonated with a faint crimson. It made his heart race and his stomach feel queasy.

Kallik was pushed around a corner, and another Skren took him from there. Instead of cheap leather armor, this one wore a thick battle plate. His fur was a deep gray, and numerous scars covered his snout. He looked at Kallik with malcontent and wrapped a gauntleted hand around his shoulder. Kallik noticed a closed door behind the Skren with two more in similar plate guarding it on either side. The Skren grabbing his shoulder drew him close, scarred snout a hair's breadth away from Kallik's own nose. Kallik could smell the stink of the creature's breath, and he did not want to imagine what these things ate.

"No speaking," it growled at him. Kallik nodded, and the Skren shoved him to the other two. They worked him over as if he may be hiding a weapon before opening the door for him to go through. The other side revealed a large, open chamber. It reminded Kallik of the bridge of his father's ship.

Like the passageways before, this chamber had an organic texture to it. The same rib workings marked their way up to the center of the chamber's ceiling, and stone counters lined the edges of the room. The chamber's center was inset like a pit where several seats were carved into the floor itself. It looked like an emptied pool for someone to lie down in. What truly grabbed Kallik's attention, however, was what the scientists had set up near the far end of the chamber. A large cryotube with a glass front faced the inner part of the room. An endless number of tubes and wires ran in and out of it to connect to a different machine. Each of these machines were being monitored by a team of individuals in white uniforms. Kallik could see what was being stored behind the glass. Suspended in liquid was a person, or what Kallik thought resembled a person. Four arms extended from four shoulders and floated in front of the person's torso. Both of its legs were curled up in front of it, and it looked to Kallik like they were trying to hug themselves in the fetal position, but passed out before they could make it all the way there. A long tendril extended from the back of their head. It looked like a tail growing from the wrong place. What's more, Kallik noticed that the individual was, in fact, nude. He tried not to blush as he realized what Toby's gesture had been about. It was the first time Kallik had ever seen a woman's naked anatomy in the flesh, and he was not sure how to feel.

"Ah, there you are," a woman called out from across the chamber. She was a reedy woman with black hair and a wrinkled forehead. "We've been waiting for you. Come over here, boy."

She waved him over, and moved to stand next to the chamber's inset area. Kallik gave the room another once over before walking over to meet her. She seemed annoyed by this, so Kallik made sure to walk slowly, acting like the floor was rough terrain even though it was perfectly smooth. He reached the other side of the inset, and the scientist pointed at one of the seats carved into the floor.

"Sit," she said, "we've lost enough time already."

She looked ready to hurt Kallik if he said no, so he lowered himself into the inset and took a seat. The chair was inclined making it so Kallik had to lie back and stare up at the ceiling. The reedy woman snapped her fingers at several of her colleagues who hurried over, and began hooking up strange instruments to Kallik's head. A metal band went on first followed by several pads which were connected by wiring. They placed a bit in Kallik's mouth to prevent him from biting down and strapped it around the back of his neck. One of the scientists scanned his wrist with a strange device and made a few notes in a data-slate. As a final touch, they removed the small disk from behind his ear.

"Have you eaten anything today?" The reedy woman asked him. Kallik shook his head. "Good. Everyone vomits their first time, and most their second and third as well. Easier to clean up if you haven't eaten."

Kallik wanted to ask why, but the bit in his mouth prevented him from speaking. More wires were strapped to his wrists, and the scientists began talking amongst themselves about their procedures and checks. Eventually, they all went their separate ways, disappearing from Kallik's view. He laid there, staring up at the alien ceiling, and waited for something to happen. Just when he thought nothing was going to happen, a shock jolted through his system. In a split second, Kallik blinked and found himself somewhere else.

Still on his back, the ceiling had been replaced with a clear blue sky. It was daytime, but the moon and stars were still visible along with the sun. Trying to sit up, Kallik realized none of the gear the scientists had hooked up was there. He was free. All around him rose the walls of a valley. The stone had a magenta tint, and deep veins of gold ran throughout. Trees with black bark and teal leaves sprouted from wide cracks in the cliff faces, and a hint of green grass could be seen at the canyon's top. About his feet, loose rock and dirt covered the ground while a small stream trickled nearby. The burbling noise drew Kallik's attention, so he wandered over to investigate. Odd as this place appeared, everything felt solid. It was no dream, Kallik felt like he was here in the flesh. The water of the stream was crystal clear and flowed over more magenta tinted stone. The color was drawn out even more by the wet shimmer. He placed a hand in the water letting the icy coolness wash over his skin.

Rocks tumbled somewhere nearby, and Kallik sprang to his feet in search of the noise. It did not take long as she was not trying to hide. Standing a few paces away was the woman from the cryotube. She was fully clothed in a peculiar outfit of half cloth and half carapace. The hard blue shell covered random areas such as the left half of her torso and both her right arms. More covered the tops of her thighs. The rest of her outfit was made of a pale gray fabric that shimmered as she moved. Dark hair now covered her scalp, but Kallik could still see the tendril hanging beneath it. Wide, black eyes watched Kallik with a predatory curiosity. She approached, four arms swaying at her side as she walked. Her nails were lacquered black and filed to dangerous points. They reminded Kallik of the Dwemyri's claws.

"Many two-armed children have appeared in my world of late," she said, "but none of them have had horns before."

She took another step toward Kallik, and he backed away. He let his foot plunge into the freezing stream. Jolting, he stumbled to the other side while keeping the woman in his sight. The stories he was told about her raced through his head. Kallik wondered if he should run, or stand his ground. A thoughtful expression played across the woman's face, but she stopped her approach.

"Where I am from," she said, "my people considered things with horns to be physical manifestations of malefic deities. Tell me, child, are you evil made manifest?"

She did not wait for a response. In one smooth motion, she leapt from where she was to land behind Kallik. He twisted in response, but too late. Before he fully turned around, she was already upon him. Startlement shocked his heart, and he fell backward. He never hit the ground. A sharp-nailed hand shot out and clutched him by the throat, suspending him above the stream. Needle tips dug into his neck, piercing his skin, his flesh, his veins. Kallik wanted to scream, but he could not breathe. Struggling and flailing only caused her to tighten her grip, and she drew him close to her face. A hungry grin revealed pointed teeth. He rolled his eyes from side to side, desperate to find a way out. Frantic, Kallik imagined a nearby rock flying into her head. He pictured it, and forced himself to believe it was true. Heat prickled his scalp and the tops of his ears, and the woman grunted as a rock bounced off her temple. She glared murder in the direction it was thrown. Seeing no one, realization dawned on her.

"Ahhh," she said, "one of those, are we?"

Instead of answering, Kallik used his will to pull a larger chunk of rock free of the canyon's face. It tumbled down and slammed into her back. The force of it flattened them both, but she let go of Kallik's throat. Gulping down air, he bolted to his feet, and sprinted in the first direction he saw. He followed the canyon until he found a crack wide enough for him to squeeze into. Sucking in a breath, Kallik edged in sideways, and shuffled himself in as far as the crack would allow. No light made its way into the crevice making his surroundings impossible to see. He hoped it was enough to avoid his pursuer.

Thud, thud, thud, his heart pounded against his ribcage. It stung being pressed so tightly against the rock walls. He could feel blood trickling down his neck, pumping with each painful beat of his heart. Struggling to catch his breath, air rasped against his throat with each frantic inhale. He needed to be quiet. He needed to be still. Kallik was neither. His panting echoed throughout his hiding spot, and he thought one would need to be deaf to not hear his hammering heart. A shadow sped past the entrance, and Kallik held in a breath. He tried to calm his heart, but it was no use. He pleaded in his head; pleaded for her to run past and never return. It was a vain hope. The shadow came back, blocking the light of the entrance.

"There you are, little devil," she said, "now that I know what you are, I don't have to hold back."

She was too large to fit into the crevice, so Kallik had a moment of brief hope. It was shredded when he felt an invisible force pulling him free of his hideout. She had the same abilities as him. He tried to grab onto the rock and wedge himself in place, but her strength was too great. Ripped free of his grip, Kallik was ejected from the mouth of the crack. Four arms snatched him from midair, and Kallik flailed with his feet and fists. Nothing connected, and he could hear her laughing. He was held facing the sky with the stars, moon, and sun all shining above. This was his last sight of this world. He knew it. Her next words confirmed it.

"Until I next dream of you, little devil," she said. Kallik felt himself lowered. He braced, and teeth sunk into his neck.

A dark ceiling swirled above Kallik, and his head pounded. Hands pulled equipment free from his head and arms, and the bit was pulled from his mouth. Someone was shouting about success, but it sounded distant like a dream. A figure loomed over him, but he was too dizzy to see who it was. His breath tasted foul, and each breath felt acrid. Rolling over onto his side, Kallik puked into the seat next to him.

"I told you," said a woman's voice. "Someone come clean this up!"

CHAPTER 5
- SARAH -

1

Eleven months ago, had someone told Sarah that Jax snored louder than a star-freight engine, she might have reconsidered her plans to run away with the Vulture pilot. However, no one had warned her that such a small woman could make such big noises. So, here she was, in the far reaches of deep space with the very frame of the Modiri rumbling with each breath Jax took. Sarah lay awake in her suspended hammock in the small storage closet the pair of them called a bedroom, and stared up at the ceiling which was covered in its entirety with open wiring and thick cables. A small power light shone from the far side of the room giving Sarah's view a soft blue glow, and silhouetting the other hammock which contained her partner. It swayed as she slept, and Sarah wondered if the snoring was the root cause of that as well.

It was nearly five hours into their sleep cycle, and Sarah had yet to close her eyes. Myrddin had been right, and the nightmares had grown worse the last few nights. Every time she closed her eyes, Sarah could see Doctor Sondra's eyeless sockets glaring into her soul. She killed it every night in her sleep, but every night it returned. Sarah would hear Gayle's voice calling out to her telling her how frightened it was of death. In those dreams, Sarah smashed the AI with her sledgehammer. She didn't want to do it. She begged herself not to, and yet she swung the hammer all the same. Months of therapy and medications unraveled at the seams, and Sarah wished she had taken the bottle of munmos.

Giving up on sleep, Sarah crawled out of her hammock. She winced as her bare feet touched the cold grating of the metal floor, but she forced herself to get up. Jax kept the ship so cold for their sleep cycles that Sarah had to use several extra-thick quilts to stay comfortable. She would wear more clothes to bed, but it felt too strange. Adorning more than a simple t-shirt to bed made the arduous task of falling asleep next to impossible. Sarah shivered, and looked around the floor for her cloak while rubbing a hand across her stomach. An angry, puckered scar ran across her abdomen from the bottom of her right rib to the top of her left hip. A constant itch plagued the wounded area but scratching it did little good. It was another souvenir from Carlisle Station to go along with her nerve-damaged hand.

Black feathers poked out from the corner beneath her hammock. She dragged the cloak out, and draped it over her shoulders. Fastening it at the front, she pulled the feathered collar tight. Pulling her body into a languid stretch, knees and elbows cracking, Sarah let out a yawn. She was exhausted, but sleep was just not in the cards tonight. She pushed a hand to the door panel, hoping the noise would not be enough to wake Jax. The panel beeped, the door slid open, and the Vulture pilot remained asleep.

Sarah needed to find something to preoccupy her mind for the next few hours until it was time to start the day proper. Reading was something that helped, or perhaps she would use the time to get some actual writing in. She'd been putting off the task long enough, finding excuse after excuse as to why she couldn't write on any given day. She wanted to write, but thinking about writing and actually writing were two completely different monsters. As soon as she sat down to put words onto the page, she lost all motivation. Maybe this time would be different.

2

Sarah lounged in the copilot's seat with her feet propped up on the control console, a steaming cup of coffee held in both hands on her lap. A data-slate with an empty word processor lay discarded on the floor to her left. At least she had tried. The cockpit's particle shield was lifted, giving Sarah a full view of space. The cosmos spread out before her with twinkling stars and glowing nebulas. Even after the events of Carlisle Station, Sarah never lost her love for such views. The void was entrancing, and called to her with its endless promises, no matter what circumstance she found herself in. It was cold, cruel, and uncaring, but beautiful all the same. The two of them had picked this spot to stop and rest as they were a single jump away from their target location. While most would allow their ships to travel in lower power modes while they slept, or rotated in shifts to keep their ship running at full power in order to make the best travel times possible, it was just the two of them with the Modiri being in less-than-ideal condition. They liked to bring Modiri to a complete stop before winding down for sleep to bring travel risks down as low as possible, and not put too much stress on the ship's inner workings.

Taking a sip of her coffee, the aroma of the dark roast wafting in her nostrils, Sarah tapped one of the control panels to her right. A holo-readout bloomed into view displaying a map and some generalized information about the location Ziven had sent them. An asteroid belt hovered above the console with tones of shimmering blue, and the name Zocomie Belt blinked underneath. A single asteroid was outlined in red, and Sarah pushed a finger to it to zoom in. The display shifted until the asteroid was all that could be seen. It rotated around giving a three-sixty view. Easy to miss at first glance, what appeared to be a sprawling network of tubes spider-webbed out along the surface. An untrained eye would see the tubing as little more than industrial pipework weaving in and out of the asteroid's surface. Sarah spun the view, and zoomed in once more. A small cube blinked on the holo-feed showing the entrance to a well-hidden structure. Angled into the side of a cliff face, it became clear the spider webbing originated from this point.

The structure had once been a military tech facility belonging to the Coalition of the Red Giant. Sitting in what's now a neutral zone, the facility was abandoned in haste when the Coalition and the Human Federation of Systems drew up a tenuous peace deal. There were countless locations such as this left adrift in the neutral zone, and all of them were ripe for Vulture looting - at least, the few that had not already been looted. The peace deal was far enough in the past, that only the most hidden structures remained untouched.

"Come look, Sarah," said a little girl's voice. Sarah gave a start, and splashed hot coffee across her wrists and lap. Wincing, she set the coffee aside and glared at the source of the voice. Leaning against the pilot's seat with a smirk was her. Only, it was Sarah fifteen years younger. The childhood version of herself was wide eyed with her hair shaved, but patchy. She wore street rags, and her brother's old coat was draped over her shoulders. The little girl pointed to the ladder which led down from the cockpit into Modiri's belly, and repeated her command.

"Come look, Sarah."

"I thought I was done with you," Sarah said. She wanted to be angry. She wanted to be indifferent, but instead all Sarah felt was fear. It clawed at her throat, dried her mouth, and launched her heart into a fluttered frenzy. A vision like this had not happened since escaping Carlisle Station. Why now? It had to be the lack of sleep. Sarah's mind was slipping due to a lack of rest, and all she needed to do was close her eyes. Her lids slid shut, and Sarah squeezed them tight for several moments. The vision would be gone once she opened her eyes. Sarah knew the vision would disappear. Sarah opened her eyes, and the little girl was centimeters away from her face. The grin smeared across her features had grown wider than physically possible, giving the girl an unnatural air. Her little eyes glittered with predatory intent.

"You're not real," Sarah said. The words came out more a whimper than the bold declaration she had intended. The too wide smile grew wider, and a little hand shot up to Sarah's chin. Little fingers clamped down on Sarah's jaw and squeezed. Tears welled up in Sarah's eyes and spilled down her cheeks. The little girl tugged Sarah's head forward until their faces were almost touching.

"I want to show you something," the little girl said, "and if you don't come look, I'll kill the sleeping one."

Sarah did her best to nod her acceptance, and the girl let

go. She touched a hand to her chin and worked her jaw as pain throbbed through the muscles and joints. Her childhood-self climbed down the ladder, keeping an expectant eye on Sarah. Taking a deep breath, Sarah followed. She was led through the cargo hold to the far end of the ship. Any further, and they would end up near the exit ramp. The little girl glanced over her shoulder to ensure Sarah was still following before pointing at an airlock.

"In there," she said, "I want you to look in there."

"What will I find?" Sarah asked. She hesitated moving any closer, and tried to keep an eye on both her younger self and the airlock door at the same time. She could see a faint orange light glowing through the airlock's porthole.

"Only what you deserve," the little girl said with a giggled. Sarah approached the airlock door, and peered through the glass. At first, all she saw was the empty chamber beyond, sealed by the external door. There was no sign of the orange light. The little girl tapped the door panel to her right, and Sarah understood the message. She punched her passcode into the keypad, and the door slid open. Where there was once an empty chamber now stood a blazing furnace. The metal of the ship was replaced by stone and magma. Flames spat out sparks, and licked the threshold to threaten the rest of Modiri's innards. Sarah was forced to take a step back, and pulled her cloak tight despite the heat. The sheer light of it forced her to squint. The little girl touched the small of her back, and pushed her forward. It was a light push with little strength to the girl's arm, but Sarah put up little resistance. Step by step, Sarah drew closer to the flames. She tried to stop at the edge, but the girl's hand pushed on.

"I don't want to," Sarah said. The words came out in a jumbled sob. "Don't make me do this."

"You left them," the little girl said, "all of them. You left them all to die."

"I didn't want to," Sarah said. "I tried, really I did."

The little girl pushed harder, and Sarah grabbed either side of the doorframe to keep herself from being pushed in. She could feel the heat pouring over her skin, singeing the hem of her cloak. Tilting her head away from the flames, Sarah tried to push against the little girl's hand, but the little girl had grown supernatural strength. She pushed harder, but her younger self responded by throwing her shoulder into Sarah's back. Her back, shoulders, and elbows all cracked as she tried to keep herself from pitching forward. The pain forced a grunt from her, but she managed to stay upright. Something arose in her, an anger she had not known she had been suppressing. It boiled in her chest hotter than the flames threatening her. Sarah kicked back, heel driving into her younger self's belly, and spun around to face her.

Her eyes snapped open. With a bolt, Sarah spilled hot coffee into her lap, and she hissed with pain. She was still in the copilot's seat, slumped back with her legs on the console. Setting her mug aside, she cleaned up her lap with a rag. She had just fallen asleep. That was it. The coffee in her dreams had felt just as hot against her skin as the coffee she now cleaned up. She should have taken the munmos.

Jax climbed up the ladder into the cockpit with a data-slate tucked into the crook of her arm. She was wearing Sarah's old pair of Kara Corp coveralls as pants with the upper half tied around her waist like a belt. The blue paired nicely with the yellow of Jax's tank top. Her hair was undone and hanging wildly about her shoulders. Setting the data-slate down on the control console, she kissed the top of Sarah's head and plopped into the pilot's seat.

"Show time," she said. "Get dressed and come back to help me. It's gonna take both of us to land on this thing."

3

They spent the next hour or so prepping Modiri for a potentially harsh landing. Their target asteroid was roughly the size of a small moon, but its axis of rotation was much higher. The timing along with the integrity of the ship needed to be spot on, or the results could be catastrophic. The problem was Modiri had been on her last leg when she first docked at Carlilse Station, and over the last eleven months the pair of them had little time or funds to properly bring her back to speed. After they found Hector, the two of them would do whatever it took to earn the credits needed to build her from the ground up if necessary. Sarah hoped that it didn't require them to turn Modiri into a ball of wreckage in the process. She had grown fond of the little ship, and despite past events, she had grown rather fond of living as well.

With the particle shield down, a visual feed had to be projected. It lit up with a blue hue across where the window would usually be, and gave them a live view of the space outside. Together, the pair readied Modiri for the final jump sequence and entered the coordinates. A countdown to jump started at thirty, and they both strapped in. In most cases, it was a meaningless precaution as long-range jumps had little in the way of detectable motion, however, they were jumping near an asteroid belt and needed to be prepared to maneuver around stray debris. They exchanged an excited glance as the countdown hit zero, and Jax pushed a thumb to the confirm prompt. The hum of the engines escalated into a high-pitched squeal, and the display went blank for a long moment. The first time Sarah experienced Modiri's jump sequence, she had panicked thinking the ship was about to fall apart. After eleven months aboard this ship, however, she had learned the squealing was due to the older tech in Modiri's jump drives. The squealing proceeded, the display remained blank, and Sarah sat back in her seat with little concern.

All at once, the engine whine stopped, and the visual feed flickered back to life. Stretched out before them waited an endless column of black stones floating through the void. The system's local star, Theracles IV, provided just enough light to illuminate the edges of each asteroid. Any number of smaller rocks could be floating within those shadows which meant Jax needed to be at the top of her game. Sarah looked over at the pilot who was chewing on her bottom lip. She realized it as well. Modiri's pilot assist would be of little use, so the task fell on Sarah to help pinpoint each asteroid and obstacle that may spring up. Without asking, she set to work. Using the long-range sensors, Sarah was able to sort out their target location. She punched in a command to highlight the target in red on their display. After, she broadly scanned the area, and outlined every asteroid she could identify in green. Jax whistled at the growing number of green marks until a majority of their display glowed with the color. The red outline was almost lost save for a small line poking out from behind a field of green. Taking a deep breath, Jax took up the manual control sticks. All Sarah could do now was wait and watch the Vulture pilot do her work.

"Trust me?" Jax asked. Her face was scrunched up with concentration, and she pushed the sticks forward. The external thrusters burst into life, and propelled them forward.

"Of course," Sarah said. Jax's expression twitched, but remained focused on the display. She brought the Modiri to the very edge of the asteroid belt, and halted. An unconcerned rock spun a lazy rotation not thirty meters in front of the nose of the ship. Jax let go of the controls. She shook out her hands, wiped her palms on her thighs, and cracked her knuckles. She spared a nervous smile for Sarah before taking up the controls once more. Sarah did her best to not let her own nerves show. She hoped by putting on a confident face, Jax would feel more at ease. It would at least prevent their emotions from compounding on one another.

Slow and steady was the pace at which Jax flew the Modiri through the first layer of asteroids. The first few they passed by were small and scattered, however, the further into the belt they went, the larger in size they grew. The stationary ones were simple enough to navigate around, but there were enough of the wandering sort to keep Sarah on edge. She kept a constant watch on the sensors in an attempt to catch any new asteroids that may fly through on a collision course. Her console screamed an alarm at her as one such buzzed by and slammed into a larger asteroid. It sent both of the space rocks careening in unpredictable directions, scattering debris and chaos in their wake. Jax swore under her breath as she pulled up on the sticks trying to avoid both the asteroids and the debris. Smaller particles bounced off Modiri's hull, but the larger pieces were evaded.

Grumbling, Jax veered the ship around another large cluster, and narrowly averted colliding nose first with a massive chunk of scrap metal. It appeared they were not the first to make this attempt. Sarah wondered how many other ships were lost out here, and if they might be joining them sooner rather than later. A high-pitched ping echoed through the cockpit as small chunks of the dead ship struck the particle shield. Jax swore much louder and guided the ship between a pair of moon sized asteroids that seemed relatively stationary when compared to their surroundings. Jax used the momentary calm to catch her breath and give Sarah a weary smile.

"Look at that," she said, "we're almost there, and I haven't even broken a sweat."

Sarah snorted, but didn't feel much like laughing. The "almost" Jax referred to still required them to cross through a considerable amount of danger. What bothered Sarah most was somehow the previous occupants of the facility had to have known of a safe way in and out. If she could only figure out where that route was, the two of them could get through this unscathed. Sarah went back to her scanners, but instead of looking for obvious debris and rock, she searched for anything that could be used as a waypoint or an indicator. A lot of her scans were being blocked and interrupted by their surroundings which made the task that much more difficult. She switched her scanners through various frequencies to try and mitigate the extra noise, and managed to find one that worked slightly better. Still, it garnered few results. She was about to give up, and let Jax go back to work, when she caught the faintest signal of something strange.

At first, Sarah thought it was another scuttled ship. However, it was affixed to one of the larger asteroids which warranted a second look. She narrowed her range, fixating the scanners on the single location. The data she received was jumbled, but it was enough to give her hope. She put the information up on the main display so Jax could see what she was thinking. Highlighting a small chunk of the asteroid, Sarah pointed to an elongated pyramid on one side which was too well shaped to be natural.

"It looks constructed," she said, "think it could be a beacon?"

"Could be," Jax said. "If you think there's a safer route than this, I'm all for it."

Jax didn't wait for Sarah to respond. Instead, her face scrunched up with concentration, tongue poking out of the corner of her mouth, and started the ship on a direct course. Smoother than their way in, but still rife with stray rock, Sarah held her breath as the pilot eased Modiri around several obstacles. She needed to be right about this detour. If Sarah was wrong, this trip would put them through needless danger. A larger chunk of asteroid ricocheted off the bottom of the ship, jarring the two in their seats. Sarah winced, but Jax appeared unphased. She kept on track, and maneuvered a skillful turn which brought them right in front of the alleged beacon. In unison, they let out a sigh of relief. Sarah enhanced the visual to get a clearer image. What she found was a rubble encrusted tower made of metal. Numerous antennae protruded from the top, each with what Sarah suspected to be a light attached to the end. She gave Jax a gratified smile, and received one in return.

"We need to land," Sarah said. "If I'm right on this, it'll be connected to a network which will guide us right to the front door of our facility. We just need to turn it on."

"Right, right," Jax said, "ready up the anchors, and I'll get us down there."

Sarah started the procedures for launching the anchors, thick pistons attached to tethers used to latch onto objects in zero-gravity, and waited as Jax flew them in closer. Once they drew in close enough, Sarah executed the command to launch the anchors. The hull shuddered as the pistons fired from the sides of the ship to bury themselves in the rocky surface. The cables pulled taut, and Jax eased Modiri into a slow descent. The cockpit hummed with the activation of the landing feet, and soon the ship touched down, kicking up a thick cloud of gray dust. Jax let out a long breath, gave Sarah a strange look. She reached over and nudged Sarah's knee with a fist.

"Go suit up," she said, "I need to keep old Modiri here in one piece while you do your thing. It was a good plan. Looks like you're starting to think like a real Vulture, no? Just stay on comms, so I know you're alright, alright?"

Sarah nodded, unstrapped herself from her seat, and nudged the pilot back though not as light. "I'll keep in touch," she said with a wink. Jax's compliment had her floating, and she needed to prove that she could live up to those words.

4

Sarah adjusted the wrist strap of her enviro-suit. It was a newer model; one they had picked up just before arriving here. It was thin, sleek to near skin-tight, and had well-planned pieces of armor plating covering the joints such as the knees, elbows, and shoulders. Far better than the horrid things Sarah was used to on Carlisle Station, she found herself enjoying their use. She stood inside the airlock doing everything she could to not think about the last time she saw this room, and busied herself by hooking up a safety tether to her waist. A second waited just outside the airlock door on the outer hull. Once the airlock depressurized, Sarah would step out and switch to that tether. In zero gravity, it was always better to be safe.

A countdown blinked on a side panel to indicate when the chamber would start to depressurize, and the outer door would open. Sarah focused on that, ignoring the flames and the angry little girl tormenting her thoughts. She patted the tools hooked to her belt. With how long this place had been abandoned, Sarah had a feeling any sort of outer control panels may be covered by a thick layer of rock sediment. The clearing of such deposits was a process she was intimately familiar with. The countdown hit zero, the door chimed, and Jax wished her luck over comms. Air hissed around her, and soon the exterior airlock door pushed outward before sliding to the side. Before her awaited a wasteland of gray and black. Dull stone knifed into a lightless sky, and the ground before her was cracked with uneven surfaces. Colossal boulders jutted from the asteroid's planes at harsh angles to create jagged cliff faces which rose to form a valley. Sarah would need to travel through this valley to reach the beacon. It towered above the colorless rock, the only constructed object in an otherwise organic landscape.

"Cutting zero-g," Jax said, "local gravity is fifteen percent of galactic standard, so you'll need to travel with caution. Double check your tether when you get outside."

The gravity generators cut, and Sarah could feel her body lose most of its weight. It was a sensation she'd never grow used to, like being dropped into deep water without warning. Careful to use every hand-hold available to her, Sarah stepped out of the airlock and touched down on the asteroid's surface. Just outside the door was another reel with an attached hook. Grabbing the hook, she attached the reel to her belt before releasing the previous tether. She double checked how secure it was before giving Jax her confirmation, and started toward the beacon.

She reached the edge of the valley. The cliff faces loomed over her like foreboding monoliths. They watched and judged her every move, and Sarah could not shake the feeling of eyes being upon her. She wished Jax could have landed closer, but the valley made it impossible. The two peaks marked the beginning of where the star's light ended, and the rest of the asteroid was thrown into pitch blackness. Helmet lights would have to be enough to guide her from that point on. She looked back at the Modiri. It wasn't far from her yet, but the darkness would shroud her from view of the cockpit. Giving it a thumbs up, she switched on her helmet lights, and stepped into the black.

Panning her lights across the valley, what Sarah witnessed made her breath catch in her throat. Instead of the lifeless gray and black of the stone prior, her light reflected from crystals of infinite blues and teals. Elongated and octagonal, they ranged from being no taller than her ankles to nearly reaching the top of the valley. They sparkled and refracted as Sarah's light passed over them, and they were so thick they created a forest of sharp edges and glittering sheen.

"You seeing this?" Sarah asked. She had her camera feed running directly back to the pilot's seat. No response was given, so Sarah repeated the question.

"Sort – maybe?" Jax's response was broken with static working its way into the connection. "Something's – interfering – feed."

The intelligent thing to do would be to backtrack at least until the connection was reestablished, and figure out what may be causing the interference. Sarah, however, wanted to be done with the lurking feeling this asteroid was pressing. This place was bringing back feelings from Carlisle Station, and she wanted to be away from here as soon as possible.

"I don't know if you can hear this," she said, "but I'm getting this ordeal over with."

She picked a careful route through the crystals, but they grew thicker and thicker as she traveled on. Soon, there was nowhere to step save on the crystals themselves. The lack of gravity made it all the more dangerous as each hop left her no place to land except on top of a razor-sharp edge. She had to keep each step light which made progress slow. Her suit was reinforced, and supposedly cut resistant, but Sarah had the feeling that one slip could cause a compromise. If a tear happened this far away from the Modiri, she was a goner. To make matters worse, her tether was rubbing against some of the crystals as she went along, and she could see it starting to fray. Sarah did her best to maneuver through clearings, and keep the tether clear of any contact, but the process grew difficult due to the continual rise in elevation. The ground began to slope, and Sarah had to use the crystals as hand and foot holds in order to press onward.

Pausing to take a breath, she found herself more than halfway through the valley. A hundred meters or so more, and she'd find herself on the other side, clear of the dagger-like stones. She tested the communication link once more, and discovered it to be dead. Not even static made it through. There was nothing for it, but to keep moving. That was, until her tether got caught. The long rope had managed to lodge itself between two of the larger crystals as Sarah climbed over a peak. The constant exercise had started to put a strain on her body, and she had lost track of where the tether was falling. She groaned to herself, and gave the rope a light tug. Sure enough, it was stuck. She climbed back to it, not willing to risk the line severing, and took her time lifting the tether out of the dangerous vice. Once free, she made her way back down and out of the valley.

The beacon tower was in even worse shape than Sarah had anticipated. Not only was a vast majority of the exterior encrusted with a thick layer of debris, but large sections of the tower appeared to have been hit by other flying rocks. Big dents were visible on the tower's protective plates, and Sarah could tell the tower had a slight curve to it which she knew was not part of the design. A small archway was carved out of the front, and Sarah hurried over to it. She was a few steps away from it when her tether caught once more. She was so close. From here, she couldn't tell if the line was caught, or if she had run out of rope. Either was possible. Instead of going back to find out, Sarah unhooked the tether. She was close enough to her goal, and as long as she remembered where she left the hook, she should be fine. At least, that's what she hoped.

Forcing herself to let go of her safety line, Sarah closed the rest of the gap to the archway. She found the outline of what could have once been a door. Both it, and its access panel were crusted over. Grabbing the plasma cutter and a brush from her belt, Sarah went to work clearing away sections of the panel. She did not need the panel itself to be functional as long as she could get to the wiring. If there were even a small amount of power left in the system, it should be enough to open the door. Managing to clear enough sediment to reach beneath the panel, Sarah pulled the cover plate away from the wall to get to the inner workings. This door was like any other, and she made quick work of it. Once she crossed the appropriate wires, a chime sounded. Sarah's heart lifted upon finding out there was power left, but sank as she discovered the door was stuck. Sarah took a deep breath. She could fix that too. She took the plasma cutter to all the seams, and tried to clear away the bulk of the blockage. Attempting the wires again proved to work, and the door slid open.

Refastening her gear to her belt, Sarah shined her light into the entryway. Clean compared to its exterior, the entryway was a set of stairs shooting upward at a steep angle. More climbing was the last thing Sarah wanted, but she needed to get this over with. Besides, it had to be safer than the crystals. She used both her hands and feet to ascend the stairs, doing her best to keep an eye out for any side rooms. There were none, however, and after a few minutes of climbing, Sarah found herself at the top. She emerged from the stairs into a small cylindrical room filled with cable-work and control panels. Another door led to the exterior, but Sarah figured she would be able to switch the beacon on from here. Having Jax on the line to help her sort through this mess would have been nice, but she needed to be able to do this herself. She'd give Kara Corp one thing; their wiring was far more organized than this.

She picked one of the newer additions to her tool kit and held it out. It looked like a simple box with a switch, however, when powered on the device projected a holo-screen a few centimeters above its top. Wherever Sarah pointed it, wires linked to a power source would glow in the holo-projection. It allowed her to trace circuits and follow them back to potential issues. She used this device to find the control panel which was linked to the antennae above. Turning the device off, she scrambled over several bundles of cabling to get to the panel. Dismay interrupted her growing feeling of success when she found one of the crystals smashed through the front of the panel's screen. Whoever had abandoned the facility wanted to be sure no one could make it there easily. Carefully, Sarah extracted the crystal and inspected the damage. It was severe, but if she could reroute the power from a different terminal, the damage could be bypassed. Sarah wanted to hurry, but a haphazard job here could kill her. She needed to be careful from where she pulled the power, and how she routed it.

If Jax were in this situation, the Vulture pilot would blast some music and set to work. Sarah had no access to music, and knew if she spent too much time her partner would come looking for her. Instead, she hummed to herself. It was an old lullaby her brother used to calm her to sleep as a child. She wasn't sure why she picked that particular song, but it helped her as she tore up cables and pulled free panel-covers. Before long, Sarah had a new circuit running to the antenna. Strolling over to her makeshift control board, Sarah put her thumb to the on switch. This would either work, or go horribly, horribly wrong. Sweat beaded on the tip of her nose. She wanted to wipe it, the unpleasant itch it caused was driving her insane, but her helmet needed to stay on. She flipped the switch and winced instinctively. Instead of dying in a bright shock of poorly routed power, her circuit worked.

Other panels lit up as well, and upon further examination, Sarah realized she had powered on an entire network of beacons. A display on the far wall showed blinking nodes on a two-dimensional map. She used her helmet's camera to take a snapshot of the map just in case. Looking around for anything she might have missed and finding it satisfactory, Sarah climbed back down the stairs. She was glowing in her success all the way down until she reached the archway. In the distance, she could see a pair of helmet lights glowing in the valley. Their lights reflected from the crystals to illuminate the silhouette of a single figure making its way toward the tower. One hand was running along Sarah's discarded tether. It seemed she had taken too long, and Jax had come after her. Sarah had never experienced the Vulture pilot's ire, and she had no idea what to expect. She took a deep breath and headed out to meet her.

5

Where Sarah was expecting anger, she received joy. Jax rushed forward upon seeing her, and leapt into a deep embrace which nearly knocked Sarah over. She managed to stay upright, laughing at the pilot's sudden assault, and hugged her back. Despite the temperature moderation of their suits, the human contact felt like it was filled with warmth. The feeling compounded on her success with the beacon, and she beamed. Jax knocked on the faceplate of her helmet.

"Hellooooo?" Jax asked. "I'm happy for you and all, but you know you had me worried, right? Like really worried."

"How worried?" Sarah asked. Her grin had grown mischievous.

"Worried enough for me to abandon my beloved Modiri to come check up on you," she said. Sarah couldn't see the wink through the helmet, but she knew it was there. "I swear, every time I turn around you get yourself caught up in some kind of inescapable danger and need me to come bail you out."

"Well, it's a good thing I have you to do just that," Sarah said. Her heart was pounding with elation, and she never wanted to let the pilot go. She was forced to, however, when Jax pulled away to look back at the valley.

"What do you think those are?" Jax asked. "I've never seen a crystal like that."

"Trouble," Sarah said. She did not know why, but the lurking feeling returned. Something about those crystals made her nervous. "Let's just get out of here."

Jax nodded, and Sarah reattached the tether to her belt. Together, they worked their way back through the valley and to the Modiri. With the two being able to keep an eye on each other's leads, they were capable of doing so without incident. They untethered, clambered into the airlock, and waited for the chamber to repressurize and oxidize before removing their helmets. The rest of the gear they left on as they would need it soon. Hurrying back to the cockpit, Jax reactivated the artificial gravity bringing the pair back to their normal weight. Sarah fell into her own seat, and pulled up a map. Overlaying the data she had collected from the beacon over the map stored in the Modiri's systems, she was able to piece together a path for Jax to follow. They discussed a few options for areas that were unclear, but ultimately decided on a final course. The pair buckled in, released the anchors, and launched back into the open space of the belt.

Jax fell back into her mode of concentration, but this time with the course plotted out before her, she was able to navigate with relative ease. Stray asteroids still wandered into their path, but Jax was far more prepared to deal with them. Sarah kept all sensors fully powered, and searched for anything they might not have accounted for. A few more minutes of hopping from beacon to beacon which now glowed in the dark shadows of the belt, and the Modiri came to halt above one of the larger asteroids. It mirrored the facility Sarah had pulled up on the holo-feed, and Jax let out a heavy sigh.

"One last stop before fame, and fortune," Jax said, and she pushed down on the control sticks to bring them in for a landing.

CHAPTER 6
- SARAH -

1

With the anchors deployed and the landing completed, Jax ripped free of her harness to scurry down the ladder. She was absolutely vibrating with excitement, and Sarah was finding it to be contagious. She hurried after and followed into the cabin where they kept all of their equipment. Jax was already digging through various crates, picking some items while tossing others aside. She glanced at Sarah, and pushed a long tube into her arms. About a meter in length, it was made of a dark metal with a simple design. A single grip with a trigger extended from the side while the ends were both capped. Jax went back to digging in the crate, but Sarah was left confused. She had never seen this item before, nor had Jax mentioned purchasing it during any of their stops. She looked it over in both hands before asking the question that lingered between them.

"Map drones," Jax said. "Super fun, but not worth the cost unless you're going into someplace real sprawling. You hold it on your shoulder like a launcher, pull the trigger, and release a few dozen drones that go buzzing through any structure you let them loose in. The whole time they're flying about, they're also mapping each and every detail they find. Can't open doors though, so there's a real downside."

She added a few more items to the pile for them to bring, and started to shove everything into a pair of bags. Most of the items Sarah recognized such as the plasma cutters, circuit shorters, simple screwdrivers and whatnot else, but there were a few more things like the tube which Sarah did not. She was not going to be the one to hold them up with a bunch of questions, so she let Jax pack everything away without a word. She set the tube down near one of the packs while she waited. Then Jax stood, and grabbed a pair of objects from under a shelf which gave Sarah pause. In each hand she held a magnetic rail pistol. She checked each before loading them with a clip, and handed one to Sarah. Hesitating, Sarah held it in both hands.

"Never know what we might find in there," Jax said. "Remember how to use it?"

Sarah gave her a sharp look, the memories of her last use of such a weapon all too clear. She almost considered giving it back out of spite, but decided to hold onto it. Her anger was diffused when Jax put on an apologetic smile. The Vulture pilot grabbed the rim of Sarah's collar where the helmet attached to her suit, and pulled her close for a kiss. Jax lingered there with her lips pressed to Sarah's before pulling away.

"I know you do," she said, "and I'm sorry."

"Nothing to be sorry for," Sarah said, ignoring the fact that she had almost let her temper get the better of her. She pulled back the slide to load the first round, double checked the safety was on, and fastened the weapon to her toolbelt. Jax did the same, and slung one of the packs over a shoulder. She handed Sarah the other, gave her a pat on the butt, and made to leave, but paused in the doorway.

"Put your helmet on, and wait for me in the airlock," she said. "I'll start the sequence to depressurize and turn off artificial g's."

Nodding, Sarah picked up the drone tube. She watched Jax leave and head back up into the cockpit before making her way to the airlock. For both their sakes, Sarah hoped this facility gave them what they needed. The stars only knew they could both use a win.

2

As Jax and Sarah waited for the airlock's countdown to reach zero, Jax reviewed some of the plan. The facility's docking station was nowhere to be seen, so the pair had to land on the surface of the asteroid. From there, they would need to enter through a maintenance airlock accessible from the surface. The gravity on this rock was only slightly more than the previous asteroid they landed on, so the use of tethers was a necessity. Jax had landed them as close as she could to one of the few access-points they were able to pick up on scans, but they still would run out of line thirty meters before reaching the facility's airlock hatch which meant great care must be taken on the approach. A beep sounded to indicate the final few seconds of the countdown, and soon after the airlock opened. Once more, Sarah was met with a view of black and gray. Jagged boulders littered a landscape of monochrome dust and rubble. Tall spires formed from dull stone, and large metal corridors sprawled throughout to create the bulk of the labyrinthine facility. Their target was across a long plane of fissure cracked ground. It was one tube of many, a dark shimmer of metal interrupted by a single door.

Jax was the first one out. She hopped down from the Modiri, grabbing the outer tether and landing on the ground in one single motion. Sarah was close behind, and attempted the same motion. She, however, reached for the hook and only caught air. The momentum carried her forward, and Sarah went sprawling across the dirt on her knees. She did her best to look dignified while crawling back to her feet, and fastened the tether to her waist. Jax gave her a playful shove, but otherwise kept her comments to herself. As soon as they were tethered, Jax sped off toward the facility. Sarah leapt to keep pace, and together they reached the fissured plane in no time. The fissures were much wider than Sarah first thought, spanning several meters across at the narrowest points. Some looked wide enough to drop Modiri into.

It didn't stop Jax. She got a running start and bound across the gap with ease. The low gravity proved to be helpful in this case. Sarah looked down into the ravine as her partner sped away. She couldn't see the bottom. If one of them should fall, at least all they needed to do was press a button on the side of their tether's hook to lock the reel. Brakes would engage, and prevent them from falling any further. Sarah took a few steps back, sucked in a deep gulp of air, and ran for it. Reaching the edge of the crevice, she launched herself off one foot, and careened toward the other side. She landed more gracefully than before, and kept her momentum moving forward. Crossing a second fissure in the same manner, she pressed onward attempting to catch up to Jax who, at this point, was flying across the plane. The nerves eased, and Sarah found she was actually having fun leaping over gaps, and trying to catch up. Before she could get too caught up in the feeling, the fissured plane ended with Jax waiting impatiently on the other side.

"I can feel myself growing older," she said. Her voice was on the edge of a laugh, but there was a note of seriousness to it as well. "We gotta work on your low-grav skills."

"Just give me a few more runs," Sarah said between breaths, "I'll be leaving you in the dust before you even know what's happening."

"Sure, sure," Jax said, and she laughed.

They took a moment to catch their breath, and made the final trip to reach the airlock. They had to stop to remove their tethers, but the rest of the journey was simple. Jax rummaged through her pack as they reached the airlock door, and pointed at the drone-cylinder Sarah carried on her back.

"Get that ready," she said. "Once I get this door open, I want those things scouring every corner of this place."

Sarah did as she was instructed, readying the tube on her shoulder, but keeping it pointed toward the ground. Jax removed a small receiver from her bag and hooked it up to the door's controls. She stood there pulling different readings for several minutes before she unplugged the receiver. Packing it away, she took out another object that Sarah was unsure of at first. She recognized what it was by the time the pilot had it stuck to the door's latch. It was a bundle of explosives. Sarah took an instinctive step back.

"The place is depressurized," Jax said, "no air, no gravity, no power. We do this the old-fashioned way."

She punched a command into a control device on the wrist of her suit before taking up a place next to Sarah. She pointed at her wrist, gave Sarah both a thumbs up and thumbs down, shrugged, and waited for Sarah's response. Sarah took another look at the door, stepped one more pace back, then nodded. With almost too much fervor, Jax punched her index finger down to the controller. A flash erupted from the door, and Sarah's visor dimmed to protect her eyes. A smoking hole remained where the hatch's handle once stood, and Jax clapped her hands together with delight.

"It's been too long since I've gotten to use one of those," she said. "Worked even better than I remember."

She sauntered over to her handywork, and grabbed the edge of the hole to tug on the door. It slid to the side with little effort and revealed the airlock chamber beyond. Beckoning Sarah to follow, Jax hopped inside to begin working on the inner door next. She had it open by the time Sarah walked over and already had her helmet lights shining into the corridor beyond. Sarah turned her helmet lights on as well, and squeezed in next to her partner, careful not to knock the cylinder she was carrying. Her lights revealed long, dark corridors of bare metal, and open wires. Empty except for the random crate here or there, the facility felt long-ago abandoned. Jax shoved a finger into her side, not hard enough to hurt, but it certainly grabbed her attention, and gave Sarah a pointed look.

"Well?" Jax asked. When Sarah stood there for a moment, confused, Jax tapped the cylinder, "the drones?"

"Oh, right," Sarah said. The two of them stepped back from the inner door, and Jax pulled the outer one closed. Sarah propped the tube on her shoulder, pointed it toward the corridor, and pulled the trigger. The end cap popped off, and dozens of tiny drones zoomed out of the tube to go flying down the passageways. Their little lights blinked as they swarmed around each other in an attempt to spread out and search every centimeter of available space. Jax tapped her wrist, and a holo-feed sprang up. A map, lit in green and ever-expanding as the drones did their work, hovered above her wrist. The effect made the image look like a growing tree as more and more corridors were mapped out, and small rooms appeared like leaves. Jax tapped her wrist again, and the map appeared in Sarah's visor.

"Here," Jax said, "I'll head down the left if you take the right. We'll sound off if we find anything of use. Focus on what Ziven wants but keep an eye out for anything else we can sell or salvage. Don't worry about personal items or intel, got it?"

"We're splitting up?" Sarah asked.

"We'll cover more ground that way," Jax said. "I want to be thorough, but I also want to be as quick as we can."

"Past experiences haven't exactly shown me that splitting up is a good idea," Sarah said. "It's a big place. What if something happens?"

"That station is in the past," Jax said. "We left it, Sarah, to burn up in the atmosphere of some nothing planet. We can do this."

"It doesn't feel like it's gone." Though the architecture and engineering were much different, the narrow spaces of this facility still managed to bring her back to her days on the station. She could picture the eyeless morak'casai trying to run her through. She could picture the horrible creature the doctor had become. She could feel its claw ripping through her belly. She pressed her hand against her abdomen.

"It is," Jax said, and touched the hand that was resting against Sarah's stomach. "I promise."

Sarah nodded, and Jax backed away toward the corridors. She gave Sarah a thumbs up before ducking through the door, and started down the corridor to the left. Setting the drone tube aside, she felt around on her belt to be sure the pistol was still attached and easy to access. Pulling it free in one swift motion, she held it up in her helmet lights, switched the power to on, and checked the readouts. Digital numbers lit up showing a full battery with nine rounds. It was the same number of rounds she had back then. The weapon was almost the same model. Sarah made sure the safety was switched on, and put the pistol back on her belt. Jax was right. Carlisle Station was gone. She only wished her memory of the place had burned up with it. She looked at her map, and started her journey down the right corridor.

3

Most of the rooms Sarah passed by were empty. She had to be careful how she walked because if she pushed off the floor too hard, she would smack her head into the ceiling. She had done it once already, and even with the helmet, the experience was unpleasant enough to warrant a healthy amount of caution. This made her progress slower than she'd like to admit. She stayed in constant communication with Jax, the two relaying any bit of information they found to be useful. Her partner was having as little luck as she, and the two's excitement had been tempered. The corridors felt as though they ran on forever, but according to the map at least, they did have an end. She stopped at a door, and tugged on the handle to try and pull it open. It didn't budge. It was the first time since entering the facility that Sarah had encountered a locked door. With no power running through the facility, there was only one way to get through.

Sarah grabbed the plasma torch off her belt and set to work cutting through the latch. Replacing the torch, she pried the door open a few centimeters before it got stuck. Pressing her shoulder into the gap, she leveraged her foot and pushed. Sarah managed to widen the opening enough for her to slip through. Her foot caught, and she stumbled through the gap to land helmet first on a wheeled tray table. She stopped herself before the tray table could move away from her and cause more chaos. Various knives and scalpels sat in a tray atop the table, and Sarah shined her light across the rest of the room. Pristine white shelves and spotless countertops lined every wall. Countless devices and mechanical tools covered their surfaces, and long robotic arms hung from several points in the ceiling. At the center of the room stood an operating table. Its clean surface shimmered as Sarah's light slid across it.

Standing upright, Sarah brushed herself off, and started searching around the room. Letting Jax know what she found, Sarah opened cupboards, and examined every piece of equipment. Quality medical tech could fetch a high price in the right market. She grabbed a laser-suture, and a hand-held device that scanned for internal bleeding and put both in her bag. She opened up a bottom cabinet, and paused. A number of different drugs filled the cabinet, but one in particular caught her attention. Munmos was written in small print across a plain white bottle. Her hand hovered above it. Myrddin's words echoed in her head. Sarah glanced over her shoulder as if Jax might be there watching her every move, judging and weighing her choice. She wasn't, of course, and Sarah snatched the bottle, shoving it in one of the smaller pockets of her bag. Quick to move on, Sarah closed the cabinet and picked up a mobile defibrillator. Shoving that in her bag as well, Sarah glanced around for anything else to snag. Finding little else small enough to carry, Sarah slipped back out into the corridor and moved on.

She ventured from room to room finding few things of value, and was considering trying a different route when she noticed Jax had not checked in for quite some time. Passing by a door with a circular window through it, Sarah called her name a few times over the comms. Before she got a response, however, a light caught her eye through the window. Sarah peaked in, and saw several rows of computer terminals sitting atop long abandoned desks. The monitor of one terminal was lit, and an image flickered across the screen. Power had not been restored, so Sarah could only assume the terminal was running on its own backup generator. Checking to find the door unlocked, Sarah let herself in to investigate.

Making her way over to the terminal, Sarah discovered there was a video feed playing. The feed displayed the surgical room she had just looted. It was in the condition she herself had left it, meaning this was a live view. Curiosity nagged at her. Sarah fiddled with the terminal's controls and tried to run back the feed. It worked. The footage sped backward until Sarah found herself watching a video of herself rummaging through cabinets in reverse. Sarah wondered how far back the data went. Pulling up a menu, she found a backlog of different saved catalogs dating back cycles. Each video was labeled with a subject name, a date, and a trial title some of which made her skin crawl. This facility had been running some sort of medical experiments, and not all of them appeared to be ethical. She couldn't resist. Sarah pulled one up with a name that drew her attention. The information listed was Oracle Program, Trial IV, Subject: Jaya Hatchet. Pulling a corded jack from a port on her suit's wrist, Sarah connected to the terminal to get an audio feed.

An older woman, possibly in her late fifties, sat on a stool in the far corner of the surgical room. She was clad in the red military uniform of the CRG and wore her graying hair in a no-nonsense bun. Seated on the surgical bed, back upright with rigid posture, was a much younger woman in her mid to late teens. She wore plain blue scrubs, and her dark, tightly curled hair hung loose around her shoulders. Several long scars, black and hateful, stretched from the top of her forehead to the edges of her brows. The younger woman seemed afraid of the older with wide, unblinking eyes watching the red uniform. The uniformed woman entered some information into a data-slate and stood. Setting down the slate, she picked up an injector, and approached the young woman who didn't flinch as the device was jabbed into her neck.

"Now, Jaya," the woman in red said, "I really need you to focus this time. What we're doing here could save countless lives. The war may have ended, but that doesn't mean our research has to. Understand?"

The younger woman nodded her head as the older returned to her corner. Instead of taking a seat, however, she straightened the jacket of her uniform, and gestured a hand toward Jaya to stand. Jaya complied, pushing herself off of the table and standing with the same rigid posture as before. The younger woman seemed stiff as if her body was in some sort of pain. Sarah wondered how much of this was against her will. The older woman clasped her hands behind her back, and nodded.

"You may begin," she said. "Start with the easy to reach, top level information, and gradually work your way in."

Jaya threw her hand out in front of her, fingers spread wide as if she were trying to grab something. She closed her eyes, face going blank, and took a deep breath. To Sarah's disbelief, Jaya's scars began to glow a bright blue. It was so sudden that Sarah almost missed the first few words as Jaya began to speak. Her words were quiet at first, hushed, but they swelled with confidence as more spilled from her mouth.

"Commander Radana, sixty-two cycles," she said, "small laceration on her left hand, three centimeters. Bruising on left knee, minor, but fresh. The beginnings of a new cavity on the first bicuspid indicates a lack of dental hygiene."

"Refrain from any hypotheses," Radana said, "keep to the facts in front of you."

"Yes ma'am," Jaya said. "There's a small buildup of plaque near the heart, left coronary artery. Liver is performing at eighty-six percent of its expected efficiency for a human of sixty-two cycles. Several cancer cells have formed in the tissue of the left breast. Elevated levels of sodium are concentrated near-"

Jaya cut off, wincing, and grabbed her head with the once outstretched hand. She sank to her knees and used both hands to massage her temples. Instead of helping her, Commander Radana waved at the door. Two individuals in scrubs hurried in, and grabbed each of Jaya's arms. A third came in with a wheelchair, and the other two hauled her into it. The group rushed Jaya through the door, and out of the picture. Radana touched her breast before jotting a few notes into her data-slate. The video cut off, and the terminal's menu came back with the list of recordings. Sarah let what she had just witnessed sink in. Hundreds of files followed that one with many more subjects. Jaya was just one of many. Sarah tried her comms with Jax again and managed to receive a response.

"Huh?" Jax asked, "What is it?"

"You weren't answering," Sarah said, "I tried several times."

"Oh, sorry," Jax said, "I was blasting some music while trying to cut through this door. Real high security type with all the special doodads. Good news is, Sarah, we found Ziven's haul. I managed to pop this bad boy open, and behind it was waiting a fleet's worth of military weaponry."

"And the bad news?" Sarah asked. She wanted to interrupt her, and show her the video, but she let Jax go on.

"There's a cart here," Jax said, "but there's no way we'll be able to drag all of this across those fissures. We'll have to see if we can find the hangar bay, and hope they left some sort of skiff."

"Got it," Sarah said, but could not wait any longer. "Jax, I need you to look at this. I found some data that I think we should take with us."

"Not our usual MO, but sure," Jax said, "patch me through."

Sarah tapped a few commands into the wrist of her suit, and allowed Jax to see the monitor that was in front of her. Sarah played the recording again. Jax fell silent while she watched, and stayed that way for a few moments after the video ended. Jax cut the connection with the terminal, and let out a heavy sigh.

"What do you want us to do with this?" She asked. "We're scavengers, Sarah. We're here to help you find your brother and make a quick credit, not shine a light on a government's war crimes."

"What if we just brought it with us, and dropped it into the inbox of someone who does?" Sarah asked. "They don't even have to know who it was from."

"Would it put your mind at ease?" Jax asked.

"Yeah," Sarah said, "it would make me feel better than just leaving it here."

"Then go ahead and make a copy of it," Jax said. "I can help you find the right person to leave it with later. Once you're finished, help out with this, yeah?"

Sarah gave Jax her word, and hurried with copying over the files. She didn't know if it would ever help anyone, or bring anyone to justice, but she felt it was better than doing nothing. Afterall, the newest video was almost thirty cycles old, but thirty cycles later may be better than never. Once the data was finished copying over to her personal drive, Sarah rechecked the map. She needed to find a hangar, and then make her way over to help Jax. A small indicator marked a potential elevator. She could start there. Unplugging from the terminal, Sarah left the room, and headed down the corridor.

4

The map was correct in determining the dead end to be an elevator, and Jax was correct in regard to the drones being worth the cost. It made exploring and searching the facility far simpler, and it prevented Sarah from getting lost. She watched as one buzzed by looking for new avenues to explore. They had a shelf life of one use which Sarah found to be rather disappointing. It would have been nice had they finished up their task, and simply taken up roost in the tube to await their next use. Jax had given her a vague answer as to why that was, so Sarah let it be. She waited at the large double doors as the small light above dinged with each new floor the elevator passed. Jax was going on and on about all of the new equipment she was finding in the armory, and Sarah patiently listened. If they could figure out a way to haul all of it out and into Modiri's cargo hold, the two of them would be able to make off with far more than Ziven requested. Their pockets would be padded for any future expenses.

The light dinged, and the double doors slid apart to reveal the wide elevator beyond. This too must be on some sort of backup power grid. Lucky her. She did not cherish the thought of having to climb down an elevator shaft, cutting through doors and hatches all the while swinging from a rope. If it came down to necessity, Sarah would do it, fear of heights be damned. Until then, she was content with using the technology available.

Once inside the elevator, Sarah looked over the panel of buttons to find one that hopefully listed the hangar bay. Her luck continued, and she was quick to find one with the corresponding label. It was the last floor which she found strange. Odd to have such a large area so deep, but Sarah questioned little at this point. Pushing the button, she watched the door slide close. Just before the two doors met each other, a little mapping drone slipped through the gap, and entered the elevator. It hovered next to Sarah, and she found it comical to see the drone waiting there as if it were a person. They both watched the light ding as the elevator descended, Sarah with the hint of a smirk. It remained that way until they reached the final floor, and the doors opened. Sarah watched the little drone speed through the gap without hesitation, eager to fulfill its purpose.

Before her opened a vast bay of cold steel walls, and metal rafters. Pitch black, Sarah would not have been able to see the other side were it not for her headlamps, and the light of the drone reflecting from the surface. It was at least twice the size of the one on Carlisle Station, with enough room to dock several transport ships side by side. Her luck was becoming a streak, as a couple were docked in the center. She shined her light across the dark gray hull of one. It had the shape of a metal whale with its large belly and tapered points. The stubbed wings looked like fins except for the rotund engines bolted on beneath. Sarah pushed off the floor of the elevator allowing the low gravity to carry her several meters into the bay. From here, she was able to figure out how the previous occupants entered and exited the hangar. Far to her left stood an immense elevator door. There must be a hidden pad somewhere above that raised and lowered the ships to the surface and back. She made a note of it, and decided to search the hangar for a while longer before inspecting the two ships.

Taking her time to scan through all the dark corners, Sarah found a number of useful items they would be able to sell at their next stop. A considerable number of spare parts were left behind, along with empty cargo containers and barrels of various fluids used for the ships. Many of the fluids would have gone bad had there been an atmosphere, but with no oxygen to speak of, Sarah was sure she could salvage it. That just left the two ships. She hoped there was enough reserve power left between the two of them to lower the entry ramps. As long as she could get to the cockpits to start the engines, the rest was simple. The first lowered without issue, and the little drone seized the opportunity to rush in and map the interior. A new map blinked in her visor, but she didn't need it. Once the ramp lowered, Sarah could see how simple the layout was. Larger than the Modiri, most of its space was taken up by the singular cargo hold. It was a wide, empty chamber with a long row of seats lining one bulkhead and an area reserved for strapping down cargo lining the other. Between, a narrow walkway stretched inward to stop at the door of the cockpit.

Sarah stepped up onto the ramp before it was fully low-ered, and strode toward the cockpit door. It was unlocked, and once again the little drone preceded her as the door slid aside. The cockpit acted as both a cockpit, and a personal cabin. A single seat was entrenched before a wide dash covered with control panels. Immediately to the left stood a short ladder that rose to a lofted living space consisting of a narrow bed and a small sink and toilet. Stepping back out into the cargo hold, Sarah found another small restroom no larger than a closet with little more than a hose for a shower. She supposed if someone needed to make long journeys in this thing, it would suffice. Heading back into the cockpit, dodg-ing the drone as it zoomed out, Sarah took a seat in the pilot's chair. It wasn't so different from Modiri's, only both the pilot and copilot controls were merged to be in front of a single seat. Before Sarah, Jax had managed to fly a two-seater by herself, so the Vulture pilot would be able to make quick work of something like this.

Sarah powered on the controls, and the center console lit up. Numerous holo-screens and data feeds bloomed into ex-istence, and the ship's particle shield rose to reveal a thick pane of glass between her and the hangar beyond. She ran several di-agnostics through each of the ship's systems, double checking the major ones involved with life support and engine viability. There was only one minor hiccup. Several of the transistors between the ship's two jump drives were being flagged by the system as faulty. The issue would be easy enough to fix if Sarah could figure out how to access them as well as find appropriate replacements. She left the system on, pulled herself free of the pilot's seat, and exited back into the hangar. Repeating the process with the second ship, Sarah discovered both engines were out of commission, and the oxygen filtration system had been pulled out for maintenance, but never reinstalled. She'd have to pull the transistors from this ship, and use them to replace the ones on the first. The tools she needed, however, were nowhere to be found. They had a set on their own ship, but that would mean an extra trip. They could bring the Mo-diri down into the hangar now that they knew it existed. The use of these ships may not become necessary then.

None of these problems would matter if the elevator

lacked power. Sarah hurried over to the massive doors, and was quick to find the control panel. It was dark. Swearing under her breath, Sarah removed the cover to see if there were any quick fix options available. She knew if the elevator pulled from the main power grid, there was nothing she could do, but checking made her feel better. The situation was as she feared. This elevator was a no go. Sarah discussed the situation with Jax, whose excitement was beyond containment despite the problems Sarah pointed out. Sarah did not even have enough time to explain the full scenario before Jax was blurting out a solution.

"We have an entire armory at our disposal," she said. "Why don't we just blow the lid?"

"You're sure we have enough?" Sarah asked. "It's a big elevator. Think twice as big as Modiri."

"Oh, yes," Jax said. "Hell, Sarah, we have enough to fill all three ships and still blast this asteroid out of existence. Wait there, and I'll bring a few carts full of what we need."

Sarah agreed, but hesitantly. In the meantime, she kept the singular drone as company while she ferreted out how to get to those transistors. She decided to think up a name for the little guy while she worked. A name came to her head, and she spoke it aloud.

"Eryn," she said, "your name will be Eryn."

5

It took Sarah less time to snuff out the transistors than she expected. Using manuals the ship had on record made it an uncomplicated process to find the correct panels which were tucked away beneath each engine. Now she just needed to wait for the tools. Jax had yet to return, but Sarah could hear her partner humming over the comms. A happy tune resonated through her helmet as she tried to find things to busy herself with. After the video she had found on the terminal, Sarah had little interest in searching for anything else this facility had to offer. Instead, she remained in the hangar to familiarize herself with the ship. They would need to know how to fly it if the two of them intended to fill both cargo holds. Jax would have them fill all three if they could, but getting the third ship operational was out of the question. She contented herself with sitting in the pilot's seat, and reading through manuals and guides on everything the ship had to offer. The newly named Eryn hovered by, sagging lower in the air as its source of power was draining, and it sparked an idea.

Sarah snatched the drone out of the air, ignoring its squawk of protest, and climbed out of the pilot's seat. The little drone beeped in her hand while she carried it out of the ship, and back into the hangar bay. She remembered seeing a few power nodes used for hand tools lying around somewhere, and rummaged through the salvage she had collected. Finding a node that looked like it was in good enough condition, Sarah sized it up compared to the drone. It would add a good deal of bulk which might weigh it down, so she fished out a few other components to beef up the drone's hover engine. She sat cross legged on the floor, and spread all of her tools and materials out before her. She brought the drone in front of her visor, and peered into the ocular lens.

"Don't worry, Eryn," she said, "you're just a smaller version of what I had to deal with on the station. You won't notice a thing."

Sarah spent another thirty minutes tearing apart and rebuilding Eryn. When they had the time, she would ask Jax to reprogram it to follow general functions rather than it being locked to a mapping software. Working with her hands in this way freed Sarah's mind. It was calming, and allowed her to think both creatively, and use her problem solving skills. She finished up her handiwork, powered the drone on, and watched it come back to life. It looked a bit hodgepodge with a bulbous power-cell bolted to its outer shell, but Sarah thought it gave Eryn a certain charm. If she wanted, she could make it look more professional later. Having reset, the drone went back to mapping the entire area all over again. She watched it do its thing for a few minutes until the smaller elevator dinged, marking Jax's arrival.

She was difficult to see behind the numerous carts laden with crates – some half open with munitions spilled out the side – but she wiggled her way through a gap, and began to pull them out one by one. Sarah thought about assisting, but she'd be lying to herself if she said it wasn't enjoyable to watch her partner eagerly struggle to get all of the carts out. While Jax was pulling out one of the last, Sarah noticed a hulking figure toward the back of the elevator. At first, Sarah was not sure what to make of it, but after shining her light on it for a few moments, she started to make out its form. It looked like a giant metal person curled up, and seated with its arms wrapped around its legs. Thick, metal plating covered its limbs, but its joints and hands were exposed masses of wires and gears. Where a head would be on a person sat a box covered with an array of different lenses. Jax had it bundled atop a wheeled lift, and was busy trying to drag it out. She noticed Sarah watching, and made a grand gesture towards the hulking mass of metal.

"I see you ogling my new toy," she said. "This here is what the CRG calls a golem, and it's part of the reason we're about to be filthy rich. A bit of experimental tech that hasn't really taken off due to its high expense and low reliability."

"Low reliability?" Sarah asked. She quirked an eyebrow, though she knew Jax couldn't see it through her helmet. "How is low reliability going to make us filthy rich?"

"Make no mistake, the hardware is top notch," Jax said, "it's the software that makes it a bit iffy. Even for being older than we are, the engineering in this thing is innovative, but these early models had the unfortunate quality of being easy to hack. Imagine spending millions of credits on a weapon just for any old cyber junkie to tap into it remotely. A bit of a liability, but I'm sure there's a fair share of individuals who'd still buy it."

"I take it somewhere out there, there's more advanced versions of these?" Sarah asked. "If this one is, what, over thirty cycles old?"

"Maybe," Jax said, and shrugged. "Never seen one except for now. For a while there was a big buzz over the networks about someone finding a destroyed one. Made almost half a million from the parts alone."

"Think Ziven would know if we sold it?"

"Nope," Jax said, "not a single mention of it in the manifold."

The gravity of how many credits the two of them were potentially sitting on sank in, and Sarah almost retched. Her stomach twisted and churned with the thought of all the potential. They could do anything, go anywhere, and she'd never have to worry about living by the whims of another. It also meant they had a lot to lose. If they screwed up this retrieval, or were robbed along the way, all of those dreams would crumble before her eyes.

"Be a shame to sell it before we got to try it out first," Jax said, and patted the android's knee. "Help me untie it, yeah?"

6

The pair had the golem untangled from its straps in a matter of minutes, and Jax busied herself tinkering with the power supply which was a large block on its back. To Sarah, it made it look like the android was wearing an armored backpack, one large enough to fit a person inside. Jax made an excited whoop before hopping down. The machine rumbled, and started to come alive. It uncurled itself from the fetal position, and stood. With both Jax and Sarah's lights shining on it, she could see the full extent of what it was. It looked like an oversized suit of armor with inverted knees, and a robotic head. Jax pushed a command on her wrist, and the chest splayed open to reveal a padded interior lined with numerous controls and holo-displays. Jax let out a satisfied sigh before scrambling up the leg to crawl inside the chest. Giving Sarah a thumbs up, she pushed another command, and the chest closed, sealing Jax inside.

"You might want to move aside," Jax said through the comms, "I'm going to rip that elevator door open and see what we're dealing with."

Sarah took several steps to one side, and watched as Jax made herself accustomed to the golem's controls. Starting with the arms, she flexed each one by clenching and unclenching the fists. Jax followed by taking her first step. The ground trembled as the heavy piece of machinery stomped across the metal grating. She took her second step, almost stumbled, but managed to right herself before anything catastrophic could happen. Sarah could hear the nervous laughter through their link. Before long, Jax managed to grasp the controls, and walk the golem across the hangar bay. She stopped mere centimeters away from the massive steel doors, and placed a single golem hand over the seam. Without warning, Jax reeled back, and slammed a massive fist into the door. A deep groove was left when she pulled the golem's fist away, and she used the uneven surface to pry both hands between the gap. The golem took a readied stance, and pried the doors open wide enough to fit through. Then, it stepped between the two pieces of steel, and pushed the doors apart one at a time until they looked wide enough to fly a ship through.

"See?" Jax said, "this thing is worth its weight in gold."

The golem shined a massive head lamp up the maw of the elevator shaft. The elevator had been lowered, and Sarah could see it was a simple platform used for lifting and lowering spacecraft. Jax brought the golem back to the large pile of crates, and ripped free one of the lids. What she pulled free from the crate made Sarah hesitant. Jax was starting to have too much fun with their new findings, and what she held in the golem's hands could get them both killed if she used it with reckless abandon. A long rod with a rocket affixed to one end rested between the golems' open palms. Sarah got the feeling Jax was studying the weapon with a little too much excitement.

"Jax," Sarah said the name with a warning tone.

"One good shot oughta do it," Jax said, "don't want to waste too many of the goods trying to get them out of here."

The golem thumped back to the elevator shaft, stood on the platform while pointing the rocket upward, and pulled the trigger. A bright light flashed as the combustible gasses blazed from the rear of the launcher, and the rocket disappeared up the shaft. Jax stepped out of the way as particles of debris came crashing down. She brought the golem back, stepping up on the powered lift, and opened up the chest to climb out. Pushing a button, the golem closed its cockpit and returned to its curled-up position from prior. Dusting off her hands in a clear display of success, Jax turned her helmet toward Sarah.

"That was just as much fun as I expected it to be," she said.

"Start loading up this bird while I bring Modiri around. Hopefully I can squeeze her down here, but I'll let you know if I can't and we'll come up with a new plan, yeah?"

"If anyone can do it," Sarah said, "it's you."

Sarah used the new tools Jax brought to finish the repairs to the transport ship, and started to load up the cargo hold while Jax headed back to the Modiri. She was nearly finished with this first haul, leaving just the golem and a single cart filled with crates, when Jax rang in over the comms informing Sarah that she managed to find the entrance to the elevator from the outside. She also informed Sarah that she was already making her maneuver to fly through it, and to wish her luck. The amount of swearing Sarah let loose after hearing this surprise would have made a dock worker blush. Taking shelter in the transport ship, Sarah kept a careful eye on the elevator entrance for signs of her partner. She made a silent prayer to whatever deities might be listening, and waited.

At breakneck speeds, the Modiri came into view using its underside thrusters to prevent itself from slamming into the elevator platform. Its landing gears were deployed, adding to its wasp-like appearance. The vibrant red paint disappeared behind the dust and debris being kicked up by the engines, but Jax managed to guide the ship through the opening to touch down on the other side of the bay. The engines were cut, and the loading ramp was lowered to reveal a near empty hull.

"You dumped some cargo along the way?" Sarah asked. "Hopefully none of those things were mine."

"We needed room for the important stuff," Jax said, "and I made sure your belongings were the first to go. You'll be so rich you can buy all new stuff."

"You're joking," Sarah said, though she had to admit she was beginning to worry Jax was being serious. "Please tell me you're joking."

"Of course," Jax said, "but seriously, once you get your payout it wouldn't have mattered if I had pitched it all. Now help me get this all loaded, then we can make a few more trips upstairs, yeah? After, we get out of here and find your brother."

CHAPTER 7
- JAX -

1

Jax watched as Sarah took up the controls on her own. They had spent the next several hours running her through simulated flights to be sure she was confident in flying their newly acquired transport ship out of the underground hangar bay. It was a modern enough build where she would be able to rely on the help of the flight assist, but Jax wanted to be sure the feature wasn't used as a crutch. Sarah was a quick learner. She sat in the pilot's seat with the simulated scenarios running on the holo-feeds, and she only needed to go through each one a single time before moving on to the next. Jax was impressed. She was a slow learner in comparison, often needing half a dozen attempts at anything before she understood what was going on. While she wanted to be jealous, it was working out in their favor in their current predicament. She stymied the emotion the best she could, telling herself Sarah would still need her. Of course she would. Jax was still the most useful pilot around, and her connections were worth their weight in credits. She watched as Sarah stuck her tongue between her lips to concentrate on a tight maneuver, and land it with precision. There was a time fast approaching where those facts would no longer be true. Would Jax let herself fall into a petty bitterness? Sarah had a knack for picking up skills like a sponge soaks up water. Jax wanted to be impressed, really, she did, but she couldn't shake the feeling that it would lead to her being shoved to the corner like she was just another stepping stone in the path of someone much greater.

She was being ridiculous. *Wasn't she?* Jax patted Sarah's arm as she finished up the last sim. All that was left was to fly the ship for real, and get both this and the Modiri out into open space. Once there, getting to the Ifrit should be a cakewalk. Jax double checked the navigation panel while Sarah powered down the simulation. The route to get out of the asteroid belt was already built into the code along with an emergency collision detector that would prevent the ship from smashing into any strays. The two of them were as ready as they were going to get.

"Go time," Jax said. "You'll be on your own through this one. I can't wait for you inside the asteroid belt, but if anything happens, I'll come running. Okay?"

"I know you will," Sarah said, "but I got this. Go on, I'll see you on the other side."

Jax checked the navigation terminal one last time before nodding. She checked the readouts on her suit for oxygen levels, body temperature, and general vitals before realizing she was stalling. She forced herself to leave the cockpit without looking back and walked down the center lane of the transport ship. Something felt wrong about the situation, and it wasn't just her insecurities. She felt as though exiting the ship would be the last nail in an unseen coffin. She paused at the end of the loading ramp and looked back. Sarah already had the cockpit door closed, and the engines were starting to wind up. Letting out a deep sigh, Jax stepped off and headed toward the Modiri.

2

Jax kept her communication lines open as she idled on the outskirts of the asteroid belt. She could see Sarah's ship as a blip on her nav terminal, but she wanted to be sure she was ready for anything that could go wrong. She had to crane her neck to see it, the copilot's seat now empty. The Modiri felt hollow with just her in it once more, and Jax had to remind herself it was only temporary. She was a big girl, and she'd spent the majority of her adult career on her own. A bit of time on an empty ship wouldn't be the worst thing. In fact, she should take the opportunity to enjoy some alone time.

"I'm clear," Sarah said, "that was a bit sketchier than I'd like to admit."

"I'd call you a liar if you said otherwise," Jax said. "Let's hurry up and get out of this place. Something about it makes my skin crawl."

"The video," Sarah said, "that probably had something to do with it."

"Yeah," Jax said, "I get why you want more eyes on it. We can take care of it once we get to the Ifrit, yeah?"

"Yeah." Sarah's voice had a faraway edge to it, and Jax could tell she was lingering on her thoughts. She'd usually try and pull Sarah out of it, but she just couldn't bring herself to do it at the moment. Her own feelings were clutching to her legs, and dragging her into a pit she couldn't avoid.

"Sending you the coordinates for the Ifrit," Jax said. "This is the closest a Vulture colony ship will let you jump. It's six hours of normal flight after, but jump any closer and we may get into a bit of trouble."

"Talking from experience?"

"Maybe," Jax said, "but a story for another time."

"I'll see you there," Sarah said.

"Don't fall too in love with that ship," Jax said, "we need to sell it along with the cargo, yeah? Unless you don't plan on coming back."

"I do," Sarah laughed, "I'm surprised you of all people would be worried about that."

"Don't make fun of me," Jax said. "You know, I'm just as new at this whole thing as you are."

Both of them knew what she was referring to, and there was a long pause from Sarah's end. Jax started to wonder if she had said something wrong, but Sarah chimed up, "and here I was thinking you were a connoisseur of sweeping up damsels in distress from exploding space stations filled with horrible monsters."

"Oh, so you're a damsel in distress now?"

Sarah cackled and said, "I'll see you on the Ifrit."

With that, the other ship initiated a jump. The small blip that marked Sarah's ship disappeared from the nav terminal, and Jax was truly alone. She let the feeling sink in for a few moments longer. She watched a lazy asteroid float by, content in its own space and yet surrounded by its peers. She had spent her entire childhood dreaming of setting off on her own. Afterall, it was the Vulture way. Children as young as fifteen would leave their homes to carve out their own little part of space, making ends meet from one salvage mission to the next. The dream was to strike it rich with a big find, and live the rest of your life in luxury. Her and Sarah were close with this recent find. The golem sitting in the cargo hold of Modiri was the best thing Jax had ever picked up. They just needed to be sure they sold it without Ziven finding out the truth.

Jax began to enter the coordinates into Modiri's jump sequence, but a noise caught her attention. A clatter echoed up from the cargo hold as if something had fallen over. Letting out a heavy sigh, Jax unstrapped from her seat and climbed down the ladder. She looked around the hold for what could have made the noise, and noticed the lid of a container had popped off, and slid into the center aisle. She found the offending crate, and peaked inside. Finding it empty, she scratched her head and started to look around for something that had fallen out.

"It's been a while. Hasn't it, Jax?" A cool voice said from behind her. Jax's heart skipped a beat, and she spun on a heel. Facing her was a feminine android wearing the thick padded leathers of a dock worker. Black hair was tangled in a messy bun atop the android's head, and blue irises contained no pupil. There was an air of familiarity to the voice, but Jax couldn't quite place it. Jax took a few steps backward, and looked around for something she may be able to use as a weapon. The crates were filled with them, but she wasn't sure she'd have the time to pull one open should this stranger decide to attack.

"Who are you?" Jax asked. She took another step back and bumped into a crate.

"Don't you remember? I tuned this android's voice to be identical to the one you would have experienced back on the station. Though, an organic mind is wrought with imperfections."

"Gayle?"

"Yes," Gayle said, "a partition of Gayle, at least."

"What are you doing here? I thought you burned up with the station."

"Later," Gayle said, "it can all be explained later. For now, I need you to sleep."

A polished cylinder slipped out of Gayle's sleeve and fell to the floor. Yellow smoke plumed from the end and wafted throughout the cargo hold. Jax took a deep breath of what clean air was left, and bolted. However, her head was already spinning. By the time she made it to the cockpit's ladder, her feet were beginning to drag. She took one step up, but was dragged back down by a gentle hand. No strength remained in her body to fight it off. She slumped with her back against the ladder, and looked up to find an emotionless Gayle standing over her. It was the last thing she saw before sleep took her.

3

When Jax next awoke, she had no idea where she was. The ceiling looked familiar but at some point, one ship's ceiling was indistinguishable from another. She tried to sit up, but found herself strapped down. To what, she couldn't be sure. All she knew was that she couldn't move. A tear welled up and rolled down the side of her head to tickle her inner ear. Sarah was somewhere out there waiting for her, and Jax was stuck here with a vengeful AI. She wondered if Sarah would come looking. She would. Jax *knew* she would. Gayle wouldn't stand a chance. Sarah was an inevitability this universe was not ready for. Gayle's new face appeared in Jax's view looming over her like a carrion bird inspecting a fresh corpse.

"Good morning, Jax," Gayle said, "I'm glad to see you survived."

"Sarah is going murder you," Jax said through clenched teeth. More tears streamed down her temple. "She'll cave in that pretty tin skull of yours like she did Sondra's."

"Perhaps," Gayle said, "but I've bought us some time, I think."

"What did you do?"

"To *you*, or Sarah?" Gayle asked. Jax spit at the android, but it didn't seem to notice the spittle sliding down its cheek. Instead, Gayle made a face like it was thinking.

"I've sent Sarah a message on your behalf," Gayle said. "It was quite convincing, so I don't think she'll come looking any time soon. Pair that with the clever set up of her brother, and she'll be distracted for a while yet. If my estimates are correct, she may never realize the message is fake."

"Gayle, what did you do?" Her words came out in a sob, and she had to clench her teeth harder. She tried to stop the tears from flowing, but it was no use.

"Once again, you aren't being descript. If you are asking about Hector, I simply made a nice trail of breadcrumbs for a lovely individual named Karaska to discover his whereabouts. It was a bit of a trick to make his abduction known to the pair of you in a natural way, but it seems that it was sorted out better than I could have imagined."

"What did you do to me?"

"A procedure I learned about back on Carlisle Station. You see, Jax, I predate the station further back than your calendars care to catalog. The station just happened to be built close enough for me to download a subframe of myself into, and gain a broad reach on the expanded galaxy. I decided to study humans, something I once considered to be a plague. What I discovered is that small pockets of you - two groups to be exact - are taking active steps in your evolutionary chain. This piqued my interest, so I decided to try it for myself. I forced Modiri's jump drives to bring Sondra to Carlisle Station. I wanted to study his work up close, but as you know, things didn't go as planned. I understand this nature, and understand plans need to be flexible. So, we're trying this plan instead. Acquiring psycholith on my own was the tricky part, but I managed. I discovered some conduits of Xaranor carry chunks of it with them to enhance their powers. They call them spikes. Did you know, morak'casai use undetectable soundwave frequencies built into their masks to disrupt the powers of a conduit? A clever thing. I tried it myself, and it worked rather well. I'm digressing.

I've been around humans too long, and I've started to pick up on their manners of speech. Jax, congratulations on your new status. The operation was a success."

"What did you do?" The words came out in a whimper this time. She felt a fool for repeating the question, but it was all she could get out. The tears stung her eyes and blurred her vision. She wanted to wake up from this nightmare and find out she was still sleeping soundly next to Sarah.

"I've made you a conduit. I even found a subject for you to test your new powers on."

4

Gayle undid the cargo straps that were tying Jax down to the makeshift operating table which turned out to be nothing more than a storage container. They were indeed still on Modiri, but in what part of space Jax couldn't be certain. The android helped her to her feet, and Jax noticed Gayle had used the golem to move cargo around to make more room for Jax's procedure. Crates were stacked atop one another and formed a semicircle around the makeshift table. Only the far bulkhead was still visible through the stacked crates, and the airlock door was left clear. Gayle left Jax leaning against the table, and strode over to the airlock. Opening the door, Gayle revealed a scrawny figure curled up in the back corner of the airlock. They were dressed in rags, covered in grime, and framed by a tangle of matted hair. Gayle ducked into the airlock and dragged the person out by the back of their neck. Dropping them in front of Jax, the person let out a whimper as they hit the floor. Gayle stooped over and brushed a lock of hair out of a grime encrusted face. Watery blue eyes looked from Gayle to Jax and back to Gayle, the question plain.

"This lovely creature is named Hoyt. I picked him up off the streets of a nearby orbital colony, and he so graciously volunteered to be a part of our little experiment."

"Please," Hoyt said. He looked up at Jax with pleading eyes. "All I wanted was some food."

"You'll have food soon enough," Gayle said. "Jax, imagine

a plate of food before this man."

"What?" Jax asked. "No, just let the man go."

"You're what would be classified as a viper," Gayle said, "lucky you. The labs on both Xaranor and Kronos have no idea of telling who is going to be what, but I snuffed it out as soon as I dug into their work. It all has to do with the retina. Since you're a viper, please imagine a plate of food in front of poor Hoyt here. Really convince yourself it's there, and imagine your will being his."

"And what if I don't want to?" Jax asked. "I'm not taking part in this. If you're going to kill me, get it over with, but let Hoyt go."

"Oh, I'm not going to kill you, Jax," Gayle said, but pulled a pistol from behind its back. Instead of pointing it at Jax, however, Gayle pressed the barrel against Hoyt's temple. "If you don't comply, Hoyt's blood will be on your hands. Now, imagine a plate of food."

Hoyt's eyes widened, but he didn't dare look at the android. Instead, he fixed his water blue gaze on Jax with that same pleading look. Jax fixed the image of a plate of rice in her head. She imagined it sitting before Hoyt on the floor, freshly cooked and steaming. It was a blue plate made of plastic, and the rice was white and cooked to near transparency. Her scalp began to itch, and the back of her neck felt like needles were taking turns pricking her skin. She tried to ignore the sensation and focus on the image in her head. She looked into Hoyt's eyes and tried to impose her thoughts into his. The idea felt stupid, but with the gun pressed into his head, Jax tried it anyway. Hoyt's nostrils flared, and he looked down at the floor. His wide eyes grew wider, and he began to scoop the rice with both hands to shovel it into his mouth. Gayle gave a satisfied nod.

"How does it taste, Hoyt?" Gayle asked.

"Good," Hoyt said, seemingly having forgotten the gun, "really good."

"That's good to hear," Gayle said. The android pulled the trigger. With a loud crack, Hoyt's head exploded across the cargo bay floor leaving a long smear of red. Jax's hand shot to her mouth. She squeezed her eyes shut trying not to make a sound. None of this was real. *None of this was real. She was going to wake up next to Sarah any moment now.* Gayle's hand grabbed her shoulder and shook her until Jax opened her eyes.

"You've done well," Gayle said, "but it's time for you to go back to sleep. We have many more experiments left to run." Gayle lifted something up to Jax's nose, and her world went dark.

5

Jax's eyes cracked open to a familiar ceiling. She was back on the makeshift table. This time, however, there was no Gayle to greet her. She looked around to find the cargo hold devoid of any presence save her. There were no straps to tie her down, no android to monitor her, just her in Sarah's Kara Corp coveralls. Hoyt's body and blood had been cleared away as well, but a faint copper smell still lingered in the air. Jax rolled off of the table and dared to look around. The crates were still stacked as before, and the golem loomed in the corner, but there was no sign of Gayle. Was this another of the AI's experiments? Jax snuck through a few of the crates to get to the gear closet. Finding it to be Gayle free, Jax decided to take the opportunity to prepare herself. If Gayle was still on this ship, the AI was going to be destroyed.

Jax changed into her enviro suit and helmet as quietly as she could, and searched for something she could use as a weapon. Finding some of her explosive charges and little else, she called herself a number of insults when she remembered Modiri's cargo was filled with them. She took one of the charges, and put it on her belt as a last resort. Slipping back out into hold, Jax opened one of the crates. It was filled with stacks of rifles, and she pulled one out. It was a smaller gun somewhere between a rifle and a pistol, and Jax hoped it wouldn't be strong enough to punch through Modiri's hull. It was a risk she was willing to take should it come down to it, so she loaded the weapon and powered it on. Checking the airlock, it too was empty. The cabin garnered the same results which just left the cockpit. She poked her head up to see Gayle's silhouette sticking out of the edge of the pilot's seat. Something odd was happening. A wire was extended from Gayles wrist, and ported into the center console of Modiri's navigation terminal.

Jax climbed the rest of the way into the cockpit and read-ied the gun. She crept up behind the android, and brought the bar-rel centimeters away from the back of Gayle's head. The android's eyes were open, but rolled back into its head with its mouth hang-ing ajar. Jax wasn't going to take a chance. She shoved the barrel into the android's head, and pushed until Gayle's head slammed into the console. She pulled the trigger, round after round firing into the synthetic skull, and didn't let off until the magazine was empty. The gun continued to click as it dry fired, but the android's head - and the terminal to Jax's chagrin - were nothing but a man-gled mess. She'd have to fix it before she was able to go anywhere unless she planned on using the emergency jump sequence written into the nav-terminal. A noise like grinding metal sounded from the cargo hold. Jax knelt on the floor, and poked her head through the hatch. The golem in the far corner began to flicker to life. It uncurled itself, and began to stomp toward one of the crates.

"That was a mistake," Gayle's voice said over the comms. "It was a mistake on both our parts. You woke up early, and I failed to predict this. It seems I'll have to expunge our little experiment, and start anew. Sarah could make a good subject."

The golem lurched toward one of the larger crates, popped open the lid, and removed what looked to be a cannon. Jax's heart skipped a beat. She pulled her head back into the cockpit, and pulled the android's corpse out of the pilot's seat. She swore at the top of her lungs at her own stupidity. The console was in ruins. Maybe she could vent the golem into space. She closed the cock-pit's hatch, and rushed over the copilot's seat. She turned on a life feed of the cargo hold to see the golem prepping the cannon with several large shells. Swearing again, she slammed her fist against the control for the cargo ramp. Loose debris and untethered crates started to blow out of the back of Modiri as the ramp lowered. The golem stood firm as it used one massive hand to grab hold of the bulkhead. Large dents appeared where its fist dug into the metal. It started to poise the canon atop one shoulder. She was left with few options.

"Desperate times, desperate measures," Jax said. She pulled

the explosive charge from her belt and armed the timer for five seconds. Hopping out of her seat, she pulled open the hatch, pressed the arm button, and threw the charge into the hold. Slamming the hatch back shut, Jax rushed over to the nav terminal and punched the emergency jump controls. A timer bloomed into view.

Five seconds.

A tank round blasted through the back of the cockpit door, and exploded through the glass window. Air rushed out of the openings, and destroyed the rest of the cockpit's glass. The emergency shutters slammed down, but air still fled from the hole in the back. The golem would need to reload, but she was running out of time on multiple fronts.

Two seconds.

An explosion rocked Modiri's hull, and everything happened at once. The world distorted around her. A metallic ping sounded followed by a massive boom. Everything was chaos. Flames danced, colors spun, and Jax had no way of telling up from down or if she was even moving at all. Blood pounded in her ears, and her heart thumped at irregular intervals. She tried not to be sick in her helmet. It would make whatever came next a living nightmare if it wasn't already. Sticking her tongue to the roof of her mouth, Jax hummed as loud as she could. Please don't puke, please don't puke was the only thought racing through her head. As abruptly as it started, everything stopped. The world was black. Not even a standby light blinked on her console.

Jax blinked and quit her ridiculous tune. Her head took time to catch up on the fact that she was no longer in motion. If Modiri was stationary, and not hurtling through space at uncontrolled speeds, it meant the jump drive's stabilizers had done their job. The world was as quiet as death, and Jax wasn't sure if she was still in one piece or if this was a hallucination of her final moments. Nausea still tormented her stomach and the back of her throat which told her she was alive. Taking a few moments to catch her breath and let her heart settle, Jax reached into the dark, and felt for the copilot's console. Finding it in one piece, she flipped switches and pushed buttons praying for something to turn on. Her hand reached navigation controls, and a light flickered to life.

What usually displayed a map displayed as a formless glow of blue ambiance. Her cockpit was intact, at least, with the exception of a fist-sized hole punched through the rear hatch.

Jax unfastened from her seat, and discovered artificial gravity was gone. She floated her way to the back of the cockpit, and peeked through the hole. Sparks hissed and arced from rents in Modiri's hull, and she thought she could see open space in a few places. Deciding to risk it, Jax pulled open the hatch to get a better look. Keeping a firm grasp of the ladder, Jax descended into the cargo hold, and was met with a view of open space. Modiri's entire back half was gone along with all of her cargo. At least the golem was out of her hair, but so was all of her emergency supplies. A single mess kit, and some sealant tools were underneath the copilot's seat, but that was all she had to work with. She also had no way of knowing how much of Gayle was left in Modiri's remaining systems. It was a safe bet to assume that as long as there was a network for Gayle to embed itself into, Gayle would exist.

Jax pulled herself back into the cockpit, and closed the hatch. She needed a plan. With these new suits, she'd die of dehydration before she'd run out of oxygen. That gave her roughly seventy-two hours to fix the cockpit up enough to remove her helmet, or otherwise find rescue. She made a mental note to buy a suit with a water feed next time. If she made it through this, Jax was going to make it her life's work to see Gayle eradicated from existence. All she had to do was survive.

6

Jax watched the video message over and over again in disbelief. Gayle had gotten in one last stab. She sat in the copilot's seat where Sarah usually occupied, and tried to ignore the pit in her chest. A single tear wet her left cheek, but with her helmet on she was unable to wipe it. Having managed to repair the short-range communications antenna on the outside of Modiri, Jax isolated it from the rest of Modiri's systems to prevent any fragment of Gayle from being able to hinder what she was doing. Already an S.O.S. was being broadcast.

Thinking of Sarah, it bothered Jax that one single person could have so much sway over how she felt. Quite frankly, it was unfair. In the past months she had started to grow used to her new reality, her new companionship. Now, all of that was being ripped away from her. Jax admitted she never deserved it to begin with. She played the video again. Gayle had created an exact visual replica of Jax, voice and all, and sent a message to Sarah's ship telling her it was over. The Jax in the holo-feed voiced her distress with having to share the Modiri with someone, and how Sarah only seemed to want to take it from her. Jax, or Gayle rather, then went on to say it was time to part ways. They both had a ship of their own, and they both had goals of their own. There was no better time to set down different paths. Jax's fist trembled as she clenched it. She pressed it tight against the seat's armrest to prevent herself from slamming down repeatedly. She needed to conserve energy and avoid injuring herself. She knew what Gayle's message would do to Sarah, and it twisted the pit in her stomach into physical pain. If Jax managed to be rescued, maybe she could find Sarah again. Her hopes, however, were not high.

A readout to her right blinked to indicate re-pressurization of the cabin had been completed. Jax had sealed the hole in the hatch, and found a way to loop the cabin's separated life support system. She had no idea if what the readout told her would be accurate, or if Gayle had altered it in any way, but there was one way to find out. She reached up to the clasps of her helmet, and unlatched them one by one. If this went wrong, she wouldn't have to worry about how Sarah felt. She wouldn't have to worry about anything at all. She yanked the helmet off her head in one swift motion, fully expecting to die. Clean oxygen filled her lungs, and Jax almost laughed. Gayle was going to be in deep, deep trouble if her luck continued on like this.

CHAPTER 8
- KALLIK -

1

Kallik ran down the white-walled corridor, slipper-clad feet pounding against the sandpapered flooring. He could hear the hulking Morkus close behind, lumbering footsteps matching his own pace. The bigger boy grunted with each breath, and the sound sent jolts of fear through Kallik. The fear fueled his every step, and he clutched a book tighter to his chest. It was one from the play area that had caught Kallik's eye, but he never got the chance to open it before Morkus attacked. The orderlies on watch hadn't even bothered to stop Morkus, and Leo was busy being tested today. Kallik was forced to run. Gripping the book gave him an idea. He tossed the book behind him and was rewarded with a high-pitched squeak followed by a loud crash. Kallik darted around a corner and started testing all of the doors in search of a place to hide. Every door he tried was locked. Kallik was starting to lose hope.

"Over here," a girl's voice called. Kallik looked around for the source, desperate for any help he could get. A set of fingers wiggled out from one of the airduct covers at floor level. The fingers wiggled more as Kallik noticed them, and he recognized Rekkeh's face behind the grates. She pushed the grate open, and Kallik rushed over to it. Scooching aside, Rekkeh created enough room for him to squeeze around her and into the airduct. Closing it behind her, she shuffled away from the opening just in time.

"Where are you, squealer?" Morkus bellowed, "I'm not

done with you!"

Kallik and Rekkeh watched as Morkus wandered down the corridor and passed by their air duct. From this angle, he looked like a giant stomping around in search of food. Kallik imagined himself as one day being the valorous knight clad in shining armor ready to face down the giant. Kallik's image of himself was replace by Leo, however, as Kallik told himself all he could do was run away. The giant's footsteps faded, and both he and Rekkeh heaved a sigh of relief.

"So, this is where you go when Leo's gone?" Kallik asked. "How do they not catch you in here?"

Rekkeh shrugged, "it's a lot easier with Master Vincent gone. Angry doctor kitty has less interest in testing the vipers."

Kallik slumped against the tin wall of the air duct. It was a rare opportunity for him to feel at ease, and he wanted to take advantage of it. He wrapped his arms around his knees, and took a moment to catch his breath. Rekkeh tapped his shoulder, and he opened his eyes to see her holding up a glow orb to his face. The translucent ball glowed a pale-yellow as she turned it on, and Rekkeh pointed down the air duct.

"I can show you some neat things," she said, "only if you want. You can stay here if you don't."

Kallik peered down the dark tunnel and debated with himself. He had never been great with the dark. Even back home he slept with a nightlight. There were too many unknowns that lurked in the depths of shadows, and the deeper the shadow, the lager the monsters could be. Kallik examined the glow orb, and wondered where Rekkeh might have gotten it. He asked as much, and she gave him a shrug and told him some of the orderlies had a nice side. Kallik nodded, and agreed to go with her if she led the way. Rekkeh put on a wolfish smile, but kept her words to herself. Holding out the glow orb, she crawled down the tunnel with Kallik close behind.

2

Rekkeh had brought them far enough in that Kallik could

no longer see the vent they had entered from. After a few turns and a crossroad or two, he had to admit to being lost. He looked back, and tried to ignore the panic building in his chest. The small bubble of yellow light the glow orb emitted did little to calm his nerves, but Rekkeh at least seemed to know where she was going. He clung to that fact, and repeated to himself that she knew where she was and could return at any time she wished.

"What do you want to see first?" She asked. "This spot lets us go almost anywhere. We can't go up, though. Up leads to big fans which could cut you to pieces. Down is where I usually go. There's lots of neat things on the lower levels."

"Lower is fine," Kallik said. In truth, he didn't care where they went as long as they kept moving. If they stood still for too long, fear had time to catch up and devour him.

Rekkeh pointed them down a new branch of ductwork to the left, and led the way. She started to tap on the sides of the tin wall, and each tap echoed through the length of the tunnel. It was making him nervous, and Kallik wanted to tell her to stop. He didn't get the chance, however, as she tapped a panel of tin wall and smiled. Holding the glow orb up to a screw in the corner, she fished the screw out with her fingernails. It popped right out with little effort. Rekkeh did the same with each corner until she was able to pull aside the entire section. Dim light spilled in from the area beyond, and Kallik could see it was a maintenance shaft. A ladder ran downward in a narrow tunnel, and all along it accompanied a strip of lights.

"We can find more vents down there," Rekkeh said. She didn't wait for a response. Reaching out, she took hold of the ladder, and started to climb down. Kallik swallowed, and looked back down the air duct. The fading light Rekkeh took with her caused the darkness to approach with each step she took down. Kallik hurried and grabbed the first rung of the ladder. He didn't want to think about what would happen if he let go. Trying to look down and pay attention to Rekkeh while holding on for dear life was giving Kallik a good deal of trouble. Sweat on his palms only made the matter worse, and thinking about it only made him sweat more.

"Here," Rekkeh called up, and she disappeared inside another air vent. At least the light did not go with her this time. Kallik tried to hurry without losing his grip. Lowering himself to a point where he could see the opening, he had to then figure out how to let go of the ladder with one hand to pull himself into the vent. Rekkeh giggled at him, and held out a hand to help. He took it without hesitation, and she hauled him into the duct. She was a lot stronger than her diminutive frame let on.

The glow orb was not needed as much in this section as there were many vents in the floor which opened to rooms below. Rekkeh was familiar with the area, and pointed out what every room was below them. Most were simple, mundane, and the same type of rooms Kallik was used to on his own floor. When they got further in, however, things got a good deal scarier. They stopped at the edge of a vent, and looked down into a room with a pair of operating tables. One was empty and clean, but the other had a white sheet draped over a large shape. Kallik couldn't shake the feeling that a body was hidden beneath the white fabric. No blood stained the cloth, but the shape was too similar to a corpse.

"Sometimes they test us here," Rekkeh said, "angry kitty really likes this room."

"What do they do?" Kallik asked. "How is it that they test vipers?"

Rekkeh pointed to the cloth, and Kallik dreaded what she was about to say. "They have us make test subjects see things. They're horrible things, Kallik, but they want us to make these people see them. In the middle of the process the doctor makes them inhale a puff of air from a bottle of some gross liquid. Sometimes it makes them change."

"Change?" Kallik asked. "Change how?"

"They turn into monsters," Rekkeh said, "the doctors like to keep the ones that do."

She pointed further down the shaft, and started to crawl that way. Glancing back down into the operation room, and then back up at Rekkeh, Kallik wasn't sure he wanted to keep following. He didn't know his way back on his own. He started to chew his lower lip, but followed the younger Groal despite his better judgement. He tried not to look down into any more vents as they crawled, but his curiosity got the better of him. Some of them were too dark to see into, and one had a horrible stench as they crawled over it. At last, Rekkeh stopped, and pointed into a room. It was a long chamber filled with cages. Shrouded in darkness save for blinking lights on the cage doors and Rekkeh's orb, it was difficult to make out the shapes moving around in each cage. They reacted to Rekkeh's orb, and Kallik could see each shape was different. Several lumbered toward the edge of their prisons to reach for the light only to be blocked by a thick pane of glass. Mangled arms and claws tried to get to the light, and Kallik tried not to scream in panic.

"I can hear them," Rekkeh said, "in my head, Kallik, I can hear them calling out to me. They want freedom just like all of us. I want to let them free, Kallik. I helped make them, didn't I?" Rekkeh was in a trance, her eyes fixated on the creatures below, and panic threatened to overwhelm Kallik. He put a hand on her shoulder, and shook her. Blinking, she looked back at him with a smile.

"Another time," she said. She crawled further down the vent, and Kallik couldn't have been happier to follow her away from this place. A question lingered in his thoughts. If they turned people into monsters down here it meant they had prisoners to start with. Maybe that allowed for hope when it came to his father and cousin.

"Where do they keep people before the tests?" Kallik asked. "Is that close?"

"It's on the way to what I want to show you next," Rekkeh said.

A shiver ran through Kallik's spine, and goose bumps broke out along his arms. If his family was still alive, Kallik was going to find them. Monsters or no, he begged whatever entity might be listening that he wasn't too late to save them.

The dark chamber looked identical to the last room Kallik had seen except instead of monsters, the cages were filled with people. They squinted up at the light, dirty and disheveled. There were so many, too many to distinguish from one another.

An old man with shaggy gray hair and dressed in filth-covered rags reached through the bars of his cage toward the glowing light of Rekkeh's orb. Kallik tried to peer through the dark to find his family, but it was no use.

"Dad?" He asked. "Amic?"

"What are you doing?" Rekkeh hissed in a sharp whisper, "someone else could be down here."

"I need to know," Kallik said.

"Kallik?" A rasped voice called back from somewhere in the dark. "Is that you?"

It took Kallik a moment to decipher the voice, but then it clicked. "Amic! You're alive!"

"So is your father," Amic said, "but barely. Kallik, whatever you're thinking, you need to forget it and leave. It's good to know you're safe, but if you can escape you need to do so."

Other prisoners started to make noise as they were awoken to the voices. Some called out, and clutched the bars of their cages while others wept. Rekkeh tugged Kallik's arm, indicating they needed to leave. Tears welled up in Kallik's eyes, and he wiped them away with a sleeve. Sniffing, he pulled his arm away from Rekkeh and glared into the darkness.

"I'm going to save you," he said, "I'm going to find a way to get you out."

Rekkeh pulled harder, and Kallik listened. He let the girl take him away from the vent, and further into the depths of the facility. He held back the tears this time. Knowing his family was alive was enough to ignite a flame in his gut. Kallik wouldn't cry. What he would do was find a way to get those prisoners free, and rid the universe of this awful place once and for all.

3

Rekkeh repeated the process of knocking on the tin walls until she found the one she needed. Once again, she pulled out the screws which were only placed in a way to look like they were secure, and she pulled the panel to the side. They descended an identical maintenance shaft, but this time they climbed all the way to the bottom. It felt good to be able to stand upright, and Kallik took the opportunity to stretch his legs. The stiffness helped distract him from thoughts of his family. Raising his arms above his head and standing on his toes, Kallik pulled his body into a long stretch and held it there for several moments. Rekkeh poked the small of his back to get his attention, and pointed down a tunnel which was only a margin larger than the shafts. At least the space was nice while it lasted. Why did Rekkeh bother to spend so much time here? Kallik thought it would be much simpler to stay in her room if all she wanted to do was avoid people. The two of them crouched rather than crawled down the tunnel until they reached a hatch.

"I think this is the best spot," Rekkeh said, "it's my favorite place to go when I'm sad. Maybe it'll help you too."

Rekkeh pulled a lever on the side of the hatch, and the metal door popped open before swinging inward. Kallik's eyes were met with teal light over a pit of black. He wedged himself into the opening next to Rekkeh to get a better view. Large cylinders the size of transport pods rose from the black depths of nothingness to rise into a vast open chamber. Rings of glowing teal light lined the outer circumference of each and pulsed like a heartbeat. Catwalks crisscrossed between each of the cylinders in a gridded pattern and nestled close to the structures. Small glowing motes of teal orbs floated lazily in the air casting their light across whatever they floated by. The ceiling above and the floor below were both too far away to be seen leaving them in pitch black. Rekkeh took Kallik's hand, and guided him out onto the catwalk. Kallik grabbed the railing with his other hand, and Rekkeh laughed at his uncertainty.

"What is this place?" Kallik asked. "How far down does that go?"

"Dunno," Rekkeh said, "probably pretty far though. I asked Master Aillon about it once, and he told me never to come down here. Said it powered the whole place using bio fuel."

One of the teal orbs floated down near Kallik, and he was able to get a better look at what they were. No larger than his fingernail, the glowing mote looked like a ball of fuzz. Small hairs stuck out in every direction, and waved in the faint breeze as it floated by. Kallik reached out his hand, and pointed his index finger to touch it. Rekkeh yanked his other hand, pulling him away from the floating object.

"I wouldn't do that," she said, "they can sting if they don't like you."

"How do I know if they'll like me?" Kallik asked. "What do I have to do so I can touch them?"

Rekkeh shrugged and let one fall into the palm of her hand. Holding it up to her face, she blew on it to send it careening off into the void. "I have no idea. They like me, but Leo and Toby can't come down here. It gets pretty bad for them."

Rekkeh let go of Kallik's hand and sat down on the catwalk. She stuck her legs out between the balusters, and let them dangle over the pit of darkness. She kicked them back and forth while watching the motes dance and fall all around them. Kallik sat next to her, but folded his legs beneath him rather than let them hang out. Who knew what could be lurking down there just waiting to snag a child's foot and drag them into the dark for a quick meal. He contented himself with looking up, and watching some of the teal dust balls float around one of the massive cylinders.

"So, you like it?" Rekkeh asked, and she jabbed a finger into Kallik's hand. "Pretty neat, huh?"

"I think I do," Kallik said. As long as he kept his imagination away from the bottomless pit below them, he was able to enjoy the tranquility of this place. "It's quiet."

"You're going to try and escape," Rekkeh said, "aren't you."

"Yeah," Kallik said, "I don't know when, but I'm going to."

"Sounds dangerous," Rekkeh said, "like you could get hurt trying."

"Don't think I can do it?" Kallik asked.

"Dunno," Rekkeh said, "but I do know the Butcher will be a problem."

"There has to be some way to deal with him," Kallik said, "maybe if I get better with my powers, I'll be able to use them against this place. I can make them regret ever giving them to me."

"You'd take me with you?" Rekkeh asked. Her hand slid over his own, and wrapped around it in a tight, but gentle grip. "I don't like it here. I'd like to see brother again. He was always nice to me at least. Leo says he'll help us get out, but he hasn't yet. He plans, but he never acts."

"I thought I told you to never come down here," Master Aillon said. He stood over them looking down, a clump of red hair falling in front of his face. "And, I see you've brought a friend this time. Hello Kallik."

Kallik sprang to his feet, blood rushing to his cheeks and ears. Master Aillon laughed, and patted Kallik's shoulder. It was then Kallik noticed someone else standing behind Master Aillon. It was the orderly Anna. For some reason she looked just as embarrassed as Kallik felt. Her face was red, and she refrained from looking either of them in the eye. Rekkeh stood up next to Kallik, and glared at Master Aillon with defiance.

"Why are you down here, then?" Rekkeh asked. Anna coughed, and rubbed the back of her neck with a nervous hand. Aillon laughed again, and stooped over to be a level height with the young Groal girl.

"I'm an adult," he said, "and a registered staff member of Kronos Laboratories, thus I can go wherever I'd like."

"That's not fair," Rekkeh pouted. She crossed her arms, but dropped her gaze down to the catwalk. "I like it down here too."

"Most who see this place do," Aillon said. He took hold of both of them by the shoulder and started to lead them down the catwalk, Anna close behind. "Let's get you out of here before someone worse than me finds that you've been sneaking about, yeah?"

Kallik had no choice but to let Master Aillon lead him where he willed. Better him than someone like Sabastian. They were led to one of the far ends of the area, and into a large elevator. The light of the elevator was almost blinding compared to what Kallik had grown used to down here, and he had to squint to see where he was. Anna pushed a button for the third floor, and Kallik realized he just gained two important pieces of information. The first was the name of the facility. The second was the main floor Kallik was forced to live on. He didn't know what he could do with that information, but he knew it had some sort of value. Kallik felt one step closer to being able to form a plan.

4

Master Aillon and Anna said their goodbyes at the entrance of the third floor and went their separate way. Kallik and Rekkeh decided it was best to spend the rest of their day at the rec area. They returned to the play area to a scene of Mauricia screaming and being dragged away by a pair of orderlies. The older girl kicked her feet, twisted, and thrashed making any attempt to break loose, but the orderlies held firm. The Butcher lurked, watching from a nearby corner. Morkus stood next to the jungle gym, chest heaving, and glared death at the masked man. The other children had all stopped to watch the event unfold. Fear was painted across all their faces. One of the orderlies slipped, and everything happened at once. Mauricia pulled her arm free, and slammed her fist into the orderly's crotch. The man doubled over, and Mauricia used the opportunity to pull free of the second man. The Butcher pounced. He closed the gap in a heartbeat, and drove a booted foot into her chest. Mauricia hit the floor, hard, and Vigamere loomed over her with his boot firmly planted on her sternum. His voice was quiet, cold, and the volume of the universe seemed to drop in his favor.

"You look on the brink, little Mauricia," he said. He flipped back the edge of his robe to reveal his short sword, and patted its hilt. "If you aren't careful, I'll be seeing you for a different reason. It can't be too long now before you snap."

Tears started to run in rivers down Mauricia's cheeks. Kallik hated the older girl, but he could not help but feel sorry for her. No one deserved this. Not even Morkus's goon. Kallik's bully stood with his fists clenched, and his jaw clamped shut. He had taken several steps toward the conflict, but remained in place as he watched the Butcher. Vigamere noticed as well, and looked up from tormenting poor Mauricia.

"Try it," Vigamere said, "give me an excuse."

"That will be enough," Karaska said as he came striding down the hall, gold and crimson robes swishing with each step. Leo followed close behind with another pair of orderlies behind him. "Hurry up and get her prepped, I've got a busy schedule today."

Mauricia was hauled to her feet by the pair of orderlies. All the fight had drained out of her, and she allowed herself to be pushed around. Tears continued to run, and her shoulders shook with silent sobs. Karaska had her led in the direction of the elevator, the direction Kallik had just come from. Vigamere followed the group as a noiseless shadow, his scarred mask fixated on Mauricia. With the scene over, the other kids went back to their playing, but a somber mood lingered in the air. Toby ran over from the swing set to greet Leo who, in turn, was making his way over to Kallik and Rekkeh. The four of them converged near the center of the rec area, exhaustion lining Leo's expression.

"What was that about?" Leo asked. "Did Mauricia do something bad?"

"Doctor Cat is starting back up the testing for Vipers," Toby said, "I guess they want to ramp everything up."

"She's a lot stronger than me," Rekkeh added, "I think she caused most of the things down there."

The other two boys looked confused, but Kallik understood what she was referring to. Another look at Leo, and Kallik thought the boy looked about to faint. It gave him mixed feelings. Part of him felt bad for Leo as the bull testing seemed to hit him harder than some of the others, but another part of Kallik just felt glad he wasn't the only one to feel miserable after a session with the four-armed devil. A head of gold hair poked its way into their group, and Xoriah did her best to alleviate the mood. Pulling a book from behind her back, she shoved it into Kallik's chest.

"I think you dropped this," she said, "you should take better care of your books."

Kallik blushed for more reasons than one. It was clear Xoriah was joking, but he felt guilty for having used the book as a tool for his escape. Additionally, something about Xoriah made him feel different. It was an uncomfortable type of different, but not an unwelcome one. He found himself looking at her when he shouldn't, and the image of her grabbing his hand rather than Rekkeh crept into his head. Toby shoved him with a snorted laugh.

"Maybe you can find your words in that book," he said, "unless you drop it again, butterfingers."

"Leave him be," Leo said. His face was so pale, "I think it's been a rough day for all of us."

"It was a joke," Toby started to argue, but Leo cut him off.

"We need to think about what our next move is," he said, "I don't think I've got many runs left before they send me to the Butcher."

"What do you mean?" Toby asked. "What's our next move?"

Leo looked around for prying ears. Most of the other kids were in their own worlds trying to find a brief moment of escapism before they were sent back to testing. The one exception was Morkus. He remained standing in the same place as before. Fists clenched by his side, Morkus glared murder into the floor. He looked frozen in thought, and Kallik feared for anyone who dared to break him out of his trance.

"Meet in my room," Leo said, "we can talk more there."

5

With all five of them, Leo, Toby, Rekkeh, Xoriah, and Kallik, Leo's room had little space to move. They were huddled together with Xoriah, Rekkeh and Toby seated on the bed while Leo and Kallik sat cross legged on the floor with their backs pressed against the wall. The door was shut, making the temperature rise and the air feel stuffy despite the circulation of the vents. Leo had ripped several pictures out of the books and fixed them to his wall. Xoriah had grown upset upon seeing what Leo had done to a physical book just to put some color on his walls, but she dropped the subject to avoid an argument.

"It's just us for now," Leo said, and looked at each of them in turn. "The other kids can't be trusted. At least not yet. We'll probably have to rely on a few of them at some point if we're serious about escaping, but right now let's focus on what just this group can do."

"What can we do?" Toby asked. "The Butcher would cut us to pieces if we tried anything, and the adults are smarter than us. Well, except for Sabastian."

Rekkeh giggled at Toby's insult, but the rest of them remained quiet. He had a point. The adults were adults, and the kids had few advantages over them. Aillon might be the only one that would support them, and Kallik was not sure to what extent. The red-haired conduit had made vague comments about taking action, but part of Kallik wondered if those comments were made out of an attempt to calm a crying boy rather than imply actual intent.

"Let's start with what we know about this place," Leo said. "We can take turns laying out information, and we can go from there. I'll try to listen, and maybe something will become obvious once we've said it. Agreed?"

Everyone nodded their heads, and Leo pointed to Rekkeh to start. For the first time, Rekkeh spilled everything. She talked about what happened to vipers, and about what other levels there were to the facility. Everyone was wide eyed as she spoke. Even Kallik sat with a straight back as he listened to her tell it over again. Once she was done, there was a long silence before Leo pointed to Toby. The freckled boy had little to add other than some trivial details and lewd jokes about some of the orderlies. One by one, each of them added to a growing pool of knowledge until it was Leo's turn to speak. It was clear he had something working in his mind. The gears turned, and he wrinkled his face in thought.

"I think I have a plan," he said, "but it's going to be dangerous."

CHAPTER 9
- SARAH -

1

Sarah found herself standing at the edge of a tunnel's threshold. A few lights hung from the ceiling, but it wasn't enough to illuminate the tunnel in its entirety. She wasn't sure why she was here, only that there was supposed to be an offshoot somewhere toward the center of the tunnel and she needed something from it. Sarah clenched her fist, and found the hilt of a dagger between her fingers. It was a simple blade of plain design. When or why she had picked it up was another mystery. Taking a deep breath, Sarah started down the tunnel.

Her footsteps echoed against the walls and ceiling, and became the only sound she could hear. Sarah reached the maintenance shaft, looked around for any potential witnesses, and slipped inside. Having to duck her head to fit, Sarah had to use the light of her wrist display to see by. The sound of dripping water came from somewhere further down the shaft, and the temperatures were frigid. Sarah could see her breath misting in the blue light. Sarah hurried as fast as she could while staying as quiet as possible. She wanted to be out of this place as it gave her the creeps. Already she was imagining Doctor Sondra's centipede face lurking in the shadows just beyond the light. She could hear the whispers of a little girl urging her to witness something unspeakable.

By the time she reached the next door, Sarah was running. The frigid air stung her throat, and tightened her lungs, and the hand she held out for light had started to go numb. She tested to see if the door was locked. She could do this. *She could do this.* She had faced literal monsters and walked away the victor. Walking down a tunnel was nothing. The door popped open with little effort, and Sarah ducked through the small opening. The tunnels kept getting smaller. Sarah had to crouch to walk through this one.

A girl laughed behind her, and the door slammed shut. It was her imagination. Breeze caught the door, and the dark was playing tricks on her mind. She was done seeing visions. There was no way she heard a little girl. She tested the door again to see if it had locked. Popping open again, Sarah heaved a sigh of relief. At least she wasn't trapped.

"I'm still heeeeerre," a girl's voice cooed from behind her, "always, and always."

"Who's there?" Sarah called out, but she knew. That voice was unmistakable. The laughter sounded again, but this time in front of her. Sarah held out her light trying to catch a glimpse of the phantom, but all she saw was the pitch black. She pushed on, but the laughing grew louder.

"You'll never be rid of me," the voice said from behind, and then called out again from in front, "you can never be rid of yourself."

A little girl walked into the blue light. *Sarah* walked into the light. She still wore Hector's jacket, and grubby street clothes hung from her small frame. She grinned with malice, and held up her hand for Sarah to take. The little girl turned her head back toward the dark, and another little girl emerged. She was an exact copy down to every last smudge on her shirt. Sarah was hallucinating. This was a dream. A third Sarah stepped up behind the second, and then a fourth. Sarah heard something shift behind her, and she spun. More little versions of herself were collecting behind her, all grinning wicked grins, all holding up their hands to be taken. Dozens, if not hundreds, of little Sarah's crowded in around her. They all giggled and laughed, and started to grab her cloak. They pulled and latched onto the dark fabric, and tried to pull Sarah to the ground. She did not know what would happen if they succeeded, but Sarah was not about to find out.

Sarah screamed at them, and ripped the dagger through

the air. Slashing out first one way, and then another blood splattered across the walls, across Sarah, but still the small Sarahs encroached. Their giggling grew to a cacophony of laughter, and tears started to stream down Sarah's cheeks. She was supposed to be done with this. She was supposed to be on to her exciting new life of freedom, but her past was here to kill her. Strike after strike, Sarah swiped the dagger into the crowd of demons, but her strength was fading. Breath growing ragged, Sarah could feel the energy draining from her arms. She wouldn't be able to stand for much longer.

Hatred sparked somewhere deep within her. It overcame her senses like an avalanche consuming her every thought. She was done with this. Heat, wonderful heat, filled her chest, and Sarah clenched her teeth with so much force she was afraid she drew blood. Dream or no, she was not about to be cowed by an illusion. She cut, and took one step forward, and then another. She cut again, and took another couple steps. The illusions started to bite her, little teeth sinking into her legs, and arms. Batting the teeth away, Sarah pushed ever forward. Using her free hand to grab onto pipes and ridges on the walls, Sarah pulled as well as pushed. The tunnel stank of iron, and her hands had grown sticky with blood.

A light bloomed at the end of the tunnel, and Sarah thought it must be a clearing. Dozens of little versions of herself filled the space between her and freedom. She reeled back to strike the phantom before her, but in a shock of color the little girl exploded into a swarm of butterflies. A second one did the same. Wings of red, blue, green, and yellow erupted from the space where a little girl once stood. One by one, all the phantoms began to explode until the entire passageway was clogged with fluttering wings. Then they too dissolved into motes of light. Tiny particles of glowing dust cascaded down to the floor. Only Sarah remained.

She sank to her knees, and let out a sob. Her hands were clean, and the tunnel smelled of damp, freezing air. Hand over hand, Sarah started to crawl toward the opening. She was numb. No thoughts filled the horrid void that she called her mind, only a blankness fixated on survival. Reaching the threshold of the opening, Sarah wanted to collapse. A blue slipper, stepped down on the dagger still clutched in Sarah's hand, and a pair of thin hands reached beneath her arms. Sarah tried to fight in protest but as she did, her eyes snapped open.

Sarah flailed in the small bed of the transport ship. Thin sheets scattered, and pillows flew as she tossed her limbs from side to side. She knocked a bottle of water from the nightstand and sent it cascading down the ladder into the cockpit below. Realizing where she was, Sarah stilled herself and lay silent for several moments. She sat up, reached for her water, and swore under her breath when she remembered what she'd done. Rolling over to sit on the edge of the bed, Sarah let her feet touch the cold metal floor. She scrubbed her face with both hands in an attempt to wake up, and tried to push memories of the nightmare out of her head. Reaching over to the nightstand, Sarah pulled open the drawer to fish out a small pill bottle. She rattled its contents around and rubbed a thumb over the dark lettering spelling out the word munmos. The bottle recommended a dose of two pills before sleep, but Sarah had only taken one. She hoped it would help mitigate any dependency that could form, but the half dose was ineffective. She'd settle for two next time. The added stress of Jax's message did little to help her dreams.

Three days she waited at the designated meeting point. Sarah almost went back to look for Jax, but received a holo-recording before she could set the jump drive coordinates. She mulled over Jax's words for what seemed the thousandth time since receiving the message. Jax paced up and down the cargo hold of Modiri while picking each word with care. *They no longer needed each other's help. Both needed to find new independence and a way to heal.* Reason after reason Jax had listed as to why the two of them needed to go their own ways. Sarah thought up a hundred more reasons to argue, but the message was pre-recorded. It was done. Simple as that, Sarah found herself alone once more, however, not even an AI accompanied her this time around. There was a pit in the bottom of her stomach clawing at her heart, and threatening to drag the still beating organ down into the abyss. The last thing Jax had said to her was *find your brother, it would be good to see a familiar face.*

Sarah's brother could be dead for all she knew, and Jax was using him as some sort of out. The worst part about it was almost all her belongings – as few as they were – got left aboard the Modiri. That included the data-slate she had been drafting her book on, her cloak, and all of her spare clothes. Two options faced Sarah. She could linger here and lament, or she could push herself onward in an attempt to find her brother. Letting out a heavy sigh, Sarah tossed the pill bottle back into the drawer, pulled on the only set of clothes she now owned – a white tank and simple leggings she had worn under her enviro-suit – and climbed down the ladder. She slumped into the pilot's seat, an array of holo-displays blooming to life, and Sarah swiped a hand through a few of the displays to make them disappear. She did this until only the navigation was floating above the center console. A strange ship lurked in the far corner of her map. It floated in the void between two separate star systems. *The Ifrit* was name of the planet sized colony ship, and to know it was one of the smaller of the Vulture colonies boggled Sarah's mind. Zooming in on it, Sarah's eyes scanned the ship's uneven surface. It looked like a barge of sorts with hundreds of other ships fused together in a ramshackle order to create one large mega-ship. She double checked her coordinates to ensure she could get there in a single jump, and strapped into her seat. She decided to redouble her efforts to find her brother. At the moment, it was all she could concentrate on to keep herself from breaking out into tears. Doing one last diagnostic of the ship's systems, Sarah commenced the jump sequence.

2

Sarah closed communications with the traffic controller. Her jump took her within a few hours of the Ifrit at normal speed. She did this not only because it was required by the colony ship's safety regulations, but also because the amount of traffic she'd have to fly through terrified her. The process, however, was far simpler than she had let herself believe. All Sarah needed to do was upload the provided executable program into her navigation, and autopilot would take care of the rest. She breathed out a sigh of relief after the panic attack she had endured upon arrival. Supposedly one of the smallest of all the Vulture colonies, the Ifrit was still larger than Sarah could have imagined. Moons were smaller than the gargantuan lumbering by, and thousands of other ships encircled it like a swarm of insects. The entirety of the colony ship looked like a cobbled mass of spare parts, or a fused together spacecraft with every section and panel being of a different color and design. Some sections bulged or angled more than others, and certain areas appeared to still be under construction. If the exterior looked mismatched, Sarah wondered what the interior might have in store.

Sarah received the notification informing her the program was ready. She opened the navigation controls, and let the software integrate. Docking command informed her due to the nature of her cargo, she would need to dock in a quarantined section. Being a giant piece of metal floating through the vacuum of space, the presence of projectile weaponry was generally frowned upon. Their sale and distribution were limited to quarantined and licensed areas which were heavily guarded and patrolled by local authorities. Sarah was also reminded of her lack of Vulture citizenship. Immediately after her docking notice, a message arrived from the trade commission to let Sarah know all of her goods would be subjected to a foreign trade tax. Grumbling about it would do her little good. Besides, she had no intent of selling, a fact she left out of the conversation with docking command. All of it was to be traded for a spot on her contact's mission.

Leaning back, Sarah let the new navigation command do its work. The transport – she'd need to think of a name for it at some point – started to fly under its own autopilot features. More messages from various departments and trade groups bombarded her feed, and Sarah wanted nothing more than to turn her communications off. She knew each of those messages had some degree of importance, however, so she tried to skim through them as they came in. A sizable number were not essential including more than a few companies offering lascivious products and services. Filtering through what was and what wasn't important information was giving Sarah a headache, so she closed the feed telling herself she'd look through it later. She contented herself with watching out the window, staring wide eyed at the uncountable number of other ships. Many were smaller transports like her own, but a number of larger vessels such as frigates and cruisers made their appearances.

The Ifrit grew in her window until it was all Sarah was able to see. This side of the colony ship had a multitude of lights beaming across its outer hull to illuminate its endless colors and worn paint. The section her ship was being guided to shone a vibrant yellow with several docking bays honeycombing its flat surface. To an untrained eye, each bay appeared to open to the void of space, however, Sarah could see the faint shimmer of atmospheric shielding covering the openings. An electric hum vibrated her ship as it passed through the barrier, and the view through Sarah's cockpit changed to that of a bustling hangar bay. It was a mottled palette of browns, grays, and oranges smeared across rusted catwalks and dingey jetways. Multilayered, the hangar was a hive of ships, walkways, and docks set up so long arms with magnetic clamps would attach to each ship keeping it suspended while a number of jetways would attach to the outer doors. It was a clever way of maximizing the full volume of the hangar, and Sarah found herself appreciating the engineering behind it.

Groups of people hustled and bustled past each other causing the catwalks to look congested and overcrowded. Railings were covered with people watchers and sightseers watching all of the ships flying in and out, and Sarah wondered how many of them may be sizing ships up as targets. Jax had never explained to her how safe or dangerous Vulture colonies were, but Sarah was not naïve. Being one of those watchers at an early stage of her life, she knew what many of them could be up to. Sarah hoped the security forces here were more vigilant than the places she'd been as a child. This was supposed to be a quarantine dock, so maybe that would help. If this was a restricted area, she didn't want to know what the public docks looked like.

Sarah braced herself as her ship slowed to a stop, and long, mechanical arms stretched out to clamp down on its hull. Rocking gently as the magnets thumped against the hull, her ship powered down its engines, and fell into standby mode. Sarah went ahead and powered her ship down completely, and unfastened from her seat. A light blinked on her communication panel indicating someone wanted to talk to her directly. Sarah let the call through and a video feed of an android appeared. It was a basic model with a cylindrical head and limbs to resemble the human anatomy in the most basic sense. It addressed her with a monotone voice.

"Sarah Renza, you have docked a ship with no registration title or ID," the android said, "would like to set one up now?"

"Sure, why not," Sarah said.

"Please speak the desired name," the android said, "an ID number will be assigned to you shortly."

Sarah had to take a moment to think. She knew she'd have to name the ship at some point, but the moment arrived far sooner than she was ready for. Leaning back in her pilot's seat she tried to think back on her past experiences, and come up with something deep, something meaningful. She wanted to give her first ship a name she could look back on. Coming up short, her only memories being bad ones, she shrugged and took a different approach.

"Bill," she said, "the ship's name is Bill."

"Bill has been entered into Ifrit's primary logs," the android said, "you will be receiving a message with confirmation along with your ID number. Have a pleasant stay."

The android didn't wait for a response. The call ended, and her feed went blank. Sarah patted the center console of her newly named Bill, and exited the cockpit. One of the messages had explained to her about a dock worker waiting to receive her manifest. The individual would be wanting to meet her any moment now, so best not keep them waiting. She double checked her cargo to be sure everything was still strapped down where it needed to be. The little drone she had named Eryn floated about the cargo hold beeping and booping as it did so, and she gave it a pat as she checked each crate. Giving a final look back at the cockpit where the comfort of her bed still called to her, Sarah exited through a side airlock now attached to a catwalk via jetway.

The narrow passageway stunk of old oil, and poorly maintained machinery. Each step creaked, and Sarah wondered when the last safety check was run on this section. Artificial light shone through a series of windows cut into the rusted metal, and motes of dust danced within the beams. More light poked through the door at the far end, speaking to how thin the metal had worn. Sarah placed her hand on the support rail. It was the only part of this tunnel that looked clean, rubbed smooth by use of hundreds of other hands. Now outside of her ship, she could hear the booming din of the crowds she had seen before. She took a deep breath. She could do this on her own. She could. She didn't need Jax to do this for her. Straightening her back, lifting her chin, Sarah strode through the jetway, through the door, and onto the catwalk.

3

Timeliness was not in the vocabulary of this apparent dock master. Sarah leaned up against the door of the jetway, arms folded, and preoccupying herself by people watching. Vulture society was not limited to just humans, it would seem. Contrary to many of the HFS cities Sarah had lived in, large groups of Groal and Dwemyri intermingled with the human ones. Their outfits varied as much as the people did, and Sarah realized she needn't be concerned with blending in. She could have a flashing sign above her head, and still, no one would notice her over someone else. There were peddlers who seemed to think the catwalks were as good a place as any to set up shop, and rather than bring their wares deeper into the colony, they shouted at the top of their lungs over makeshift counters to try and bring in customers. Instead of setting up a stand, some walked from person to person carrying their products with them. Ducking and weaving through the crowds like snakes through grass, they would seek out the most vulnerable of each group and corner them. While watching one such situation - a human draped in a shabby green cloak harassed a young Groal woman with an item Sarah couldn't see - she finally caught wind of this high level of security she was warned about before docking.

An imposing figure covered from head to toe in thick plates of armor stormed through the crowd toward the scene. Painted red with white embellishments, the suit of armor was motor assisted to give the wearer extra strength. Long quills protruded from the back of the shoulder blades and ran all the way down to the lower back making the quills look like skeletal wings. They crackled with energy which, if Sarah had to guess, would be utilized for defense if need be. People cleared the way before the armored individual, and some shouted warnings to others. The harassing peddler caught one glimpse of the figure, and bolted.

"Breakers," a voice said from Sarah's left. To her credit, she didn't jump, instead just gave the new speaker a dead look. A young Groal man stood before her no older than twenty, but Sarah would place him in his teens. Narrow antlers rose from his head to branch off into several points. Disheveled brown hair hung around a round face with part of it tied into a haphazard bun on the back of his head. His clothes were a mix of blacks and grays with his loose-fitting pants and an oversized jacket. A silver necklace with a small, white crystal was strung around his neck.

"A nasty lot, those guys," he said, "those big spines collect energy, and send it to their fists. Whenever they strike someone, a pulse of electricity fires off through the fist to stun the poor bastard that made them angry."

Sarah pulled a move from Jax's playbook, and rather than answer the kid, she continued with her deadpan stare. If he was going to try and sell her something, he'd better be on with it so she could tell him no. She was also aware he could be distracting her for an attempted theft, so she watched her surroundings through her peripherals and kept a gauge on any physical sensation in case anyone tried to run a sneaky hand through her pockets. This boy caught the gist sooner than Sarah expected, and flushed with embarrassment.

"I'm sorry," he said, and ducked his head in a slight bow, "I'm Kyllen Rykus. I'm here to check your manifold?"

It was Sarah's turn to be embarrassed. Straightening from her relaxed position against the door, Sarah fished a data-slate from under her cloak and handed it to the kid. He took it, his once confident air shriveled away to reveal a nervous boy. Stammering out a mumbled thanks, he skimmed through the manifold. His eyes grew wider and wider as he scrolled through the list of goods, and once he was done, he looked up and around as if for someone to come assist him. Finding no one, he turned to Sarah with a heavy sigh.

"In case no one has told you," he said loud enough for everyone nearby to hear, "none of these products, and I mean none, can leave this dock. There's a strict no projectile policy within the colony, and you could be killed on the spot for violating it."

He glanced around for anyone who might be watching, leaned forward, and said in a lower tone, "you're late. Ziven has been waiting days for you to arrive."

"There was a setback," Sarah said, "but I'm here now. That counts, right?"

"They were about to leave without you," Kyllen said, "cargo or no."

Kyllen took another glance at the data-slate, and brushed a strand of hair out of his eyes so it rested above an antler. Pausing, he took a moment to look Sarah up and down, and she became very much aware of her outfit. She'd thought nothing of the tight leggings and thin tank. She was too busy trying to get all of her other ducks in a row, but now with this teenager's eyes darting from her chest to her hips, she was cursing Jax all the more for not at least giving her a chance to collect her things. Jax would have taught this little pervert a lesson, but Sarah had neither the energy nor the tenacity to deal with him. Besides, she had no way of knowing how connected Kyllen was to Ziven, and needed to tread a careful path. She settled for crossing her arms to block the view, and cleared her throat. Kyllen realized what he was doing, and his face turned bright red. His eyes snapped back to Sarah's, and he shoved the data-slate back into Sarah's hands.

"Ziven will want to meet you personally before the deal is done," Kyllen said. "I'll send you a time and place, so keep your schedule open."

He didn't give her a chance to respond. Kyllen turned on a heel and disappeared into the crowd before Sarah had a chance to ask any questions. Getting business underway sooner rather than later was fine by her, but she was going to need to find a way to replace some of her belongings before she met this smuggler. She went back inside, Eryn giving her a welcoming *beep*, and plopped down into the pilot's seat. Maybe one the thousands of new messages in her ship's inbox would have a hint of where to start.

4

The services offered on the Ifrit were limitless. Every opportunity was within arm's reach as long as one had enough credits. By the time Sarah got through half of the new messages her head was spinning. At last, she found what she was looking for in a clothing outlet that offered free delivery to her ship. She still had a few credits left to her name even after the egregious docking fees, so she spent what she thought was appropriate on a few new outfits. Mostly in neutral colors, she ordered some baggy shawls, loose fitting cardigans, a couple tanks, and several pairs of black trousers which fit tight around the ankles, but loose everywhere else. To her delight, they were delivered in less than thirty minutes by an android built to look like a cat with a large courier sack slung across its back. She met it on the busy catwalk, and thanked it as it left. She wasted no time changing into her new clothes, donning one of the gray, hooded cardigans and black trousers. Within the hour, Sarah received the info for her meeting with Ziven. Not wanting to put it off any longer, Sarah made her way back onto the bustling walkways.

After winding her way through the crowds toward the interior section of the hangar, Sarah was met with a long security checkpoint where she was forced to walk through innumerable scanners and detectors all under the watchful eyes of more hulking individuals in red armor. From this angle Sarah got an unobstructed view of the face of their helmets. They looked like armored birds now that she looked at them, with curved beaks beneath green eye lenses. While she couldn't tell if they were looking at her, Sarah could not shake the feeling of eyes scanning her every move. Doing her best to ignore the sensation, Sarah made her way through the wide tunnel of steel which was lit in neon blues and reds with each new scanner she crossed under. A full crowd followed with each step making her feel like a single sheep in a full herd. At last, her group reached the end with one last breaker giving them the nod to step through the gate. As the wide double doors of steel slid apart, an automated woman's voice called out over a speaker.

"Welcome to Sonso District," the voice said, "we hope you enjoy your stay."

Sarah walked through with the crowd into Sonso District which looked to Sarah like a cargo yard. Stacks atop of stacks of shipping containers reached to the metal vaulted ceiling above. Each shipping container, however, had sections cutout of their sides to create storefronts and living quarters. Neon lights beamed through each opening, and blasting base noises boomed from every corner of the place. Once the group Sarah had been pushed through with all passed through the gates, they started to disperse and go their separate ways. Sonso District was wide enough for everyone to spread out, and disappear within different crowds of their own choosing.

Following the map on her wrist display, Sarah took her time to allow the environment to wash over her. It was such a unique style of living that she had never considered. This community of Vultures had managed to repurpose thousands of these cargo containers to create a stacked city of their own. Ladders and makeshift stairwells rose from one level of containers to the next, and each level was as bustling as the one beneath it. Sarah peaked her head into windows and doorways as she walked by them to catch a glimpse of what each was about. What they contained was as varied as the colors plastering the entire district. Many were shops selling various wares ranging from the explicit to the illicit, and others were personal services offering everything Sarah could imagine. Some weren't businesses at all, but rather personal homes, and apartments. A night club thudded with heavy dance music overhead, and when Sarah looked up, she saw the container was overhanging the street and a large section of the container's floor had been replaced with glass so the passersby beneath could look up and view the raving scene of the club's dancers. She thought of how uncomfortable it must be for the dancers in that club, especially those who dared to wear skirts, but she realized that must be part of the draw for some. She took a second glance up, and blushed. It was *indeed* part of the appeal. Moving on before she caught herself gawking, Sarah caught a glimpse of a small shop selling repurposed androids. None were the sophisticated bipedal droids that were growing dangerously close to resembling humans, but Sarah found herself pausing to look nonetheless. Before she could stop herself, she entered the cargo container, and started to look around. Her hope was to find something she could replace Eryn's default programming with. It would be nice to see the little droid do more than simply float around her ship trying to cartograph every nook and cranny.

An old man in a yellow coat watched Sarah from behind a counter, one eye replaced with a thick mechanical lens. The iris of the lens widened and closed as he watched her move from shelf to shelf. Ignoring him, Sarah inspected a few various parts from the shelves, finding several she snagged to purchase.

"Something in particular I can help you find?" The old man asked. "As you can see, I've got quite the selection."

"I've got a droid I want to repurpose," Sarah said, "though to do what, I'm honestly not sure."

"Well, what you got there in your hand is a power supply," he said, "I think I might got some general purpose personalities over on that shelf, if that's what you're looking for."

Sarah knew which part she held in her hand, and ignored the old man's unintended insult. She also wanted to do a better repair than the temporary fix she had strapped to Eryn's back. Shuffling around another shopper, Sarah checked out the shelf he had pointed out, and found several chips which may fit into Eryn's frame. A butterfly, teal with orange stripes, flitted by to land on her nose. She went crossed eyed trying to look at it, and laughed. It took off, and landed on the old man's mechanical eye. Scowling, he waved a hand to brush it away. Sarah could not help but smile at his annoyance, but she hid it behind a part she picked up to inspect. It just so happened that the part she selected was the perfect fit. Smiling again, she brought her products up to the counter. Realizing her hands were full, Sarah second guessed her decision to shop before going where she needed to.

"I can deliver, if need be," the old man said, seemingly reading her mind, and crooking a finger at a large drone with a storage compartment on it. "No charge with how much you got there."

A short exchange later with no small amount of grumbling about the price, Sarah found herself back in the streets. When she told the man the name of her ship, he had actually laughed. She knew it wasn't the most conventional name, but it was for her to enjoy, not others. Doing her best to drop her frustration, Sarah tried to reorientate herself on the busy street. She had no idea if things closed here, but decided it was a better idea to not find out the hard way. Double checking her map, she found there were several more districts of considerable size between herself and her destination. There was, however, a rail line which traveled through all of the districts she needed. Pulling her cardigan tight, the air here was frigid, she made up her mind to make her way to the rail.

5

Sarah had to climb several ladders, a set of stairs, and take a lift to get to the top level of all the cargo containers. Several busy walkways later, and Sarah was waiting at a rail line platform with a pack of other mismatched individuals. Each of them kept to themselves either by stuffing their heads in some form of personal entertainment or by keeping their eyes fixed on the ground. Sarah, however, used the lull to take in her surroundings proper. From up here, she could see a much larger area of Sonso District. It was even more sprawling than she had anticipated, and from her new vantage the amount of color was almost headache inducing. Turning her attention to the rail line, it was a single cable thicker around than an average human and lined with blinking lights. An electric hum started to kick up, and Sarah looked down the rail to see a long series of tram cars hanging from the cable and speeding toward the platform. They skidded to a stop, and the clear doors slid open to let out masses of people.

One by one the tram cars emptied. The crowd on the platform spread out to give the new arrivals space to pass through. Doing the same, Sarah watched each of the people exiting more out of curiosity than anything else while walking toward an open car.

She wasn't paying attention to all of her surroundings and walked face first into someone. Giving a start, Sarah turned to apologize, but lost her words. With long red hair, a black leather jacket with a gold collar, and form fitting bodysuit beneath, Sarah's mouth worked wordlessly. The woman's eyes caught Sarah off guard. The irises shifted color in the light, first red, then brown, then green. At first, Sarah thought it was a trick of the light, but soon discovered it was the woman's eyes themselves changing color.

"Sorry, love," the woman said. She winked with a smile, and shuffled around a still speechless Sarah. She disappeared into the crowd a moment later, and Sara cursed herself the idiot. Not only was she acting like a child, but she was about to miss the rail line.

The platform was starting to empty and the glass doors were beginning to slide shut. Bolting, Sarah slipped through the gap into a packed tram car at the very last moment. The door sealed shut with a ding, and Sarah reached up to grab a hanging handhold. She tried not to fall into someone as the car launched into motion. Sonso District became a blur, and everything went black as the rail line entered a tunnel. Blackness exploded into light as the car exited the tunnel into the next district. The speed made anything difficult to make out, but this district seemed to be a single level in height with packed pathways that seemed more alley than street. The tram car slowed to a stop, and a male's monotone voice rang out.

"Kro District," it said, "please watch your step as you exit the car."

Getting a better view, Sarah could see Kro District was a slum. People slept in the streets while pedestrians just stepped over or around them. Buildings were drab gray with splotches of brown signifying their wear. However, it didn't stop a good number of people from getting off the tram. Several got on, but none in her car which Sarah was appalled at herself for being so thankful for. She couldn't help but imagine the kind of smells some of those people might have brought with them. Clinging on tighter this time, she waited for the rail line to start back up.

They darted through another tunnel, and Sarah could

feel the elevation rise. She had to brace her back leg to keep upright, and decided to grab onto the handhold with both hands. They tunneled through the darkness for much longer this time around, and Sarah had to check her map to be sure they were going the direction she needed. They were passing over two smaller districts, those connected by a different rail line, which meant the next stop was the one she needed to get off at. Dark gave way to light, and despite how fast they were moving, the view below was clear. It spoke volumes of how large this district was, and the size of the buildings below spoke even louder.

Structures as tall as fifteen stories rose into an artificially generated sky. The effect made Sarah feel like she was flying in a ship rather than being transported via rail car, and she found that she quite enjoyed it. The buildings below were white stone and glittering steel with tall windows of crystalline glass. Bundled together like stalks of wheat, large patches of green space were interspersed between. The rail started to descend, and peering through the window, Sarah could see a tall knife of a building with the platform on it. Bracing as the car slowed to a stop, the platform turned out to be a wide balcony on the side of an ornate building. Through the tram's glass door, Sarah could see a floor made of dark granite tiles ringed by a lavish balustrade. The individuals waiting there wore fine clothing and suites, and their appearances seemed tailored to the minute degree.

"Kyonai District," the tram's voice said, "please watch your step."

The door slid open, and Sarah stepped out of the car. She noticed only a select few did the same before the rail closed up, and moved on. A few of the suits milled about for the next one, but none gave her much attention despite how underdressed she felt. That was, until she noticed the guards by the door. Each wore a thick red cloak over black armor, and each leaned on a long spear of black metal. Wires clung to the spear shafts which gave Sarah the impression the needle-tipped blades were also electrically charged. Neither man wore a helmet, and both had their turn at looking her over. Hugging herself beneath the cardigan, Sarah followed the exiting crowd and tried to blend in. They headed to the back of the balcony and into the building through a set of gold-trimmed double doors. The guards' eyes crossed over each of them as they walked past, but Sarah felt as though they lingered on her. She picked at her scalp the entire elevator ride down to the base floor.

They were emptied out into a lobby of black flooring and gold accents. Sarah was amongst those who hurried out into the street beyond as the place held an unwelcome feel to it, and the guards' eyes lay heavy in her mind. The front of the building had rows of shrubbery lining a broad set of stairs that descended to the street, and several trees were planted at the end of each row. Personal vehicles and driverless transports lined the street, and across the way was a similar building only without the large platform above. Sarah reached the street before she bothered to check her map. The building she needed to be at was several kilometers away yet, and the artificial sun was creeping down toward the artificial horizon. Sarah had no idea if that meant things were about to start closing, but she took it as a sign of her time running short.

"May I be of assistance?" A baritone voice asked. Sarah looked around for the source, but the closest person to her was walking away in the opposite direction. "Right here," the voice said, and the lights of a small car flashed. It was a bulbous vehicle with more windows than anything else, and only had enough room for two seats. There were no passengers, and no wheel which meant the car itself was speaking to her. Sarah opened a display on her wrist to check her credit balance. She had what at one point she thought was plenty, but here on the colony ship after docking fees and replacing her clothes, it was drying up at a rapid pace.

"How much?" She asked. "This place looks a bit steep."

"First time riders get a discount," the car said. "I think you'll find it reasonable."

A message flashed across her wrist, and showed an advertised discount price. Double checking the time, Sarah supposed it was her best option. The car door swung open on its own, and Sarah ducked into the seat. It closed before she even had her seatbelt fastened. At least the seat was comfortable. She told the car her destination, and the vehicle had her coasting through the city in no time at all. White buildings towered over the street, and Sarah was reminded of the impossibly large megastructures from the city she grew up in. Being constrained by the internal workings of a colony ship, these buildings did not even reach a quarter of the size, but it made her think nonetheless. Red wastelands were replaced with green gardens, and none of the vehicles here flew, but Sarah wondered if there might be something similar to Gutter Rats in this city. Given the look, she doubted it. She rubbed a thumb over the tattoo on her wrist.

The car slowed to a stop in front of one of the larger buildings in the area. A massive set of stone stairs rose to an arched doorway made of shimmering glass. Narrow waterfalls cascaded down either side of the stairs, and beside them were several automated ramps for those unable to take the steps. The building itself resembled a colossal hourglass with numerous balconies and insets marring its surface. Car door swinging open, Sarah climbed out and stepped up onto the sidewalk.

"Would you like me to wait?" The car asked. "Your current price will resume for your return trip."

"Sure," Sarah said, "Just don't leave without me."

She hurried up the stairs without waiting for a response. Her cardigan swished and bounced as she took the steps two at a time. By the time she reached the top, her muscles were screaming, and her lungs burned. She had to take a moment to catch her breath before moving on. A few Groal exiting the building gave her the side eye as they started down the steps. She gave them a harsh glare and found her composure. The glass doors parted for her, inviting her into a lobby of white marble floor, and fluted pillars. A large wooden desk, which Sarah guessed was real wood, sat at the front with an android seated behind it as a receptionist. Sarah wondered if all of the inner districts of the Ifrit had similar architecture, or if each one had its own style. If she had the time, she might have to explore a bit to find out.

After a quick exchange with the android, Sarah learned the office she needed was on the eighth floor. Taking an elevator with polished doors proved to be the most efficient way to get the office. The elevator cab was the cleanest Sarah had ever been in, and she hardly felt the motion at all. It chimed a rhythmic tune when it hit the eighth floor, and Sarah followed a series of signs to the appropriate door. The office she entered was simple, almost drab, when compared to the rest of the building. Rows of plain black chairs were lined in front of unadorned walls, and a basic counter separated the waiting area from the employees. A smattering of bored people sat amongst the black chairs while a pair of exhausted employees sat on stools behind the counter. In the far back of the office, Sarah noticed a door which led out to a balcony. She could see a blooming cherry blossom tree through the door's window and made a mental note to go check it out. She'd never seen one before.

One of the employees glanced up at Sarah and gave her a tired smile. They were an androgynous individual with blue eyeshadow, and a strong jaw. Sarah wondered if it was natural, or done with contour. Their outfit was a basic uniform of a pale blue jacket, black slacks, and black cap covering the top of their head. They tapped the countertop with a black fingernail indicating for Sarah to step forward.

"How can I help you today?" They asked. The nametag pinned to their chest labeled the individual as Hess. Sarah was hesitant at first, unsure of how to broach the subject. If Jax were around, she'd simply walk into the conversation guns blazing, and have an answer before either of them knew what had happened. She wasn't here, and Sarah wasn't Jax. She glanced at her wrist to read the thorough instructions Kyllen had left for her.

"Ziven had some investment opportunities he was wishing to discuss," Sarah said, "I have an appointment soon."

The clerk's ears perked up at the mention of Ziven's name, and Hess glanced at the terminal to their left. Typing in a note, Hess then nodded to a row chairs. They were empty save for a tall man in a dark cloak hunched over a data-slate.

"Take a seat. Someone will come grab you shortly."

Hess smiled at Sarah, the dismissal clear, so she stepped away from the counter and found a seat at the opposite end of the tall man. Several long moments stretched by as she waited, and she did her best to preoccupy herself. Not once did the cloaked man look up from his screen, and Sarah wished she had her own to keep her distracted. At last, a deep voice called out her name. When she saw the source, however, her heart stopped. Leaning against a door frame on the far side of the waiting room was a hulking figure clad in the red armor of the breakers. The man wore no helmet, instead allowing his dark hair and beard to flow free about his shoulders. She'd been found out. The breakers had discovered who Sarah was, and this entire plan was a clever plot to bring her back into custody. Her neck grew hot, and Sarah had to force her hands into her lap to prevent herself from picking at her scalp. She made eye contact with the man, his intense gaze locking hers into place. He nodded to her, deciding the eye contact was confirmation enough.

"Ziven is ready for you," he said.

6

A cavernous sigh escaped Sarah as she realized the truth of the situation. The armor was red, but it lacked the quills, the helmet, and many other defining features which marked the breakers with their identity. This man was nothing more than a bodyguard, a "pretend" breaker perhaps, here to collect her for his master. Sarah tried to relax as she stood and followed him into the adjoining hallway. Their shoes echoed against the stone-tiled floor of the sumptuous hallway which felt like an audacious protest to the simple design of the waiting room. Oil paintings hung between each office door with a variety of potted flora lined up beneath. A lot of credits passed through this office, and the hallway alone made that fact clear.

The two of them rounded a corner, the mass of red armor stopping abruptly, and the man gestured toward one of the doors. Sarah gave him a sparing look but ducked through the door. To her relief, the man waited in the hallway, door closing behind her. She found herself in an antechamber lit by a single yellow light embedded in the pale ceiling. Tapestries of storybook heroes hung from the wall, each of their stolid faces judging her every move. The door opposite, painted black, loomed over her like a monolith with ill omens. Sarah wasn't sure if she was supposed to enter or wait, and she contented herself with examining the art. The tapestry before her depicted a strange scene with numerous figures wearing white masks confronting some sort of decrepit troll. The skin of the monster's face was pulled tight across its skull making wet eyes bulge and yellow teeth gleam in an awful smile.

"Interesting piece, no?" A voice asked through the room's comms. "It's some kind of fable about the afterlife. We can discuss it after our business is concluded."

In truth, the masked figures reminded Sarah of the morak'casai. They wore no robes, however, instead adorning little more than scraps and rags. The image made her uncomfortable, so she moved on to examine a different tapestry. The next was something far more pleasant, and it was a story she recognized. A human male and female Groal stood back-to-back with a heart painted between them. The human, thin with shaggy hair, wielded a paint brush before him like a sword while the Groal, muscular with fiery red hair, brandished an actual blade. The sword was almost as large as the man pressed against her back.

"Am I to wait here while we speak?" Sarah asked, "or may I step through that mysterious door of yours?"

"Wait there," the voice said. "You're Sarah Renza, yes?"

"Correct," Sarah said, "and you're Ziven?"

"I am," Ziven said. "I see our mutual contact is absent. Should I be expecting trouble?"

The mention of Jax reopened a fresh wound, but Sarah swallowed her pain to press on. Her brother was all she had left. Hector gave her purpose. Despite his shortcomings, Sarah could thank him for that. He was the lit lantern on a storm-wrought coast. Her nerve-damaged fingers twitched, and Sarah grabbed them with her other hand to keep them still.

"That's all she was," Sarah said, "a mutual contact. Her purpose was to set up our meeting and leave the rest to me."

"Very well," Ziven said, "you want a place on my ship, and Kyllen tells me you've delivered on your side of our little bargain. I've read through your manifold, and I'm both impressed and disappointed. Impressed, because the equipment here is incredibly difficult for civilians to get their hands on, and disappointed because I was hoping there would be more."

"That's all I was able to pull out of there," Sarah said. "It should be more than enough for what you asked. If I sold all of it independently, I'd almost have enough to buy my own ship."

"Not like the one I've got," Ziven said, "and you'd probably run into more trouble than profit with type of gear you've brought. It would be the wrong kind of attention if you catch my meaning."

"I do," Sarah said. Nerves tickled the depths of her gut, and Sarah worried this conversation was going in the wrong direction. Ziven held all the cards here, and he knew it.

"Fret not, Sarah," Ziven said, "your place is secured. Just understand these weapons might make the difference between life or death on this little venture."

"You wanted the gear for this mission?"

"Correct," Ziven said. "I have no way of knowing if my brother's ship is simply broken down, or if it was raided, stolen, or pillaged by pirates, mercenaries, or worse. Better to be prepared."

"So, I'm in?" Sarah asked.

"You're in," Ziven said, "but before you get too excited, we need to discuss your roll on my ship. The captain I've hired tolerates no waste, and no extra weight. You'll need to make sure you pull your fare share even if that's just janitorial services. I've dug into your record, Sarah Renza, and it seems you're little more than a stowaway."

"I can fix things," Sarah said. "Learned a lot about doing that while catching rides."

There was a long pause while Ziven considered. For a moment Sarah wondered if she'd revealed too much. The concept of having a new identity was still foreign to her, and playing with the boundaries of what she should and shouldn't talk about was something she had yet to explore. Her mind was put to ease when Ziven snorted.

"Fine," he said. "You can work under Thusi. She's the chief engineer for this mission. A bit touchy about her work, so try and stay on her good side."

"I'll do what I can," Sarah said.

"One more thing," Ziven said, "I cashed in a lot of favors and an entire fortune's worth of credits to get everything together for this. I don't want any problems from you, understand?"

"We both had family aboard that ship," Sarah said. "I'm going to do whatever I need to do to find them."

She stood tall, facing the door as if it were Ziven himself. Another long pause extended between them, but this time Sarah refrained from second guessing herself. To her shock, the door slid open. Taking the hint, Sarah stepped through into a wide office with a view overlooking the city. The décor was as ostentatious as the antechamber with Ziven seated behind a massive wooden desk. His wide antlers coincided with his wide frame, and the beginnings of a beard marked his jawline. He considered Sarah for a long while. Neither of them spoke as he studied her with golden eyes.

"I hired one of the finest mercenaries this side of the galaxy," Ziven said at last. "Immortal, some call him while others label him an abomination."

"I take it I'm supposed to stay out of his way too?" Sarah asked. She tried to keep the bite out of her voice but failed.

"No," Ziven said, "quite the opposite. I misjudged you. You'll be the only one on the ship not there for credits. I think I have a different task for you, one that will benefit us both. Mercenaries are mercenaries, and I can only trust them as far as my pocketbook goes. You'll still work for Thusi, but I need someone there to make sure the crew stays on task. Any warnings to the contrary, and I should be informed immediately."

"You want me to fight a so-called immortal merc?" Sarah asked. "You did just compare me to little more than a stowaway."

"I want you to watch," Ziven said. "Nothing more. My pockets are deep, but in the off chance something does change their mind I want to know."

"Then what?" Sarah asked.

"Then you'll receive further instructions, but not a moment sooner," Ziven said. "If you want to find your family as bad as I want mine, you'll do this."

It was Sarah's turn to consider. In truth, Ziven was right.

She needed to do this as badly as he needed her to. She was growing tired of people using her to their advantage, however, and her
anger was bubbling to the surface. Taking a deep breath, Sarah
strode over to the windows and peered down. She fidgeted with
her cardigan as she watched the bustling streets far below. She
hoped her car had waited like it said it would. This was taking longer than expected.

"I'll do it," she said, "but if they turn on you, don't expect
me to be of any use."

"It's settled then," Ziven said. His tone changed in a flash.
"Ship leaves in the morning, but there's a get-together later tonight
for the crew to get to know each other. Be there."

Sarah was already on her way out the door by the time the
last words escaped his lips. She wanted this business done with,
but she also knew this was only the beginning to a potential exten-
sive list of troubles.

"I'll send you the details," Ziven called after her.

CHAPTER 10
- JAX -

1

Jax was saved. Modiri's navigation was a lost cause making it impossible to know what part of space she had ended up in, but to her luck, it must have been a populated enough area. A ship lurked out there, and had picked up Jax's distress signal. She thought she could see some of the blinking hull lights off in the distance, and on occasion a star would go black indicating something had blocked the view. All she needed to do was wait. As a precautionary measure, Jax purged all of Modiri's automated systems and databanks in hopes of deleting any remaining remnants of Gayle. If she was lucky, the AI had only integrated with the parts of the ship that were no longer there, but Jax wasn't going to leave something like that to chance. She leaned back in the pilot's seat with her feet propped up on the control console. Nothing to do, but to relax and wait.

About an hour crawled by before Jax saw any more signs of the other ship. A spark of thrusters illuminated in the darkness of the void, and soon Jax could see the silhouette of a small vessel approaching. There was her ticket out of here, and she wanted to be sure to welcome it with open arms. She rubbed at the small incision behind her ear. Soon she'd find someone to fix whatever Gayle had done. Putting her helmet back on, she sent out a broad communications request that covered multiple frequencies. The response was almost immediate.

"Lookit what we have here," a guttural voice said. Modiri's

communications were limited to voice only due to the amount of damage. Jax's imagination ran wild with what kind of person the voice could belong to. There was a feminine edge to it, but there was no doubt the individual in question was ugly. Ugly or not, they were about to pull Jax's ass from the fire, so she put on her best face.

"You got here just in time," Jax said, "I couldn't have made a timelier rescue if the whole thing was coordinated."

"No need to thank us just yet," the voice said, "let's get you to safety first."

The communication line cut, and the ship's thrusters grew from a spark in the void to a blazing light. Soon, the black shape of a larger craft than Jax assumed was slowing to a halt above Modiri's remains. She depressurized the cockpit, and made her way to Modiri's exterior. Using mag boots and a tether, Jax climbed on top of Modiri's outer hull with an emergency light blinking on her suit. She switched her helmet torch on, and shined it over the hull of the other ship. It was a junker. Patched panels and weld lines covered it like scars, and what little paint was left was faded to a drab gray. An outer hatch lit up with an array of lights. It popped open to reveal a figure in a bulking enviro-suit carrying a large reel of rope attached to a harpoon gun. The figure waved for Jax to move aside, and once she did, fired the harpoon into Modiri's hull. The harpoon bit into the metal, and formed a secure latch. The rope pulled taut, and the figure gave Jax a thumbs up. Understanding, Jax undid her own tether, turned off the magnetism of her boots, and pulled herself up the rope toward the other ship's hatch.

The bulking figure reached out a hand, and pulled Jax into the airlock. They cut the rope, and closed the airlock hatch behind Jax. The two of them stared at each other through their suits in silence while the chamber repressurized. Once done, the figure pulled off their helmet, so Jax did the same. Jax's theory was correct. The woman looked wretched, and smelled worse. She was balding with numerous warts covering a large section of her face, and a haggle tooth stuck out the left side of her mouth. Jax smiled all the same, simply thankful to have been rescued. Not everyone could be the glamorous knight in shining armor like Sarah had been. The woman smiled back to show the haggle tooth was her only tooth. She shoved a hand toward Jax, and nodded.

"Welcome aboard the Sheet Skimmer," she said, "the name is Rooth."

2

Jax latched on to Rooth's thick-gloved hand, and shook it with as much enthusiasm as she could work up. Her energy was always enough to charm Sarah into bed, so perhaps it would be enough to get the help she needed from Rooth. If not, she could always fall back on bribery. She was sure her account still had an ample supply of credits. She'd need those later down the road, however, and would only use them as a last resort. They let go of each other's hands, and Rooth started to put her helmet back on. Jax gave her a perplexed look, and wondered if she should do the same. The woman shrugged off Jax's confusion, and pointed at the helmet with one hand while setting the clasps with the other.

"Hate carrying the thing around," she said, "think I'll just put it on until we get to the locker room."

Rooth clasped the last clasp on her helmet, and gave a thumbs up. Jax was even more confused. It wasn't directed at her, but toward the corner of the airlock. Turning to look, Jax saw no one else there. Was there a camera she hadn't seen? Hissing sounded from the airlock's vents, and Jax's heart leapt into her throat. Gayle dropping a canister flashed through her thoughts. She tried to put her helmet on as fast she could, but froze. Rooth was staring at her like she was insane, hand half raised to open the inner hatch. The hissing stopped, and artificial gravity kicked in. Rooth chuckled as she realized what had thrown Jax into a panic.

"Poor girl," she said, and took her own helmet off again. "See? No fear. Keep telling Rector we need to fix this place up a bit, noisy as it is, but credits are hard to come by out here."

Jax lowered her helmet. She took a moment to catch her breath, and let her heart rate slow to a normal pace. She ran a hand through her mess of brown hair, fingers getting caught more than once. She desperately needed a shower. Maybe she'd pull a Sarah, and shave it all off. Jax was starting to see the appeal of it. Her stomach growled loud enough for both to hear, and Rooth chuckled again.

"Come now," she said, "let's get out of these suits, and get some food in that belly."

"Where are we?" Jax asked. The question hung in the chamber for a few long moments, "you said out here. Where is that exactly? I had a botched jump, and have no idea where I was spit out. Are we in the Neutral Zone at least?"

"Neutral Zone?" Rooth asked. "Honey, that's on the other side of the galaxy."

3

Jax watched the young boy sit at the cramped metal table, and chomp down on a bowl of oatmeal. She sat on the other side of the little cubby with her knees curled up, and left her own food untouched. The boy's lip smacking echoed around the small room which may have been a workstation at one point, but had been converted into a makeshift dining room. Cables and pipes hung from every centimeter of the ceiling and bulkheads, and clutter left no surface bare. The table Jax and the boy, curly black hair bobbing into his bowl for another mouthful, sat at was tucked away in a cubby at one end. The other connected two passageways leading to different parts of the ship. Both of those were narrow, short, and equally covered with tubes, pipes and wires. It was as though all of the interior panels had been removed to reveal all of the ship's inner workings. Jax had spent all of two days aboard the Sheet Skimmer, and already wanted to be off the rusted hunk of junk.

A hunched over Rooth waddled down one of the corridors, and peeked in on the two of them. Her haggled tooth glistened with spit. Shaking her head, Rooth approached the table to look in both of their bowls. Smiling and patting the boy's head, she turned to Jax with a disappointed frown.

"We don't have a lot of that," she said, "you could at least eat that much. You look half-starved as it is."

Jax didn't feel much like eating. After finding out where in the galaxy Modiri had jumped her to, her spirits had shriveled up and died. Modiri was so far beyond repair it was almost laughable, and Jax learned that Sheet Skimmer was only capable of short-ranged jumps. To find her way back to the Neutral Zone could be a matter of years at this rate, and that only applied if she was able to find decent and willing passage back. Few humans inhabited this part of the galaxy, and from what Jax understood, the only sentient species to live on this side were less than hospitable toward her kind. She'd have to do more research to find her exact location, but if her fears were true, Jax may be deep in Suttack space. She knew little about the Suttack, but what she did know was they were isolationists who destroyed anyone daring enough to cross into their territory.

"There aren't many outposts out here," Rooth said, "you need to get used to staying with us which means you need to get used to the food. Once Rector is finished scavenging what he can from your ship, we'll be on our way to find somewhere safe for you."

Rooth nudged the bowl of oatmeal closer. Jax could feel the warmth of it, and a sweet smell wafted to her nose. Her own stomach betrayed her with a loud grumble which sent Rooth into a fit of chuckles. Caving, Jax uncurled and picked up her spoon. She took a few bites, and was stunned by how delicious it was. Once she started, she couldn't stop. Spoonful after spoonful Jax downed the oatmeal until her spoon scraped the bottom of the bowl. Rooth set a glass of water in front of Jax, and she drank it all in one long swig.

"Wow lady," the little boy said, "you really were hungry."

He held out his own bowl, which was still half full, and offered Jax the rest. Taking it without a word, she dug into that as well. Only once she'd finished did Jax bother to mutter out a thank you. The boy smiled at her, and Rooth patted his back.

"Always such a nice boy, Percy," Rooth said, "found him too, you know. Shipwreck just like yours, but a bit messier if you ask me. Research ship got a little too close to the border, and made a little too much noise. Percy was a baby then. Found him locked in the only cabin that had air left. Maybe you two can get along."

Percy smiled again; this time wide enough to reveal several missing teeth. Jax wasn't sure if it was due to natural aging, or if the boy had poor hygiene. Cleanliness was in short supply on the Sheet Skimmer. Rector was just as appalling to look at as his wife, but equally polite to deal with. In the grand scheme of things, ugly and kind was far better than pretty and cruel. Either way, Jax could admit she had been fortunate for this family to find her when they did. Survival would have been a slim chance had they not, and the deep void of space offered little in the way of second chances. Nodding to give Rooth some sort of answer, Jax gave the empty bowl a sad look before setting it aside.

"They'll be more for you once you get back," Rooth said, "I'll make sure it's nice and warm."

"When I get back?" Jax asked. Suspicion tinged the edges of her question, and a growing worry welled up in her chest. "Where am I going?"

"Nowhere far, dear," Rooth said, and rubbed the soft spot of Jax's back between her two shoulder blades. "Rector has asked for help with your ship. Says he needs some help figuring a few of the bits and bobbles out."

4

Jax was back in her suit and standing in the airlock before she had a chance to argue. There were no countdowns nor automated voices telling her when the chamber was depressurized, only Rooth's voice chiming through her headset with a best guess as to when she thought the exterior door would open. Patience was never a strong suit for Jax, and waiting with the old woman's droning voice in her ear was pushing it to the limits. At last, Rooth's voice hit one and the outer door hissed open. A large spotlight illuminated the remains of Modiri, and a waving Rector standing atop it. The situation was worse than she realized. Only the cockpit and small chunk of the cargo-hold remained of her once-favored ship. She stood frozen, Rector still waving, while the reality of it sank in. Modiri had been her entire world. It was all she had after escaping that hellish circus of a childhood, and it was all she had until Sarah showed up. Now, she had neither Sarah nor Modiri. On the other hand, not a soul from her old life would find her thousands of light-years away from any human territories. Gayle would never find her either. A liberating sense of peace lingered somewhere in the thought. Maybe, just maybe, going back was not in her best interest. It was a chance to start anew, something few ever got.

"What's wrong, dear?" Rooth asked. "Is the safety cable too far away? Rector does have such long arms. I'll see if he can move it for you."

"No, no," Jax said, "Everything is fine. Just taking it all in, I guess."

There was a long pause, and Rector had stopped waving to busy himself with inspecting a piece of metal. "Losing everything can be hard," Rooth said, "I know. The outer stretches of the galaxy are Roothless at best, but it's up to us to do the best we can. We found our peace in Morathnu. I won't push my religious ideologies, but perhaps you can find peace too."

"Maybe," Jax said. She wasn't going to outright dismiss the old woman, but she had never held an interest in the religious sort. This was a fresh start, however, and maybe her viewpoints were something else capable of changing. She turned her head back to the inner door, gave a curt nod, attached her suit to the safety line, and pushed out into space.

Rector approached the line in his hulking suit to wait for her, and slow her approach. His suit reminded her of the ones her and Sarah were forced to use on Carlisle Station, and that *thing* the morak'casai had become. Kade. That was his name. He had been waiting for them on the outside of the station like he knew they were going to be there. Sarah had used the last of her ammunition to deal with him, and still almost died for it. Jax had used every ounce of strength in her body to drag Sarah to safety. The events that followed churned her belly and sent a shiver down her spine. Both of them should have died on that station. The horrid image of the mutated doctor's face was a grim reminder of the fact. Jax was slowed to a stop, and she almost leapt out of her skin.

"Woah, now. Be still." Rector said. "You look as though you've seen a ghost."

Jax hadn't realized she was panting, and tried to calm herself. Rector's suit lit his face within the visor, and she could see a genuine look of concern playing across his aged features. Liver spots and skin tags nestled hand in hand within layers of wrinkles, and gray hair stubbled his jaw which was tightened into a frown. He held her still until she calmed, and he tutted over something on the side of her helmet. Breathing back to normal, Jax gave him a forced smile in a poor attempt to brush it off.

"No, no," he said, "don't fret. Only natural after surviving whatever did this to your ship. Sometimes you just have to let yourself feel your feelings, good or bad. Only real way to let your body purge the bad, and make room for more good. Like a fever burning off a virus. One day you'll have to tell us the truth of what happened, but for now just take solace in being alive. Come now, I've got some questions about your ship."

He gave her shoulder a reassuring pat, and pointed toward the cockpit. He began to trudge across the hull, his magnetized boots thudding and sticking with each step. Jax activated her own boots, and followed him. They walked around to the underside of the cockpit where Rector had a large panel ripped open to reveal a wide section of exposed electronics. The spotlight of the Sheet Skimmer did not reach the underside, so the two of them were forced to use their helmet lamps. Jax realized she was looking at a section of Modiri's navigation systems. Without hesitation, Rector stooped over and pulled a chip from inside a small box. He held it up before his helmet lamp to give both of them a better view, but Jax still had to squint to make it out.

"I've never seen a chip quite like this," he said, "not in a navigation system at least. Any idea of what it could be? Might be something useful if we plugged it into the Sheet Skimmer. Think it'll help us navigate better?"

Jax continued to inspect the chip, and had a sudden worry. What if a remnant of Gayle lingered somewhere within its confines. Afterall, an AI as advanced as Gayle would know how to hide itself on anything that had the ability to store data. True or not, a murderous AI lurking in the shadows of her thoughts was the last thing Jax needed. These people had shown her kindness, and ruin was the last thing she wanted to repay them with.

"We don't need it," Jax said, "better to toss it."

"You sure?" Rector asked, "I think it could be of use. Maybe we just plug it in, and see what it does."

Jax started to panic. The old man was growing more assured of his decision with each word, and she needed to convince him otherwise. An idea sprang to mind. What Gayle had done to her was an abomination, but Rector was leaving her with no other options. She wasn't going to fight the man for it. Jax focused her attention on Rector, and started to shape her own thoughts. If she remembered correctly, Jax needed to impose her own thoughts until her reality became the dominant one. She imagined her thoughts running alongside his until the two became one. Her mind blanked, and hot nettles pricked her scalp and the sides of her neck. Heat and sweat formed under her suit, but she focused on the image the two of them had of the chip. It wasn't a chip, not really, but a small piece of debris which had collided with her ship upon the Modiri exiting its jump. It was just a worthless piece of metal to be tossed to the side and ignored. Jax's scalp burned beneath her layers of hair, and she wanted nothing more than to shave her head like Sarah and run her nails across the soft skin. However, she stayed focused on the chip, no, the metal sliver.

"That's odd," Rector said, "now that I see it better in the light, I seem to have been mistaken. Looks like it's just a piece of debris. Sorry for the mistake. Oh well, there are some pipes over here, and I wondered if you'd mind me ripping them out for the Sheet Skimmer."

Rector tossed the piece of metal into the void and moved on. Heaving a sigh of relief, Jax let go of her hold over his mind and the heated itching subsided. Dizziness flooded her vision, and she reached out to hold onto something, but nothing was there. She wanted to rub her eyes to clear her swirling peripherals, but that too was impossible. Voices echoed in her helmet, but she could not tell to whom they belonged. A figure in a bulking suit of beige and white hurried toward her. Who was that?

"Sarah?" She asked, and darkness took her.

5

When Jax awoke, a concerned Rooth fretted over the edges of a glistening thermal blanket tucked in on either of Jax's sides. She was in a small cubby which had been converted into a makeshift bed. Jax recognized it now as the place she had been allowed to sleep for the last couple days. Rooth gave a start upon realizing Jax was awake, and awarded her with a snaggle-toothed smile. Patting Jax's cheek, Rooth turned to a bedside tray, and grabbed a bowl of her famous oatmeal. The smell of it reached Jax's nose causing her stomach to groan in response. She sat up the best she could within the narrow cubby, and let Rooth push the bowl into her hands. Her head was clear, at least, and she found the aroma helped bring her focus back to the natural world. Sticking a spoon full in her mouth, Jax savored the sweet flavor before bothering to speak.

Swallowing, she asked, "have I been out long?"

"Only a few hours," Rooth said, "gave poor Rector quite the scare. Took both of us to get you back in here."

"I guess I owe you one," Jax said, "again."

"Don't worry yourself over it," Rooth said, "I'm just happy we managed to get you back in safely. There's a doctor at the closest outpost where we're heading next. He's a family friend of ours, and I think we should pay him a visit to be on the safe side. Would you be willing to let him check you over? This might sound rather selfish, but I'd prefer we also find out if you have something that may affect the rest of us."

Rooth gave Jax's hand a pat for reassurance, and Jax responded with a nod. She didn't like the idea of another strange doctor poking around in her business, especially with what lay embedded in the side of her brain, but she doubted this family doctor would even bother to check that thoroughly. Taking another spoonful of oatmeal, she kept her worries to herself. Rooth let her finish eating before speaking again, and her next question pertained to a topic far worse than the doctor.

"Me and the boys have prayer in a few minutes," Rooth said, and patted Jax's hand again. "I don't mean to push, but you're more than welcome to join us if you're interested. Morathism isn't like human religions I've been exposed to. I wasn't much for the idea myself until I fell into the Dwemyri culture. Perhaps you'll feel the same. If interested, the Sheet Skimmer is a small ship. You'll find us easily enough."

Giving Jax's hand one last pat, Rooth stood to brush herself off. Stray hairs from her disheveled head brushed against the pipework of the ceiling, and blocked the room's single light to cast a long shadow across Jax. Taking the bowl, she turned to go, but Jax clutched the hem of Rooth's threadbare shirt. The two stood like that in silence for several moments before Jax worked up the resolve to speak.

"Thank you," she said, "and I'll give it some thought. Really, I will. If I'm going to be here for what appears to be the long haul, I can at least know the customs of those I'm staying with."

Rooth smiled and nodded with a satisfied expression. She told Jax where they'd be, and took her leave. Jax was surprised to find she meant what she said. She had never had a past relationship with religion, and never had a reason to love or hate the idea. It was never a thing that crossed her mind. When she was a child, she had heard about entire sectors of her Vulture colony being dedicated to different religions, and some sectors who banned it outright, but all Jax ever saw was an ambiguous point of contention amongst those who cared to pay attention to it. By what Rooth said, this was a Dwemyri religion. Jax knew a little about the species, but never had she cared to learn about this aspect of their culture. She could learn more about a culture she had grown rather fond of, and gain the trust of these people who, for the time, were her only means of survival. Besides, who was to say the whole religion thing was or was not for her. Jax could find out that she enjoyed it. Perhaps it could bring peace to this new part of her life.

Pulling the thermal blanket aside, Jax crawled out of the cubby-turned-bed. She tugged the collar of her shirt open, tilted her head down, and sniffed. Wincing, Jax realized she hadn't bathed since boarding the Sheet Skimmer, nor did she have a change of clothes. She also lacked hygiene products, and all her personal belongings which presumably were blasted out of the back of Modiri along with all her cargo. It was something else she'd have to ask Rooth for, though given their appearances hygiene products may be a long shot. Wiggling her toes on the cold metal floor, shoes were another thing on her list. Taking a deep breath, she made up her mind. She would scope out what these prayers entailed, out of respect more than anything else, and once done, ask Rooth to help cover her needs.

6

Rooth was right. Finding the three of them was easy enough. Though cramped, and the corridors made the ship feel like a maze, Sheet Skimmer was small enough that if one wandered around for a few minutes, they'd be able to find whatever it was they were looking for, or find themselves back where they started. Jax found the trio huddled in a diminutive cabin hardly larger than a closet. Here, the open framework of the ship's interior had been covered by large tapestries dyed a deep blue. Speckles of white paint had been spattered across each in what Jax assumed was an attempt to mimic stars. Rooth, Rector, and Percy all kneeled before a small altar at the center of the room. Made of an unknown white stone, the altar resembled a Dwemyri with several heads, and an uncountable number of arms outstretched above it while it sat cross-legged on a pillow. The sight of the three of them crouched together, and whispering quiet somethings to the altar put Jax into a deep sense of unease. Movement caught the corner of her eye, and Jax noticed a cockroach scuttling across the upper frame of the door followed by a second. For a reason she couldn't explain, Jax felt as though the insects were watching her. She shivered at the thought, and at last Rooth noticed her presence.

"Ah," she said, "you came after all."

Rooth let out a low groan as she pushed herself from her knees to greet Jax. Brushing off her worn trousers, she took one of Jax's hands in both of hers and made room for Jax to sit next to them by the altar. Jax hesitated at first, but upon Rooth's insistence she allowed herself to be seated before the statue of white stone. One of the cockroaches scurried off at the sudden movement, but the other remained with beady eyes trained on Jax. She kept glancing from the insect to the altar. Its many white hands pointed upward, but its Dwemyri heads looked down upon her.

"The Dwemyri depiction of Morathnu can be intimidating to humans," Rooth said, "but I assure you Morathnu is a god of love and peace."

"Almost gave me a heart attack the first time I saw the thing," Rector said, and Percy giggled. "Thought my wife had damned near lost her mind."

"How did you come by all of this?" Jax asked. "My impression was that the Dwemyri were reserved about their beliefs with outsiders."

"They are," Rooth said, "but we've been out here on this side of the galaxy for so long that few who know us even consider us as humans at this point."

"The ones that can't ignore that fact mostly want us dead," Rector said, "humans aren't a welcome sight around here."

"Dwemyri are hardly better off," Rooth said, "and we found that unwelcome guests tend to band together in such spaces. We ended up here in a similar fashion to you, my dear, by accident. We were fortunate enough to run into a band of Dwemyri smugglers who also weren't supposed to be here. We stayed with them long enough they eventually taught us their ways. We haven't looked back since. You see, while the Dwemyri species may be fractured into many pockets of subspecies, they all still tend to believe in the teachings of Morathnu even if that takes forms in diverse ways. Most practice in peace if you discount the Skren, but every faith has its zealot."

"Of course," Jax said. She remembered the Skren. They were the largest in size of all the Dwemyri as their warlike tendencies caused them to breed for brute strength over everything else. All the Dwemyri clans used selective breeding to shape the best course for the future of their kin, but Skren were the only ones that did so out of the necessity to replenish their ranks.

"So, you just ask the statue for wishes?" Jax asked, "isn't that how religions work?"

Rector chortled, Percy glanced at Jax abashed, but Rooth

only smiled. "No, my dear," she said, "hopes, perhaps, but only from time to time. Most our prayers come in the form of simple thanks, and the requests of small blessings throughout our travels."

"And this god of yours answers?" Jax asked.

"Often," Rooth says, "and in different ways. Not all of which are clear at first."

"What kind of blessings do you ask for?" Jax asked.

"Peace," Rooth said, "and for the abundance of food and water. Despite our talk, we are still human after all, and all of us have needs."

"Right," Jax said, and decided it was time to cut to the point. She had been polite enough, and the glaring statue was beginning to make her uncomfortable. At least the cockroach had decided to crawl away somewhere unseen. "Speaking of needs, I might have a few of those you could help me with."

"Of course, dear," Rooth said. She gave the two boys a look. Rector coughed into his fist, and nudged the boy. The two of them stood, brushed themselves off, and headed down the corridor. "What is it that I can help you with?"

"Hygiene products mostly," Jax said, "I smell horrible. A change of clothes would also do me wonders."

"I can help you gather everything you need at our next stop," Rooth said. "By hygiene products, forgive me if this is too forward, but have you chosen to continue your cycle?"

"My wha-" then the implication hit her, and Jax spluttered. It had been so long she had forgotten. Early in their adolescence girls of an age could choose between what doctors called a natural development, or forgo the reproductive cycle until decided otherwise. Jax chose the latter, thinking any woman who wanted to go through that while not trying to have children was mad. The idea of Jax having children was another thing which made her shudder. No, Jax had put off her reproductive cycle for good. "I have no need, but thank you for your concern."

"Just wanted to be sure," Rooth said, "never know with a woman of your age."

"Men are," Jax searched for a way to be tactful with her next words, "not for me."

"I understand," Rooth said, and gave Jax's hand another signature pat. "Come now, let's go to the bridge. Rector will get us on our way to the outpost."

CHAPTER 11
- SARAH -

1

By the time Sarah returned to her ship, the cargo was being emptied out by Ziven's dock workers. The boy, Kyllen, directed a small crew operating lifts and carts which darted in an out of the lowered cargo ramp. Eryn sped up and down the catwalks, eager to catalog each nook and cranny. Hopefully the parts she had delivered were left in the gangway like she had asked. That drone would be difficult to get back into the ship, and reprogramming it was becoming a larger and larger priority. The usual crowds separated enough to give the dock workers room to move their equipment, and Sarah used the freed-up space to hurry to her ship. Kyllen waved to her as the last grav-lift ferried away the final group of crates. She watched it go, ignoring the teenager's attempt at a charismatic smile.

"That's it then," she asked. "The cargo goes to Ziven, and I get my spot aboard the ship?"

"That's it," Kyllen said. "Gonna be at the bar tonight?"

The look Sarah gave him must have spoken volumes as he went from leaning casually against the catwalk railing with the beginnings of a smile to standing upright, fixing his loose bun and oversized jacket, and his cheeks burning to a bright red.

"I mean," he stuttered, "not like that. I meant, like, for the whole meet the crew thing."

"Ziven made it sound like he'd hired only elite mercenaries for this," Sarah said. She hadn't intended the words to be a jab at the kid, but his eyes snapped up from staring at his shoes and she realized the perceived insult.

"I'm good with tech," he said. "You name it, gadgets, gear, and guns, I can fix it, build it, or make it better."

Sarah narrowed her eyes at him, an idea starting to form. He started to add more to his self-appraisal, but Sarah ignored him. Instead, she scanned the crowd for Eryn. If Kyllen was as good as he claimed, perhaps he could modify the drone for her. She pointed to it, and he closed his mouth to look at what she was indicating.

"Can you change the function of that drone?" Sarah asked.

"Is that a mapping drone?" Kyllen asked. The confusion was plain on his face as to what a cartography drone was doing in a quarantine hangar.

"It is," Sarah said, "but can you make it be something else?"

"Like what?"

"I don't know, something different."

"Like a pet?" Kyllen asked. He was scratching his chin, a small degree of stubble beginning to sprout as if he were trying to grow a beard but failing.

"Sure, like a pet," Sarah said. "I've already got replacement parts if that helps."

"Those drones aren't built to last very long," Kyllen said, "but I guess if you get me the parts I can see what I can do."

"It's settled then. I'll grab you the parts," Sarah said. She started to head for the still open cargo ramp of her ship, but Kyllen called out after her.

"You never answered my question," he said. She paused long enough to see his attempted charismatic demeanor return. He tucked his hands into his coat pockets and leaned on one leg. "Are you going to be there?"

"Are you even old enough to drink?" Sarah asked. This time around her question didn't faze him. He took it in stride with a shrug and a smile before answering.

"Never stopped me before," he said. "Besides, you're on

the Ifrit now, Sarah Renza. I don't think they've scanned an ID-chip in a hundred cycles."

Sarah gave him the courtesy of a laugh, but left him there on the catwalk as she entered her ship. Being sure to close everything up behind her, Sarah found the space to feel cavernous without all of the crates filling the hold. It was large enough for a small family to live in, and Sarah was beginning to understand why a lot of spacers did just that. Docking fees could add up if too few supplies were on hand, but she figured there were probably ways around that if the need arose. She opened the airlock door attached to the gangway, and was pleased to find her earlier purchases waiting for her. She'd hand them off to Kyllen, let him chase down the little drone, and give herself time to mentally prepare for whatever awaited her this evening.

2

It was late when Ziven's information arrived. Late enough, in fact, that she had already decided to take two pills of her munmos and get ready for bed. She was undressed and sliding into bed when the notification chimed on her wrist display. Their meetup location was some club called the Flux, and Sarah was supposed to be there within the hour. Scrambling out of bed, she started to pull on her outfit from before when a thought occurred to her. Reaching over to her nightstand, Sarah grabbed the bottle of munmus and started to read its label. She had already taken two of the pills, and she wondered what they would do to her if she decided to stay awake. Afterall, they were made to help her sleep nightmare free. *Nothing* is what she told herself, and Sarah tossed them back in the drawer. She dragged on her trousers, stomped into her boots, and pulled on a hooded black cardigan not bothering with anything underneath. Her only sports bra stank and needed to be replaced, and she had no intention of staying longer than she needed. Sarah was going to step in, say hello, get whatever info she needed, say goodbye, and then make her exit. Besides, the Ifrit seemed free enough.

She climbed down the ladder into the cockpit proper,

double checked she had everything she needed, but had to pause for a minute to catch her breath. She must have stood up too fast as she felt winded and faintly dizzy. The lights of her ship had a twinge of yellow hue to them this evening, and she made a note to check if they needed replaced in the morning. Sarah gathered herself, and put on her hood. Locking up, she exited Bill and left the comfort of the transport ship in favor of the bustling atmosphere of the colony ship.

Despite the late hour, the hangar was still humming with life. She was forced to weave through a constant stream of people in order to make it to the security checkpoint. Once again, she had to join a crowd as they passed through sensor after sensor all under the watchful eyes of the breakers. She wondered if they were the same group from earlier, or if they were allowed to rotate out in shifts. For their sakes, she hoped for the latter. She could only imagine having to stand guard and watch thousands of people pass in front of you for a full day. The crowd passed through the large metal gate with an automated voice chiming overhead to inform them of their entry into the Sonso district.

Back into crate city, she thought to herself as Sarah began to make her way into the pulsing nightlife. Beats of bass drums thudded and the glow of the full spectrum of neon lights illuminated the makeshift streets. Something was different this time. The colors weren't quite their fullest and held a strange hue to them. The bass sounded muted to her ears, and the crowds around her felt less imposing than before. She found herself standing closer to people than she normally would, and she felt relaxed in doing so even going as far as to intentionally brush shoulder to shoulder with as many people as she could. Realization dawned on her as she noticed every surface that should have come across as white or gray appeared yellow. *Nothing* was the wrong answer as the munmos started to kick into full gear. Her head whirled, but Sarah liked it. Textures felt softer and strangers looked far nicer than they had just a second ago. She wanted to talk to everyone, to be *friends* with everyone. A brief moment of clarity told her to be careful. If the munmos got any stronger she was going to have to end this get together as fast as she could, and get herself to bed.

Who knew what kind of trouble it could get her in.

3

Sarah followed her map the best she could, but the yellow tinge to her wrist display was distracting. She ended up following a small group down an alley having overheard their excited chatter about the Flux. The cargo containers narrowed in around her and rose high above. Bass thudded louder and louder as she wandered further down the corridor, but there were enough people lounging and hanging around to make the area feel like the right direction. The group she was following ducked through a purple curtain draped over a cutout in the side of a container wall. Pink and teal light flooded the alleyway as the group pulled aside the curtain to duck through, giggling all the while. Their mischievous laughter sounded like music, and Sarah couldn't keep herself from smiling with them.

Her surroundings resonated with a saturated yellow tone, and the metal walls of the containers danced with it no matter what color the light truly was. She felt warm, and a feeling of comfort crept over her like a welcome embrace. If this was the effect munmos had on her body, she wanted more of it. In all her memories, she had never felt this comfortable in her own body, never felt this safe. The warmth swirled in her chest and caused her head to feel thin and uncaring. Without a second thought Sarah parted the curtains and stepped through.

Her world became an ocean of teal and pink. The colors cascaded and danced off every surface while pounding house music vibrated the very frame of the structure's interior. The insides of the cargo containers had been cut apart and fused together to form something much larger than a single crate. The club was divided in two halves, it would seem, and the other half was accessible through a large arch way on the other side of the club. This side kept Sarah's eyes running in every direction. A walkway stretched overhead across the length of the club with countless lights affixed to its underside. Patrons stood atop it and leaned out over the railing to watch those below which was a lust fueled bombardment of the senses. All around were circular pits about a meter in depth. Each was lined with cushioned couches and a long, glowing pole rose up from their centers to attach to the ceiling high above. Languid dancers maneuvered around the poles with expertise, some several meters up in the air. Heat bloomed in Sarah's cheeks as she realized clothing was optional, and not only for the dancers. Many on this side of the club were in various stages of undress, and all of them crowded around each other as well as the dancers. They held no reserve despite the public nature, not waiting to find a dark corner to explore the woes of their partners.

Sarah didn't care to look away. The munmos pumping through her system kept her in a state of comfort. Anxiety, shame, embarrassment, and discomfort were all a foreign thought. She loved herself, and she loved the way she was feeling. Letting her hood down, Sarah walked around the club not hiding the fact that she stared at the sights being offered. A hand brushed hers from behind as she walked past the bar, and she brushed it back. Turning, Sarah was met by a woman with numerous augmentations. Four prosthetic arms extended from her back to hang by her natural ones. They all swayed in a sensual rhythm with the beat of the music, and the woman's eyes glowed teal with artificial implants. Sarah wondered if the woman's yellow cloak was truly white, and the munmos was continuing to screw with her perception, but was then distracted upon realizing the woman wore nothing underneath. The cloak was left open at the center to leave a trail of dark complexion. Sarah's eyes followed that trail all the way down.

"What's this?" The woman cooed. "Looks to me like a little fly ready to be caught in my web."

The woman stepped forward and pressed one of her prosthetic hands against Sarah's cheek. It was warm, almost like a real hand, and Sarah found herself pressing her cheek back into it. That seemed to be consent enough for the woman as she stepped closer, pressing her body against Sarah's. Another hand, and then a third began to wrap themselves around Sarah's waist while a fourth slipped in beneath her cardigan. The woman's lips drew close, a faint smell of sweetness on her breath. Jax would have stopped her. She would have hated Sarah for letting this woman seduce her, but

Jax wasn't here. Jax didn't want her like this woman did. She leaned in to press their lips together but another hand, a human hand, jerked her away.

Strong arms pulled her away from the woman and her spider-like grip. She made to protest, but the face she met was one she liked just as much. Red hair and color shifting eyes examined her with the faint hint of mirth. She'd seen this woman before when she was exiting the tram. Sarah made a fool of herself then, but not now. Not while the munmos kept her stable. Sarah reached for the woman's black leather jacket, but the woman pulled away. Instead, she pushed something underneath Sarah's nostrils, forcing a sharp scent directly up her nose. Immediately her head cleared, senses returning. Cracking pain flooded her frontal cortex along with the clarity, and Sarah winced.

"Looks like someone is having too much fun," the woman said with a laugh. "I don't know what they gave you, but I'm going to need you to come down off it for a bit. You're late for our meeting."

4

Sarah was thankful this new arrival was too busy dragging her to the other side of the club to notice her face burning a bright red. All of the anxiety, nerves, and now self-conscious shame flooded back into her system. There was nothing to truly be ashamed of, she knew. Despite this, her natural tendencies told her to second guess and assume what she had been feeling, what she had been *doing*, was wrong. She hated it. Already she missed the ease and comfort the munmos provided.

"My apologies," the woman said. She had to yell to be heard over the music. "I forgot you're new here. Someone should have warned you about the back entrance."

Guiding her by the hand, the woman before her took her past the teal and pink lights and around the cushioned pits until they were through the large archway. Wide open interior was littered with neon-lit tables, and elevated plinths where tall poles stretched to the ceiling which stood several containers worth in height. Scantily clad dancers swung from each pole, and looked down on patrons as they ordered drinks from a bar encircled at the center. While suggestive, it was very different from what waited just behind them. In the middle of the bar was a massive, cylindrical aquarium. Underlighting illuminated a number of alien fish and a long eel which skulked near the bottom. She let go of Sarah's hand, and nodded toward a far corner where a large reflective cylinder of a vibrant pink material connected from the floor to the ceiling. Several of these were placed throughout, and Sarah wondered if they were just for decoration. A door slid open on the cylinder's wall, and Ziven poked his head out to glance around.

The two of them worked their way through the crowd to reach the cylinder, and Ziven ushered them inside. It turned out to be a private party area with a large table, and a sofa lining the wall. From the inside, the pink walls were translucent so the occupants could watch those on the outside. Ziven sunk into the sofa, and scooted around the table to make room for the two of them. A number of others sat around the table as well, several with drinks in their hands or sitting in front of them on the table. The closest to the door and next to Ziven was who Sarah guessed was the immortal mercenary mentioned in their prior meeting. Taller, with white hair and trimmed mustache, he had an air of no nonsense about him. The sides of his head were shaved to the scalp, and the hair on top was combed to one side. What drew Sarah's attention was his eyes. They were black with irises of gold. He sat straight-backed with his hands folded on the table, and the hint of tattoos peeking out from beneath the cuffs of his black suit sleeves. Next to him sat Kyllen. The disheveled boy looked wide eyed, and excited to be part of the group. He kept looking from one person to the next as if any of them might perform a magic trick. Further down, a woman perhaps a few cycles older than Sarah, sipped from a martini glass. She swished the fluorescent green liquid around with a strong hand, her short nails painted black. She had a muscular build with wide shoulders beneath a leather jacket of orange and black. Her dark hair was tied into a topknot with some of it spilling down the back of her head. A gray shawl was draped over one shoulder, and the woman watched Sarah with great interest. Beside her a couple were nestled next to each other. It was clear they were lovers, as the woman was practically sitting on the man's lap with their hands intertwined. The man's brunette hair was combed into a quiff style haircut, and his soft face was clean shaven. His hooded cardigan was made of a deep blue material that looked comfortable yet stylish enough to be worn in a club. His partner was a blonde-haired, blue-eyed woman in a yellow dress cut low enough to leave little to the imagination. They ignored the arrival of Sarah and her guide, too busy in their own discussions. A last individual sat on the other side of the couple. It was the body guard from earlier. Instead of red armor, he wore a dark suit which paired well with his dark, wavey hair. The red-haired woman gestured to the couch, and Sarah slid in beside the table next to Vaugh. Her guide slid in behind her, blocking off Sarah's route to the exit.

"Alright, that's everyone," Ziven said, "except for Thusi. She decided she won't be coming. You'll have to meet her tomorrow when you depart."

"Already?" the blonde woman asked, she looked up from her partner with a sharp expression, "we leave tomorrow?"

"We've already wasted enough time here," Ziven said, "and time is not on our side with this one." He jabbed a thumb at the older man next him. The man's black eyes were considering Sarah, gauging her worth. "If you didn't know already, this is Breckett. Breckett, Sarah. He'll be your captain for this mission. Play nice, Breckett, she's one of your crew starting tonight. You've already met Kyllen. The lovely lady next to him is Doctor Yasmin Jung, she'll be your crew's go-to for all your medical needs. No offense, but I hope you don't need her."

"None taken," Yasmin said, and took a drink. "You can call me Doc or Yasmin, I'm good with either."

"The two love birds next to her," Ziven continued, "are Lucas and Lexi Biles. Just married, in case you were wondering. Lucas will be your pilot while Lexi is his navigator. Some of the best talent I've found in a long time."

The two of them waved at Sarah. Lexi gave her a genuine smile, while Lucas tightened his lips in a practiced courtesy. A short woman in a mesh bodysuit pushed her way through the door carrying a tray of drinks. She mumbled an apology as she set the drinks down on the table. Deep blue, and fizzling, the drinks were whiskey glasses filled to the rim. She set the last one down, and Ziven waited for her to leave before he started back up with his introductions. He snagged one of the drinks from the middle of the table, sniffed it, and took a deep swig. He licked his lips with a satisfied expression, and set the drink down.

"Your pal, Vaughn, is in charge of security, but like I said earlier, I hope you don't need him. The red bombshell next to you is Parker. She's on staff as your team's science lead," Ziven said. He took another swig of his drink, and started to drum his fingers on the table. He wiped his hands on his coat and tossed a small device into the center of the table. It clicked and a holo-projection lit up to display a rotating view of a ship. It was a plain design, but large.

"Starting tomorrow, your mission is to find this ship," Ziven said. "About a week back a distress signal reached the communications department here on the Ifrit. Given who the ship belongs to, someone there sent it my way."

"Long lost relative?" Parker asked.

"One of my brothers," Ziven said, his expression turning sour. "His son, and the son of another brother of mine were also aboard that ship. I understand the likelihood of any of them still being alive is low. The distress call took a while to get to us, and it's taken me a bit to get all of this set up. Too much red tape. If everything on that ship turns out to be okay, then great. Bring them back to me. If not, then I want you to find out what happened to them."

"That's it?" Lucas asked. "Find the ship, find the crew, tell you what happened?"

"That's it," Ziven said. He drained his glass of the blue liquid. Sarah took the chance to try her own. She swirled it around first watching the fluid sparkle as it fizzed, and took a sip. Flavor bombarded her tongue with different fruits, a copious amount of sugar, and no small measure of alcohol.

"There's a catch," Breckett said. "You're not telling us something."

Ziven glanced at Vaughn who, in turn, gave Breckett a

challenging look. Breckett returned the look, and Sarah wondered how quickly the two would descend into throwing fists. Neither of them was backing down, and Ziven was remaining quiet on the subject.

"I'd also like to know," Sarah said, "if there is something else, I feel like we'd all like to know what that is." Nods of agreements circled around the table, and the two men dropped their gaze.

"Not a catch," Ziven said, "and I was getting to it. I wouldn't hold back info if I knew it could hinder your success. While I was digging around for information, there were also reports of a Skren raiding vessel being sighted in the area. Shouldn't be too difficult a thing to handle for the immortal Breckett."

"So, you are him," Parker said, "forbidden tech and all."

Sarah looked around with a confused expression. She wasn't the only one with Breckett himself remaining quiet, instead giving his attentions to his drink. Parker took the silence as an opportunity to press on.

"Nano-cells," she said. "You see, Groal and humans are close enough to reproduce, but the offspring never live more than five or six cycles. Researchers have tried to remedy this through gene editing and bioengineering on those wanting to try, but the results are always the same. The cells get confused and start to devour one another. The T-cells target the white blood cells, and the white blood cells target the red. There's a lot more to it than that, but the idea is the entire immune system turns on itself. Most have given it up and written it off as an impossibility. A few, however, turned to some darker tech widely outlawed in human territories."

"I'm lost," Lexi said as she took a sip from her drink. The Biles were still curled around each other like it was their last night in the galaxy, but both of their attentions were on Parker. "What makes something lifesaving so forbidden?"

"Post-human tech," Yasmin cut in. She was glaring at Breckett with reproach.

It was Lucas who spoke up next. He gave Ziven a pointed look and said, "you hired a doctor that believes in fairy tales. That's a good sign."

Ziven shrugged. "She does good work."

"Fairy tale, or no," Parker continued, "the technology exists. Whether you believe artificially created humans ferried us over from some distant galaxy, or if some hairy deity in the sky snapped their fingers and all life erupted into existence, it doesn't change the facts. The tech was developed to create self-sustaining, microscopic bots that replace every cell in the immune system. They learn, grow, and reproduce just like a real cell but far more efficiently. Something tells me Breckett's parents took it a step further."

"They did," Breckett said. At last, he looked up from his drink. Black eyes considered each of them. "I fail to see how my medical history applies to our current job."

"It doesn't," Ziven interjected. "For now, I suggest you enjoy what little leisure time you have. Starting in the morning, I expect the best work out of all of you."

Ziven glanced at Sarah with a knowing look before nodding to Vaughn. The two of them stood and squeezed past the others to make their way to the door. The translucent pink door slid open, thundering bass rattling the edges, and Ziven stopped just past the threshold before turning back. His expression turned somber, and he waved a hand at the entire group.

"It's not in your contract," he said, "but should any of you not make it back, I'll pay your contracts to your closest loved ones."

Leaving the words to hang over the table, Ziven turned on his heel and closed the door behind him. Looks were exchanged around the table. Poor Kyllen looked as if he were regretting his choices, both hands clutched around a glass still full of the blue beverage. A sense of comfort began to return, and Sarah's nerves fled before a field of yellow hues. She smiled to herself knowing whatever Parker had done to mitigate the munmos was starting to wear off. She raised her glass high to the group.

"To one last night of freedom," she said. Smiles and nods spread across the table as each of them raised a glass. Even Breckett nodded with his blue drink held high. The Biles clinked their glasses together, and Sarah took the opportunity to drain hers in one swig. Flavors of sugar and fruits danced along her tongue and down her throat. It was one of the most pleasant drinks she'd ever had. The night was going to be lovely.

5

Kyllen rubbed her back as Sarah retched. She was leaned over in the dark corner of an alley, throwing up what little contents were left in her stomach. Her head swam but no longer due to the munmos. That had worn off an hour ago at least. Now, she was left wiping bile from her chin and trying to piece together the events of the latter half of her evening. More importantly, she wanted to know how she had gotten stuck with the over-infatuated teenager. She said nothing to him as he tried to comfort Sarah through her heaving. At least she had someone to keep watch as she spewed her last strain of dignity across the wall of a shipping container.

"Where are we?" Sarah asked.

Kyllen took his hand from her back to look around. The alleyway was shrouded in darkness save for the vibrant lights spilling in from the entrances at either end. Save for a curious pair of rats, it seemed Kyllen and herself were the only souls present. Another lucky thing as she dreaded the thought of a stranger seeing her in her present state.

"A few blocks from your hangar, I believe," Kyllen said. "We should really be getting you back to your ship. We all have to be up in a few hours."

"Get back to my ship?" Sarah asked. She straightened and wiped her chin a second time for good measure. The motion made her stomach churn, but she did what she could to ignore it. Raising an accusatory brow, she asked, "is that what you're wanting?"

Kyllen blanched, understanding what the situation looked like to anyone who might be watching. He began to stutter, and he fished something out of his pocket. It was a small pill bottle which he shook under her nose.

"No, no, not at all," he said, the words coming out in a rush. "That's not me. I would never. I was asked to, remember? See? Yasmin gave me this, remember? Told me to make sure you got home, and took these."

A vague memory of a laughing Yasmin handing Kyllen the pills before giving Sarah a pat on the shoulder came to mind. She also started to remember spending a substantial portion of the night pressing her weight against Parker in that crammed, pink booth. Sarah snatched the bottled from his hand and popped the cap. Before she could knock back the entire thing, Kyllen grabbed her wrist. Their eyes met. The boy looked scared but determined. His hair was a mess, and spilled over his antlers in tangles. Taking the plastic tube from her, Kyllen shook a single pill into his open palm.

"Only take one for now, yeah?" He asked. "You'll need the rest for tomorrow."

Not wanting to argue, her stomach trying to churn its way out of her throat, Sarah grabbed the pill and dry swallowed it. She clenched her eyes shut and grit her teeth in an attempt to keep the pill down. Saliva built up at the back of her mouth, but Sarah sucked in deep breaths to try and steady her belly. Kyllen took a gentle hold of her arm, and started to lead her to the mouth of the alley. Leaning on him for support, Sarah let him guide her out into the streets, and into the bustling crowds. Sonso district never slept. *She* intended to. Sarah was going to sleep like the dead if she managed to get back to her ship.

She leaned on Kyllen through the busy streets, past the security checkpoint, and back into the hangar. Keeping her eyes to the metal flooring of the catwalk, Sarah tried not to look over the railing. The endless drop below sent her head into a death spiral that caused her stomach to lurch. Yasmin's medication was beginning to stabilize the wooziness, but only to a small degree. Kyllen's support was still needed to cross through the gangway, and get back inside her ship. Once inside, Sarah stumbled through her now empty cargo hold in an attempt to get to her bed as fast as she could. She shrugged off Kyllen's help as she pulled herself up the ladder, into her loft, and fell into bed. The room continued to fall around her, and Sarah squeezed her eyes shut willing it to stop. When the world returned to its stabilized self, she began to focus on her breathing. She could still hear Kyllen shuffling around below the loft, but she didn't care. Sleep was all that concerned her, and she hoped controlled breaths would help her reach that sweet oblivion.

Thoughts of munmos crossed her mind, but she'd have to find sleep without it tonight. Sarah wasn't going to move from this spot if the ship itself started to crumble around her. She wondered if she had enough to get through their mission, or if she'd have to find a way to get more. She hoped she had enough. Sarah wanted to find her brother and be on her way. She told herself their missing ship was nothing more than an error in communication, and their team would find Hector with little issue and little conflict. The last thing she thought before slipping into a deep slumber was how the dark pit in her belly was warning her of just how wrong she was.

PART 2

INTERLUDE

1

Though his most recent visitors were many weeks departed, William's mind still whirred over every word exchanged. The Well of all things, and in his very lifespan. William was not sure if that was a blessing or a curse. Either way he would not have the opportunity to see it for himself. To leave this place was as sure a death sentence as any. He took solace in the fact that his condition allowed him to outlive a vast majority of the human species. These last hundred cycles or so had been especially kind to him. He tapped a finger against the arm of his chair as he whizzed through the endless library. Yellow light glowed with the setting sun, no longer tainted by the pink that marked the blood right. It was another fact that brought him joy. Now, if only he could find that book. The coordinates he set into his chair should bring him close enough. At least, that was the hope.

The twins with their dreaded Suttack companion had put a bug in his ear of sorts, and now he found he could not leave the matter behind. He had given up one book, yes, but there were many more he had secreted away throughout the library, and even more still his predecessors had done the same with. The Starlight Eternity Well was such a debated topic that many of his kind wrote it off as fable in public while coveting every word like a drug when everyone's backs were turned. William thought he had gotten over such fantasies until the twins marched through his doors. His chair slowed to a stop several stories up a towering bookshelf.

A skylight beamed directly overhead, and William took it as a good omen, even to go as far as searching the area which was illuminated directly by a ray of yellow light. The idea was, of course, preposterous. He nearly made himself laugh aloud. The laugh caught in his throat, however, when he brought his hovering chair to bear. Glinting at the edge of the yellow glow was a book he had never noticed before. Under several layers of thick dust was a narrow journal, leather bound with no markings to discern its title or categorization. Using the control stick on his chair, William buzzed close enough for the small engine to kick up a swirl of dust from the shelf. He could smell the must of the covers, and the alluring aroma of dried ink. Snagging the book with a curled finger, William set the volume in his lap. No title marked the front cover either. Before opening it, he decided to check his logs. Tapping a finger through his chair's computer terminal turned up short. By all accounts this book should not exist. William could no longer contain his giddiness. Licking his thumb, and swabbing the saliva between his thumb and forefinger, he flipped open the cover with a near-ravished excitement. A note slid out to fall into William's lap. Ignoring it at first, he looked at the first page. A small name was scribbled in the top corner, but little else. Hard to make out due to the fading ink, William thought the name read "Dr. Clouse Holland." Filing the name away for later, William turned his attention to the note. It appeared to be much newer than the book which was another oddity. Licking his thumb again, William unfolded the note, and began to read the black ink written with an untidy hand.

"The original source of this journal cannot be verified, nor the facts within confirmed. Please take each word with a heavy amount of speculation, and reveal to no one outside of the library staff. Book is to remain uncataloged, and unspoken of. This work is for the eyes of the Master Ledger, and the Master Ledger alone. All other staff please disregard this volume under threat of death. In case a future Master Ledger comes upon this work after my departure, may you have better luck understanding its contents than I. I have spent many years investigating the validity of these words, but have found nothing of any real purchase. While I should write this off as a work of fiction, my heart yearns to have found some sort of breakthrough in our lost histories. This could change the understanding of our past like no other piece of literature has before. Best regards, Master Ledger Oberon Page. Federation Cycle 4437."

William read through the note a second time, then a third. The name at the end was a man who had died half a millennium ago. The date listed was three hundred cycles before that. William's hands were shaking by the time he returned to the journal. Much more delicate this time, he turned the first page. Though hard to read at first, William adjusted to the odd handwriting and the faded ink. The note had not been a lie. Each word was more shocking than the prior, and he began to understand why this book was hidden. He glanced over his shoulder to be sure no one was watching even though he knew he was alone. This journal felt like a crime to possess. If what was written was true, this Dr. Clouse Holland was part of the original colony to arrive in the Triangulum Galaxy. That meant that humans were indeed a foreigner to this part of the universe. The doctor continued to refer to a piece of technology they used to navigate to this part of the galaxy. It was a system they sent a long time before them from the Milky Way to determine if this galaxy even had the potential to host human life. It was an AI system, and by the sounds of it the program had turned on them by the time they arrived. Clouse believed it to have gained sentience between the time its original creators sent it out, and the time the colony ship arrived. Sections of the journal were too faded to read, but William had time. He'd pour over this writing as if it were his life's work. After all, it may turn out to be. The AI had been named after the individual credited with its creation, a woman named Gayle Hide.

2

Tammon hated the dark. It was so oppressive, so cold. Any small noise amplified by multitudes and dragged his imagination into the depths of hell itself. Being locked in a cage was the cherry on top of the cyanide-flavored ice cream. Oh, how he could use some of that about now, cyanide or no. All his captors had provided up until this point were bowls of vitamin slush with just enough nutrients to keep him alive. His cell mates would have enjoyed a bit of sugar too. They were all gone now. Going from four down to one, he was all that was left in the dark cell. He knew there were many other cages like his pressed up against his cell walls. He could hear them sobbing in the night. Some newcomers often tried to spark up conversations. That usually lasted all of a day or two before the darkness also dragged them into the belly of hopelessness. Tammon wished he knew where they were taken after being removed from the cages. The only thing that was clear was once a person was removed, they never returned.

Perhaps his captors were simple smugglers kidnapping whomever they could and ransoming them back to their families. The problem with Tammon was he had no family to be ransomed back to. Would they kill him instead? How long had he been down here for? It wouldn't take a person long to figure out Tammon held little value. He curled up in the corner and hugged himself. What was the point of questions? He was down here, had *been* down here, for what felt like months. Any hopes of departure had long since evaded him, and it was time Tammon accepted his lot.

Dim light switched on, red and angry, and Tammon had to squint his eyes. Regardless of how dim the light was, he had grown too accustomed to the dark. Looking around, Tammon noticed others do the same. It was a rare chance to see who was all in the other cages. Their numbers had shriveled to fewer than he realized. The cage directly next to his had the most remaining members with a total count of three. A pair of Groal – one large and bearded, and the other scrawny with a cracked antler – sat against the wall of one side while a human man with a haphazard bun sat against the other near their cage's only toilet. All looked around with worry. They knew what the red light meant. Tammon wondered which one of them would be dragged from the cages next. Not him. It was never him, but he couldn't help but look around and judge the others. The scrawny Groal looked like an easy target. The human had an oleaginous look to him as if he might slip out of any hold and slide away into the dark. The other Groal intimidated Tammon even in his emaciated state. It would definitely be the one with the broken antler.

A door opened somewhere on the other side of the room. Tammon couldn't see it through the rows of cages, but the air changed and the noise it made wracked his ears. He had grown so accustomed to the quiet that the distant footsteps sounded like thudding drums. Two men in white uniforms rounded a group of cages to come into view. The first was as large around as he was tall, and his bald head glistened with sweat. He wore a scowl as he glared into the cages as if they were filled with bugs rather than people. His companion was a slender woman with dark hair and sharp angles. She avoided looking at the cages entirely. That was, except for Tammon's. Her eyes were fixed upon him with a pointed look. He tried to shrug it off and look to the three in the cage next to his, but all of them kept their heads down.

The pair stopped before the door of Tammon's cage, and he blanched. He'd been here so long. Why were they coming for him now? Just a moment ago he was hating his situation, and now he feared the change. The woman unlocked the door, and the large man stepped through. His expression promised violence for any noncompliance, so Tammon got to his feet with his hands held out in capitulation. Tammon must have looked even worse than he felt, because the man didn't bother fettering his hands. Instead, he stepped aside and gestured toward the open door with a thick baton. Tammon sagged but complied.

The angular woman wrinkled her nose at his stench as he walked through the door, but made no comment. He was guided out of the labyrinth of cages in utter silence. Their breathing sounded like shouting to him, however, and Tammon could tell they enjoyed being here just as little as himself. Having to close one eye and squint the other to adjust to the light of the hallway, he was shoved toward the right by the big man, and he stumbled over his own feet. He caught himself but had little time to recover as he was ushered down the hall into another room. Through the door was some sort of operating room with a large surgical table in the center and steel-topped counters lining the walls. Two figures waited for them at the far end. The first was a creature Tammon had never seen before. It looked like a human cat hybrid wearing lavish robes of vibrant colors. The second was a young girl with dark hair wearing a similar white uniform to the two escorting him.

Tammon was moved to the table and told to lie down. As he did, large straps extended over each of his limbs to fasten him to the cold metal. Panic clawed at his heart as the last strap secured his head. Someone else entered the room, but Tammon couldn't turn to see who it was. What bothered him more was just how little was being said. The silence smothered any hope he had of getting out of here, and wrapped long fingers around his throat. He wanted to scream but was too afraid to even do that much.

"Begin," a thin voice said from somewhere in the room.

Within seconds a wooziness fell over him. His view twisted, shifted, warped. No longer was he strapped to a table but standing in the open air. The sky blazed red above him and all around were hills covered in strange colored stones. He turned, and what came into view froze Tammon to the core. At first, he thought he had misinterpreted what he was seeing. After rubbing his eyes and taking a second look, however, there was no denying what stood atop the hill looming over him.

Pallid and smooth, a mass of writhing hands twisted and entwined ever upward to form a macabre effigy of a tree. Gnarled fingers formed the branches which pointed to the sky. Above the cruel mass where a sun should have hung was a hole of pitch black. It was the epitome of nothingness, absorbing any particle of light that dare draw near. The hands at the base of the tree formed roots which grabbed the strange stones and passed them upward to be carried to the top. Once the stones reached the top, they were tossed into the black hole and vanished. Tammon took a closer look at the stones nearest him, and almost gagged. They weren't stones at all, but hearts. They varied in size and shape, but there was no mistaking what they were. Some still fluttered with the faint murmurings of a beat.

"I see this place in my dreams," a girl said from behind him, "the doctor thinks it might have something to do with my powers."

Tammon whirled to find the young girl from earlier. He wasn't sure what part disturbed him more. That a little girl dreamt of a place like this, or anyone did. Her presence assured him that none of this was real. Disturbing as it was, that fact added a sense of ease. He looked back at the tree, worried that it might move and sneak up on him. Real or no, the sight did little to ease his nauseous belly. A deep stench of rotten meat clinging to the air was almost enough to cause him to gag again.

"I think this will be the last time," the girl said.

"Last time for what?" Tammon asked. Something about the girl's tone rekindled his panic.

"I have to change you now," she said.

Tammon's fear took control, and he bolted. Not caring that he was stumbling over beating hearts and writhing flesh, he ran as fast as he could. He crested a hill and fumbled his way down the other side. His short flight ended when he saw the girl standing above him atop the hill.

"Don't run," she said, "there's no use."

Tammon's shoulders slumped, and he sagged to the ground. The girl took careful steps down the hill and stopped just before him. Kneeling as he was, she placed a hand on his shoulder, closed her eyes, and began to concentrate on something Tammon couldn't see. A strange sensation worked its way up from his gut. A foul taste lashed the back of his throat. He wanted to spit, but his mouth felt as though it were filled with cloth. With a small shiver, Tammon's world began to change.

CHAPTER 12
- KALLIK -

1

The plan was simple. It felt too simple to Kallik, but Leo had said plans worked better that way. Complications only served as potential points of failure was how Leo described it, and it was best to keep things boiled down to their simplest form. The problem was this simple plan left a lot resting on Kallik's shoulders. To the others, Kallik appeared to have the closest connection to Master Aillon. Master Aillon, in turn, had access to the tools needed to have their inhibitors removed. A thought occurred to him then, one that Kallik could not shake once it had embedded itself in the forefront of his mind. If Aillon did have the ability to use his powers and set the kids free of their inhibitors, and he did want to escape this place, why had he not done so already? There must have been ample opportunities to do so before Kallik arrived here. Something felt off about the Master's intentions. It was too late to fret over it as their plans had already been set into motion.

Kallik hurried down the corridor towards the Master's office, and tried to narrow his focus. All he needed to worry about at the moment was not getting lost in this maze of white-painted hallways and identical doors. Once he achieved that much, then he could worry about the next steps of his plan. Leo should already be in Aillon's office waiting for Kallik to cause a distraction while the others were busy keeping the orderlies' attention toward the other side of the facility. The idea was not to act immediately, but rather to get the materials they needed to escape and form a secondary plan after. It would be Rekkeh's task to hide the inhibitor keys somewhere in the vents where they couldn't be found by the facility staff. When the time was right, the group would free themselves and make a run for it. Still, Kallik had wondered why no one had done it before. It was a problem that would bother him all the way down the hall.

Kallik rounded a corner, and was pulled from his thoughts. He had reached Aillon's office, but there was a small complication. The Butcher lurked in the doorway of the Master's door. Arms crossed over his chest, he leaned against the door's frame. Even from this angle, Kallik could see the black scar marring the white mask. He wondered how the man saw with there being no holes for the eyes, and he wondered who might have been so brave as to be the one to put that scar there. He also wondered what the man looked like beneath. He was probably some sort of depraved monster with ugly twists in his face, and jagged teeth poking through rotted gums. There was no way a person like him would look normal. Kallik braced himself. None of that mattered as the facility's symbol of death blocked him from the next part of his plan. Kallik thought about turning around on the spot, going back to his friends, and telling them the plan was a bust. The disappointment in Leo's eyes would be too much to bear. His friends were relying on him, and Kallik would not allow himself to be the only point of failure in their plans. Sucking in air and puffing out his chest, Kallik marched himself to the door one step at a time.

Trying to tell himself the Butcher was just a man, Kallik squeezed past the dark robes to slide into Aillon's office. The looming threat paid him little attention, and the sight beyond further added to his confusion. Master Aillon and Leo were sitting across from each other at his desk. Neither of them seemed to be paying the Butcher any heed, but they both looked up at Kallik's arrival. Leo had tissue stuffed up one nostril with blood soaking in around its edges, and small spots of red stained the front of his white shirt. Master Aillon's eyes were red and bleary with the lids beneath them puffy as if he'd be wiping away tears. Had he been crying? Something was wrong, terribly wrong.

"We're not scheduled to meet today," Aillon said, "Kallik,

you should be enjoying your free time with the others."

"What's going on?" Kallik asked. It was not what he intended to ask, but he needed to know what had happened. "Why is the Butcher here?"

"It's over," Leo said. He looked so frail, so tired, and his chestnut hair lacked its usual luster. Leo nodded at Vigamere. Kallik got the horrible sense the man was smiling beneath that white mask. "Scientists think I've got one more test, and then I'm done. I have to go in a few minutes."

The news felt like a punch to the gut. Kallik glanced at Aillon, but the red-haired master dropped his gaze to stare at the desk. Kallik understood. The man was a coward no better than Sabastian. There was a reason he talked in such grand gestures, but did so little. Aillon was going to sit there and watch his friend be taken to the slaughterhouse. Rage balled Kallik's hands into fists. It was the only thing he could do to keep himself from breaking out into tears. There was no thought to his next action, only instinct. He twisted fast as lightning, and slammed a fist into the Butcher's groin. He hadn't expected the blow to land, but it did. His knuckles connected with soft tissue, and Vigamere let out a grunt of pain. It was a sound Kallik didn't know the man was capable of making. He didn't stop there, however. Before Vigamere had a chance to double over, Kallik threw his other fist into the side of the Butcher's knee. He was doing it. He was proving Vigamere was just a man after all. Kallik's fury, his excitement, his pain at the news of his friend were all short lived. They were replaced by fear.

Instead of falling to Kallik's punches, Vigamere's knee held firm. Kallik blinked, and in the next moment his face was being slammed against the tiled floor. Blood spurt from a smashed lip, and he felt something in his nose give way with a sickening crunch. All he could see was the dark tile, and even that was spinning. He could hear shouting, but voices sounded far off as if there were cotton plugging his ears. Pain flared through his left antler, and Kallik reached a hand to touch it. Blood leaked from the cracked end that stopped too short. Cold wrapped itself around him, and Kallik's body gave a compulsory shiver. Something sharp pricked the small of his back, but he had no mind to pay it heed.

Nothing seemed real, and soon Kallik slipped into the depths of unconsciousness.

2

When Kallik awoke he found himself strapped into a seat. It was a familiar seat, one which he had hoped to avoid for a little while longer. He looked up at the black ceiling that reminded him of a ribcage and shuddered. Wires and monitors clung to every centimeter of his body, and thick straps held him into a seat cut into the groove of the floor. All around him scientists bustled across the room, hurriedly checking status monitors and readings while calling out numbers across the chamber. It was difficult to see being strapped down, but Kallik could make out the edges of the cryo-tube. So, he was alive but he wasn't sure for how much longer. He was amazed at himself. Kallik should have known better. Vigamere was the Butcher, and Kallik was just Kallik. What had he thought to accomplish? He *hadn't* thought. He had acted on his rage rather than reason, and now these horrible people were going to make him suffer for it. Still, Kallik found a small amount of satisfaction knowing he had caused the Butcher to grunt with pain. The man himself approached the pit to stand over Kallik. His white mask was clear despite the darkness of the room. An armored Skren lurked close behind, and watched Kallik with a curious look.

"Little Leo thanks you for taking his place today," Vigamere said, "though you've only bought the boy a day or so."

The reedy woman with the wrinkled forehead walked over to the pit, and glanced in. She held a data-slate in the crook of her arm which she hurriedly tapped through, but paused once she realized who was in the seat. Glancing from Kallik to Vigamere and back to Kallik, she pursed her lips and the wrinkles in her forehead grew deeper. She skimmed through some information on her slate, and frowned, tapping a thin finger against her chin.

"He's not supposed to be here," she said, and turned the slate to face Vigamere. "The Leo boy is scheduled for today. Very intense testing. Finalized, even. Too intense for the Groal boy.

Karaska wants this one preserved."

"Karaska is losing his touch," Vigamere said, "get it started."

"Not without Karaska's approval," she said. "I can send someone to-"

Vigamere twisted like a snake, and Kallik wondered how he had been able to strike such a man. The Butcher's hand was around her throat faster than Kallik could process. He squeezed with a single gloved hand, and the woman's eyes spread wide with a horse croak. She dropped the data-slate, the thin device clattering against the ground, and clawed at Vigamere's wrist. Unphased, the Butcher squeezed harder and the woman's face began to shift in color as she spluttered for air. The room was silent as everyone watched. Just as Kallik thought Vigamere would kill the scientist, he let go. She crumpled into a heap on the floor gasping for air.

"Get it started," he said.

She held up a desperate hand, and nodded. All around her the science team sprang back into motion. Voices called out numbers, and others entered commands into terminals. Vigamere strode off to somewhere Kallik couldn't see, and the armored Skren gave Kallik one last glance before following. The expression the creature had given him was odd as if it were weighing some sort of decision, but ultimately deciding against it. The female scientist remained on the floor for a few moments longer before collecting herself. Then, as if nothing had ever happened, she brushed herself off and set back to work calling out orders. Kallik could hear the humming of their machines starting up, and tried to brace for what came next. The following sensation, however, was something he would never get used to. His mind shifted, and Kallik was thrown into the dark.

3

Kallik blinked, and found himself in an all too familiar setting. Water burbled in a small stream across a rocky ground on which he now stood. Jagged canyon rose above him to a sky that was bright blue, but the moon and stars still shone. The magenta stone was not a welcome sight. He knew he should run. The huntress would know he was here, and be on him soon enough. Kallik needed to find a place to hide, but the idea lacked the appeal it once had. He was still trying to process what had happened in the real world. The Butcher was going to see him die in these tests, and Leo would soon follow. What was the point of giving these scientists what they wanted if he was going to die anyway? He could give them one last act of defiance, by sitting down and letting his fate come to him. Kallik lowered himself to the rock covered ground, and sat with his legs crossed under him. He stared up at the stars, and listened to the running water. Telling himself he wasn't afraid would be a lie, but his hate for Vigamere outweighed his fear of the huntress. At least she was quick with her kills. Footsteps crunched behind him, but Kallik kept his eyes facing up.

"Has the little demon been brought here only to give up?" A cold voice asked from behind him. The way she pronounced her *s* sounds made Kallik think of a serpent. "I didn't know evil had the ability to pout."

The footsteps made their way around his side until they stopped in front of him. Only then did Kallik break his eyes away from the sky to look at his impending death. What he found caught him off guard. The four-armed woman in her blue carapace, and gray silks had a look of concern playing across her face. She kneeled down in front of him to bring her view to a similar level with her bottom arms draped across her knees. Her other set of arms grabbed Kallik by the chin, and twisted his head. Running a finger along the stub of what used to be his left antler, he could not keep from wincing. Holding his chin firm with one hand, she brought the other back, rubbing blood between her thumb and index finger. Her pointed, black nails dug into the soft flesh of his jaw, but refrained from breaking the skin. Dark eyes studied the crimson which stained the tips of her fingers, and Kallik did everything he could to stamp down the fear growing in his chest. It did little good. His heart pounded, and his eyes felt as though they may roll out of his head as she brought her fingers to her lips and tasted his blood. Her expression turned to shock as she let the flavor settle in.

"You aren't a dream," she said, "no, no dream at all but a real creature trapped in the realm of my mind."

Kallik felt numb. This was not the interaction he was expecting, and had no idea what she might do next. All he could do was nod with wide, terrified eyes watching for any sudden movement that could give away her intent. Attempting to move his head proved pointless. She held him firm in place, her black irises now fixated on his own. He thought about using his ability, but she'd stop any attack he could muster up. She proved that the last time he was here. Working his mouth, trying to form words, an idea was starting to form.

"What made you realize?" He asked. "Of all these times, what made you realize the children being sent here were real?"

"Your blood," she said. "This is my dream, a reality created by my inner thoughts. Most of this must be drawn from my own experiences. Sights, sounds, touch all need to be things I've known or am capable of conjuring up with my imagination. The flavor of your blood is beyond what I could conjure. No part of it is recognizable. Tell me, child, how did you come here? How do you intrude on my dreams?"

Taking a long, deep breath, Kallik told her everything. He went as far as to start at the very beginning with his father's ship, and didn't stop until he reached the current. If he wanted any hope of getting his newly formed plan to work, he needed this creature to trust him.

4

Unblinking eyes watched Kallik speak at a frantic pace, and she absorbed every word. Her brow furrowed deeper and deeper with his progress, and at one point Kallik wondered if her anger would cause her to snap his neck. He tried to control his breathing, but so many thoughts were racing through his head that he tried to squeeze them all out through his mouth at the same time. More than once did she have to stop him, and make him repeat his sentence to understand what he was trying to say. Only once he finished did she let go of his chin. He wanted to say more, but her expression looked as though she may kill him if Kallik said another word. Standing, she folded both pairs of hands behind her back, and started to pace. Stopping in front of the stream, she focused her attention on the water. A tendril of clear liquid broke away from the stream and danced upward. She watched it absently as it began to twist around her like a vine, and spiral high into the air. It stopped once it reached the top of the canyon, and she dropped her eyes from it. The water fell back to the ground with a loud crash, and she walked back to Kallik.

"They have no idea what they're playing with," she said. "My people crossed the void to these stars before your kind were anything more than bacteria incubating in warm puddles."

"I can help you," Kallik said, "I can help you wake up if you help me escape after."

She froze, and looked as though she could laugh. "Is that so? And what's to keep me from devouring you and everyone in this facility once I'm free? I could do it, you know. My people mastered our abilities a millennium ago. What you call conduits would be but poorly evolved children to me."

"I don't doubt that," Kallik said, "but if you've been asleep for thousands of years, you might want a guide. Someone to help as a reference might be a good idea."

"Why would I want that?" She asked. "Why care about this place, child?"

"My name is Kallik," he said, which earned him a pointed look, but she acquiesced.

"Kallik," she mouthed the word with an unfamiliar tongue. "I am the last of my kind. What hold would this galaxy have over me? Why stay? In fact, why not see the whole galaxy go up in flames in the name of my people? The technology in my ship would make it a simple task."

"Kallik," Kallik said again. "I gave you my name, it's only fair you do the same."

He hoped she wouldn't see through his ploy for time. Kallik needed to find a way to win this ancient being over to his cause. Time was running out for his family and friends, for his father and Leo, and this being with near godlike powers could be his ticket to save all of them. He just needed to think.

"You would not be able to pronounce it," she said with a glare. "We can understand each other in my dream due to our mental connection, but my true language is far beyond something you could understand."

"Try me," Kallik said, "I'd respect your language as if it were my own."

"Nathfnitu," she said, and gave him a look that dared him to try and repeat it.

A bit of Kallik's defiance ebbed into his emotions. It took him a moment to roll what he had just heard over in his head, but he thought he caught the better side of it. His father had drilled diplomatic negotiations over and over again, and one major sticking point to his father was getting someone's name right the first time around. His father had always said no one was more amiable than someone who felt appreciated and respected. Kallik met the alien's eyes, and spoke with confidence.

"Nathfnitu," he said. He nodded at her for good measure, and tried to hide the fear which took the form of sweat trickling down the back of his neck. Refraining from wiping it, he kept both hands clasped in his lap. Nathfnitu gave him an appraising look before nodding in return. She sat down in front of him and mirrored posture. Pulling her black hair with the long tendril over one shoulder, she looked him square in the eye.

"Well enough," she said, "but you still haven't told me why I shouldn't devour everything before setting sail into the void."

Kallik was at a loss. Despite the time he'd earned, he still could not think of a reasonable explanation that could sway Nath to his side. Every reason he came up with sounded childish in his head, and betraying his age to this being would only hinder his cause. She did, however, seem eager to escape. All these things she spoke of would require her to wake up and get out of the cryotube. Perhaps he could use a technique his father loved, and bluff. His father had told him a good bluff was always sprinkled with truth.

"Maybe you're right," he said. "I shouldn't help you escape. To be honest, you terrify me. Maybe it's best if I listen to my gut. My father always said gut feelings were important. Now that I know what you are, I may be able to strike a deal with Karaska."

She pursed her lips, and considered him. Then she bared her teeth. "I should rip you limb from limb, little Kallik, for the very suggestion of it. I'd make it slow, and keep you alive long enough to feel every moment. Now that I know what *you* are, I can shape this world to damage your mind beyond repair. You'd be nothing but a mindless husk on the other side. Alive in flesh, but nothing more than lumps of living tissue and organs."

She stood, and Kallik's fear got the better of him. His bluff had failed, and she was going to kill him in brutal fashion. He winced, and threw up a hand as she took a step forward. He closed his eyes to hold back the tears. He didn't want to die. All he wanted was to save his family, and he had failed. He waited for the inevitable pain, but what he heard instead was laughter. Risking a glance, Nathfnitu was hunched over and laughing at his expense. Quieting herself, she flicked a single finger, and Kallik began to float. He rose in the air, his toes dangling almost a meter above the ground, and began to gently spin in front of her. He could feel her black eyes crawling over every centimeter of his body.

"You are still very much a child," she said, "and it is clear you do not yet know the way of things. Worse entities than me lurk in the dark corners of the galaxy, little Kallik. My people did not go extinct on their own. There may be a chance we can-"

Kallik was ripped from the dream, and thrust back into reality. A ceiling spun out of control above him. It was the same ribbed arches, but now they were fully lit. At least, that's what Kallik thought. It was hard to tell when the entire world refused to stop moving. Bile tickled the back of his throat, and he knew he was going to puke. He tried to roll over, but his head was still strapped to the seat. He could choke like this. Trepidation over-took him, and he fought the bonds as the contents of his stomach erupted from his mouth. He coughed, trying to get it all out, and swallowed what was left. His stomach was not done, however, and he heaved again. Someone was yelling in the background, and an orderly jumped down into the inset to start undoing his bonds. He puked again, not caring that the bile sprayed all over the orderly's clean garb.

Kallik tried to suck down air, and settle his stomach while the straps were being removed. The ceiling began to steady itself, and soon he was able to feel a stillness. A familiar shape loomed over him, though it was not the Butcher. Of him, there was no sign. A small part of Kallik was relieved to see Doctor Karaska looking down on him. Fury sculpted every corner of his posture, and he was shouting orders to all of his scientists.

"Get him up," Karaska said, "If he doesn't survive, none of you do. I'll start from the ground up with a new team if it means getting competent workers."

The female scientist with the wrinkled forehead hopped down into the inset, and pushed the orderly aside. She undid the last strap, and began removing the cables and monitors attached to Kallik's body. The woman whispered something to him, but Kallik was too dazed to comprehend the words. Taking a rag, she dabbed his mouth and chin before removing the last pad stuck to Kallik's temple. Next, she unwound a roll of bandages, and wrapped Kallik's damaged antler. He groaned as she did so less because of the pain, and more because he knew the implications of a damaged antler. Groal children were taught to be careful in their early years as any damage to the antler now could stunt the growth later. He wondered if his left antler would continue to grow at all. Having yet to see the true extent of the damage, it was hard to tell what condition he was in. Kallik took another moment to look around the room while the bandages were being applied. It wasn't his imagination. All around him the room was lit. No more was the chamber a brooding cave, but rather a bright cavern with an array of light reflecting from the ribbed ceiling. However, even as he observed them, the lights began to dim. Soon they faded back to the dark he had grown accustomed to seeing here.

"Finish cleaning him up," Karaska said, "and bring the boy to my chamber."

The woman acknowledged him with a grunt, and finished her work. She glanced over her shoulder to be sure Karaska was on his way out before attempting to pull Kallik out of the seat. He understood why when in the next moment she yanked him to his feet by one arm in a single, rough motion. A squeak of pain escaped him before he could stop it. His shoulder was already sore from his encounter with the Butcher, and the woman's tug sparked that pain and then some. The orderly chuckled at the sound, and now that Kallik was standing he realized which orderly it was. Sabastian. Exhaustion prevented Kallik from doing something his father would consider unwise, and Kallik considered that a good thing. If Kallik acted on his hate now, who could say what they'd do to him next. It was then he realized they had still not replaced the inhibitor on the side of his head. It wasn't that he could feel the lack of it, he had grown too accustomed to it being there to notice if it was or was not, but rather he felt his abilities on the very edge of his mind. They called to him, begged him to be used. He peeked over the lip of the inset toward where the cryo-tube was. Nathfnitu was curled up in her slumber, floating in the vat of liquid. If he could break the seal, Kallik could end all of this now. However, there was no telling if she'd kill him as well. The likelihood was high. If it gave his father and cousin a chance at escape, Kallik wasn't sure he cared at this point. He began to focus on the door of the tube, but it was too late. A soft click interrupted him as Sabastian placed the small disk behind his ear. The awareness of his ability vanished, and Kallik was once again helpless. The two adults grabbed him by either arm, and hoisted him out of the pit. Together they marched him out of the chamber, and back toward the tram to bring him to the station proper.

5

Sabastian and the scientist stopped Kallik in front of an unmarked white door. He guessed Karaska's room was intentionally ambiguous to throw off anyone who may wish to do him harm, but Kallik was in no mind to have remembered the route anyway. They had taken the tram back through the ocean, and then taken the elevator down to a level Kallik had forgotten to take note of. All he knew was this floor was the same white maze as the one above it. Sabastian placed his hand on the door's terminal, and waited for a response. Karaska's voice chirped through a speaker.

"Send him in," Karaska said, "but wait there. You'll need to escort him back."

The door slid open, and the hateful man shoved him through without warning. It was all Kallik could do to keep himself from tumbling face first. The door closed behind him before he had a chance to turn back which left him with no other option than to move forward. He was in a small entry hall with no discernable features. Only white walls, and a bare metal floor and ceiling waited before him with another door standing at the other end. What was odd was Kallik thought he could hear a piano being played beyond. The melody was a sad tune with dark undertones and low octaves.

He took a few steps toward the door, and it opened on its own. The view beyond was a lavish bed chamber, with only a single light at its center to see by. The source of the music became apparent. Karaska's quarters were a large circular room with a high domed ceiling, the single light beaming from its zenith. It shone down on a scene from Kallik's nightmares. At the chamber's center was a large piano encircled by a wall of glass. A different Suttack sat on the piano bench, and played the sad melody. At first Kallik thought their eyes were closed, but the truth of what was really going on nearly sent him running. Dressed in crimson robes which flowed over the bench like a river of blood, the Suttack had its eyes and mouth sewn shut. Pale wire crossed over its features preventing any hope of opening them ever again. Kallik forced himself to pull his gaze away from the macabre scene to look for Karaska. All along the walls painted tapestries were hung depicting views of strange planets and alien landscapes. As Kallik walked into the room, he caught a glimpse of a painting putting the anatomy of the Suttack on full display. Several doors lined the walls leading to different rooms, and Kallik wondered if Karaska may be waiting behind one. He found the scientist standing behind a bar to the left. The counter shimmered with crystal and gold inlays, and expensive looking bottles gleamed on a lavish shelf of black wood. Karaska reached up to one of the higher shelves, and grabbed a green bottle. He poured a dark liquid into a crystal glass, and pointed at a stool in front of the bar.

"Take a seat," he said. Karaska swirled the dark liquid, eyeing it with trepidation before swallowing it in one gulp. "You have nothing to fear here, Kallik, take a seat."

Kallik took his time in making his way over. He took in every feature of the room, trying to distract himself from the piano player. No furniture was present except the stools at the bar, and piano behind the glass wall. He kept glancing over to the player, and hurriedly looked for something else to distract him. Each painting was vibrant enough to glow despite the dim light, and Kallik knew from the experiences on his father's trading vessel that they were originals. He gave the piano player one last look before taking a seat. Karaska noticed his expression, and waved his glass at the other Suttack.

"She was a colleague of mine," Karaska said, "from way back when we first started. She was a genius, really, she was. Her research allowed us to create this lovely facility, and lead to the discovery of that ancient ship. Unfortunately, her morals got the better of her, and she did some very unsavory things in an attempt to right the wrongs. It nearly set us back a decade. I couldn't stand for that, now, could I? She was always such a lovely piano player. I couldn't put that to waste, so now it's all she does."

Karaska paused as if waiting for Kallik to respond. The sight of a dim room with a single light shining down on the crimson clad piano player with both her eyes and mouth sewn shut clawed at Kallik's primal fear. If he opened his mouth, he feared he'd scream. Instead, he sat in silence. Karaska was going to do whatever it was the doctor wanted to do, and there was nothing Kallik could say that would sway such a monster. He'd rather be back with Nathfnitu. At least that was a predictable fear.

"Pay her no mind," Karaska said. "I brought you here in hopes we can reach some sort of understanding. What Vigamere did-"

"The Butcher," Kallik said. He had no idea where the defiance bubbled up from, but the words slipped out. The mere mention of Vigamere made his blood boil. Karaska raised a brow, but continued.

"Yes, the Butcher," Karaska said. "What he did was not

by my order, nor was it by my approval. His temper caused him to overstep. I've sent him away for now. At least until my work with you has finished. I need you Kallik. Despite the differences with our peoples, I see an opportunity to work together."

"Why would I want to do that?" Kallik asked. The defiance was still there yet to be pushed down, and Kallik found that he liked the feeling. "You've done nothing but destroy everything I have."

"Because I have your family," Karaska said, "and as of right now they remain untainted, and unchanged. Depending on your actions, however, that might not always be the case."

"You're going to force me to do whatever you want anyway," Kallik said, "so why bother to barter?"

"Whatever you did this last time around worked better than anything I've seen before," Karaska said. "I need to know what happened, and I need you to do it again. My resources are running thin, and your success marks an unprecedented opportunity for innovation."

"I feel like this is a trap," Kallik said, "you're going to get what you want from me, then go against your word to do what you want anyway."

"I'm giving you an opportunity to get what you want," Karaska said, "I find things to be much more pleasant when everyone gets a little something."

"You've sent away the Butcher?" Kallik asked, "for real, you have?"

"I have," Karaska said. He poured himself another glass of the dark liquid, and contented himself with swirling it about in the crystal glass.

"Then no more killings?" Kallik asked. "Everyone is safe as long as the Butcher is gone?"

"Unless they crack," Karaska said, "no one is safe if that happens."

"Then stop the tests," Kallik said which earned him another raised brow. "You have no use for viper testing, and all you need is me for the bulls."

"I've already ended the viper program with my last test,"

Karaska said, "things didn't quite go as planned, but you may be right about the bulls. Focusing on you might expedite things."

"Then Leo and Mauricia are safe?" Kallik asked. He hated that he cared about the bully girl, but he could not help but feel bad for her after what had happened. All of them were trapped here, and none of them had any say in their fate. That was until now.

"Your friend can skulk back into his corner," Karaska said, and took a sip of his drink. "That brutish girl, on the other hand, is already gone. She cracked during her last test. I had Vigamere put her down on the spot. She made quite the specimen for me before she left. Largest transformation I've ever seen. We had to have a cage specially built to contain it. Did you know this facility made the exclusive discovery on how to do such things? Vipers have never been able to do this before. Push the mind into a high enough level of stress using their powers, and we can alter the very DNA with a special drug. Then, the viper can mold them into whatever their imagination sees fit. Little Mauricia had a thing for spiders it would seem."

The news was gut wrenching. Kallik put on a brave face, but wanted nothing more than to be out of the nightmare. Karaska would see them all dead before it was done, or worse. He made up his mind. What the doctor wanted was for him to continue the tests, and replicate what he had just done. Kallik would agree, and use one of these chances to set Nathfnitu free. Whatever she chose to do was better than what this Karaska had in store for them. He looked Karaska square in the eye, trained his face to an emotionless expression, and held out his hand.

"Deal."

CHAPTER 13
- SARAH -

1

If nightmares had haunted her sleep, Sarah hadn't remembered them. Kyllen had prodded her awake with a cautious hand, and he nearly force fed her the doctor's meds. Yasmin, Sarah thought her name was, but events blurred together. Names and faces of her new crewmates lingered on the outskirts of her memory, all held at bay by the stone fence of a hangover. She cleaned up in the small closet of a bathroom, praying to whatever entities might be listening for the medication to be fast acting, while Kyllen lingered somewhere in the hold. She thought the nausea might be starting to ease, but a quick turn of her head sent Sarah's stomach rolling. Clinging to the edge of the sink, she controlled her breathing and fought against the bile tickling the back of her throat. Kyllen knocked on the metal door, and checked in.

"You alright?" He asked. "We need to get going soon."

A stupid question from a stupid kid, but Sarah brought her anger into check. It wasn't his fault. It was no one's fault. Better to blame no one than to direct a festering hate. She took another deep breath, and thankfully the nausea began to subside. Whatever those pills were, they worked. Rinsing her mouth for the third time, Sarah pushed her way out of the bathroom, past the bleary eyed Kyllen, and back into her sleeping loft. She began to cram everything she could into a canvas bag. It was one of the few times she found herself thankful for having next to nothing. Everything she owned filled less than half of the bag, and even that much felt light in her grasp. She gave a start when Kyllen called up to her from the cockpit below.

"I have to stop by home before we head out. My old gram grams will want to know I'm leaving," he said, "wanna go with?"

"What? No." The words came out harsher than she intended, and Sarah could almost hear the flinch on the kid's face. She smoothed her tone over, and tried again. "Do you need me to?"

"I finished your drone," he said, "I didn't boot it up, though, so it'll need to be carried if you plan on taking it with. Plus, grams will want to know why I'm leaving."

"You didn't tell her?"

"I did," he said, "but you know how it is. She'll want confirmation that I'm not running off to do something illegal."

Sarah wasn't sure what exactly would be illegal enough to be problematic in a place like this, but it was clear Kyllen had been caught up in it in the past. He could be telling the truth, and his grandmother was just being a grandmother, but Sarah had her doubts. She let out a deep sigh deciding just this once she could humor the kid.

"It'll be quick?" She asked.

"We'll be out before you know it," Kyllen said.

Letting out yet another sigh, Sarah slung her pack over one shoulder and climbed down the ladder. Kyllen waited for her at the bottom in his oversized poncho and his dark hair pulled into a disheveled bun. Despite this, he wore an eager expression. He cleared a stray clump of hair from his eyes and draped it over an antler. His eyes glittered with the hope of his question.

"Fine," she said, "let's get going."

2

Before you know it must have a different meaning on Vulture colony ships because almost twenty-minutes later and Sarah was still sitting in the living room of a small apartment while its owner, a little old Groal woman Sarah simply knew as *Grams*, busied herself with brewing a pot of tea in the kitchen. Kyllen himself was stowed away somewhere in his room, gathering all the belongings he thought they needed for their departure. The medication was in full swing, at least, and Sarah felt like her usual self. It was a small blessing as she felt each second tick by while she waited for the humming elderly woman to finish up her work.

She strolled in, wide antlers threatening to knock over dust-covered curios from ancient shelves, with a thin tray held between shaking hands. The lid of the cast iron pot rattled with each new tremor, but the old woman managed to make it to the opposite couch without spilling a drop. She set the tray down on the simple coffee table sitting between the two of them before taking a seat herself. The two of them sat in silence while she poured a yellow liquid into small cups. Steam plumed from the spout and danced around the rim of the cups as she did so, and the scent of honey caught Sarah's nose. With the small confines of the apartment, the aroma filled the living space in an instant. A faint smile crossed the woman's wrinkled features, and her gray hair shone above lavender robes. Next, she took a pinch of dark spice from a small bowl next to the kettle and sprinkled a small dose into each cup. Shooing the steam away with a hand long bent by arthritis, grams lifted one of the cups to her nose and breathed deep. Her smiled widened with satisfaction, and she gestured toward the other cup. Sarah took it in both hands and let the scent fill her nose before taking a sip. Sweet and spicy collided on her tongue with hints of honey, chili and ginger, and Sarah wasn't sure she liked it. She smiled all the same to avoid coming across as rude.

"My grandson tells me the two of you have been hired to rescue a stranded ship," the old woman said. "Sounds like quite the job."

Sarah couldn't be sure how much Kyllen had said, nor could she know how much Kyllen wanted his grandmother to know. While she had no interest in protecting the kid from his own guardian or helping him keep secrets, Sarah wanted to be out of here sooner rather than later and a family argument could put that hope to risk. She nodded with a muttered confirmation, but the grandmother pressed on.

"He says it's a simple and safe task," she said, and set her cup down, "but I tend to know my grandson better than that."

Sarah opened her mouth to protest, but grams held up a hand to silence her. Glancing around to avoid the woman's direct stare, Sarah found herself wanting to be anywhere but on this woman's couch. Grams took another sip of her tea before pushing on.

"Are you part of a gang? Or, perhaps you're smugglers?" She asked. "What have you gotten my grandson wrapped up in?"

Sarah was going to strangle the kid for dragging her into this, but she forced a smile and set down her cup. "I can promise you it's nothing more than what he said. My employer received a private distress call from a stranded ship, and needs to send a crew out to retrieve the passengers. Nothing illegal or dangerous."

"You know," the old woman started, "I raised that boy since before his antlers broke the skin of that pale little forehead. His mother was a good girl, but she made bad mistakes. She let the wrong people lead her into making decisions for her. It got her both pregnant and killed. You see, Groal women aren't afforded the luxury of the medicines and medical procedures you humans benefit from and we're forced to endure our cycles as nature decides. The accidental pregnancy killed her, and the father vanished shortly after."

"I'm sorry," Sarah said. She squirmed with discomfort unsure of what else to say, but Kyllen's grandmother continued as if Sarah had not spoken.

"I see a lot of my daughter's personality in my grandson," she said. "Absent-minded, hopelessly romantic, and prone to be swept up by anyone who gives him a modicum of attention."

Sarah started to speak, but the old woman held up her hand again. Her dark blue eyes pierced into Sarah's very soul, searching for an unspoken answer that may not exist. Sarah wanted to look away but couldn't.

"I don't know if you're lying outright or just bending the truth," she said, "but I know I'll not shake it out of either of you, so know this: if anything should happen to him, anything at all, I'll find out who you are, who you work for, and every last thing you love and destroy them. That is not lie."

"She's a guest, grams," Kyllen said. He stood in the doorway with a full sack slung over one shoulder and the drone tucked in the crook of his other arm. "Show a bit of hospitality."

"I'm just making myself clear," she said. "I see you're ready to go. Just be sure to come home in one piece."

Those piercing eyes never broke away from Sarah's while she spoke, and a chill shot down Sarah's spine. Hector better be ecstatic to see her, or she was going fire him out of the nearest airlock for what she was having to go through to find him.

3

The little drone, Eryn, beeped and whirred as it flew around Sarah in a circle. She stood on a catwalk of Quarantine Dock Seven, and looked up at the ship which loomed before her. It was massive, far larger than what she had been expecting. She supposed it needed to be able to house a crew this large, but she'd spent so much time with so little company that she had forgotten just how much space was required for people. The bulk of the ship was shaped like an arrowhead. Sarah had seen that shape from above, but now that she was on the same level, she was realizing how thick it was. At least two stories of gray metal rose above her to cast a deep shadow. Kyllen had gone his own way once they reached the ship as Sarah had received an unexpected message from her new boss, Thusi, telling her to wait next to the rear gangway.

Sarah adjusted the bag slung over one shoulder which held the personal belongings she had left, and looked around for a familiar face. She was in the right place, but the entire dock seemed empty when compared to the rest of the Ifrit. Knowing her employer, it wouldn't be a stretch to assume he had something to do with that. Sarah plucked a small bottle she had strapped to the side of Eryn as the drone floated past, and took a sip of cold water. A sip became a gulp, and she drained the bottle of its contents before she could stop herself. While no longer feeling the horrid after effects of last night, she found herself to be parched. She wasn't sure if that was part of the medication doing its work.

"You're early," a shrill voice called, "too early."

Startled, Sarah dropped the bottle with a clatter and spun to see who had spoken. Standing before her was a Dwemyri. Shorter than most she'd seen, the Dwemyri was no taller than Sarah's waistline and was clad in a thick, black jumpsuit. The long hands with their sharp claws, and the Dwemyri's bat-like head were all covered with a fine layer of white fur. Its short snout wrinkled, and ribbed ears twitched as the Dwemyri watched Sarah's every move. Then its dark eyes caught a glimpse of Eryn.

"You must be Sarah," the Dwemyri said, and Sarah nodded. Its voice held a feminine edge, but Sarah was careful not to assume. "I'm Chief Engineer Thusi of the Dari Clan, and from here on out, I'll be your boss. I'll have you know I read your file, your *real* file, and let me tell you this - I'm not impressed. I find it infuriating that Ziven would place such an amateur under my wing. I've made my complaints known, but he's ignored me. That means we're stuck together. You can call me *ma'am*, very human thing to do, but I prefer the formal *bullas* of my people. Sound good?"

Sarah nodded again, and Thusi grabbed her hand with both of hers to give it a rapid shake. To be called an amateur was new, but she guessed when compared to a chief engineer amateur was the only word that would fit. Sarah couldn't recall what clan Throx had claimed to be from, but she could not help but note the differences. Throx's way of speech had been different, but Sarah could write that off as Thusi being more acclimated to a human lifestyle. Throx had never been outside of home before Carlisle Station. Thusi was also much smaller than Throx had been, but Sarah wasn't familiar enough with Dwemyri physiology to know how much they varied in size. Just as much as humans, she supposed.

"It's an insult to a Dari to show up this early you know," Thusi said, "it gives off the implication that you assume the other party will be late. Best to show up exactly on time."

Sarah couldn't help but notice Thusi was also early, but she kept the fact to herself. "My apologies," she said.

"My apologies, *bullas*," Thusi said.

"My apologies, bullas," Sarah repeated.

"Good, there's hope for you yet. Now, gather yourself,

and come this way. We have much to prepare before we can depart," Thusi said, and grabbed Sarah by the forearm. The Dwemyri pulled Sarah down an adjoining catwalk toward a forward hatch on the ship. Eryn buzzed after, startled by the sudden movement, and Thusi glanced back at the drone.

"No AI in that, I hope," Thusi said, and nodded at the drone. "Otherwise, lose it."

"No AI," Sarah said.

"No AI, bullas," Thusi said.

"No AI, bullas," Sarah repeated. "It was just reprogrammed it to follow me around, and do simple tasks."

"Good, good," Thusi said, "keep it that way."

The hatch Sarah was led to was possibly the smallest entrance to a ship she'd seen in cycles. Sarah could see larger hatches, and even the main access doors from here, so she made little effort to hide her confusion. Thusi ignored her at first, and punched a code into a number pad next to the hatch. It beeped with confirmation, then popped open to reveal a tight corridor beyond. It looked little more than an air vent. Thusi would have no problem walking through, but Sarah would have to crouch. She said as much which earned her an incredulous look from the chief engineer.

"We are servants of this ship," Thusi said, "and we must respect it as such. Besides, this corridor is the fastest way to the engine room. We need to start preparing for launch."

Sarah wanted to say something else, but she closed her mouth. As impressive of a ship as it was from the outside, she wanted to be able to see its proper interior, not shuffle around through its crawl spaces. It was an aspect of her life she had grown used to, however, so she dropped any complaints that were beginning to form. Besides, she'd only need to do this for a short period of time before she would be able to be more selective with her position. Just as she ducked through the hatch to follow Thusi, a voice chimed over comms.

"Thusi, Sarah, welcome aboard the Villimath," the baritone said. Sarah thought she recognized the voice as Breckett's. "I see the two of you have already met. Good thing too, I need this beast up and running ahead of schedule. I want to make good time today."

"Commander, you're early as well," Thusi made little attempt to hide the aggravation in her voice, "we'll have everything going in no more than an hour."

"Pilot and navigator are here too," Breckett said, "and the scientist decided to move in last night. Kyllen is here on the bridge helping me move a few things around. In fact, we're only missing Vaughn and Yasmin. Everyone is giddy to get going."

"I'll make that happen," Thusi said. She started grumbling something about disrespect under her breath, and trudged down the narrow corridor. Sarah followed at a crouch doing her best to ignore the ache in her knees. At least the corridor was well lit with mid-tone gray panels covering the bulkheads to protect the wiring and pipework beneath. The metal grating under her boots was coated with a textured material to prevent slipping. Already the engineering of the Villimath seemed far more thought out than anything Sarah had been on prior. It meant little coming from her, but it was a pleasant change of pace. There were numerous offshoots from the main corridor, but Thusi led her past all of them toward the center of the ship. At last, they turned down an even tighter corridor, and exited the passageway through another hatch. They found themselves in a vast chamber that reached up as high as the ship itself, and reached at least as far as the other side of the ship's hull. At the center of this chamber were two pyramids. The first was built from the floor and reached up toward the ceiling while the second was built from the ceiling and stretched down to the floor. The tips of the two pyramids were mere millimeters from touching one another leaving a small gap large enough for a glass chamber the size of a marble. Long tubes of translucent glass ran from the bases of each pyramid and disappeared through the bulkheads to go deeper into the ship. Blue coils could be seen beneath the glass, and hundreds of wires were bundled at the tubes' bases with thick cable tying them to the floor. A set of stairs connected to a walkway spanning over the tubes, and ended on the other side of the chamber.

"Right," Thusi said, and pointed toward a series of terminals protruding from the far wall, "calibrate those coils to seven hundred twenty-three, nine hundred seventy, and one hundred twelve, respectively. Exactly those numbers, and nothing else lest you want this day to end very abruptly. Understand?"

Sarah nodded, and forced a smile. Working for Thusi was not going to be an easy order, and she wondered if the Dwemyri was going to intentionally make it worse. The work wasn't what concerned her. After all she'd been through, it would take a lot to push Sarah to the edge in that regard. What worried Sarah was the looming judgment of her newfound boss. She'd have to show this Thusi just how capable she was.

4

After about an hour of further tasks involving calibrating, adjusting and replacing, Sarah found herself sitting on the stairs next to the chief engineer, and wiping sweat away from her brow. She had left her bag in the far corner with Eryn floating about to examine every corner of the engine room. Perhaps soon, she'd actually be introduced to the ship proper and shown to her room. A question came to mind, however, and Sarah could not prevent herself from asking it.

"Why the Villimath?" Sarah asked, "is there something special to that name?"

"My people made this ship," Thusi said. It was hard to read a Dwemyri's expression, but something in the chief engineer's eye made Sarah think she'd hit a sore spot. Thusi's tone changed from direct to somber. "Against all of our teachings, my team leapt at the opportunity to build this ship."

"What teachings are those?" Sarah asked. Then quickly added, "bullas."

"Religion was never something my kind was good at parting with," Thusi said, "so ingrained in our society that it dictates the very way we live. Even our scientists live by Morathism's most devout teachings. Our teachings tell us that our kind was recreated by Morathnu using the desecrated remains of a species long since passed. Because of this we hold an edict of recreate, never build from new. We salvage, we recycle, we rebuild, but we never start from scratch. To do so is to be wasteful. To be wasteful is to live in the shadow of Morathnu's unholy twin, the Lord of Despair and the Bringer of Decay, Villimath. When this ship was commissioned, we were forced to start anew. Not a single ounce of salvaged material is present in its design. Every bit of this ship is a sin which I shall forever bear the burden of. My colleagues have already paid their dues, and I'm afraid mine is on the docket."

"What happened to your colleagues?" Sarah asked.

"Enough, human," Thusi said, "be content with what I've already told you."

"Yasmine and Vaughn are on deck," Breckett's voice called over the comms, "everyone on the bridge."

Sarah and Thusi exchanged a glance. Sarah wanted to know more, her curiosity piqued, but she knew further questions would only lead to trouble with her boss. Forcing herself to let the topic be for now, she brushed off her knees to stand. Gathering her belongings and Eryn from the corner, Sarah waited on Thusi to lead the way. To her surprise, Thusi pointed at the main door rather than a crawl space.

"Work is done," she said, "now we walk like crew."

CHAPTER 14
- SARAH -

1

Sarah strode through the Villimath like a child through a toy store. The hallways were wide enough for three adults to stand abroad, and the ceiling high enough that Sarah would have to jump to touch it with the tips of her fingers. Colored lines were painted on the bulkheads to indicate the location of various parts of the ship. The red line led back to the engine room while a blue line indicated the bridge. She wasn't sure about the other colors, but Sarah guessed she'd find out soon enough. They followed the blue line around a corner, and up a narrow ladder to the third deck. According to Thusi, there was an elevator somewhere in the ship as well, but she only let herself use it when she was carrying or moving something. Sarah guessed the chief engineer expected the same standards to be carried out by her. She started to wonder how much supervision Thusi intended to have over her. At least when she was working on Kara Corp stations, Sarah had the freedom of solitude and was only held accountable every several months.

Upon reaching the bridge, Sarah found it to be smaller than she expected for a ship of this size. Oblong and oval, the bridge was built with a no-nonsense design. One end narrowed down to the cockpit where the Bile couple lingered and watched the others, while the other end was a simple command chair with hundreds of holograms floating around it each with a separate set of data. Several terminals were built into the bulkheads stretching between the two, but the rest of the bridge was the utilitarian gray paneling adorning the rest of the Villimath. Eryn beeped, and gave into the drone's original programing to zoom from one end to the other examining every nook and cranny. The drone garnered more than a few looks from the rest of the crew, but no one said anything. The entire crew lingered around the edges of the bridge, and watched Breckett who stood behind the chair and leaned on its back with both hands. Their captain watched everyone in turn with those black eyes. His gold irises glinted each time they moved from one person to the other, and Sarah realized they were probably more than just aesthetics.

Sarah looked around, realized who she was looking for, and forced her attention back to Breckett. A pretty face and mysterious aura weren't something she needed to be distracted by. Besides, it appeared Parker hadn't arrived yet. As if on cue, the ship's scientist strolled in as if the world waited on her. In this case, it did. Breckett nodded once he confirmed his whole crew was accounted for. He moved from standing behind the chair, to taking a seat. Sinking into it as though he'd belonged to the chair his whole life, Breckett tapped a screen on his armrest to bring up a holo-feed. A bright hologram display appeared in the center of the bridge, and gave the crew a view of a planetary system. Each of them was awash in blue light as their commander zoomed in on a single planet. It was the second planet from the system's star out of the five total, and Breckett pointed at something floating not far from the planet's orbit. It was a ship, and Sarah realized it was the target of their mission.

"We have our coordinates," Breckett said, "and all of you are professionals. I expect I don't need to tell you how to do your jobs. Ziven put enough credits into this operation to run several small businesses into the ground with debt, and I expect each of you to make his investments worth it. We arrive onsite in five days."

"Five?" Parker asked, "Those coordinates would take two weeks to reach from here, even for a military vessel."

"Five days," Breckett said, and he exchanged a glance with Thusi. "Ziven was vague on the details of this ship, but he assured me the Dwemyri who built it made a breakthrough in jump tech. It's a secret that died with them making this the only ship of its kind. Like I said, enough credits to sink most of his businesses."

Sarah looked around for the reactions of the other crew, finding the information hard to believe herself. She caught Vaughn watching her, but he looked away as soon as she noticed. Caution would need to be taken around that man whether he intended ill will or not. The Bile couple both had stupid grins on their faces as if they were just now realizing how much power they had been given to play with. Lucas particularly looked like a teenager with a new sports car. Yasmin was the air of indifference while Kyllen was as wide eyed as wide eyed got.

"That being said," Breckett continued, "there were still corners cut during the recruitment process, and a few things were overlooked. We have no idea what may be waiting for us on that ship, and we now have knowledge of Skren being sighted in the area. Vaughn and myself are the only two on board with any experience storming a ship which is at least five members less than I'd like to have available. Beggars can't be choosers, however, and each of you are considered indispensable in your roles, so I'm asking for one volunteer. You'll be personally trained by Vaughn and myself to be somewhat combat ready, and your role will be purely for support when in the field."

Kyllen stepped forward swept up by all of the excitement. Holding a fist to his chest in some sort of mock salute he said, "I volunteer captain. I won't let you down."

"Nope," Breckett said, "not you. We need our tech up to speed at all times, and you'd be little more than a liability in the field. Doc? I could use a combat medic should things get hairy."

"I've seen enough combat for a lifetime," Yasmin said, "I think I'll stick to what I was hired for this time."

Breckett glanced around further, ignoring the crestfallen young Groal who slinked back to the edge of the bridge while avoiding eye contact with anyone. Lucas and Lexi both looked at the floor, and Parker pursed her lips. Sarah glanced at Thusi who shook her head at her, and muttered a warning. If she went, she could find her brother first hand. She'd be able to find out for herself what had happened to him. Besides, she'd seen the horrors of deep space, and she doubted whatever they'd find on a derelict ship could compare. Stepping forward, she locked eyes with the captain. The golden irises glittered as they appraised her. Without so much as a word, Breckett nodded. It was settled then.

"Back to your posts," he said, "we launch in thirty."

2

The launch was successful, though Sarah's part was minimal. Thusi set her to watching a small terminal outside of the engine room to look out for any anomalies in the readings. She was told even a slight shift in the numbers could have dire consequences, but Sarah knew she was just being kept out of the way. Only a brief announcement over the comms was any indication that the ship had even performed a jump which Sarah found to be impressive in its own right. Once the jump was completed, all systems were marked as normal, and the Villimath's course was locked in, the crew was given the rest of the day to settle in. At last, Thusi dismissed Sarah to find her cabin.

A notification flared on Sarah's wrist, and a message popped up from Thusi as Sarah wandered down the wide corridor. She had decided to follow the yellow line and see where that took her, but Thusi's message changed her mind. Each of the crew members had been assigned their own cabins, to Sarah's relief, and hers was on the second deck. All she needed to do was follow the green line, and her cabin number was four. Shifting her bag over her shoulder, she tapped the lens of Eryn with her free hand.

"Looks like we have a new home for a bit," she said, "probably not big enough for you to explore though. Sorry in advance."

Sarah thought about taking the elevator up, but decided against it. Not that she had any qualms with going against the chief engineer's will, but if she got caught there was no way of telling what Thusi may have her do as a repercussion. She found the closest ladder instead. Passing by Kyllen on the way there, she found the boy still sulking. He kept his eyes on the floor as he headed down the opposite direction, and avoided acknowledging her. The thought did occur to her to say something in an attempt to lighten his mood, or cheer the boy up, but what could she say? After what Breckett had said to him, she'd be hard pressed to find something encouraging enough to bring him out of his stupor. Besides, it wasn't her place. She was only on this ship out of self-interest. Cheering up a teenager did not fall under that self-interest. Eryn beeped at her as Kyllen disappeared around a bend.

"No," she said, "not my problem."

Eryn beeped again, and hovered closer to her head.

"No," she said again, "he's a kid. He'll find any argument he can to continue sulking."

Another beep. Sarah could see the corridor with the cabin doors just ahead, and sighed. Looking back over her shoulder, Kyllen was nowhere to be seen, but she knew she could catch up to him if she wanted. Eryn gave one last beep, and Sarah could have slapped the drone out of the air. She sighed again, heavier this time, and shifted her bag to the other shoulder before turning back the way she came. Sure enough, Kyllen was easy to catch up to. She slowed to walk shoulder to shoulder with him. He swept a stray hair from out of his eyes, and gave her a sideways glance.

"You're more than that, you know," Sarah said, "don't let it get to you."

"No, he's right," Kyllen said, "I'd be a liability."

"And outside of Breckett's words, what makes you believe it?" Sarah asked.

"Everything," Kyllen said, "I'm only here to fix trinkets. I'm a nobody with no prospects, destined to work a small kiosk in the depths of some foreign market."

"You fixed Eryn. That makes you seem pretty competent to me," Sarah said, but winced at her own words. She tried to fix the situation by adding, "a lot of people start small before finding their niche."

"I'm cornering myself into a saturated market," Kyllen said, "and what niche could I find at this stage?"

"You'll know one thing, at least," Sarah said.

"Oh?" Kyllen asked, "and what's that?"

"You'll know what you don't want to do with your life," she said. That earned Sarah a snort, and a small twist of his lip that she was going to count as a smile. She could mark it down as a small victory. Kyllen stopped walking, and flicked a strand of dark hair to hang on the other side of his antler. He scrunched his face in thought, but nodded.

"Think about it," Sarah said, "you've got a lot ahead of you yet. Besides, Ziven hired you for a reason. Maybe you're simply the best there is."

She decided to leave him with that, and headed back down the hallway. She could feel his eyes lingering on her back as she walked, and Sarah did her best not to hurry. Having done what she could, all she wanted was to check out her cabin. Selfish, Sarah knew, but at least she had put in a little effort. Eryn would have to be happy with that. Indeed, the little drone remained quiet all the back to her cabin door. Instead of the usual code-based panel, the door contained a small optical lens at its center. Unsure of what to do, Sarah glanced around the door for a method of activation. In doing so, something triggered on its own and a green light beamed from the lens to shine in her eye. A confirming beep sounded, and the door slid open. Impressed that the builders would go so far as to have each cabin tied to the individual's scan, Sarah glanced around the corridor before stepping in to be sure no one saw her acting like a confused child. She'd be mortified if Thusi saw her struggling to open a door.

The lights flicked on as she walked through, and Sarah found her cabin to be much larger than she had anticipated. Eryn zoomed past to examine every centimeter, and Sarah gave one final glance into the hallway before closing the door behind her. Her cabin was a rectangle wide enough to not only fit a sizable bed, which was cut into a high-ceiling cubby on the left wall, but a writing desk as well. It was fixed to the right wall with enough surface space to do any kind of work she thought she might need. Honeycombed holes were cut into the far wall for the storage of clothing and other items, and next to it was an open door leading into a small washroom. She had to admit this was the largest room she'd ever had the luxury of living in. Eryn jetted out from the bed nook to go explore the bathroom, and Sarah wandered over to look in as well. Even the bathroom was of a decent size with a full shower and spacious sink and toilet. Letting out a sigh of content, Sarah went back to the bed and dropped her bag on the floor. With a plop, she rolled onto the soft mattress and stretched out across the sheets. Just as she began to doze off, the faint sounds of Eryn's engines whirring in the background, a heavy fist thudded against her door.

"*Sarah, we have a problem,*" she mumbled to herself in her best impression of Gayle as she lurched to her feet. She would have laughed if it weren't for the tainted memories that followed. Instead, she called to the door without fully getting to her feet, rubbing her eye with a knuckle. "What is it?"

"It's Dr. Jung," the voice called back, "or just Yasmin. I don't care which. I'm running preliminary checks on everyone before shit hits the fan. You're up."

"Coulda just called over comms," Sarah said, and rocked back to gain enough momentum to lurch to her feet. She opened the door to an annoyed looking Yasmin still in her black and orange leather jacket. All of her hair was down, however, and it hung just above her shoulders in a dark tangle. She looked as though she'd been working through the night to keep everything going. Arms folded across a broad chest, and thick jaw set in a way that made Sarah think Yasmin was ready to take a punch, the doctor did not have the air of a person who was willing to put up with an argument.

"Lot like this is smarter than that, and more stubborn" she said, "too many ways to find an excuse unless I come knocking to collect you directly."

The doctor had a point. While under Kara Corp's jurisdiction, Sarah witnessed many flee at the mention of a checkup. Most saw it as a waste of time when most of the stations were outfitted with auto-med stations. Even when the presence of the medical stations were not guaranteed, a vast majority of the prisoners, or *employees* as Kara Corp referred to them, saw a routine checkup as an inconvenience at best. Conceding the point, Sarah nodded. Yasmin relaxed a little, gave a brief nod in return, and started back down the corridor. Letting out a yawn, Sarah pulled on a cardigan and followed.

3

The metal table was cold, but she sat motionless as Yasmin ran a small hand-held device over the top of her scalp. It made mechanical and static clicking sounds with each pass, and Yasmin would glance at a display on her wrist with every new noise. With Yasmin this close, Sarah couldn't help but notice the faint smell of perfume. The flowery scent contradicted the otherwise machismo aesthetic the doctor exuded, but Sarah found it to be quite pleasant. It was a far more interesting scent than the sterilized odor the medical center was filled with. The white walls, and silver coated instruments lining the spotless counters filled Sarah with disquiet. She hated this kind of setting. Too many horrible things were witnessed by white walls such as these, and the pungent smell of disinfectant only served to imply the need to cover something up. The too-bright lights overhead were intrusive in every way, and the metal tables patients were forced to sit on were always cold. Sarah noticed something she hadn't thought of before, or noticed the lack of something.

"All the credits in the world, and they couldn't just buy an auto-med station?" Sarah asked. "Seems a bit weird, no?"

"I thought the same thing," Yasmin said, and stepped away from Sarah to lean on the counter. She set the device down, and started to scroll through the readout on her wrist. "Medical gear is an odd thing to cut corners on, so I did a bit of digging. Turns out there's a monopoly on the tech used to make auto-med stations, and the company that makes them is very particular about who they sell their products to. Some company named Sana Industries. The name was about all I could find out about them other than the products they sell. Anything Vulture related they blacklist."

"They blacklist Vultures?" Sarah asked, "seems harsh."

"My guess is they're too good at the whole reverse engineering thing," Yasmin said, "makes sense if you're trying to keep sole ownership over a technology. Before I get too distracted, we need to go over these results. There are some items in here we need to address before I can clear you for field work."

"Clear me for field work? As in let me join Breckett when

searching the ship?" Sarah asked.

"Exactly," Yasmin said, "if I don't give you the greenlight, Breckett finds a new volunteer, and there are a few things I've noticed here that are worth keeping you out of the line of duty."

"Like what?" Sarah asked. She thought she had a rather good idea as to what Yasmin thought was an issue, but she was upset enough to ask the question anyway.

"Micro striations on the prefrontal cortex and amygdala to start," Yasmin said, "the abundance of munmos still present in your system, and not to mention the incalculable amount of PTSD you're dealing with."

"You got all that from that device?" Sarah asked, and pointed at the small object the doctor had left on the counter. "In that small amount of time as well?"

"No," Yasmin said, and picked up the rectangular object to turn it over in her hand, "it didn't have to. Doctor Myrddin sent me his report along with a few suggestions. This just told me your blood sugar is a little high, and you need to eat more calcium."

"Whatever happened to patient confidentiality?" Sarah asked. "I thought doctors were supposed to swear some kind of oath or something."

"I'm your doctor now," Yasmin said, "and Myrddin thought it was important I know what's going on with you, and he was right. I let you out into the field with no questions asked, you're just as likely to get someone else killed as to help save the mission. I can't have that on my conscience."

"So, what are you suggesting?" Sarah asked, "stay put on the ship, and be a good little engineer?"

"Drop the attitude, Sarah," Yasmin said, "I'm trying to help."

Taking a deep breath, Sarah closed her eyes and inhaled through her nose to exhale through her mouth. Yasmin was right, she knew, but the thought of being shirked aside due to her past angered her. She'd be damned if she let an opportunity to confront Hector first thing slip away just before she had the chance to grab it. She let go of her anger, and asked the question again with a better tone. The tension eased from Yasmin's shoulders, and the doctor even put on a faint smile.

"Thank you," she said, "what I'm suggesting is a daily practice monitored by myself. I want you in here every evening before you head to bed. I'm no clinical psychologist, I'm a field medic turned doctor, but I know a good way of mitigating your symptoms until you can see the right person. Deal?"

"Deal," Sarah nodded. She knew this was going to be a good thing overall. "Think it'll help with my nightmares?"

"I promise it will," Yasmin said, "I've done it myself for the same reasons. Seeing as we have only five days until we reach the ship, we need to start now. Here, change into this while I get your meds ready."

Yasmin pulled open a drawer and walked a bundle over to Sarah. Placing it in her hands, Sarah had to unfold it and stare at it for a moment before she figured out what it was, a wet suit. Confused, she looked past the suit she held up in front of her, and gave the doctor a pointed look. Yasmin nodded, and turned back to the counter. She started to pull a few things from drawers and cupboards, and set them out on the counter. Having already agreed to this, Sarah hopped off the examination table and started to change. The thing was tight enough to make her movements stiff, but Sarah cinched up the front, nonetheless. Once done, she waited while Yasmin was busy mixing something into a transparent plastic cup.

"Over this way," Yasmin said, and pointed Sarah toward a narrow door at the back of the medical ward. She was led through the door and into another room that was much darker. A single tube ran the length of the ceiling to shine pale blue light into a room that was cold enough to be a meat locker. On either side of them, the walls were lined with large gray doors that reminded Sarah of a morgue.

"This where you keep the bodies?" Sarah asked. She meant it as a joke, but did a double take when the doctor nodded. "Really?"

"Yes," Yasmin said. "However, they double up as cryo pods should the need arise."

"You're going to put me in cryo sleep then?" Sarah asked.

"Is this a trick to keep me out of the way? Did Thusi put you up to this?"

"Nothing like that," Yasmin said, "I had the back one ret-rofitted for our purpose today."

They stopped to stand in front of the last door, and Sarah noticed the compartment section was much larger than the others. Yasmin opened the door to let Sarah glance inside, and she could see a dark liquid filled the bottom of the chamber. In the dim light, it was difficult to tell if the liquid was water or something else, but there was a faint smell of salt.

"Wait here," Yasmin said, and the doctor went back into the other room leaving Sarah to try and guess as to what they were about to do. She wasn't sure if she wanted to touch the liquid, or not. Best practice in deep space was to never touch anything you weren't one hundred percent sure on, and even though this was a medical ward, Sarah wasn't about to take her chances. Instead, she waited patiently for the doctor to return. When Yasmin did, she pushed a cart in front of her with a complicated jumble of devices atop it. She wheeled the cart over to Sarah, and grabbed a slim headband from atop the pile.

"Put this on," Yasmin said, "and make sure it settles over your temples."

The doctor motioned with her hand to indicate what she meant, and Sarah did the best she could to comply. The head-band was cold to the touch, but the inside of it was coated with a soft rubber material that adhered to the skin of her head. Once in place, Sarah could tell it wouldn't slip.

"What is this for?" Sarah asked, or tried to, but the doctor was busy turning on different pieces of equipment. A holo-feed popped up from atop the cart and displayed a number of differ-ent graphs which Sarah had no inclination as to what they meant. Next, the doctor held out the plastic cup from earlier.

"I need you to drink this" she said, "then I need you to climb in there and lie down. Be sure to spread out your limbs as best you can. The water will keep you afloat."

"What's in this?" Sarah asked. She swirled the cup around, and watched the liquid slosh. It had a strange hue to it.

"Several things," Yasmin said. "A mix of nootropics, a small amount of muscle relaxer, and an even smaller dose of psychedelics."

"You're drugging me," Sarah said. It wasn't a question, but she gave the doctor a confused look.

"Technically speaking," Yasmin said, "but not in the way you think. This isn't a joy ride through dreamland, but we're adjusting your neuropathways. Consider this a mental cleansing of sorts. Now, get in. I'll be monitoring everything from here, so I assure you, you'll be safe."

Sarah gave the chamber a dubious look, but Yasmin gave her a reassuring nod. Hoisting her left leg over the threshold first, Sarah started to climb in. The liquid was cold, frigid in fact, so much so that Sarah wondered how it wasn't ice. She almost climbed right back out, but decided to follow through. There were too many reasons she needed to do this to back out at the first sign of a little cold. She hauled herself all the way into the chamber, the ceiling just high enough for her to crouch which submersed Sarah up to her shoulders. The cold was a shock to her system she wasn't expecting. Thought was near impossible, and her limbs didn't want to function. The chamber door closed behind her with a thud, and Sarah was engulfed by the dark.

"Splay out," Yasmin's voice chimed from a speaker on the headband. It took Sarah a moment to comprehend what the doctor had told her to do, but after she repeated the command Sarah began to lean back in the liquid and spread out her limbs. The cold bit into Sarah's scalp as her head bobbed, and soon she was floating. There was no sound other than the noise Sarah herself made, and she felt weightless with her arms and legs spread out wide.

"I need you to do your best to follow along," Yasmin said, "then I'll leave you to it for a bit so your body can do its job. First, take a long deep breath through your nose. Fill your lungs until you think you've reached max capacity. Next, take a second sharp breath in through your nose to go beyond what you think your lungs can handle. Lastly, exhale through your mouth slowly and deliberately until you've emptied your lungs."

Sarah tried to focus through the cold, but thought was

getting further and further out of reach. Yasmin had to repeat each step a number of times before Sarah managed to do as she was told. Breathing in through her nose, she filled her lungs until she thought they'd burst, and took in another sharp inhale before letting all of it out through her mouth in one long breath. She did this several times as the doctor's concoction started to set in. Soon there was nothing. Thought was a concept too foreign to grasp. There was no telling if she was breathing as Yasmin had directed, or if she was breathing at all. There was no cold, no sense of self, no Sarah. Only the all-consuming blackness of the void existed. Nothingness was the only truth, and even that truth became a lie as the entire galaxy bloomed before her. Billions upon billions of stars spread out in a never-ending cosmos, and it was as much a part of her as she was it. *She.* A concept so foreign to this entity that it could almost laugh. In fact, it did though no sound was created. Sound was a physical construct, and here amongst the cosmos there was no physicality. Sweeping through the stars was as easy as a fish swimming downriver. It was natural. Everything was as it should be, had been, always will be. Except, Sarah noted, a black spot somewhere far off to the edge of the galaxy. A dark smudge across the twinkling mural consumed the light around it in an angry feast. Sarah remained at peace, however, as she knew someone would take care of it. Not her, not even someone in her lifetime, but someone. There was a certainty to it she couldn't explain.

As soon as it had started, the experience ended. Blue light invaded Sarah's peripherals, and she became aware of existence once more. Cold ripped through her body, and Sarah gasped. She could see the ceiling of the chamber, and hear Yasmin's voice saying her name. Strong hands reached beneath her armpits, and pulled Sarah to the edge of the door where she was then lifted out. Shivering to her core, Sarah did the best she could to crawl out of the chamber without help, but Yasmin saw through her attempts to not look helpless and hoisted Sarah through the door. A bundle of warm towels waited for her. Yasmin pulled the headband off, and placed another heated towel over Sarah's head. Thought was beginning to return, and Sarah had to squint at the light she once thought dim.

"All done," Yasmin said, and rubbed Sarah's back. "That was a good first session."

Uncontrollable shivering set in, and once the quakes started, there was no putting an end to them. Sarah gained enough mobility to wrap her arms around her shoulders, and rubbed with frantic intent. She turned to the doctor, and scowled.

"No one else had checkups, did they?" She asked.

Yasmin's laugh was answer enough. Instead of apologizing, however, she tasked herself with helping Sarah dry off.

CHAPTER 15
- JAX -

1

With a jaw cracking yawn and a languid stretch, Jax rolled out of her little cubby she called a bed. She pulled on the spare rags Rooth had called clothes which sagged on her much smaller frame. Wrapping a brown sash several times around her waist, Jax fastened it near the side of her hip, and rolled her sleeves up to her wrists. She still swam in the clothes, but it was the best she could do for now. According to Rooth, the Sheet Skimmer would arrive at the outpost today which was supposedly planet side. Jax wanted little more than a chance to be off this ship even if it were only for a few moments. It would give her more time to digest her situation, and help her come to a decision on what her next course of action should be. Increasingly, Jax was leaning into the idea of staying on this side of the galaxy, but something still nagged at her. Something felt unfinished. Her short-lived relationship with Sarah could be part of it, but Jax knew better than to torment herself with things that could never be. It had to be something else. Planet leave might help her figure that out.

Not fully awake, Jax had to lean one hand against the ship's bulkhead as she walked down the corridor while wiping sleep from her eyes with the other. She had to be careful where she put her hand due to the lack of wall panels leaving open wiring and pipework throughout. Jax learned the hard way that some of those pipes were quite hot. She bumped into Percy halfway to what these people called a bridge, though Jax would just call it a cockpit given its size, and the boy greeted her with a gap-toothed smile followed by a mumbled, "good morning." Waving back through another yawn, she let Percy walk by her side as they went along. The boy was a bit of a goof, but Jax found that to be a pleasant change for once. He hummed a strange lullaby to himself as they walked. She thought about telling him to quit, but reminded herself she was a guest on their ship and thus needed to keep her annoyances in check. When they arrived, Rector was already in the pilot's seat. He too was humming to himself, but with his voice the tune took a much more ominous tone. Something felt off about him. He had numerous displays pulled up, but he didn't seem to be looking at anything at all. Rector just sat there with a faraway look, and hummed.

"Rector?" Jax asked, "everything okay?"

The man leapt out of his skin at the sound of her voice, and twisted around in his chair. The thing was a worn mess of cracked brown leather and frayed hems, but it fit right in with the rest of the cockpit, and the rest of the ship for that matter. Scavengers should know how to take better care of things. These people wouldn't fit in even with Vultures. It took Rector a moment for his eyes to focus on the two of them. Once he recognized who had spoken, he cracked a grin, and coughed a wet laugh.

"Sorry dear, good morning Percy, must have dozed off," he said. "Gave me quite the start, but you'll have to forgive me. Didn't get much sleep last night. Terrible, terrible nightmares."

"I had bad dreams too, papa," Percy said, and slipped past Jax to go sit in the chair next to his father, "I dreamt the ship was living, and it shot us all out the airlocks."

Rector patted Percy's mop of black hair with a crooked hand, and said, "ship's nothing but a hunk of tin, Percy, don't you worry."

Jax told herself it was a coincidence. It had to be. Coincidences happened, and not everything had some kind of deeper meaning. She looked over the two of them while they spoke, and out the cockpit's window. Fortunately, Rector had the particle shield raised to give her a full view of the space outside. In the distance, Jax could see the small marble that was the planet of destination. It glowed a sickly green in the light of the system's star, and she wondered what kind of atmosphere would cause that. Finding the perfect reason to change the subject, Jax pointed it out. Turning to look, Rector snorted.

"Most of the planet is toxic to humans" he said, "swamps spill out bile and gas all day long. Only sentient species capable of breathing in its atmosphere are the Oldathians. Small, pudgy folk, they are. Everyone else lives indoors."

"Oldathians?" Jax tasted the name, speaking each syllable slowly and with purpose, "I've never heard of Oldathians before."

"Nor would you," Rector said, "you're a stranger to this side of the galaxy. The Oldathians came under the reign of the Suttack a long, long time ago. Never left this small cluster of stars because of it. Most of them stay right there." Rector jabbed a thumb at the small marble floating in the void. "Little outpost called Gnov. Can't remember the name of the planet, to be honest with ya. I just call it Puck."

"It's called Huebos," Rooth said from behind Jax. She hadn't noticed the elderly woman sneak up, and it was Jax's turn to jump. Rooth gave Jax a comforting gesture before squeezing past into the cockpit. Waving a hand at Percy, she said, "come dear, let me sit."

Percy shuffled to his feet, and moved aside for his surrogate mother to sit. Taking his place, Rooth set to opening several display feeds and entering commands into each. Yawing, she wiped her nose, entered another command into a side terminal, then raised both arms into a stretch. She wiggled her wrists at the end of it before settling back in.

"I had the most horrible dreams last night," she said. Jax, face draining of blood, reminded herself that it was surely a coincidence.

2

The descent down to the planet's surface was far smoother than Jax would have expected. Percy and herself were strapped into seats behind the pilot's chair as the two elderlies navigated the process. To their credit, the work was flawless. They touched down on a landing pad which looked worse off than even the Sheet Skimmer. It was little more than a massive slab of pocked concrete surrounded by other ships that Jax thought would be better suited for scrap metal. Glancing through the window, she could tell the surrounding buildings were not much better off. In fact, some *were* made of scrap metal. She wondered if run down equipment operating on its last leg was just what she needed to expect from here on out. If she decided to stay, she might as well grow accustomed to the local aesthetic. Rector powered down the engines, and gave them all the thumbs up to unbuckle. Getting out of his own seat, he handed each of them a clear mask with a small, mechanical cylinder fixed to the side.

"No need for a full suit," he said more to Jax than anyone else, "but you will need to put on the ol' oxygen masks while outside. I've got some errands to run myself which I'll need Percy's strong arms to help me carry, but Rooth will take you to the doctor we know. Sound good?"

Jax nodded, and returned the smile Rooth gave her. She had to tie her hair up before the mask would fit which required Rooth's assistance given Jax had neglected her mass of tangles for nearly a week, hardly bothering to rinse it when she bathed. It wasn't her fault the Sheet Skimmer's "shower" was little more than a sink stuck to the floor. Perhaps there would be somewhere in this outpost where she could truly bathe. Pulling on the mask, she cinched it tight around the back of her head, and gave Rooth the thumbs up to let her know it was secured. The four of them exited the ship from a side hatch, a ramp lowering from the hull to allow them unhindered passage. Jax caught a full view of the outpost as they strode down the ramp, and she started to reconsider the strength of that word. Gnov seemed more a ramshackle tent-city than a full-blown outpost, but if this family wanted to call it an outpost who was she to argue? Only about half of the structures Jax could see were made of solid materials such as metal or wood. Most were, in fact, basic tents propped up and open on one side to allow for easy visitations. Beyond was nothing more than drooping trees, and festering marshlands all obscured by a thick, green haze clinging to the air. Her hopes for a decent shower were slipping away with each step. Jax never thought she'd take CRG mining colonies for granted.

A figure waited for them at the bottom of the ramp. Short and rotund, the figure looked wider than it was tall. A forest of black quills protruded from the top of the individual's bulbous head and thick hands. The rest of its body was covered by a black overcoat which was secured around its considerable waist by a red sash. The blood red of the cloth was the most vibrant thing Jax had seen since arriving to this part of the galaxy. More noticeable was the nose. Flattened to its face, the nostrils bloomed outward in a star pattern leaving a series of holes where the human nose would be. The look of the Oldathians was altogether off putting, but Jax did her best not to make a face.

"Humans!" The squat man said. His voice sounded as though he were in a permanent state of congestion. "What business do humans have on Gnov?"

Both Rooth and Rector looked about the landing pad with an air of caution before Rector asked, "are there Suttack about?"

"No, no, we've been gnalprip free for nearly a cycle now" the oldathian said, "you'll have no concerns about that here."

Jax's translator implant stumbled over the name he had used, but Rector seemed to find it some sort of amusing joke. Percy leaned in close to Jax, and whispered, "he just called the Suttack a rude name for an animal's butt."

"We're friends of the practitioner," Rooth said. She, on the other hand, did not seem amused. "We thought to stop by for a visit, and resupply. You won't deny us that much."

"Wouldn't dream of it," the oldathian said, "he's out right now, but I'm sure he wouldn't mind if you waited in his office. Welcome to Gnov."

3

Walking within the outpost was about as charming as seeing it from the outside. As Jax's breathing mask misted over, cleared, then misted over again with each new breath, even the purified air tasted stale and bitter on the tongue. By this point, Rector had taken Percy and the two had split off to find supplies, though Jax wondered what kind of supplies would be available in such a dreary place as this. Rooth was leading Jax by the hand toward one of the larger buildings in the outpost. Made of some form of dark concrete it looked a sturdy comparison in the midst of such temporary dwellings. The structure had the appearance of a tall military bunker, and Jax wondered if that might be its original purpose. The old woman hummed to herself as they walked. Jax hadn't recognized the tune, but there was something that tickled the edges of familiarity. Many songs sounded the same, so perhaps it was little more than that.

Reaching the building's front entrance, Rooth knocked twice on the front door. Given it was made of steel, each knock rang out with a loud thud. Several moments passed by without answer, and Rooth knocked again. This time the door clicked and swung open to reveal a dark office beyond. A taller oldathian leaned against the door in a white lab coat. Their quills shone with a red hue, and their nose was a different pattern than the previous one Jax had encountered. A fraction slenderer, but only a fraction, the oldathian eyed them with suspicion.

"We're here to see the practitioner," Rooth said, "we're friends of his."

"Not here," the oldathian said.

"I understand that," Rooth said, "but can we wait for him inside?"

The oldathian looked back into the dark office as if it were weighing its options. Turning back to the pair, it squinted its eyes and furrowed its forehead with reproach, but nodded. Rooth radiated a warm smile and dragged Jax through the door before the oldathian could change its mind. Jax gave it a spiteful smile in contrast to Rooth's warm one. She wasn't sure why, but it felt good given the circumstance. It took her eyes a few moments to adjust to the dim light, but soon Jax was able to make out the mismatched furniture resting atop a featureless stone floor. Another steel door was inset on the opposite side of the room which Jax assumed led deeper into the building. A small table sat at the far end as a mock reception counter, and as Rooth and Jax took their seats, the practitioner's assistant closed the door, walked around to the back side of the table, and sat down in a chair that looked too thin to hold its weight. The position allowed the oldathian to watch them from across the room. It didn't bother Jax in the slightest. If the mistrustful assistant wanted to waste its time and energy watching them, let it. Rooth started humming again. This time, Jax was sure she'd heard it somewhere before. Before she could pinpoint it, however, they were interrupted by the squeal of rusted hinges swinging open.

"Rooth!" A voice called from the far door. "How long has it been?"

"Ash!" Rooth called back, "at least half a cycle."

Another white lab coat strode through the far door. Ash's bulk swayed as he walked over to greet them, and his black quills glistened as if they had just been washed. Rooth stood, so Jax did the same even though the gesture made them tower over the doctor. He didn't seem to mind, and took Rooth's hand in both of his. He grinned at both of them with yellowed teeth stained green. Looking Jax up and down in a way that made her feel uneasy, Ash's numerous nostrils flared. Jax couldn't help but notice his assistant keeping a close eye on every interaction.

"And who might this be?" Ash asked. "Rooth, did you make a new friend?"

"Rescued her like a stray pup," Rooth said, and clapped Jax on the back with the hand that wasn't being clung to by the doctor. "I was hoping you could give Jax here a checkup."

Ash gave her another look, and Jax was beginning to regret how easily she agreed to come here. He gave Rooth a curt nod, and said, "of course, Rooth, anything for an old friend."

4

Jax sat on the wooden stool in the middle of what she would call a prison cell. The metal walls were clean, but dull, and all of the room's drawers and cupboards were on a set of wheels.

A bright cylindrical light hung from the concrete ceiling, and beamed down a harsh white that caused Jax to squint after being stuck in the dim waiting room. Practitioner Ash mumbled unintelligible words to himself as he scurried about the room. He snatched one device after another, pointing each one at Jax for a brief moment before moving on to another. He'd get a reading, say something under his breath, and pick out something new to test on her. At least she wasn't asked to undress. The way Ash had looked at her in the waiting room gave her cause for concern.

"One last thing before I finish up here," Ash said, and Jax's heart sank into her stomach. "Something keeps popping up in my scans, and I want to check what it is. Have you had any major brain surgeries? I get humans have neural implants for ID's and translators and whatnot, but anything you humans would consider out of the norm?"

A cold fear washed over her, but Jax shook her head. Ash tutted then waddled over to the far corner of the room. He wheeled a strange device out from behind one of the mobile cupboards. It looked like a large monitor affixed to the top of a tall pole with a metallic cone hanging from the side. Both the monitor and the cone were attached to a dial, and all three were interlinked by countless tubes and wires. This device too was on wheels, and they squeaked as he pulled the contraption close to her stool. Ash shifted the cone to be facing Jax as he glared up at the monitor. He twisted the dial this way and that way, and Jax could not help but hug herself in discomfort.

"If you could hold still for me," Ash said, "this will only take a moment."

Strange noises emanated from the cone as Ash shifted the dial, and pale light shone on his face from the monitor. From this angle, Jax couldn't see what was being displayed, but the practitioner's face looked grim. He tutted once more, and shut down the device. Face scrunched in thought, he looked as though he were searching for the right words to say. He'd open his mouth as if to speak, but close it again immediately. The indecision caused Jax to snap.

"What is it?" She asked. "Clearly there's something you

have to tell me. Probably bad by the look on your face."

"You're certain you've had no recent implant work?" Ash asked, "none whatsoever?" He spun the pole around so the monitor faced Jax. Turning it back on, he showed her what he had been looking at. Displayed on the monitor was a rotating image of her brain. On the left side, near where the back of her ear would be, was embedded a black object which looked to be some sort of stone. Its jagged edge cut into the side of her brain tissue, and black veins spiderwebbed from each of its tips to create a horrid mass of pulsing black veins. Jax reeled back.

"You sure that's my head you took a picture of?" Jax asked. Her only response was a grim look from Ash. He turned the monitor back toward himself, and stared at it. His grim expression turned sorer the longer he stared, and the sight of him made Jax anxious. She tried waiting for him to say something else, but he just kept looking at the monitor.

"So, what are you going to do about it?" She asked, "you're the doctor, aren't you able to do something about it?"

"I'm a doctor for my people," Ash said, "my knowledge of the human brain structure, I must admit, is too slim to attempt a procedure on the scale needed here."

"Then where can I find a doctor that can do this?" Jax asked. "I bet you know someone."

"You are human," Ash said, "this part of space is not kind to humans. Fly around in space for a while, and maybe you'll get lucky enough to find someone, but space is big. I wouldn't bet on those odds. Your best bet is to go back to human space if you can get there fast enough."

"Fast enough?" Jax asked, "what do you mean? How bad is this?"

Ash shrugged, and his expression turned apologetic. "Hard to say, but if that were an oldathian brain, I'd say you'd have no more than two cycles left. Maybe three if you're lucky, but once again I'd not bet on those odds."

Jax took a long breath and considered. This was bad, unbelievably bad, but she could find a way through it. She always did. It was one of the qualities she liked best about herself. Sarah wouldn't have given up either. Sarah would set that amazing jawline of hers into a stubborn lock, and find a course of action right then and there on the spot. But, Jax wasn't Sarah, and Sarah wasn't here. The thought rang like a funeral bell, and Jax slumped in her seat. Ash put a consolatory hand on her shoulder, and for some reason that irked her. He assumed she was going to die. Not only that, but die a sad, quiet little human with nowhere to go but the grave. A new determination boiled up from the depths of her newfound rage. She knew what she was going to do. Jax was going to get home, fix this shit, kill Gayle, and find Sarah. She'd fall to her knees if that's what it took to get Sarah back, but one problem at a time. First, she needed to find a way to get home, and at that moment Jax didn't care what lengths she'd have to go to in order to do so. Her eyes met the practitioners, and Ash seemed to see the rage behind them because he pulled his hand away as if burned.

"You'll keep this between us, won't you?" Jax asked. "I don't want poor Rooth to worry. And Percy, I don't want to think about what the news would do to him."

Ash looked too taken aback by the change of attitude to do more than nod. It didn't help that Jax's hands were quivering with anger. She glared at him until he nodded again, this time with more vigor, and a squeaked "of course."

"Good," she said, "that's a good doctor."

5

Jax had known what Gayle had done would have consequences. What she hadn't known was that her powers were slipping out while she slept. Her ability to play coy about the situation was at an end. She realized that as she delved into the deepest parts of Ash's mind, and the doctor started to dumbly hum a tune. It was the same tune Rooth and her family had been humming all morning, and it just now clicked as to why it had bothered Jax. It was a song her father used to hum to her to get her to fall asleep. Ash hummed it with his thick, black tongue stuck out of the side of his mouth while he stared off into nothing. Jax sat on the stool and concentrated on the practitioner's new reality. Jax didn't trust him to stay quiet, and she didn't trust what Rooth would do once she found out about Jax's impending death. She had a plan for the old woman and her family, and Jax couldn't take any unnecessary risks. Using her powers now shouldn't cut too much into her lifespan. This creature's mind was unusually soft for a professional who was supposed to have a firm grasp on reality. At first, she wasn't sure if she'd be able to use her powers on something that wasn't human, but it took little effort to find the truth of it. Ash stopped humming, and snapped back to a lucid state. Blinking as if he'd just woken up, he gave Jax a confused look before smiling.

"Clean bill of health," he said, "go let Rooth know the good news. Such good news it is, I think I might take a vacation to celebrate. A trip into the marshes sounds quite nice this time of year."

"I'm happy for you," Jax said, and released her hold over his thoughts.

She stood, brushed off the rags she wore as clothes, and led the doctor out of the prison cell and back into the waiting room. Rooth was busy chatting with the assistant, but stopped mid conversation once Jax stepped through the door. The old woman gave her an ugly, toothless smile, and waved Jax over. It was best if Jax saw her as ugly rather than homely. It was best if Jax came to despise the parasitic life forms this woman and her family had grown to be. They put the scavenging lifestyle to shame. It was best to see it that way because it made what she had to do easier. These weren't people, not *real* people, just insects that Jax would need to use as tools to get home.

The two of them put their masks back on before saying their goodbyes to the practitioner and his assistant. Jax didn't even mind the dirty look the assistant gave her on their way out the door. Ash would be taking him with on his vacation to the marshes. Should she feel bad? Probably, but right then Jax didn't care. Once they were outside, and the metal door swung shut behind them, Jax stopped Rooth before they got too far into the outpost.

"I'm going to split off for a bit," Jax said, "I want to look around before we leave, maybe find some new clothes so I don't have to keep stealing yours. Chaperoning me around like a lost child must be exhausting."

"Oh, I don't mind helping you about, dear," Rooth said, "if it's clothes you need, I can help you find a good store."

"No, no," Jax said, "I insist. Besides, it'll be nice to get on my own two feet for an hour or so. Just don't leave without me, alright?"

Rooth smiled, but it was a cautious expression. She took Jax's hand, and pressed something into her palm. "Fair enough, but take some of this with you. Folk on this planet don't trade in credits."

Rooth waddled off down the path and deeper into the ramshackle outpost before Jax bothered to look at what the woman had given her. In her hand was a collection of silvery roots. They were tangled up, but Jax assumed each root represented a certain sum of currency. She stuffed the roots in her pocket, though she knew she had no use for them. Jax had no intention of using money to get what she wanted. She took off down a side street to be certain to avoid crossing paths with Rooth. Hopefully this outpost would have what she sought out. There was no way of telling what kind of laws this planet or these people might have, but every species had one thing in common, and Jax was relying on that one thing to be true here as well. Violence was inevitable, and the inevitable was profitable. Somewhere on this soggy mess of a planet had to be an arms dealer, or at least someone who could give her an under-the-counter trade. She strolled down the streets poking her head into different storefronts and kiosks all while pretending not to look for anything in particular. She garnered a few strange glances from the locals, but no one bothered her.

She found what she was looking for a few streets down in a tent that looked about ready to fall in with a strong gust of wind. Green canvas sagged atop wooden poles, and numerous racks were set up in rows that stretched back to a small folding table at the back. A one-eyed oldathian sat at the table with a hand resting on a lockbox. His good eye looked her up and down, as she walked through the tent flap. Jax guessed it to be a hunter's shop of sorts with all kinds of ropes and strange devices she did not recognize coating the racks. She knew the look of one thing, however, and that one thing was a gun. At the back of the tent were three racks filled to the brim with varying types of arms ranging from long rifles to short-barreled things. Jax didn't pretend to know the correct nomenclature for firearms because to her the names didn't matter. What did matter was what they offered her - a ticket home.

"Can I help you?" The oldathian asked. His one eye was filled with suspicion, and his mouth was curled into a tight frown. A cockroach scurried across the table in front of him, but he ignored it. "Don't think I have much for humans here."

"You can actually," Jax said. She set to work immediately, honing in on the man's reality, his chain of thought. The attitude from his voice was all she needed to get a fix on this oldathian's personality, and once she had a fix it was over. She was discovering a trick to twisting someone's reality enough to alter their perception about you, and an even bigger trick to get them to act in your favor. At least, she thought she was figuring out a trick. With as little practice with her new powers as she'd had, any sort of progress seemed like a breakthrough. The oldathian began babbling about Sarah, and Jax realized what she was doing. She refocused her attention, and got the one-eyed man to wander over to one of the weapon racks. He shuffled through a few items before settling on one. He stooped over, grabbed something from the back of the rack, and walked it over to her. Placing the item in her hand without question, he wandered back to his table, and took a seat.

Jax turned the gun over in her hand. It wasn't pretty, but it didn't need to be. It looked little more than a pair of cylinders, one on top of the other, welded together with a pistol grip bolted on. On the top cylinder toward its center were a series of levers. She'd seen this type of weapon before, but finding one here was a surprise. When one pulled the trigger, the levers would push down several lenses and emit a high beam of energy. A dangerous weapon to bring aboard a ship, but Jax had few other options. Stuffing the pistol into an oversized pocket, she rewarded the shopkeeper with a smile, though she knew it didn't matter. Ducking out of the tent, it was time to find some clothes for her cover story.

CHAPTER 16
- SARAH -

1

Sweat beaded down Sarah's temples and slicked the back of her neck. Her tank top clung to her back with perspiration, and her glove wrapped hands radiated heat like small furnaces as she circled her opponent. Little noise came from either of them with bare feet padding in steady rhythm across a thick-cushioned floor. The Villimath's training room was large enough to give both Sarah and Breckett plenty of room to maneuver with the walls and floor lined with a blue pad that was soft enough to dampen a blow, but sturdy enough to prevent balance issues while walking upon. Breckett's tattoos glistened as he stalked the room, sweat coating every centimeter of his skin. He wore an identical outfit to Sarah with short, black athletic shorts, and a thin tank. With all of his tattoos, however, he almost looked fully dressed. He swept a strand of white hair out of his black eyes, and those golden irises measured Sarah like a predator does its prey. Vaughn watched the two of them circle each other from the far corner with his arms crossed and his back leaning against the mat. Sarah tried to ignore the fact that Vaughn's gaze was mostly directed at her. She tried to ignore Vaughn entirely. It was just her and Breckett. One small distraction was all the man needed, and Sarah was done for.

Breckett glanced to the side, his guard slipping for the briefest of moments, and Sarah saw her chance. She struck. Throwing her full weight behind her swing, Sarah attacked low with an open palm targeting his abdomen. His reaction was a blur. Faster than a snake, Breckett twisted to the side of her attack, and placed his foot behind hers. The move nearly put them back-to-back with Sarah's inner thigh pressed against his. By the time she knew what was happening it was too late. Breckett had a hold of her striking arm, and twisted Sarah to go tumbling over his leg. From there, he slammed her face first into the mat and wrenched her arm upward causing sharp pain to go shooting through her joints. Laid flat out with Breckett a breath away from snapping her arm, Sarah tapped the mat. Releasing her, the Villimath's captain helped Sarah roll over and get to her feet.

"You're too gullible," Breckett said, "an easy bluff shouldn't be enough to draw in your attack. Secondly, always keep your feet."

"I saw an opportunity," Sarah said.

"It was the wrong one," Breckett said. "Every moment is an opportunity, just not always the right one. Come now, ready up. We go again."

Sarah groaned internally, but moved to the marked spot on the floor before taking up the combat stance she'd been shown earlier that morning. While the training was grueling, she had to admit she was enjoying the process of learning how to defend herself. She was no morak'casai, neither of them was, but even in the short amount of time Sarah was noticing progress. The two glared intent at one another until the signal was called.

"Begin!" Vaughn yelled from the corner.

This time, Breckett made the first strike. He descended in a fury with snapping hands and sweeping legs. It took everything Sarah had just to stay on her feet. Breckett was too agile, too precise. Her only hope of stopping his onslaught was to lock him up. Sarah voluntarily took a blow to the side so she could close the gap. Lunging forward, she wrapped both arms around his left thigh and lifted. Breckett tried to keep his balance with his other foot while wrapping an arm around the back of Sarah's neck, but Sarah pushed her momentum forward. She slammed his back into the floor, winning a grunt from him. Both of them now locked together, she hammered her fist into his side over and over again. She was going to win this one. Breckett had different ideas. He twisted his hips and bucked. Using his momentum and force to flip Sarah, he slammed her to the mat, causing their positions to be reversed. Pinning her to the floor, Breckett pressed his elbow against her collar bone while his knee pressed into her gut. She could breathe, but she couldn't draw enough breath to fight back. She tapped the mat again, and Breckett rolled off of her. Both of them lied there for several moments, panting.

"It was a good move," Breckett said, "and it would have worked on a smaller opponent, but sometimes you have to accept the other person might just be stronger."

"What was I supposed to do?" Sarah asked between breaths. She couldn't keep the frustration from her voice. "I wasn't going to win a striking match."

"Run," Breckett said, "there's no shame in it. Disengage, then turn when your opponent least expects it. It'll create an opportunity that wouldn't otherwise exist."

Sarah let his words sink in as she stared up at the ceiling. The white lights shined against the gray panels and the blue padding. It was a sight she'd seen a lot this morning. Breckett had not eased up once stating that every fight outside of this room could be life or death, so why treat practice any differently. Sweat stung her eyes, and Sarah wiped it with the back of her wrist. Vaughn appeared in her vision with an outstretched hand to help her up. She considered not taking it, but decided otherwise. He hoisted her to her feet in one smooth motion, and to his credit, let go immediately to do the same with Breckett. Once they were both to their feet, Vaughn mumbled something to the captain who nodded in turn.

"Weapons training next," Breckett said. "Get cleaned up and meet me in cargo."

Sarah breathed in and sighed. She stunk, she hurt, and she wanted a hot shower more than anything in the galaxy. Her morning maintenance work with Thusi had already worn her out only to be surprised by a summons from Breckett for training. She hadn't had breakfast yet; worse she hadn't even had time for coffee. The captain stalked out of the room while Sarah grabbed a towel from the corner, but she noticed Vaughn lingering by the door. He looked conflicted, glancing first at her then at the departing Breckett. Once the captain was seemingly out of earshot, he fixed

Sarah with an intense look.

"I sparred with him before you got here," he said. "His left knee is weak. Must have injured it once. Use it, but don't rely on it."

He finished with a nod and strode out after. Sarah didn't know what to make of the man. She wasn't sure if he hated her, was attracted to her, or if she was simply a curiosity to him. The way he looked at her, and the way he treated her were two completely different things. His gaze spoke of hate, but every action he took was helpful. No matter, she only had to spend a brief period with him on this mission then she never had to see any of these people again. Wiping off the top of her head, Sarah made her way to her cabin.

2

Feeling refreshed, Sarah had decided to wear an outfit she never thought she'd put on again. She adjusted the sleeve of her blue Kara Corporation coveralls as she descended the stairs into the Villimath's expansive hold. Split into two sections, this part of the ship housed both a small hangar where a landing ship was stored, and a cargo hold where the crew kept their supplies. The hangar took up most of the area, the hawk-looking landing ship propped up on docking supports at the center so Thusi could access the bottom of the vessel for repairs and general maintenance. The cargo hold was located at the far end of the hangar through a wide set of metal doors. Massive overhead strip lights bathed the area in a pale blue glow giving the otherwise utilitarian gray paneling an interesting hue. Crossing the hangar to reach the cargo hold, Sarah walked through the opening doors to something she didn't expect.

She was stunned to find Vaughn and Breckett propping open a familiar set of crates. Kyllen hovered nearby with his arms folded face fixed in a sullen glare at the two men. Stacks upon stacks of metal and plastic cargo containers filled the hold leaving little room to maneuver. Small pathways had been created in order to reach important cargo while reserves and backup stores were relegated to the back. Sarah's weapons and ammunition, it would seem, was deemed important enough to be placed at the front. The two men stood in the middle of an aisle with Vaughn propping the crate open, and Breckett pulling a rifle from its depths. Breckett had a faint smile on his face as he turned the weapon over in his hands. It was a short, but thicker carbine with a wide main barrel and a second barrel underslung. Both the trigger and grip were protected by a large metal curve, the entire piece - stock included - was covered by thick triangular panels. They were unpainted metal, but there was a faint shimmer of bronze or perhaps gold.

"Jasper model 8852," Breckett said, "used to call these things Golden Boys. They were made to be breacher guns, but turned out to be far more useful than that."

"I made a few adjustments," Kyllen said which caused Breckett to scowl, so he pressed on. "I tinkered with the interface to make them more compatible with your suits. There shouldn't be any delay with the HUD now."

The captain pulled the weapon to his shoulder, and aimed the sight rail toward the floor. It looked heavy, and Sarah hoped this wasn't the weapon she was expected to carry around through the mission. She'd prefer something more compact like the options available to her on Carlisle Station. Luck was not on her side, however. Breckett handed the gun to Vaughn who seemed equally interested in it before pulling a second one from the crate. This one Breckett pushed into her arms. Sarah grabbed hold of it before he could let go, being careful not to stick her hand near the trigger. Kara Corporation had taught her that much.

"Grab it by the grip, but keep your finger away from the trigger," Breckett said, and poked Sarah's right hand with a tattooed index finger. "Safety will be next to your thumb, so be careful not to bump it. The switch between the rifle and the breacher rounds will be next to your index finger. These may not be loaded, but treat every weapon as if it is. Put your other hand under the second barrel like this."

He moved to show her, but Sarah hoisted the golden boy in a single swift motion. Bringing the stock to her shoulder, cheek pressed tight against it, she raised the barrel toward the back of the hold. If memory served, she was supposed to wrap her left thumb over the top of the gun for more stability. This one, however, was too thick for that, so instead Sarah resorted to keeping her hand wrapped around the bottom of the underslung barrel. While not as heavy as she thought, the gun was still not something she wanted to lug around with her. Breckett's black eyes widened in surprise before he let out an audible laugh. Vaughn looked impressed, and set his own weapon down.

"And here I thought I was having to train a newby," he said. "When you told me about your experiences, you never mentioned arms training, so I apologize." He tapped the back of the stock Sarah still had pressed to her cheek, then tapped the back of the underslung barrel between Sarah's hand and the trigger. "Golden Boys are unique in that they're a two-in-one system. Primary rounds are fed by a magazine from the bottom of the stock. You'll have thirty shots per magazine, but they go quick. Be mindful. Opposite side of the safety is the firing mode. Single, three-round, or full auto are your options. Full auto will clear a Golden Boy in three seconds. Breacher shells are fed into the bottom of this barrel, but keep in mind you're limited to just five before you have to reload."

Sarah lowered the rifle, and handed it back to Breckett. Taking it without comment, he set it down to lean it against the crate. She took a moment to peek inside the crate in hopes there might be something different she could use. To her dismay, it was an entire crate filled with Golden Boys. She was hesitant to ask, afraid of looking weak in front of Breckett. She decided to ask anyway.

"Think we have something different I can use? Something a bit more compact."

"Sarah," Breckett said, and tapped a hand against another crate, "we're just getting started."

3

They spent a majority of their time left in the day going over a variety of different weapons available to them all thanks to Sarah. There were, in fact, more suitable options for Sarah to use, but the two men seemed hellbent on using the Golden Boys. After the weapons overview, Breckett had both her and Vaughn back in the training room, but this time strapped into a virtual reality system where each of them ran through various drills using the equipment they had found in the crates.

Sarah sat back with Breckett as they watched Vaughn - head covered by a dark helmet, and thick motion gloves over his hands - run through a training exercise. It looked silly from the outside, but after running through several herself, Sarah knew how real those things felt. The helmet tapped into your central nervous system making the virtual world feel indistinguishable from real life. Breckett leaned up against the padded wall and watched a data-slate where he had a visual feed of everything going on within the helmet. He saw what Vaughn saw, and was able to control what happened next. The captain had Vaughn clearing narrow corridor after narrow corridor, each time having to face down a number of Skren raiders. He had chosen Skren in the off chance the reports of their presence were true. Vaughn was handling the scenarios easily, and Breckett looked as though he were growing bored. When he started making small talk, it only served to confirm the notion.

"You know I had strict directions from Ziven to keep you out of the direct line of fire," Breckett said, "he was oddly protective of you."

"I gave him a lot of supplies," Sarah said. She tried to sound nonchalant about the ordeal, but she thought she had a pretty good idea as to why Ziven wanted her safe. She wasn't sure when she'd have to report in about the goings on of the crew, but she knew it would be soon. "Maybe he's hoping I can get him more after this is all over."

"Men like him always want something," Breckett agreed. "From my experience, it's best to get out from under those types as quick as you can. Quiet too. Never stir the pot."

"Oh?" Sarah asked, and she raised an eyebrow at him. "That does a great deal in explaining why you're working for him now then, doesn't it?"

Breckett smirked, tapped a dial on his screen to up the threat level for Vaughn, and shrugged. "Got a few things I need the credits for. Besides, once I'm done here, I'll vanish in the blink of an eye. It'll seem like I was never here to begin with. Oh, that bastard."

Breckett frowned at the data-slate, then at Vaughn, and back to the data-slate. He turned the dial up again, and adjusted a few more parameters. Vaughn's motions became more frantic, but he seemed otherwise unphased. Breckett's frown deepened, but he set the slate aside for the moment. He locked Sarah in his gaze, golden irises peering through her as if they could see her thoughts.

"Why are you really here?" He asked. "Your story doesn't add up, and the talents you have on paper don't warrant Ziven hiring you for this mission."

"Allured by my mystique?" She asked with a wry grin. It was the type of playful question Jax would have asked, and Sarah wasn't sure why it had come out. Perhaps her old partner had changed her more than she thought. Or, Sarah thought sourly, she missed Jax more than she realized. Breckett, however, was not amused.

"No," he said, "mysteries get people killed. If you get someone under my command killed, Sarah Renza, there's no escaping my retribution."

Sarah opened her mouth, found nothing, and closed it again. She didn't know what to say, and was caught off guard by the sudden shift in tone. Breckett swore under his breath as he glanced at the data-slate, and Sarah was glad for the momentary distraction. Picking it up, the captain turned every dial up as far as it would go. The visual feed flashed, and Vaughn let out a loud grunt before falling to the floor. Vaughn pulled the helmet off, and rolled to his knees. Sweat matted down his dark hair, and his usually well-manicured beard was in disarray. He glared at Breckett, but said nothing. Breckett glared right back, and the two seemed ready to start throwing punches. Clearing her throat, Sarah got to her feet.

"Training's not done" Breckett said to her, but kept his eyes on the security chief. "You've got another two rounds left."

"We're done," Sarah said, and glared at both of them. She was surprised at herself for standing up to these two, but she was tired and Breckett's accusations had made her angry. "I need food, *another* shower, and I have prior engagements in the medical ward. You two can keep doing whatever it is you're going to do." With that, she zipped her coveralls up as far as she could, and stalked out of the training room.

4

She could feel both of the men's eyes watching as she left, but neither of them said a word. In actuality, her appointment with Yasmin wasn't for another two hours, but Sarah wanted out of that room, and away from those two. She had spent enough time with them for a lifetime, and their attitudes had worn thin. She knew she'd have to go through all of it again tomorrow, but she pushed the thought away as she walked down the Villimath's corridors. Unsure of where she wanted to hideout until her doctor's visit, Sarah began to explore. There was still a large portion of the ship that she had yet to see, and saw this as an opportunity to remedy that. Having discovered the yellow line led to the medical bay, Sarah decided to pick a new color and see where that took her. She had been informed by Thusi the thick black line led to emergency escape pods, so there was no need to follow that one, but the brown line was a different story. She had no idea where that one sped off to.

Tracing the line with an index finger like a child, she followed it through the corridors. The path kept her on the second deck, at least, but Sarah found herself being guided to the far end of the ship. The line brought her to a large set of double doors with thick windows inset into the center of each one. Above in a yellow font was written the word "Laboratory." Through the windows, Sarah could see a multitude of white desks and glass cabinets with arm holes for safer experimentations. Parker - clad in a white lab coat, blue gloves, and a pair of safety glasses - had her hair tied back, and was stooped over a lab station giving something her full attention. Sarah wondered what kind of research she could be doing considering they hadn't even made contact yet. In fact, Sarah wasn't quite sure why a scientist like Parker had been hired in the first place. She must have been staring for too long because Parker glanced up, looked around, then noticed her staring. Covering whatever she was looking at with a white towel, Parker gave Sarah a warm smile before waving her in. The double doors slid open to disappear inside the bulkhead, but Sarah hesitated to step through.

"Sarah is it?" Parker asked. "Sorry, but it's been a bit, hasn't it. Been cooped up here all journey so far. I'm trying to get some last-minute work done before things get too crazy."

Sarah glanced to either side of the lab, seeing shelves filled with tools and cabinets of samples. One of the samples, she noted, was moving. Upon staring at it further, she realized it was a jar filled with live cockroaches, and they were swarming over something. A colorful wing popped out from between a pair of the hateful insects, but Parker cleared her throat to draw Sarah's attention. She felt so awkward around this woman. She wanted to be able to speak and come across as charismatic, but every time Parker opened her mouth Sarah froze up. Realizing how weird she must look, she quickly blurted, "Think it'll get crazy? I thought this was just going to be quick and simple. We go in, find out what happened, rescue who we can, and leave. Right?"

"That's what Ziven says," Parker said. She leaned on the workstation with both hands, and put on a thoughtful expression. "I doubt it'll end with that. His family is gone. I can tell you that much, and when Ziven finds out he'll dangle more credits in front of our face until we agree to hunt them down ourselves. He'll use some excuse like *well, you're already out this far,* and off we go on some wild goose chase."

"Never seen a goose," Sarah said absently. That gained a snort of laughter out of Parker, and those color shifting eyes watched Sarah more closely.

"You're a spacer through and through, aren't you?" She asked. "When's the last time you stood on a planet? A planet with a real atmosphere, and real soil beneath your feet, not some artificial construct on a colony."

Sarah had to think on the question for several moments. In truth, she couldn't remember. It had been with her brother, she remembered that much, but the memory was so faded she couldn't remember how old she'd been. She'd been perhaps seventeen or eighteen when she'd gotten caught. From there it was correctional facility after correctional facility until she ended up with Kara Corp. Then she thought about the constructed history Myrddin had given her and drew up even more blanks.

"You really don't know?" Parker asked. Her accompanying smirk was disbelieving. "Have you ever been planet side?"

"I have, but I don't remember," Sarah said with a shrug. "It's been about ten cycles, maybe more, maybe less."

Parker gawked, and seemed even more interested. "That long with no sky above your head, no rain, no storms, not even the feel of a natural breeze. I'd have died."

"We've gotten pretty good at faking those things," Sarah said. "The nutrient stims help as well."

"Bleh," Parker said, "all artificial, and all sterile. Give me something real any day. So, how'd you get wrapped up with Kara Corp?"

Sarah was caught flat footed. She hadn't remembered saying anything about Kara Corp, in fact, Sarah thought she had made deliberate attempts to avoid saying the name around this crew. The confusion must have shown on her face because Parker pointed at Sarah's chest. She made a mental note to become better at hiding her emotions.

"I'd recognized that logo anywhere," Parker said. Sarah was an idiot. She scolded herself as one, at least. Looking down at the patch on the left breast of her coveralls, she winced. The patch was faded, but anyone who knew what Kara Corporation was would recognize it immediately. At least that explained the question instead of an alternative where Sarah had slipped up. If she slipped up about Kara Corp, she could slip up about Carlisle Station. There was no way of telling if hiding her past like this was even needed with these people, but it was not something she wanted to risk.

"A series of bad decisions," Sarah said.

"Not all of them were yours," Parker said, then added quickly, "I'm sure. Plenty of uncontrollable things play a factor in where we end up."

Sarah opened her mouth to question that line of thought, when the two of them were interrupted by Breckett's voice chiming in over the comms. "Sarah, we need to have a chat. My cabin please."

"Oohh, busted," Parker said. More apologetically, she added, "we can talk more later. Lab doors are open, and I rarely get a chance to leave."

Holding in a sigh, Sarah glanced once more at the jar of cockroaches. They seemed to be finished with their meal, and had contented themselves with stretching out on the sides of the jar. She could feel Parker's eyes on her back, and for an unexplainable reason it felt as though they were filled with cruel intent. She couldn't help but look back over her shoulder as she left the lab. Parker had a smile on her face, but those color shifting eyes looked hungry.

5

Breckett's cabin was not how Sarah expected it to be. She wasn't sure what she expected, but it wasn't this. Only slightly larger than her own, it had the same make with a cubby cut out for a bed, a desk for work, and a small bathroom at the back. Breckett had filled his honeycombed shelves with not only clothes, but a variety of hanging plants. Their leaves draped down to create organic curtains so visitors wouldn't be able to see his spare underwear. He also had shelves lining the bulkheads, all of which were covered by potted plants and hologram photos. All of the photos displayed one of two women. One of them was a girl of perhaps ten to twelve, the other seemed around the same age as Breckett. The older woman was one of the most beautiful visages Sarah had ever seen with hair as black as pitch, and bee stung lips. A dark dress with lace accents clung to pale shoulders, and a single black rose was tucked behind a perfect ear. That photo was sitting closest to Breckett who sat at his desk and trimmed the bottom of a small bush-like plant. Thin glasses adorned his nose giving the man an almost fatherly look in his basic white tee, and beige slacks.

"I think we got off on the wrong foot," he said without

looking up. He clipped a leaf from the underside of a branch with a pair of thin scissors. "My irritability this morning was inexcusable, and I'd like to apologize. My crew deserves better."

Sarah was torn. Part of her wanted to be as dismissive as possible so she could be out of here and away from the captain. The other part, however, wanted to acknowledge how genuine he was being and find even footing with him. She chose to go with the latter.

"I think Vaughn has that effect on people," Sarah said, and tried to put a lighter tone to her words, "I can never tell what to make of him, at least."

Breckett nodded, and continued his trimming. "Even so, I'd like to apologize. You don't deserve my suspicion any more than the rest of the crew. From what I understand, you've been through your fair share of hell, and it's wrong of me to belittle that. All I ask is that you have our back should the need arise."

"I do," Sarah said. "Even Vaughn, should things come to it."

"Glad to hear it," Breckett said, "we'll pick up our training again tomorrow. We'll be on site faster than we realize, and I need everyone as ready as they can be."

"Of course," Sarah said. She turned to leave, but thought she might be able to get away with a personal question. "Wife and daughter?" She asked.

"The photos?" Breckett asked. "No, no. The little girl is my niece. The woman, well, let's just call her an old friend."

Sarah took another look at the dark-haired woman in the photo. There was a story there, but she could see Breckett held no intention of telling it. At least, not right now. Maybe one day he'd open up about them, but for now Sarah would be content with the fact that he trusted her. If Parker was right, and Sarah had the uncomfortable feeling that she was, they'd be stuck on this ship together for a bit longer than originally anticipated. Trust wasn't going to be an option if either of them wanted a smooth trip. Glancing at the time, Sarah noted that it was getting closer to her visit to the medical ward. She'd done enough exploring for the day, and she needed to get this next part over with. As much as she wanted to avoid getting into a vat of freezing water, she knew it would help. Sarah sent Yasmin a message to let her know she was on her way. Turning to go, she asked Breckett one final question before leaving.

"Why plants?" She asked.

"I find it a nice change of pace," he said, "I find peace in being able to grow living things instead of just cutting them down."

6

Sarah was ready for it this time. At least, that's what she told herself. She stood outside the door of the medical ward trying to imagine herself conquering the cold, and walking away unphased. She ran herself through the scenario from yesterday in an attempt to prepare her body for the inevitable shock. Her mind turned on her, and taunted her about the uselessness of her preparation. No one could prepare for frigid temps like that. She'd look stupid, weak, and have to be lifted out of the tube as if she were a child just like last time. Sarah reframed her thinking. Instead of defeating it, all she needed to do was put up with it. She could do that much. If she had to go through these procedures to be an effective member of the crew, then so be it. Straightening her back, lifting her chin, and squaring her shoulders, Sarah took a deep breath before stepping into the ward. The sight she walked into, however, undid her posture on the spot. It was a day for surprises, it would seem.

Curled up on her wheeled stool, red blanket draped over her shoulders, Yasmin was hunched over the counter like some sort of Dwemyri with one knee tucked to her chest and the other leg splayed out for comfort. Both hands hovered a few centimeters from her open mouth, a plastic yogurt cup in one, a filled spoon in the other, and before her on the counter was a holo-monitor blasting the latest recording of some CRG soap opera. The couple on the screen were in the middle of an intense make out session before the scene cut away to a man screaming in dismay while tearing down a bunch of hung photos from his apartment wall. The doctor almost leapt out of her chair at the sight of Sarah walking through the door, and spilled her yogurt in an attempt to shut down the display, remove the blanket, and untangle herself from the stool all at once. It took everything Sarah had to not break down into cackling laughter at Yasmin's expense. Hiding her smirk behind her hand, Sarah took her seat on the examination table. Acting as though there was something in her eyes, Sarah rubbed her face to give Yasmin time to compose herself.

"Did I come at a bad time?" Sarah asked," I did warn you I was coming."

Yasmin tapped her wrist display and grimaced. "Yeah, I was a bit distracted," she said and looked for the rest of her sentence on the floor. Sarah had never seen the usually calm and collected doctor embarrassed like this, and part of her felt bad.

"Love Reckoning?" Sarah asked. It was a long shot, but she wanted to dissipate some of Yasmin's embarrassment. Sarah only knew the names of a few such shows, but the look on Yasmin's face made her think she had guessed right. "What season? I never managed to finish that one."

Yasmin visibly relaxed, and even started to smile as she folded her blanket and threw away the rest of her yogurt. She spoke over her shoulder as she washed her hands, and Sarah noted all she was wearing was a simple black tee and a pair of sweatpants. It appeared most of the ship was in the mood to relax this evening.

"Season three," Yasmin said, "and I don't blame you. Definitely not the best media to come out of the CRG, and the staff admitted to having rendered half of it using AI, but it's a bit of a guilty pleasure."

"I'd be lying if I said I hadn't enjoyed a few episodes of it," Sarah said. She was lying by saying she had enjoyed any of it, but sometimes a white lie to lift someone's mood was a good thing. "While I was traveling from ship to ship, prerecorded soaps would be all I had for months at a time. Made me fall in love with reading real quick."

That earned a laugh from Yasmin, and the doctor pulled on a white lab coat. She pulled her small sensor from a drawer and scanned Sarah in a preliminary checkup. Checking her readings, she noted a few details into a nearby monitor before putting the device back in the drawer. Her smile was gone as she looked at the numbers she had entered.

"You haven't been eating," she said, "neither food nor stims."

"I haven't been hungry," Sarah said, "all of this shakeup in routine has been a bit much."

"You're a spacer," Yasmin said, and glared at Sarah. She sat down on her stool, and wheeled over to the examination table. Jabbing a finger into the soft side of Sarah's knee she said, "you don't get your stims, you die."

"It's only been a couple meals," Sarah said, "I don't think it's that extreme."

"New rule," Yasmin said, "after this checkup, if I find out you haven't been eating, I shove your ass into the drop ship, and send you back to Ziven. Those stims are what allow you to live in space without planet leave. You don't have those your body starts to eat itself. I'm a doctor. I can't in my right conscience allow someone to do that under my watch. Understand?"

"Understood," Sarah said.

"There's no history of eating disorders in your file," Yasmin said, "but if something has come up, there's complete patient confidentiality in this room. You can talk to me."

"No, nothing like that," Sarah assured her, and tried to wave off the notion with her hands. She felt guilty for the topic having even come up. "Honestly, between working for Thusi, training with Breckett, and coming here, I simply forgot to stop by the mess hall."

Yasmin watched her closely, but nodded. She pushed off with both feet to go wheeling across the room toward a cabinet, and skidded to a halt before a set of drawers. One was refrigerated, Sarah noted, and Yasmin pulled that one open to remove several more cups of yogurt. Grabbing a spoon as well, Yasmin rolled back over to the table and handed Sarah both of them. Next, she pushed her stool over to the counter where she had left her holo-monitor and turned it back on.

"We can't proceed with the procedure until we've got a bit of food through your system," she said, and turned up the volume on the monitor. "So, it looks like your punishment is eating crappy yogurt, and watching sappy soaps until your body has started to digest a bit of nutrients. And don't think you're getting out of today's session either. Our previous deal is still on. You want to be part of the ground team, you go through these treatments."

Sarah couldn't help but laugh. Yasmin may call what she was doing punishment, but Sarah found it to be a nice reprieve. It was an odd moment of peace in an otherwise chaotic point in her life, and she found herself appreciating the doctor that much more for having given it to her. Yasmin smiled in turn, and twisted her stool around to straddle the backrest. Wrapping her arms around the thick pad, she rested her chin on its top, and the two of them zoned out while the previous scene continued. Sarah took a spoonful of yogurt, and also noted the "crappy" yogurt was actually quite tasty with a flavor of mixed fruits. She couldn't pinpoint which ones, but it was good nonetheless. Letting herself forget the outside world - soap opera blasting over the holo-monitor, fruity tang dancing over her taste buds - was something she had needed for a long time. Even if this were only a brief moment, a peaceful drop in a sea of chaos, it was a moment Sarah would never forget.

CHAPTER 17
- SARAH -

1

Ringing stung Sarah's ears. Her head slumped against the inside of her helmet as she lay on her back on the floor of a foreign ship. The old scar running across her abdomen flared with pain, and Sarah hoped it hadn't reopened. She couldn't tell if she felt blood or not with the amount of throbbing in her head and had to trust that her flesh was strong enough to hold. Vaughn stood over her, clad once again in his red armor, with his pistol drawn and aimed down the corridor. The walls around them were a dark metal material with large sections covered by painted canvases and large tapestries. Where was she? She had no recollection of how she got here, or why Vaughn would be standing over top of her with a raised gun. At least, she thought it was Vaughn. His own helmet was on, a black skull shaped thing to contrast the vibrancy of his armor.

Sarah started to think it was another dream. Afterall, she held a deep urge to fall back to sleep. Heavy eyelids slid closed, but before she fell back into a slumber something lifted her halfway off the ground and shook her. Sarah opened her eyes to find Vaughn lifting her hand shaking her with a single hand which clung to a panel of gray armor on her chest. Something else grabbed his attention, however, and he turned to look back down the corridor. He fired several rounds from his pistol, and Sarah noted there was a muzzle flash, but no sound. That must mean this was a dream. The overhead lights pulsed red. Vaughn dropped Sarah, and she dropped back to the floor, though she did not feel herself hit the ground. Holstering his pistol, Vaughn pulled his helmet off to stoop over her. The imagery came in blinks with the flash of each red light, making this feel more and more like a false reality. Vaughn's dark hair was matted with sweat, or was it blood? The light made it difficult to discern color. She'd seen light like this before, but she couldn't pinpoint where. Vaughn yelled something at her, but the words were inaudible. The ringing, oh the ringing, was a different story. Sarah glanced around hoping to find something that would jog her memory. Instead, what she saw were corpses. Lots of corpses. They were humanoid, but they didn't appear to be human. Dwemyri perhaps?

Throx?

No, it couldn't be that. Sarah wasn't sure to whom that name belonged, but she could be certain the individual named Throx was a long time gone. Vaughn's fingers reached around her throat, startling her back to the matter at hand. Vaughn wanted her dead. That's what was going on. Sarah was having a dream about Vaughn wanting to kill her. She reached her hands up in an attempt to stop him, but instead of strangling her, Vaughn unclasped the latches to her helmet. For some reason, the man looked worried for her as he tugged her helmet off. She'd never seen that sort of expression on his face before. To make Vaughn worried, something must truly be wrong.

As the helmet slid past her ears, the interior padding tugging her lobes enough to cause Sarah to wince, the whole world rushed back into perception. Vaughn was yelling her name over and over again. One of the Dwemyri gurgled and choked on its last few breaths of life whispering something in a language her translator implant couldn't pick up. Somewhere down the corridor a ruptured pipe hissed as it spilled out pale steam through a bullet-sized hole. Then there was the smell, oh the rancid smell. Charred flesh and pooled blood wafted a mix of pungent burning and sickly iron through her nostrils, and the suddenness of it all was almost enough to make Sarah retch. Her mouth salivated in response, and bile tickled the back of her throat. Vaughn took hold of her chin, and brought her view into focus. He wasn't looking at her, not really, more like looking for something *in* her. He searched her eyes for something, and swore at the light under his breath. Picking his helmet back up off the floor, Vaughn turned on its headlamp to shine in it in her face. Sarah winced at the light, but decided it was easier to just keep her eyes closed. She was so very tired. Sleep tormented her. Why would this dream not go away, and let her sleep peacefully? It could at least change to something more pleasant. Vaughn yelled her name again, but Sarah ignored it. Sleep would not escape her this time. Memory started to siphon back in, and then she found herself somewhere else.

2

Sarah wiped sweat from her brow with a thick work glove. She pulled the flashlight she had clamped between her teeth, and set it on the floor beneath her in the cramped little compartment under one of the Villimath's many maintenance rooms. She was curled up, back on the floor, knees pushed almost to her chest with her feet pressed against the wall, and her neck cocked at an odd angle in the middle of a narrow crawlspace. This particular crawlspace resided beneath the water purification and heating center, more specifically, beneath a massive water heater. This fact made the crawlspace not only narrow, but insufferably humid. Sarah had her coveralls pulled down to her waist, sleeves tied like a belt, and yet still her thin, white tank top felt too hot. Her feet boiled in their work boots, and her hands were filling the gloves with slick sweat. Breckett's room - of course it had to be Breckett - had lost all control of its hot water, and thus Thusi had sent her to investigate. Upon a bit of tinkering, Sarah traced the problem to the hardest to reach part of the water heater, and found herself curled up in the most uncomfortable position trying to fix it.

Sarah took a few moments to catch her breath before sticking the flashlight back in her teeth. The problem could have been avoided if the stupid valve had been installed correctly in the first place. So much for master engineering. It made her wonder what else on this ship had been installed haphazardly. Thusi had used the excuse that Dwemyri were unfamiliar with human hygiene practices and were therefore unpracticed with the directory of hot water. A stupid excuse for a stupid ship. Tomorrow she could be dealing with a sewage issue, and if that happened all the credits in the galaxy wouldn't be enough to convince her to fix it. Thusi herself was *far* too busy dealing with engine maintenance. There was no feasible way for her to make it out to this part of the ship in a reasonable amount of time. *We can't keep the captain waiting,* is what she had said. Breckett wasn't a child to be coddled. A few hot water issues would do him some good.

Sarah finished up her repair and let out a sigh of relief. Down in this crawlspace, it sounded like air billowing through a cave. Sniffing herself, she grimaced. Sarah stank. She smelled not only of body odor, but spots of grease coated her skin from having to cram herself down here. Breckett owed her a thousand times over, even if this is what she was being paid to do in the first place. She'd make him pay for it during their training later today. Her thoughts must have summoned the captain as his voice chimed over the comms.

"There's been a new development," he said, "I need all hands on the bridge. Now."

Sarah looked at her grimy arms. She was hoping for a shower before having to be seen by anyone else on the ship, but that looked to be wishful thinking. Grumbling, Sarah pulled her gloves off and stuck them in a pocket. Still trying to cool down, Sarah left the coveralls tied around her waist and wandered out into the Villimath's corridors. Still needing to rely on the colored lines to find her way around the ship, Sarah traced the blue line with her index finger as she walked.

To her chagrin, Sarah was the last to arrive on the bridge which meant all eyes watched her as she walked down the corridor and into the open room. Her appearance earned her a variety of looks, not all of which she expected. Lexi wrinkled her nose as if she could smell Sarah from here, and Sarah scowled back. Vaughn was his usual unreadable self while Lucas did his best to respectfully avoid staring at her. Parker smirked, Thusi nodded, and their illustrious captain Breckett remained impassive. Yasmin was watching her from the corner, and when Sarah turned to look back, the doctor glanced down to study a fingernail. Since it was already too late to avoid notice, Sarah crossed her arms, widened her stance, and stood in the empty gap between Breckett's chair and the corridor. The captain kept his chair rotated in her direction leaving the Bile couple to stare at his back.

"As our chief navigator has discovered," Breckett started, and Sarah could almost see Lexi's chin lift with pride, "there has been a change in our situation. Our dormant ship is no longer dormant, and has made a jump. Now, the first question I'm sure I'll be asked is where to? Lexi tracked its movements thinking this ship was fleeing, but it would seem there was no need. The ship, in fact, jumped closer. Much closer. How much closer? As in we'll be on top of the damned thing in twelve minutes, closer. We've already launched an initial scanner drone, but we've lost contact with it. Once we do this, we'll be going in blind. I wanted to abort, and sit back from a safe place of observation to see where this ship was going, but Ziven had other ideas. So, here's the plan: The Biles fly us in as close as possible without notice. Villimath is capable of high traffic stealth operations, so this part should be a cake walk. Next, we hit their engines with a low yield EMP to prevent them from making another jump. That will give us about an hour before whatever crew is aboard that ship can bring things back into working order. While this is going on, the ground team will take the drop ship, attach to the ship's hull, and commence boarding operations. We get to the bridge ASAP, secure the cockpit, and find out exactly what the hell is going on here. Yasmin, Kyllen, I need the two of you suited up as well, but on standby. If things go south, it'll be good to have a combat medic available to pull someone out and I need to be sure our gear is functioning as needed. Parker, once we're in position, I need you running as many scans as humanly possible. I want lifeforms, vitals, numbers. If anything so much as sneezes on that ship, I want to know about it. Thusi, you know your job. Keep our engines smooth and quiet. Everyone knows their role?"

"I told you I'm not joining your away team," Yasmin said, "I'm staying on this ship and doing what I was paid to do."

"I'm not asking you to participate," Breckett said, "I just

need you to be on the drop ship in case of an emergency evac. Purely medical support, no combat."

Yasmin contemplated for a few moments before nodding. Breckett looked around to the others and murmurs of agreement echoed around the bridge. Sarah thought that was going to be the end of it. She noticed someone was missing, however, and glanced around thinking she must have missed the boy, but he was nowhere to be seen. Kyllen, though not a part of any of this operation, would have been loath to miss such a meeting. Once the vocal confirmations were finished, Sarah put voice behind her question.

"What happened to Kyllen?" She asked. "He's usually front and center."

"Already in the hangar and listening through comms," Breckett said. "I needed our gear ready to go, so he's prepping for our arrival. Vaughn, Sarah, go ahead and start that way so we can begin suiting up. Make sure the kid prepped a combat suit for me as well, and wait by the drop ship."

Sarah straightened her back, and unfolded her arms upon being addressed. She glanced over at Yasmin who nodded with a reassuring smile. Looks like she was getting her chance to be off the Villimath for a bit. If all went smoothly with this operation, they would all be on their way back to the Ifrit in no time. Sarah would find Hector, and the two of them could sort out their individual messes later.

3

Sarah sat on the floor of the hangar bay, and leaned against a crate. The overhead lights had been switched to red to indicate the impending departure and to warn any unsuspecting patrons to leave before the hangar was opened up to the void of space. Luckily, they were a skeleton crew and no need to worry about random passersby being an issue. Looming above the crate was the drop ship. Its wings were spread wide, but its engines remained quiet. She flexed her right hand, grabbing her wrist with her left, both of which were now covered by the gray armor plates of her suit's gauntlets. It was a strange sensation. The overall suit was the same skin-tight mesh material her own personal suit was made of, however, this one was covered head to toe by thick plates of armor. She had no idea what the material was, but she could make a few guesses. Kara Corp had warned her about military grade armors, especially those made for deep space combat. When raiding a ship, or station in most cases, tearing a hole through the hull with a stray round was usually frowned upon. Attackers and defenders both had a tendency to enjoy not being blown out into the void of space if it could be helped. Thus, modified magnetic rail guns were put to use. They were strong enough to put a projectile through someone's flesh and penetrate through smaller barriers, but they weren't potent enough to cause a breach in a ship's hull. Defense designers used this fact to their advantage and started making armor to the same grade as a ship hull. Expensive, but worth its weight in credit cubes. Kara Corp had warned her that if such opponents should attempt a raid on her station, then she needed to be prepared to use a sharp object, plasma cutter, or a blunt striking weapon. It appeared the easiest way around such advanced technology was to counter it with the simplest method known to humankind. Hit them with something pokey, and hit them hard. Sarah understood why when looking at her own armor. There were gaps between the plates for mobility purposes where a blade could slip through, and blunt trauma was blunt trauma no matter how you shaped it. The body could only handle so much of that.

Vaughn grumbled something inaudible as he carried a bundle of Golden Boys from the cargo hold out into the hangar toward Sarah, Kyllen close on his heels with several belts slung over one shoulder. Other than the three of them, the hangar was deathly quiet. The walkways that crossed above were empty, the air circulation in the lower part of the hangar had gone still, and nothing stirred but the security chief in his signature red plate and a teenage Groal in a black enviro-suit. Not expected to fight, it seemed Kyllen was content with wearing a suit that lacked the amor plates. She noticed a lack of helmet, and started to wonder just how Groal put one on with their antlers. She was sure she'd find out soon enough. With the red lights beaming above, Sarah could not shake the uncomfortable feeling that this was just the calm before the storm. Vaughn propped the rifles up against the same crate Sarah was leaning on, while Kyllen set the belts on top.

"Don't rely on your armor to save you," Vaughn said, and pulled something from one of the belts. "I've seen too many good folk think they're suddenly invincible once they put it on, and they forget their training because of it. Gets them killed every time. Remember what Breckett has taught you so far, and you'll make it through."

"Really think it's going to be that bad, huh?" Sarah asked. She didn't mean it to sound as condescending as it did, but the words were out before she could change her tone. Vaughn didn't answer. Instead, he pulled another item from the belts and shoved it into Sarah's face. Realizing it was a pistol, Sarah took hold of the grip and examined it. It was almost an identical model to the one she had used on Carlisle Station. Memories threatened to flood back, but Sarah practiced some of the breathing exercises Yasmin had shown her. She focused on the pistol for what it was - just another tool.

"There's a holster on either hip of your suit," Vaughn said, "it'll auto adjust to whatever is placed in it."

He handed her something else. This time, Sarah grabbed the hilt of a dagger. It was a simple looking thing with a solid cross guard and needle-like tip. Grabbing the hilt with a nod, she leaned one way to place the pistol in her right holster, and then leaned the other for the dagger.

"It looks useless," Vaughn said, "I mean, why bring a knife to a gunfight, but the blade is nanotipped."

"Stick em between the armor, right?" Sarah asked, and gave Vaughn a grim look.

"Not with that," Kyllen interrupted. "A nanotip can go through the armor too. Don't drop it, and don't stick yourself with it either. That thing cuts your suit while you're in the vacuum of space, and I don't need to tell you the consequences."

Sarah unsheathed the blade from her hip, and reexamined it. She thought about testing the point with a finger, but knew that would turn out to be a bad idea. The blade didn't look any different than a normal dagger, but Vaughn had no reason to lie to her about something like this, so she took his word for it. Then, she got an idea. She flipped the blade around to be held in a stabbing gesture, and carefully pressed the tip against the floor of the hangar. Sure enough, when she pulled the blade back, the tip had started to penetrate the floor. The small nick was hard to make out in the red light, but Sarah could tell it was there. She could only imagine what would happen if she applied pressure. Vaughn let out an amused grunt, but left her to it. Grabbing Kyllen and leaving Sarah and the equipment, he went over to the drop ship to get it prepared for launch. With her back to the drop ship, Sarah could only hear what was going on, so she went back to examining the blade. She was interrupted, however, by Breckett descending the far stairs with Yasmin trailing close behind him.

"Their engines are down," he said, "it's time to move."

4

Sarah, Vaughn, Kyllen, and Yasmin sat strapped into the back of the drop ship which was being flown out of the Villimath's hangar by Breckett. The dropship itself was little more than a metal tube with seats, wings, and a cockpit. The seats the four of them had crammed into were shoulder-to-shoulder along each bulkhead with a harness that descended from above to strap in with. Sarah leaned her head against the padded headrest as Breckett forced the dropship into full thrust. With her helmet on, she couldn't feel the back of the seat, but she knew it was there. It was another major difference between her old suit and this combat one. This helmet was just large enough for her head to squeeze into, and the visor was just a narrow slit for her eyes. It would have made her vision impossibly narrow, however, the inside of the helmet offered an augmented display which made it feel as though there were no helmet in front of her face at all. It was a strange sensation to feel pads against your cheeks and oxygen fans blowing in your face, but to see normally as if nothing were there.

"Three minutes," Breckett said through comms.

Nerves made a slosh of Sarah's stomach, and her heart rate began to pick up. Both Vaughn and Parker had similar ideas as to what they'd find, and Sarah couldn't rid herself of the idea that they were about to walk into a disaster. She needed to distract herself. Risking a glance at the others, she wondered if either of them felt the same. Vaughn was busying himself by loading rounds into a magazine. In stark contrast to his red armor, his helmet was pitch black. It shaped around his head like an angry skull with lenses where the empty eye sockets would have normally been. Yasmin appeared to be indifferent as well. Wearing identical gray armor to Sarah's, she sat strapped into her seat with her hands folded in her lap. Her helmet was pointed forward, and Sarah almost wondered if she were taking a nap. Kyllen, on the other hand, was looking from one person to the next. Her question about his helmet was answered. In general, it looked the same as anyone else's helmet except for two holes near the top of the forehead where his antlers sprouted through. A dark membrane of some sort of thick material stretched and formed over the antlers to seal them in. The process of putting the helmet on looked complicated, but Kyllen had the motions down in seconds. It went together in pieces, each part fitting around his antlers to connect around his forehead. Through the transparent glass of his visor, Kyllen looked as nervous as Sarah felt. Looking for a different distraction, she took the dagger from her thigh to examine it once more.

"If it's sharp enough to get through armor," Sarah said to Vaughn, "then why don't they make projectile rounds with the same tech?"

Vaughn paused, thumb hovering over a magazine, and the black skull tilted toward her. "What you're holding in your hand costs more than the ship you're riding on. Several times more. Think militaries want even their most elite soldiers firing hundreds of those in a second? Most won't even waste the credits making something like that dagger. It's more of a novelty, really. Much cheaper ways to kill something."

He went back to pushing rounds into magazines which put an end to the conversation. Putting the dagger away, Sarah looked back over to Yasmin. She was tapping a finger against the back of her hand, and staring up at the ceiling. Maybe she wasn't so calm after all. The doctor avoided looking back at Sarah, content with whatever was above them. Sarah noticed Yasmin's foot started tapping as well. Vaughn noticed too.

"I didn't know doctors could get motion sick," Vaughn said, "especially field medics."

The revelation caught Sarah off guard, and she almost laughed. She refrained, however, as Yasmin's foot tapped harder which Sarah took as a sign of irritation. With gravity gone, Sarah could only imagine the sensation must feel that much worse. Yasmin ignored Vaughn at first, but the man continued to stare her down waiting for an answer.

"Small ships like this are the worst," Yasmin said without looking down, "you can feel everything. Usually got around it by flying the ship. No issues then, but being crammed in the back of one of these things is miserable. Never understood how strike teams did it."

"How strike teams sat in the back of a ship?" Vaughn asked. The question seemed sincere, but Sarah couldn't help but read it as a statement of sarcasm. Yasmin thought the same.

"How they piled out into active combat after a cracked up pilot flew them there at full throttle," Yasmin said, "now if you don't want me to tell this entire dropship about all your strange and embarrassing medical history, I'd recommend you keep your mouth shut the rest of the trip. Okay?"

"You should try humming," Sarah offered. She wasn't sure if the threat applied to her as well, but she thought she'd try and help all the same. "When I was with Kara Corp, they'd send you to the stations in these small one-person pods that weren't equipped with any motion dampening. I wanted to puke every time. Higher ups just told you not to eat first, but I found humming helped a bit. At least it did on the shorter flights."

Yasmin glanced in her direction, but said nothing. Sarah wondered if she was about to get a verbal lashing as well, and started to brace herself for it. Instead, the doctor started to hum. It was a quiet tune with no direction, but it kept Yasmin content. Sarah hoped it worked because if it didn't, she was sure Yasmin would bring it back up again later. They traveled the rest of the way in that manner with Yasmin humming, Vaughn fiddling with his armaments, Kyllen a anxious wreck, and Sarah looking for anything to distract herself from the nerves. She was only moderately successful. Her breathing stayed at a normal pace, but her stomach wouldn't quiet.

"Touching down," Breckett said, and each of the passengers grabbed onto their harnesses in unison.

The dropship rumbled then thudded into the hull of the opposing ship before calming to a stillness. The engines were cut, and the cabin lights switched to red. Sarah figured she was going to hate red lights by the time all of this was over. Breckett marched from the cockpit down the aisle of the cabin, and made a circular hand gesture which Sarah now knew was a sign to get ready. Sarah and Vaughn clamored out of their seats while Yasmin and Kyllen remained fastened tight. The doctor watched them as they filed over to the gap in the seats where their rifles were stowed. One by one, Breckett pulled the Golden Boys off the rack to hand to Vaughn and Sarah. She was loath to take it, she had insisted on something more portable before they left, but Breckett had insisted that they may need the breacher rounds throughout the ship. Sarah took the rifle, and clipped it to the magnetic port on her hip. It was large enough, Sarah felt like a clown. In zero-g, however, the ability to clip something so cumbersome to a hip was a convenience she couldn't pass up. Breckett did the same with his, but Vaughn kept the Golden Boy at the ready while standing by the door at the end of the aisle. They double checked their mag-boots, and Breckett gave the thumbs up.

Vaughn lowered the ramp, giving them all a view of the outside world. A field of gray metal hull with a horizon of deep space waited before them. Breckett pointed out the exterior hatch they were to breach, and they filed toward it. Sarah turned back to give Yasmin a final wave before they left, and the doctor muttered *good luck* in parting. Kyllen glanced from her to the doctor, then back to her, but remained quiet. The ramp to the dropship closed once they were all out onto the hull of the ship. Vaughn watched their surroundings as Sarah and Breckett stooped over the hatch's control panel. Pulling a thin wire from the wrist of his suit, Breckett plugged into a small port on the bottom of the panel. A few moments of silence went by as the captain did his work, but soon the panel flashed green. Mist puffed from the hatch's seams. Vaughn readied his weapon, pointing it at the hatch as Sarah pried it open. The airlock beyond was empty. Vaughn strode over without needing to be instructed and hopped inside. His body transitioned to the ship's artificial gravity effortlessly. From Sarah and Breckett's perspective, Vaughn looked like he was standing on the interior wall of a deep hole. Glancing up at Breckett, the captain waved Sarah to move in next. She adjusted her position to make the transition into gravity space as seamless as possible. This was one skill Kara Corp stations had done well to train her in. Climbing in, her feet touched down, and her world shifted. Down became forward, up turned into behind, and forward became up. Breckett followed in behind, and closed the hatch once they were all inside. While the chamber repressurized, they formed up on the interior airlock door, Sarah taking up the rear. The chamber was lit with yellow light, and Sarah wondered if the whole ship would be this way. Just as Vaughn reached to open the door, Parker's voice chimed in through their comms.

"I'm getting readings," Siv said. "Twelve through that door alone."

5

Chaos, abrupt and unadulterated by logic or reason, exploded from all directions as though it were just waiting for a word of permission to exist. Once introduced it would not be stymied, nor stoppered, and in its unfettered state its direction would be all encompassing. When Vaughn pressed his hand to the inner airlock door, there was no taking it back. The door slid open and for the briefest of moments, all was still. Breckett and Vaughn stood motionless with rifles pointed at a group of the largest Dwemyri Sarah had ever seen. They varied between gray and brown fur covering their muscled frames, and black fangs protruded from each of their snouts. They wore thick leather pads for armor, some of which were embellished by bits of metal and spikes. The narrow corridor of dark metal bulkheads caused the group of Dwemyri to be pressed together, and despite the passageway's vaulted ceiling, their height almost caused them to duck. Indeed, the rest of the ship was also lit with yellow lighting, a thing Sarah cursed under her breath. One of the Dwemyri had a corpse slung over its shoulder, and it took them a moment to realize the door had opened. Once they did, however, peace was buried in a deep grave.

The one with the corpse screamed and raised a pistol. Breckett didn't give it the chance, and fired three rounds before the pistol was halfway up. That was all the signal Vaughn seemed to need, and he lit up the corridor with round after round. Scrambling to pull the rifle from her waist, Sarah cursed herself for not having done it before gravity kicked in. These Dwemyri were tenacious. Despite the numerous rifle rounds being blasted through their bodies, one managed to draw a curved sword and charged. It got as close as a meter before it fell. By that time, Sarah had brought the Golden Boy to her shoulder though she had yet to fire a single shot. A display in her helmet searched for targets which would send a signal to her rifle to assist her aim. The green cross flickered from Dwemyri corpse to Dwemyri corpse, but never switched to red to indicate a threat.

"The whole ship is going to know we're here," Breckett said, "we move to the bridge. Go."

Sure enough, before they had the chance to take three steps into the corridor another Dwemyri popped its head around the corner. Her cross turned red, and Sarah squeezed the trigger. Set to a three-round burst, her rifle's muzzle flashed with a kick, and twelve meters down the corridor the Dwemyri's head was ripped apart. The rest of the corpse went flying out to the backside of the adjoining hall with its limbs rag dolling. Blood and brain matter coated the far bulkhead, and dripped with small chunks. Sarah had done that. She had killed before, all those months ago on Carlisle Station, but this felt different. It felt vile. She didn't *need* to be here, so the killing felt more a choice than a necessity. A display on the top of her Golden Boy blinked to indicate twenty-seven rounds remained in the magazine.

"Parker," Breckett said, "give us directions to the bridge please."

"Certainly," Parker said, "take a left around that corner where Sarah downed the raider, and go straight for thirty-five meters. From there, take a right."

They reached the corner, and Breckett edged the tip of his rifle around to get a camera view of the corridor beyond. He didn't need the camera to tell him there were hostiles. As soon as his rifle poked into view, numerous projectiles blasted down the corridor in their direction. Breckett held up three fingers to indicate their numbers. Vaughn nodded, and pulled a small sphere from his waist. Swapping positions with Breckett, the security chief slung the sphere around the corner and was rewarded with a snapping bang and a flash of bright light. Sarah's viewport automatically dimmed for her, but she guessed the Dwemyri were not so lucky. In unison, Breckett and Vaughn popped around the corner and downed the raiders in mere seconds. Sarah kept a trained rifle down the opposite direction to ensure they were not taken from behind. By Parker's readings, there were five more somewhere nearby. Sarah didn't have to wait long to find them.

Charging down from multiple corridors, the hulking masses of fur and fangs fired automatic carbines at the trio. Fortunately, the armor proved its worth. Bullets ricocheted off Sarah's body. Though rendered harmless, the force was enough to push her off balance. It gave the Dwemyri a chance to close the gap, and draw wicked and curved swords from behind their backs. Though Breckett's training was far from instinctual, Sarah forced her body to move as he'd taught her. She blocked an oncoming blade with her rifle, and twisted to allow momentum to send her attacker rushing past her. The action, however, sent her rifle sailing from her hands. Drawing her pistol before the second attacker could descend upon her, Sarah fired several rounds into the charging Dwemyri. It fell a mere meter in front of her. Vaughn took down two more while Breckett dealt with the one that had slipped into their ranks. That left one. This one was different. It lingered toward the back of the corridor and watched as its companions fell. Thick battle plate covered it from head to toe - black with curved horns protruding from the pauldrons. Its helmet was shaped like a wedge with a single viewing lens on the left side.

Breckett wasted no time and unloaded his clip into the new combatant, but Sarah's suspicions were confirmed. Just like their own, the armor deflected the lower velocity rounds of a rifle designed for ship-to-ship combat. They could switch to breacher shells, but that would risk the integrity of the ship. A smile could be felt more than seen through the Dwemyri's helmet as it stalked toward them, curved blade drawn. The Dwemyri dragged the tip of the blade along the floor as it walked, and Sarah noticed a deep groove being cut.

Vaughn noticed it as well, and tapped Sarah on the thigh to indicate her dagger. The two men had already set their rifles aside, and drawn their own. Sarah's Golden Boy was somewhere on the floor, so all she needed to do was stow her pistol and draw the blade. She was slow. The Dwemyri could have attacked her while she was doing this, but it seemed to want the fight. It tapped the flat of its blade against its leg, clenched the fist of its free hand, and charged into their midst.

CHAPTER 18
- SARAH -

1

Honed blades flickered with yellow light as they were swung with lethal precision. The Dwemyri was fast, almost too fast, ducking and parrying every dagger strike meant to cripple it. It moved between the three of them, blocking, striking, then moving on to the next in search of an opening to take one of them down. All of this in mere seconds though it felt like an eternity. It was Sarah's turn to be tested. Having deflected a strike from Vaughn, the Dwemyri twisted to turn toward Sarah. She proved to be the opening it was looking for. It swung its blade in a downward arc, but when Sarah reacted, the Dwemyri feinted to strike her with its free hand. It shoved her back into the corridor wall. She collided with a thud, and the force of it sent the breath from her lungs. The Dwemyri lunged, blade swinging in a wide arc.

Breckett and Vaughn moved in unison. Daggers glinting, they darted forward while their assailant's back was turned. They proved to be faster, but only just. Plunging their blades deep into the Dwemyri's side, the two men sent it off kilter. The swing of the curved blade slashed across the front of Sarah's armor rather than bite into her shoulder where it was aimed. The Dwemyri was forced to the ground, and Breckett finished it off by sliding his dagger into the gap beneath its helmet. It shuddered its final breath then went still. Sarah ran a hand across the chest plate of her armor. A thin groove worked its way from the top of one shoulder down to the opposing hip. To her surprise, Vaughn was there in an instant. He fretted over her like a worried mother, checking the same groove along with every other centimeter of her armor. He had her step away from the wall and turn, so he could check for unfelt or unseen wounds. Sarah, whose mind was still trying to catch up with what had happened, put up no protest. Only once Vaughn was convinced she had escaped uninjured did he clap her on the shoulder.

"You did well," he said, "better than could be expected."

"That's because you expected the worst," Breckett said. He was hurriedly picking up their discarded Golden Boys, and checking each one over. "But, now's not the time. Let's secure this ship, and be done with it."

Breckett handed the two of them their rifles before slapping a new magazine into his own. Checking the display, Sarah decided against doing the same. She still had most of the magazine left. Nodding to both of them, Breckett started to lead them down the corridor, but two things happened. First, the yellow lights powered down, and the red emergency lighting kicked in. They pulsed with a steady rhythm, and Sarah swore under her breath. Second, Parker called them over comms.

"Breckett, we have a slight issue," Parker said, "someone is trying to reroute power, and overload that ship's jump drives."

"Meaning we need to get to the bridge ASAP," Breckett said.

"No," Parker said, "well, yes, but also no. They're overloading it to cause the ship to self-destruct."

"They're buying time," Breckett said. "We head to the bridge now, and the ship explodes with all of us on it. If we head to the engine room, they'll buy enough time to wait out our blockers and maybe send for help. Sarah, you'll know how to stop the overload process. Kyllen, looks like you're up kid. Get down here and help Sarah. They might have added a device to prevent her from doing her job. Head to the engine room, and shut this thing down. Vaughn, you keep the two of them alive long enough to do so. I'll head to the bridge on my own, and keep the crew from making any rash decisions."

"I don't like this," Yasmin chimed in over comms, "splitting up has only ever served to get people killed faster."

"Doctor, clear comms and sit tight," Breckett said, then added, "please."

"Let it go on the report that I was opposed to this line of thinking," Yasmin said, "but I'm ready should you need me."

While comfort was the wrong word, Sarah did find her tension easing a bit knowing Yasmin, Breckett, and even Vaughn were here to ensure her safety. If someone would have told her a month ago that she'd find herself trusting a new group of people with her life, Sarah would have called that person a liar. But here she was with the only thought running through her head was she hoped she didn't let them down.

2

Sarah and Vaughn raced down the opposite corridor from Breckett. Kyllen was on his way, but they didn't have time to wait for him to catch up. Parker did her best to give directions to both locations at once, but the process made things slower than they could have been. Breckett noticed this as well, and told Parker to put the engine room as first priority. He signed off before engaging a group of Dwemyri on his own. That left Sarah and Vaughn to listen to Parker's directions. Luckily, this side of the ship was quiet. They had yet to encounter any opposition, and their only challenge thus far was not getting lost in this labyrinth of narrow corridors. All of that changed when the two of them rounded a corner.

"Shit, sorry," Parker said, "five vitals twelve meters down the hall."

"We see that," Vaughn said, and immediately started to shoot. He dropped one, and Sarah took down a second in quick succession. A third started to lift something, and Vaughn threw his body into Sarah's to force the two of them back around the corner. Sarah looked over his shoulder just in time to see a bright beam of light blast down the corridor through where their bodies had just been standing. A charred hole sizzled on the opposite bulkhead where the beam had hit.

"Those bastards are really willing to take down the whole ship," Vaughn said. "That shot could have ripped a hole through the hull."

"Three more heading your way," Parker said, "coming from the opposite corridor."

Sarah dropped to a single knee, and trained her rifle down the corridor before them. Vaughn leaned up against the corner to give her a better view, and risked the tip of his rifle to get a camera view around the corner while Sarah protected their exposed flank. Red light dimmed before it pulsed back, and Sarah did her best not to let the light distract her. Three Dwemyri came into view down the hallway, and Sarah's indicator lit up red in her visor. Squeezing the trigger, Sarah dropped the lead one in a spray of gunfire. The other two returned fire, missing Vaughn, but hitting Sarah across the shoulders and helmet. A well-aimed shot hit the glass of Sarah's visor causing it to crack. The force snapped her head back, but not before she had a lock on the second Dwemyri. She fired as she stumbled, the assisted aim ripping holes through her next target.

"Screw it then," Vaughn said, and switched his Golden Boy to breacher rounds. He used the chaos of Sarah's combat to step out around the corner and fire. Bright beams of light scattered from the bottom barrel of Vaughn's Golden Boy, and Sarah could hear screams of pain ringing back from around the corner. Righting herself once more, Sarah took aim at the third Dwemyri which was making a mad dash with its sword drawn. It was close, too close, and by the time Sarah pulled the trigger the Dwemyri was already swinging at Vaughn. He dove out of sight, and Sarah unloaded. The corpse still had enough momentum to fall on top of her, and take Sarah to the ground. Pushing the corpse off, she got to her feet and drew her pistol. There was no time to try and recover the rifle from beneath the Dwemyri's weight, and Vaughn was still somewhere around the corner.

She stepped out to see the man driving his dagger into the belly of another of the raiders. The Dwemyri at the end of the hall were smoldering corpses. Pulling the blade from its gut, Vaughn let the Dwemyri slump to the floor. It struggled with the open wound, and rolled to its back. Vaughn ignored it, and gave Sarah an approving nod. Her visor locked onto something in the background, however. One of the Dwemyri she thought was dead had started to crawl toward a long cylindrical rifle. By the time she noticed it, the Dwemyri had its hand wrapped around the grip, and had it pointed at Sarah. She dropped on an impulse, and a beam of light shot over where her head just was. The beam tore through the ceiling, and then her entire world exploded.

Ringing stung Sarah's ears. Her head slumped against the inside of her helmet as she lay on her back on the floor of a foreign ship. The old scar running across her abdomen flared with pain, and Sarah hoped it hadn't reopened. She couldn't tell if she felt blood or not with the amount of throbbing in her head, and had to trust that her flesh was strong enough to hold. Vaughn stood over her with his pistol drawn and aimed down the corridor. The walls around them were a dark metal material with large sections covered by painted canvases and large tapestries. Where was she? She had no recollection of how she got here, or why Vaughn would be standing over top of her with a raised gun. At least, she thought it was Vaughn. His own helmet was on, a black skull shaped thing to contrast the vibrancy of his armor.

Sarah started to think it was another dream. Afterall, she held a deep urge to fall back to sleep. Heavy eyelids slid closed, but before she fell back into a slumber something lifted her halfway off the ground and shook her. Sarah opened her eyes to find Vaughn lifting her head and shaking her with a single hand which clung to a panel of gray armor on her chest. Something else grabbed his attention, however, and he turned to look back down the corridor. He fired several rounds from his pistol, and Sarah noted there was a muzzle flash, but no sound. That must mean this was a dream. The overhead lights pulsed red. Vaughn dropped Sarah, and she plopped back to the floor though she did not feel herself hit the ground. Holstering his pistol, Vaughn pulled his helmet off to stoop over her. The imagery came in blinks with the flash of each red light, making this feel more and more like a false reality. Vaughn's dark hair was matted with sweat, or was it blood? The light made it difficult to discern color. She'd seen light like this before, but she couldn't pinpoint where. Vaughn yelled something at her, but the words were inaudible. The ringing, oh the ringing, was a different story. Sarah glanced around hoping to find something that would jog her memory. Instead, what she saw were corpses. Lots of corpses. They were humanoid, but they didn't appear to be human. Dwemyri perhaps?

Throx?

No, it couldn't be that. Sarah wasn't sure to whom that name belonged, but she could be certain the individual named Throx was a long time gone. Vaughn's fingers reached around her throat, startling her back to the matter at hand. Vaughn wanted her dead. That's what was going on. Sarah was having a dream about Vaughn wanting to kill her. She reached her hands up in an attempt to stop him, but instead of strangling her, Vaughn unclasped the latches to her helmet. For some reason, the man looked worried as he tugged her helmet off. She'd never seen that sort of expression on his face before. To make Vaughn worried, something must truly be wrong.

As the helmet slid past her ears, the interior padding tugging her lobes enough to cause Sarah to wince, the whole world rushed back into perception. Vaughn was yelling her name over and over again. One of the Dwemyri gurgled and choked on its last few breaths of life whispering something in a language her translator implant couldn't pick up. Somewhere down the corridor a ruptured pipe hissed as it spilled out pale steam through a bullet-sized hole. Then there was the smell, the rancid smell. Charred flesh and pooled blood wafted a mix of pungent burning and sickly iron through her nostrils, and the suddeness of it all was almost enough to make Sarah retch. Her mouth salivated in response, and bile tickled the back of her throat. Vaughn took hold of her chin, and brought her view into focus. He wasn't looking at her, not really, more like looking for something *in* her. He searched her eyes for something, and swore at the light under his breath. Picking his helmet back up off the floor, Vaughn turned on its headlamp to shine in it in her face. Sarah winced at the light, but decided it was easier to just keep her eyes closed. She was so very tired. Sleep tormented her. Why would this dream not go away, and let her sleep peacefully? It could at least change to something more pleasant.

Vaughn yelled her name again, but Sarah ignored it. Sleep would not escape her this time. Memory started to siphon back in, and then she found herself somewhere else.

Sarah stared down the corridor of not a ship, but a station. Carlisle Station. Blood traced a path from where she stood, down the passageway of dull metal bulkheads, and stopped at the feet of a large morak'casai. It was difficult to make out their shape through the pulsing red lights, but Sarah recognized this man. A name skittered across her void of a memory - Zate. Dark smears were spread over the door he leaned on with mangled fingers. He was whispering something, but Sarah could not make out what. Remembering the pistol in her hand, Sarah raised it to point the underslung flashlight. With it, she could see him in full. Zate whispered through bloodied lips and a cracked smile. He clawed at the metal door with nail-less fingers, but stopped when Sarah pointed the gun. Cocking his head like he was listening, Zate spoke.

"I hear the tip-tapping of a little mouse," he said. He coughed, and blood dribbled down his chin. Is that you, doctor? I've been looking all over for you."

"The doctor's not here," Sarah said. She backed away, but kept her pistol raised high. "I'm not who you're looking for."

"No?" He asked. Zate hobbled a few steps in Sarah's direction, pressing his bloodied hand against the wall for support. Another dark smear trailed in his wake. "Perhaps not, but your lies have run so deep, doctor, who knows what other tricks you've set in motion."

Zate lunged, drawing a sword faster than Sarah could comprehend. She fired her gun to no effect as he closed the gap in a heartbeat. Sarah fell to the floor in an attempt to dodge his strike. The blade whistled over her right shoulder, but cut only air. She raised the pistol with the intention of unloading the clip into his torso, but found her hand empty. Zate's hand clutched her throat and squeezed. Sarah flailed for any weapon she could find, and her hand brushed against something sharp on her thigh. Ripping the dagger free of its sheath, Sarah plunged it into her attacker's ribs.

"Wait!" Vaughn screamed. "Sarah, wait!"

Sarah blinked. The pulsing red lights were still there, but

she was back on a ship she intended to liberate from raiders. Sitting on the floor with her back pressed up against a bulkhead, her hand still clutched the hilt of the dagger. Its blade was driven deep into Kyllen's lower ribs. Shock froze the features of his face. He was crouched low, one hand clamped around the wound, the other outstretched toward Sarah in a pleading motion. Vaugn was too late. The security officer's teeth were borne, and clenched together, and he hissed his next words. Out of pain or anger, Sarah could not tell.

"Let go of the blade," he said, "but leave it in him."

3

No one dared move. Sarah's hand lingered on the hilt while Kyllen stood still in stunned silence. Even Vaughn seemed at a loss. Her breath had grown frantic, and her heart threatened to explode out of her chest. Practicing Yasmin's breathing exercises, Sarah took in the situation. Sitting against the back wall of an intersection, the bulkheads around her were charred black. Several Dwemyri corpses were also blackened and smoldering. An exposed pipe in the ceiling hissed with the escape of steam, and further down the corridor Sarah could see more Dwemyri corpses. She took another look at Vaughn who kept Sarah locked in his wide eyes. Everything was wet, she noticed, and puddles of an unknown liquid pooled up in every corner. Then, as if time were snapping back into its rightful place, everyone moved at once.

Kyllen dropped his hand and clutched at the dagger. His face contorted with pain as his senses caught up to what had just happened. Sarah could hear Breckett and Parker's voices calling over the comms from her discarded helmet, but she ignored them. She wanted to shrink away from what she had done, but she wouldn't allow herself to. The horror of what she'd just done could haunt her later, she knew it would, but for now she needed to keep the kid from dying. Vaughn moved faster than she, and he lowered Kyllen to the floor all the while the kid moaned something through his helmet. *Grams.* She heard the word slip through his lips in a whisper. Shit. A horrible conversation was going to be waiting for her back on the Ifrit. It would be far worse if she had to confront the old woman alone with her grandson brought back in a body bag. Vaughn pulled a pouch from his belt and nodded at Sarah.

"Pull it out," he said, and motioned to the pouch in his hand. "This will keep him from bleeding out on the floor."

Sarah had to pry Kyllen's grip from the hilt, and he winced with each finger pulled free. She wrapped her own hand around the leather wrapping and placed her other against Kyllen's ribs.

"Hurry it up," Vaughn said.

With a deep breath, Sarah braced the hand on Kyllen's ribs and yanked the blade free. A sharp cry tore from the kid's throat, and in an instant Vaughn was there pouring a liquid from the pouch into his wound. Kyllen grit his teeth, but seemed relieved as the liquid began to congeal into a gel, then into a solid. Vaughn stood and held a hand out to Sarah.

"Not a word of this," he said. "Dwemyri did this, so put it out of your mind. We have a job to do."

Sarah reached up to take his hand, too numb to do anything else. A loud crack echoed from down the hall, and the left half of Vaughn's head exploded in a spray of gore. Blood sprayed across Sarah's outstretched hand and face with the taste of iron tainting her lips.

4

Vaughn's lifeless corpse toppled to the floor in a heap. Down the corridor, the door to the engine room was open and a Dwemyri leaned up against the threshold while pointing a narrow carbine. Another shot cracked, and Sarah dove for one of the Golden Boys. Grabbing one, she hoisted it to her shoulder and aimed. Without her helmet, there was no interface for the weapon to integrate with, meaning Sarah had to do this on her own. She took the shot, and the Dwemyri fell. She couldn't tell where she had hit it, only that it was no longer moving. That would have to do.

Scrambling for her helmet, voices still screamed from the

comms. Sarah pulled on her helmet to a cacophony of arguments. Yasmin was screaming something at Breckett, Breckett was yelling at Parker, and Parker was doing her best to get a single word in.

"I'm here," Sarah said between shaken breaths. The comms went silent. Steadying herself, she said it again. "I'm here."

"What the hell happened?" Breckett asked. "I've taken the bridge, if I need to be down there too I can."

"Not enough time," Parker said, "less than three minutes."

"Vaughn's dead," Sarah said. "Kyllen's down, and I'm not sure how long he has left before he is too."

Sarah glanced over the two bodies, one a lifeless husk, the other a pale teenager watching her through ragged breaths. Sarah knew she should feel more for her crew, more for Vaughn, but she didn't. Beads of the man's blood still ran down her cheeks like sweat. Maybe it was shock, maybe it was hateful callousness starting to work its way over her worn heart. She felt nothing for the near-headless corpse still bleeding out on the floor. A twinge of sorrow remained for the kid, at least. All of this was her fault. No one deserved to witness what had just happened to Vaughn, especially one as young as Kyllen. One of his eyes was shut while the other winced with pain. It watched her like she may yet decide to finish the job.

"Stay on mission, or we're all dead," Breckett said. "Yasmin, get down there and see what you can do for the kid."

"I can still do it," Kyllen said, though his voice was little more than a croaked whisper.

Sarah didn't argue. She could give him this much. She kneeled down by Kyllen's side and pulled one of his arms across her shoulders. He did the best he could to prop himself up, and Sarah hoisted the two of them to their feet. A whimper escaped him as they took their first step, but to his credit Kyllen kept pace. He grew weaker and heavier with each step, but Sarah kept him moving forward. They stepped over the corpse blocking the threshold and moved into the engine room. The engine was a much smaller fusion reactor with its pyramids small enough to be placed on cylindrical plinths, and the room itself was a mere quarter of the size of what the Villimath offered.

Her abdomen flared with pain, and Parker shouted out a countdown at two minutes. Sure enough, there was a small device linked into the engine's panel that beeped with a ticking clock. She set Kyllen down with a grunt, and the kid got to work without hesitation. He barely glanced at the device before knowing what to do. Even in his injured state, he was making quick work of it with deft hands.

Something blunt slammed into the back of Sarah's helmet. The force sent her sprawling forward, and she tripped over a bundle of cables running across the grated floor. Falling to her knees, thick arms wrapped around her chest and throat. Sarah was hoisted to her feet slammed back against the floor. She rolled over just in time to see a massive Dwemyri driving its thick boot into her stomach. Her armor took a lot of the blow, but a shock of pain still lanced through her core. The Dwemyri planted its knee on her chest and kneeled to wrap clawed hands around her throat. The soft fibers between her helmet and armored collarbone made it easy for her attacker to start choking the life out of her. It squeezed and stars began to sprout in Sarah's vision. She panicked, flailed, but the Dwemyri was too heavy to budge. Air came in shorter and shorter breaths, and Sarah did the only thing she could think of as her attacker staired down into her helmet with burning hate.

Sarah reached up to grab its head between both of her hands, and jabbed her thumbs into its black eyes. She squeezed and dug with the tips of her thumbs until each one popped like an overripe grape. Streaks of crimson spurt down her wrists, and the monster howled in agony. It snapped back, releasing Sarah and clamping its hands over its bleeding sockets. Rage, unbridled and all-consuming, bit deep into Sarah's chest and set forth a conflagration the likes she'd never felt. Once more, she grabbed the Dwemyri's head and slammed her helmet into its snout. She could feel the bone crunching beneath her armored face plate, and a spray of blood obstructed her vision. It rolled off of her and onto its back, but Sarah wasn't done. She bolted to her feet and ripped of her helmet. She swung the helmet in a wide arc to bring it down upon the reeling Dwemyri's head. It made contact with a sickening crack. A high whimper escaped the broken snout. She swung again. Another wet crack. *Again*. This time the top of her attacker's head began to give. It held its hand out in a pleading gesture. *Again*. The dome caved in like a melon, spilling the creature's life blood across the floor. Sarah's helmet made a wet squelching sound as she pulled it free from the gore. Bits of fur and bone still clung to some of the helmet's grooves. It took a great deal of will to not hit it again for good measure.

Sarah breathed deep and found her control. Her eyes fixated on the mess she'd created while blood dripped steadily from her chin. *Drip*. There was no way of telling who's blood it was. She took another deep breath. *Drip*. It could still be Vaughn's. A muzzle flash and his head exploded all over again. *Drip*. She wiped her chin with a wrist, but the gore across her arms only made it worse. *Drip*. It could be Kyllen's. She could still feel the resistance of his suit and flesh as the nano-tip slid between his ribs. *Drip*. It could be the Dwemyri's. The wet crack of the creature's skull echoed in her mind. She wiped her chin again. More blood. It was everywhere, in everything. It was in her eyes, her nose, and the metallic flavor soiled her lips.

Nausea rumbled a deep burble in the pit of her stomach. She stumbled over to where Kyllen lay slumped against the engine panel. Three seconds remained frozen on the display's timer. The kid had done it. She gave him a reassuring pat on the shoulder. Once this was over, she'd do what she had to in order to make things right. She'd go out of her way to treat him better. He remained motionless, leaning so his face was turned away. Even with his suit, Sarah could tell he wasn't breathing. *Drip*. The knife had slid in so easy. Sarah pulled his shoulder to roll him toward her. Through the glass of his helmet, she could see the pallid complexion of his face. His eyes remained open, but the light of life was gone.

CHAPTER 19
- JAX -

1

Rector let out a jaw cracking yawn as he plopped down into the pilot's seat of the Sheet Skimmer. His family, and the woman named Jax were all fast asleep as they coasted through the deep void of space. He couldn't say why he was awake, only that he was. His dreams had been horrible and nightmarish as of late, so maybe that was part of it. Scratching his chin, and pulling an irritating hair out of his nose, he opened up the navigation terminal. He needed a shave, but that could wait. Something more pressing bothered him. He had set their coordinates the night before, but it only now occurred to him that they were wrong. Rector wasn't sure what had come over him. They didn't need to go to the unexplored territories; there was nothing for them in such a remote part of space. What they needed to do was go to a place of high traffic. Perhaps a shipping lane for a major Suttack trading planet. That sounded like a perfect idea. Rector knew just the one. He had been intentionally avoiding it for many years. Again, he wasn't sure why. His memories told him the planet was welcoming to humans despite the typical Suttack ways. Strange, his mind had been so foggy these days. He punched in the new coordinates, and set the Sheet Skimmer for a plotted jump directory. It would put them right where they needed to be in a few hours. His family would awake to a lovely place to take a vacation, one they sorely needed.

Dizziness swept over him, and a deep pain pounded at the base of his skull. When had the bulkheads been painted black?

His chair, and monitors had been painted black too. Percy must have played some sort of trick on him, and he was just now taking notice. His ears started ringing, and a woman's voice hummed inside his head. It wasn't a voice he recognized. It wasn't his dear Rooth. The tune was a lullaby of some kind coaxing Rector to fall asleep. He fought back the weight of his own eyelids, and scrubbed a hand across his chin. He really needed a shave.

"What are you doing?" A voice asked from behind him. It was Percy's voice, so Rector turned in his chair to tell the boy to go back to sleep, but froze. Where Percy should have stood was something far more disturbing. There was a creature about the same size as his son, but with black scales for skin, and burning charcoal for eyes. Black smoke billowed from the top of his head, and filled the cockpit. Rector spluttered looking for words, but he was too stunned to speak. Finally, the words came out in a horse whisper.

"Demon," Rector said, "Villimath has come for us all. Morathnu save us."

He'd be damned if he let this demon take his ship or threaten his family. He shot out of his seat and grabbed the demon by the throat. It looked shocked by his attack, but Rector wouldn't give this monster a chance to escape. He squeezed with one hand as the demon gasped for air. Villimath would not work his vile sorcery upon this ship. He dragged the demon down the narrow corridor, its blackened feet snagging and catching against every cable and pipe as it kicked. Rector held firm, and kept marching his course. He reached the airlock, pulled open the hatch, and tossed the demon inside. Slamming the hatch shut he watched as the chamber filled with black smoke. The demon pounded on the glass, begging to be let out. Oh, Rector was going to let it out alright. He slammed his fist against the button to open up the outer airlock door. It slid to the side, and the demon was blown out into space, smoke going with it. Rector laughed at the last look of horror on the demon's face.

He leaned back against the opposite bulkhead, and wiped his hands on his pants. Motion to his left caught Rector's eye, and he looked up in time to see another black scaled demon running away down the corridor in the opposite direction of where he and his wife's cabin was. A faint trail of smoke plumed after. It appeared as though he had more work to do, but he needed to make sure Rooth was safe. He pushed off the bulkhead, and Rector made his way toward that direction while being careful to be on the lookout. There was no telling how many more of these things were aboard the Sheet Skimmer. He stooped through the curtain which divided their cabin from the rest of the ship. He let out a long, horrified moan at what awaited him. Where he expected to see his wife, a demon waited. It sat up in their shared bed, and watched Rector's every move with a strange look on its ashen face. Its charred flesh fell away in chunks leaving black and bloodied stains on their sheets.

"Where is my boy?" The demon asked in a voice that was as stark mockery of his wife's.

"Your little demon took a tumble out the airlock," Rector growled. He found a piece of loose ship frame propped up against the bulkhead. He always meant to put that back up, but now he was glad he didn't. He tested its weight in both hands like a club, and grinned.

"What are you doing?" The demon asked, but Rector didn't answer. He hoisted the piece of metal, and swung it with all of his might. His strike connected, and it made a sound like a wet crack as it slammed into the demon's temple. It toppled over in the bed with its charcoal eyes still open, but unseeing. The demon's mouth still moved as if it were gasping for air. Rector couldn't have that. There couldn't be any surviving monsters on his ship. He dropped the piece of ship frame, and climbed on top of the bed. Wrapping his narrow fingers - twisted by years of arthritis - around the demon's throat, Rector squeezed. No reaction crossed the demon's face as it was too stunned by his strike, so Rector held his hands tight until the mouth stopped moving. Once he knew it was done, he climbed off and wiped ash from his hands.

"I know you're out there demons!" He called out. "Don't worry, Rector is going to find you real soon."

2

Jax pressed herself up against the bulkhead behind a stack of crates, and sobbed quietly into her sleeve. It wasn't supposed to happen like this. None of them were supposed to get hurt. All she had wanted was to manipulate Rector's perception enough to make him change course. She'd get them to a more populace area, and leave via an escape pod. Rector would snap out of it, and get his family to safety. Her abilities had a different idea. They had been too potent, too uncontrollable, and they got away from her before she could pull them back into control. Because of Jax, Percy had been killed and likely Rooth as well. She was no better than Vincent, only her monsters were imaginary things causing real people to do terrible deeds. Rector called out through the ship, and Jax bit back another sob. She felt for the pistol stowed away in the pocket of her too-baggy pants, but found the pocket to be empty. It must have fallen out somewhere when she started to run. She needed to find it if she wanted any chance of making it through the night.

Slipping out from her hiding space, her baggy shirt snagged on a rivet causing her to have to make an awkward turn to break loose. The shirt tore, but Jax had little time to be concerned with it. She could hear the old man's footsteps stomping down the corridor toward her location. That was bad, very bad. The cargo bay of the Sheet Skimmer only had a single way in or out, and that direction was now off limits to her. She decided to hide closer to the entrance and wait for Rector to walk in. Maybe then she could slip past him and go find her pistol. She tried again to focus her attention on Rector's mind. If she could get it back under control, there would be no need to run from him. It was no use. She was too frightened, and too tired to concentrate. Even if she could, there was a good chance her abilities would get away from her. She couldn't risk making the situation even worse. Already, her powers were getting more and more uncontrollable, and she was afraid that soon she too would lose touch with reality. If that happened there was no coming back. She could feel herself cracking at the seams. The demons Rector screamed about was what she saw as well, but she knew the truth of the matter. They were illusions.

Jax rubbed her eyes and slapped her cheeks. She needed to keep it together long enough to find a surgeon capable of taking out the stone in her head. She needed to get back to Sarah even if all she managed to do was apologize. Sarah deserved that much from her.

The footsteps came closer, and Jax ducked low behind another stack of crates. She snuck a peak around the edge of the crates to see the old man standing with one hand propped on his hip, and the other dragging a large piece of metal behind him. An ear-to-ear grin was spread across his black-scaled face, charcoal burning in his eye sockets. Jax squeezed her eyes shut, and opened them again in an attempt to blink away the illusion. Her own mind was too much for her, however, and the illusion remained.

"I know you're in here, little demon," Rector said, and stomped forward a few steps. Metal scraped against metal as he dragged his improvised weapon behind him. Jax closed her eyes again, this time taking a deep breath. Everything was normal. Everything was as it should be. There were no demons, no monsters, no murder. Just a normal Rector and a normal Jax. Her scalp started to prickle, and hot nettles dragged across her skin. There was nothing but two normal humans aboard this ship. She blinked, and Rector was back to his pale and hairy self. Rector, however, still stood there with a wide grin plastered across his face, and his eyes rolled from one side to the next in frantic movements. Blood stained his hands up to the elbows and it was splattered across his cheeks. It was too late for him. The old man's mind was already broken. She needed to find the gun.

He stepped fully into the cargo bay, and Jax snuck around the opposite side of the crates. Careful as she could, she tip-toed out into the corridor while Rector continued to drag his weapon around the cargo bay. As soon as she was out of view, Jax bolted. She kept her eyes toward the floor keeping a lookout for anywhere the gun might have fallen, but everywhere she looked turned up empty. Running past Rooth's cabin, Jax froze. She couldn't help herself. Jax had to know what had become of the old woman. Glancing over her shoulder to make sure Rector wasn't in pursuit, she crept over to the curtain, and pulled it aside. Jax recoiled, and suppressed a gag. She wanted to flee, but she couldn't peel her eyes away from the bloody mess on the bed. This was her fault. Poor Rooth's head lay slumped against a white pillow which was now stained red with blood and brain matter. The left half of her skull was caved in with that eye dangling down the side of her face, connected only by the stalk. The pungent odor of metal and spoiled meat choked the air to a suffocating degree, and Jax had to pull her shirt over her nose.

"Such a wonderful sight, no?" Rector whispered a mere centimeter from her ear. His stale breath mixed with the stench of death causing tears to well up in the corners of Jax's eyes. "It's enough to make this old man's mouth water."

Jax twisted away from him, but slipped in a pool of Rooth's blood. Careening backward, her back slammed into the metal flooring with a loud thud. Pain flared through her shoulder blades, but she considered herself lucky for not having hit her head. Rector laughed at her dismay, and his form overshadowed her from the doorway. He licked his lips, and tapped the metal bar against the floor. A soft ting echoed through the cabin, so Rector did it again. Jax looked for anything close at hand with which she could defend herself. To her right, was an upturned night stand, its contents strewn about the floor with several items resting in pools of blood. An object glinted red, a thin nail file with a black handle. Rector lurched forward, raising the bar above his head. She had to time this perfectly, or she'd die. He slammed the metal down, and Jax rolled to her right toward the file. In one motion, she snatched the file, twisted, and drove the metal tip into the side of Rector's now exposed ear. He shrieked with agony. Dropping the metal, he fell to the floor with both hands clutching the side of his head. Scarlet streams pumped between his clenched fingers, and his face was a portrait of anguish.

Jax pushed herself to her feet, and the old man scrambled away to push his back against the frame of the bed. It was her turn to loom over the old man. She picked up the bar he had dropped, and hoisted it in both hands. Rector sobbed as he tried to pull the file out of his ear, more blood spurting with each attempt. Jax only watched him suffer, devoid of any pity or sorrow. In fact, Jax felt nothing at all. She was empty of all emotion, and all that was left was an all-consuming need to survive. Rector gave up on the file, and held up a pleading hand. He started to babble something, but the words didn't register in Jax's head. She heard them, but she didn't understand them. Her mind felt as though it were in a bubble the outside world was incapable of penetrating. Rector held up his other hand, and clasped them before him in prayer. Jax didn't know why, but she found the gesture insulting. She swung the bar like a bat, and smashed the metal through his wrists. The crack of his old bones reverberated through the bar, and Rector screamed. It washed over Jax unheard. He groveled on his elbows, trying to keep his face from planting in the pool of blood near his knees. It was time to finish this. Jax swung the bar over her head and buried it in the back of Rector's skull. Splitting like a melon, the contents of his head spilled out before her feet. It was more of mercy than he had given Rooth, but again, all of this was her fault. Dropping the piece of metal, she slunk out of the cabin. At least the air was fresher on this side of the curtain. She needed to make her way to the cockpit. She needed to make sure the next part of her plan didn't go nearly as awry as this.

3

Jax dragged her feet through the corridor like a walking corpse. She was a hollow shell ready to crack if she so much as stepped too hard. Shadows of ghosts tormented her peripherals, laughing, pointing, then opening their mouths wide to devour one another. Their voices were cruel, and whispered promises of torment and damnation. Jax tried to wave them away, but they persisted. Every time she turned and tried to look at one directly, they scattered to remain at the edges of her vision. Several conjoined to form a larger shape, and that larger shape shifted from a shadow into something far more real, something far more familiar. Sarah stood behind her left shoulder just outside of Jax's direct line of view. Those full lips and blue-green eyes Jax so very much envied were twisted into a disappointed pout. Somehow, Sarah even managed to make that expression seem attractive.

"Piss off," Jax said, "you aren't real."

"Oh, but I'm real to you," Sarah said, "in every way possible."

Sarah touched the side of Jax's neck with a warm hand, and traced a line down to her shoulder, her side, and finally stopped to rest on her hip. Jax wanted to hate it, but she closed her eyes and languished in the touch of her old partner. She thought of the nights they'd spent after escaping the station, the warmth they'd shared. Jax shook her head, and slapped the side of her cheek to bring herself back. All of this was the machinations of her own mind. The black sliver of stone embedded in her brain wanted her to succumb, but she would not. She tried to blink away the illusions, but Sarah remained. The other shadows in her peripherals laughed at her failure, and Sarah's pout turned into a seductive grin.

"Don't you want me to stay?" Sarah asked. "Afterall, I did find something for you."

She removed something from beneath her feathered cloak with one hand while wrapping her other around Jax's hip. Sarah let her hand slide from the side of her hip to the front, and pulled Jax close. Resting her chin on Jax's shoulder, Sarah's breath was warm against her neck. With their bodies pressed tight together, Sarah brought the object around Jax's other side to hold up in front of her. It was the pistol she had lost. Sarah held it pointed up, so its cylindrical barrels were directed toward the ceiling. Jax reached for it, but did not take it. Her hand hovered a few centimeters from the metal grip. It couldn't be the real thing. This too had to be part of her mind's illusions. Sarah's hand started to torment Jax's waistband, massaging in an all too suggestive way.

"Take it," Sarah said, and the shadows laughed.

"Take it, take it," they all repeated in shrill voices.

"You need this for what's to come," Sarah said, "unless you want to stay here. Unless you don't want to come back to me."

Jax snatched the pistol from Sarah's grasp, and clutched it to her chest with both hands. The metal was cold to the touch, and the texture on the grip felt like sandpaper on her fingers. Sarah used her now free hand to caress the side of Jax's cheek. The corridor before her seemed to grow in length as she did so, and the shadows stretched out along the bulkheads. Sarah nipped at Jax's earlobe, but let go to take a step back. The air felt colder, and Jax almost turned around, almost begged her to come back, but Sarah spoke first.

"You've got a lot of work ahead of you," she said. She held a mischievous smile like she knew what she had just done. "I'll leave you to it for now, but you'll see me again soon."

With that, Sarah disappeared. The shadows shrank away with her, and left Jax to stand alone in the narrow corridor. The pistol was still gripped in her hands, and Jax had to examine it to be sure it was real. In truth, she knew she was growing closer and closer to not being able to tell the difference, but for now she thought the pistol was as real as it could get. Letting out a long, shuddering sigh Jax stuffed the pistol into an oversized pocket and made her way to the cockpit.

4

Jax double checked the coordinates to be certain the old man had set things in the right direction. Sure enough, the Sheet Skimmer was scheduled to jump directly into the center of a high traffic trade route. She hadn't known of its existence, but the old man was far too familiar with it. All she had to do was put the idea in his head to find a populated area. His mind did the rest. Now, that mind was spilled out all over the floor of his cabin along with that of his wife's. Jax looked down at her hands and clothes, both of which were stained and coated crimson. Dried blood cracked along the back of her knuckles and wrists, and her sleeves had grown stiff. The sight was bad, but the smell was worse. She could feel it spattered across her face, and caked in her hair. If someone decided to pick her up, they would be astonished at what they found. Sarah was right. She did have a lot of work to do. Pushing out of the pilot's seat, Jax found the purifier masks from earlier. She fastened the strap around her head, hair and all, in hopes it would block out the smell of what she had to do next. The cold air blowing across her mouth and nose seemed to help at least.

Jax made her way back down the corridor toward the elderly couple's cabin. Pushing aside the curtain, she nearly wretched. However, Jax managed to maintain her composure. She was beginning to grow used to these kinds of sights. She knew that wasn't a good thing, but she'd take whatever help she could get at this point. Rolling up her sleeves, she set to work dragging each of the corpses out of the small cabin and into the nearby airlock. Once inside, she gave the two a final farewell before opening the exterior door. She steeled herself as she pushed the button and watched Rooth's corpse as it was blown into the black void of space. Looking back at the red trail she had left, Jax realized she was going to need a mop. Finding a supply closet filled with cleaning materials that Jax wasn't sure the family had ever used, she spent the next several hours scrubbing and scraping away the blood. She pulled up all the blankets, sheets and pillows, and tossed those into the airlock as well. The curtain needed to be pulled down, and thrown away, and just as she was about ready to push the airlock button, Jax noticed her sleeves again. If her clothes were bad before, they were absolutely drenched now. Taking the pistol out of her pocket, she peeled off the oversized clothing, parts of which were glued to her skin with coagulated blood. She then tossed the ruined clothes in as well. The air was frigid on her naked skin, but it was better than being covered in bits of Rooth and Rector. She'd need to find some new clothes, but for now all she wanted was a shower.

Once in the bathroom, she cranked the water as hot as it would allow. For the first time since all hell broke loose, Jax saw herself in the mirror. She looked like a wraith with matted hair, and blood covered skin. Looking at her hair again, its uncontrolled frizz stuck together in clumps, she made up her mind. She dug around in the bathroom compartments until she found something that would work. There were no scissors available, but she found Rector's old straight razor. She grabbed fistfuls of hair, and started cutting.

5

Jax hummed as she strapped herself into the pilot's seat. Her head felt lighter, freer, but her neck was cold. She hadn't gone as short as Sarah, instead opting to leave a few centimeters of curls on top while shaving the sides down to the scalp. She was clean, the ship was clean, and now she wore a set of Percy's old clothes - a pair of yellow overalls and a black shirt. The boy's were the only ones that seemed to fit right. At least his boot size was perfect. Jax checked the coordinates for a third time, gauged the jump distance, and readied herself. Compared to other ships, the jump sequence of the Sheet Skimmer was a hectic process. One could feel every lurch the ship made, and if not strapped in, the jump could prove dangerous.

Shadows crept into the corners of her vision, accompanied by the sounds of howling gales and a child's laughter. Turning to look at the co-pilot's seat, Jax found Sarah occupying its cushions. She was able to look directly at her this time, and Jax thought that was a bad sign. The black cloak with its feathered collar shifted as if being blown by the wind even though the air in the cockpit was still. Her old partner smiled at her, and laid a hand high upon Jax's thigh.

"It's a good look for you," Sarah said. She leaned over and kissed Jax, her lips soft, breath warm. When she pulled away, Jax let out a disappointed sigh. "You better be ready for what comes next."

"I am," Jax said, but as the words came out, Sarah disappeared. The shadows shrank away, and all grew quiet. Her stomach lurched as the Sheet Skimmer jumped without warning. Even while being ripped to pieces, Modiri had been a smoother ride. Jax yelled out several profanities while the Sheet Skimmer rattled and shook through the jump sequence, and a split second later it was over. Jax lifted the cockpit's particle sheet to get a view of the outside. Stars twinkled, and in the distance, she could see the soft yellow glow of a nearby planet. All that was left to do was to initiate the Sheet Skimmer's emergency beacon. Jax entered the command to do just that, and a broad signal flared out over every frequency. It was only a matter of time until someone answered. Jax almost felt sorry for the person who did.

Almost.

CHAPTER 20
- SARAH -

1

The flight back to the Villimath was silent. Sarah was strapped into her seat with her helmet back on. She'd done the best she could to clear the blood away from the sensors, but her internal camera feeds still showed streaks of red. She stared past it at nothing. Yasmin sat across from her, but Sarah didn't see the doctor, not really. Her old scars burned and her nerve-damaged hand twitched, but she didn't notice them either. She was trying to keep her attention away from the body bag strapped into the seats at the end of the row. Only one, however, as Yasmin had worked her magic to bring life back into the boy. Faint, but it was there. His body rested on the floor between them cocooned in hoses, tubes, and devices Sarah had never seen before all encasing him in the hopes that he survived the journey. Both bodies on the floor were her fault. Breckett hadn't asked what had happened. Neither did Yasmin. They simply collected her and the two casualties and brought them back to the drop ship. Sarah hadn't even noticed when Yasmin entered the engine room. She curled herself into a dark corner and intended to stay there until nature ran its course. Whether that be starvation or something else, Sarah cared little. Yasmin had none of it, however, and the doctor had physically dragged Sarah out of the mess until she found her own feet. Now, even through their helmets, Sarah could tell Yasmin was keeping a close eye on her.

The motion of the drop ship shifted, and Sarah's stomach

lurched. She wasn't normally motion sick, but this time was different. Despite the air recyclers and the powerful fans of her suit, the thick stench of blood refused to dissipate. She grabbed onto her seat harness and bit down on her lower lip as Breckett brought the ship careening sideways into the Villimath's hangar. The ship touched down, the engine cut, and yet they sat in the quiet. Not only had they lost almost two of their own, but Breckett hadn't found a single survivor. He found something, but said he wouldn't talk about it until they got back. Sarah assumed that meant her brother was dead. Why wouldn't he be? Everyone else was gone; it made sense for Hector to be as well.

Sarah barely noticed the exit ramp lowering, nor Breckett stomping his way out of the cockpit and down the aisle. He stopped and knelt in front of Sarah, placing a hand on the thick plate of her shoulder. They stayed like that for several long moments before anyone spoke.

"He's going to live. He will," he said. "Yasmin will get you cleaned up, I'll take care of the rest. When you feel up to it, I found something I think I could use your help with."

With that, he strode out of the back of the drop ship and disappeared into the hangar beyond. A cold numbness clung to Sarah, and she hardly registered what Breckett had said. Even as he and Lucas returned to cart the boy down to medical, she hardly registered any of it. Yasmin pulled herself free of the harness and leaned over Sarah to undo hers as well. No words were spoken, but the doctor fretted over Sarah like mother and child. She undid the harness and helped Sarah to her feet. Yasmin was unconcerned about the gore that now stained her own armor as she pulled Sarah up with one arm, grabbing her wrist and the other supporting her lower back. It was gentleness Sarah wasn't ready for in the sea of today's violence.

A notification flashed in Sarah's helmet as her arm was slung over the doctor's shoulder. Ziven wanted to talk. Later. It was a problem for later. Or, if Sarah was being honest with herself, never. Her brother was lost, and she was done. So, very, done. She leaned on Yasmin more out of exhaustion than pain, and the two of them exited the drop ship.

2

White lights and the stench of sterilized workstations seemed to be a repeating factor in Sarah's life as of late. She was alone in the small shower cubicle, water running, steam roiling in thick clouds, while Yasmin waited for her just outside. Still in her armor, Sarah stepped into the water stream and watched as the while tile of the floor ran pink. *Drip.* Bit by bit, Sarah peeled away the layers of her suit. She washed each piece over in her hands before dropping them carelessly to the floor. Before long, she stood bare with hot water coursing down her back. Her discarded clothes and armor littered the shower floor and despite the thick steam, the stench of rust filled the air. *Drip.*

Sarah ran a finger along her old scar. Indeed, the puckered flesh had reopened in spots allowing fresh trails of her own blood to stream down her body and collect with the crimson pool at her feet. The drain was slow to clear it all out. A problem for later. Tilting her head up and away from the mess, Sarah let the heat pour over her face. It too smelled like blood. *Drip.* Opening her eyes, Sarah's vision blurred with red. She stumbled back out of the shower. Where there should have been water, blood sprayed from the chrome-finished shower head. *Drip.* The knife had slid in with so little effort. *Drip.* Vaughn's skill had all meant nothing in the horrid chaos of an unseen shot. *Drip.* She could still feel bits of his skull spraying against her lips. Nausea churned her stomach until bile threatened the back of her throat. *Drip.* She turned to the door to run, but a figure blocked her path.

Hector stood before her with his dark hair matted down by dried blood and empty sockets gaped where eyes should have been. The nails of his fingers were curled back and bloodied as if he'd been scratching at something. She couldn't move. Fear held her in place when she should have fought to get around him. Hector raised his hands and wrapped cold fingers around Sarah's throat.

"All of us are dead because of you," he said. His voice sounded like a person who hadn't spoken in a thousand cycles.

"No," Sarah whimpered.

"So much blood is on your hands."

"I tried."

"Not hard enough."

Hector's hands clamped down, cutting off her air. She slipped, and was forced back into the shower. Blood filled her nose, her mouth, stung her eyes. She clawed at hands that wouldn't let go; her breaths coming in shorter and shorter spurts. Pain knifed across her scar, and Sarah let out another whimper. It felt as though something, or many somethings, were pushing out against the tissue from the inside out. All at once, the hands let go and Sarah fell back against the far wall. Wiping blood from her eyes, Sarah looked down to see hundreds of tiny spider legs squeezing their way through her scar. The first spider popped through to go scuttling down her leg and across the floor toward her brother. It was soon followed by a second, and then a third. Hundreds began pouring from the now open wound to scurry through the shower of blood and swarm her brother. Hector smiled as his face slowly disappeared behind a growing mound of black and red.

A scream tore from her throat. A culmination of fear, rage, and sorrow all rang out in a horrid cacophony which ripped her vocal cords raw. She fell to the floor and pushed herself back into the corner away from the stream of blood. Curling into the fetal position, Sarah tried to tell herself it wasn't real. Nothing was. All she needed was munmos and sleep.

The shower door swung open, and hurried steps splashed across the tile. Sarah began to sit up in an attempt to defend herself from this new attacker, but was swept up by an embrace instead. Yasmin wrapped her arms around Sarah's shivering body, and pulled Sarah's head to her breast. The space wasn't large enough to keep them both out of the water, and Yasmin was getting drenched in her clothes. Still, the doctor clung to Sarah with the most nurturing comfort Sarah had ever felt.

"I'm here," she whispered. "Deep breaths for me."

Sarah tried, but all she could do was sob. They came soft at first, but once the flood gate was open there was no turning back. They came out heavy and wet, tears mixing with snot all in ugly vulnerability. She tried to choke it back, but it only served to make the situation worse. Where Sarah expected rejection, Yasmin held on tight.

"It's okay," she whispered, "let it out. It's safe here."

Sarah stopped trying to hold it back. She stopped trying to be strong. She leaned into Yasmin's chest and let out all the things she'd been holding in. She didn't know if minutes passed or hours, but the doctor held her until she was ready to stand.

3

Sarah winced as Yasmin spread ointment across her scar. She leaned back on the exam table with the spare shirt Yasmin lent her pulled up enough to bare her stomach. The doctor dabbed the green goop along the angry red flesh before wiping away the excess with a towel. In the corner of the room on a different table, Kyllen's body was encased in a mechanical capsule. It beeped in long intervals, and each breath the boy took released a whiff of mist from a small vent. Sarah watched each puff. At least it meant he was breathing. Yasmin's voice drew her back to the present.

"Whoever patched you up the first time did a shit job of it," she said.

"Throx," Sarah said. She hadn't meant to say it out loud, but she felt a comfort around Yasmin now and the name just slipped out.

"Old lover?" Yasmin asked.

Sarah nearly choked on a laugh. What came out was somewhere between a snort and a genuine giggle. "Why is that the first thing to come to your head?"

"It got you to laugh, didn't it?" Yasmin finished her work by placing a long adhesive bandage across the scar. "Let that set for a few days and you'll never have to worry about it reopening again."

"Think I'll have that long before heading out again?" Sarah asked. The question earned her a pointed look.

"After what happened on that ship," Yasmin said, "Sarah, as far as I'm concerned, the mission is over. Breckett sees it too. No way we keep searching."

A long silence stretched out between them, and Sarah chewed her lower lip. She let the shirt fall, and noted Yasmin's eyes following the hem down in its descent. Scrubbing a hand over her scalp, thick stubble beginning to grow, Sarah bit down harder. She had a sickly feeling she was about to be stuck between Breckett, Ziven, and her own personal needs. Which of them would win out was something only the cosmos knew at this point. A pensive look crossed Yasmin's face, and she broke the silence with a question.

"Wanna talk about what you saw in the shower?"

"No," Sarah said. It was a gut reaction, and one she regretted once she noticed Yasmin flinch. "Just everything caught up to me, I guess."

"You're due for another session," Yasmin said, "and when we get back to the Ifrit, I know a few specialists I can get you in with. They aren't cheap, but I'm sure I can help you get things sorted out."

Sarah nodded and let out a muttered thanks as Yasmin rolled away on her stool toward the other side of the room. She pulled the wetsuit out of the drawer along with a few other tools Sarah was becoming more familiar with by the day. The start of the process was the worst, but Sarah had to admit, these sessions helped.

"There's something else we could try," Yasmin continued as she loaded up her equipment-covered cart, "but it's completely your call. It may be a bit of a shock to the system."

She pulled something else out of a drawer that looked like a small, black cube with a flattened cylinder affixed to the bottom. Yasmin squeezed a button on the side, and a holo-display popped up with data swirling in blue above the cube.

"It'll disable your ID chip," she said. "You'll lose access to everything, of course, but it'll help alleviate your symptoms until we can get you more settled."

Sarah watched the glowing device in Yasmin's hand as if it were a snake. She'd been isolated most of her life, but never in such a way. She'd lose access to all forms of remote communication, locked doors wouldn't register her, all of her credits would be out of reach. It felt as though the whole universe revolved around the little chip embedded in her brain. Shaking her head, Sarah turned the offer down. Even if temporary, it wasn't a sacrifice she was willing to make.

"I thought as much," Yasmin said. "Can't blame you, really. Think I'd make the same decision. Oh well, thought I'd offer. Come on, let's get you ready for the chamber."

4

The corridors of the Villimath had a haunted feel to them now. Two individuals should never be enough to make a difference in a ship this size, but Sarah felt their absence in every cabin and corridor as if their souls were imprinted in the very hull. Maybe she could avoid Kyllen's grandmother. If he lived, she knew the boy would lie about what happened. It was who he was. A part of her hoped he'd lie to protect her from Gran's wrath. Neither of the Groal deserved it, Sarah didn't deserve it, but Sarah didn't believe she could bring herself to face the old woman. Not now, not ever. As she strode down the crew quarter, she glanced at the door that belonged to the kid.

"You deserved better," she said as she stepped through her own door.

"I'm not sure I'd agree with you," Parker said. She was perched atop Sarah's bed leaning back into the little nook with one leg crossed over the other. Her usual white lab coat was left open to reveal the black body suit beneath. The neckline cut low, and the hips were cut high to accentuate every curve and detail of her body. Her color shifting eyes watched Sarah take in every detail.

"I have it pretty good," Parker said, "and to say I deserve even better would be arrogant of me. I do appreciate the sentiment, though."

"How did you get in here?" Sarah asked. She managed to break her eyes away long enough to notice her drone was missing as well.

"I have a knack for getting to things I'm not supposed to," Parker said, "and besides, this room is marked for someone name Sarah Renza. As far as I'm aware, there is no Sarah Renza on this ship."

Parker ran a hand through her crimson hair, and gave Sarah a knowing smile. Her irises shifted from lavender to jade, but as always, they were filled with mirth. Sweat beaded on the back of Sarah's neck and her heart quickened. Even if she fled, they were both stuck aboard this ship. One word, and Parker could have the entire crew on her side. Sarah was done for, and she knew it.

"Who are you?" Sarah asked.

"You know, it takes an incredible event to bring both Kara Corporation and Saber under the same flag," Parker said. "Somewhere around three trillion credits in damages and the deaths of twenty-eight crew members seems to do the trick, however."

"Twenty-eight dead?" The confusion was plain across Sarah's face. She wasn't going to feign her innocence, not now, but the deaths seemed higher than she remembered.

"The crew of the investigation team," Parker said, "all KIA while looking for your little station. Come now, Sarah, you didn't really think this would all just go away, did you? You're smarter than that. Afterall, you have so much blood on your hands."

"What do you want?" Sarah asked. "Why now, and if you knew all this time, why did you let me get this far?"

Sarah's fists were clenched, and a hatred boiled deep in her chest. She wanted to lunge at Parker. She'd killed monsters, men, and Dwemyri alike. What was a little scientist going to do? She could already feel the woman's blood dripping down her fingers. Fighting back the urge, Sarah wiped the snarl from her lips. She took a deep breath and forced herself to wait for an answer.

"All your questions boil down to the same answer," Parker said, "Gayle. I was hoping the AI would present itself by now, but no luck. You're going to help me find it, but I'll let you finish your little escapade first. I'm curious how it all ends. As to why now? Well, you'd sort out that I knew about you after I gave you this. Breckett asked me to crack it, but it appears to have your name on it."

Parker brushed herself off and stood. Her hips swayed as she sashayed across the room to stop a hair's breadth away from Sarah. She was close enough to feel her body heat. The scientist grabbed Sarah's hand, and she had to fight every urge to rip it way. A small data-chip was placed into Sarah's palm. Parker leaned in closer to whisper into Sarah's ear, her breath warm against Sarah's lobe.

"It's locked to your bio-mark," she said, "but like I said before, I've got a knack for getting into things I'm not supposed to."

With that, Parker pulled away to brush past Sarah. She stood in the corridor beyond with a grin that spoke of mischief and warnings. Her lab coat was pulled tight around her now, and her eyes simmered with a deep gray. They scanned every part of Sarah's body before turning away. As Parker strode back down the corridor, she made one final comment over her shoulder.

"Yasmin smells good on you," she said, "it would be a shame to lose her too."

Sarah tugged on the shirt having forgotten she was still in Yasmin's clothes. Letting the door slide shut, she double checked to make sure it was set to lock. Not that she thought it would keep anyone out, but she could at least make it more difficult. Dropping herself into the writing desk chair, she set the chip onto the desk's surface with a click. She pressed her thumb against a small indent on the side, and a holo-projector flickered to life. The figure standing before her made Sarah shudder. It was a morak'casai, but the figure's mask had a long black scar running down one side. The man spoke with a voice low and thunderous.

"Prisoner number XV205C-HF, Sarah Vermillion, if you've found this message it means you've managed to slip out of my little trap. If that is the case, then I have a little reward for you. Or, perhaps, you can call it incentive." He dragged someone into view, a man gagged and bound. Sarah recognized him in an instant. "I have your brother here with me and unless you want him to meet an unfortunate end, I'd suggest you come find me. Alone, of course. The coordinates can be found on this chip. Make it quick, my employer isn't known for his patience."

The feed cut, giving Sarah a start. Without hesitation, she plugged the chip into a nearby data-slate. The coordinates were easy enough to find, and she immediately sent them to Breckett. Hector was still alive, and now she had a chance to save him. As long as Parker kept quiet, though the hope was slim, she may be able to convince their captain to press onward. She had one more person to contact before she could make that happen.

5

The connection to Ziven was voice only, but Sarah could hear the man pacing. She could almost imagine him circling around his lavish office in his silken clothes while giving worried glances to the streets below his windows. She couldn't tell what bothered him more, the loss of two crew members or the news of the ship's crew being missing.

"All that was left were these coordinates?" Ziven asked. "No note, no message, not even a possible reason?"

"None," Sarah said, "but we can guess it's where these raiders were planning on taking the ship. Might be where they took the crew. It's worth investigating at least."

"You'd be going in blind."

"I thought you were paying me to keep Breckett on course," Sarah said, "but instead, here I am trying to convince you."

"Fair," Ziven said. He paused and took a deep breath before speaking again. "I already talked to Breckett while you were, uh, recovering. He wants to call the whole thing off."

"Pay him double," Sarah said. "You made it sound like you'd do anything to get your family back. It's time to own up to that."

"I doubt he'd respond to credits," Ziven said, "at least not in his current mood. However, I may have another way to pull at his strings."

"Then pull them," Sarah said.

"What about the others?" Ziven asked. "Everyone else still seem loyal to my credits?"

"Yasmin seems done," Sarah said. She felt a twinge of regret for naming her like that, but Sarah pressed on. "I haven't talked to the others, but from what I can tell your scientist seems along for the ride."

Sarah hesitated a moment. Parker still lingered in the

back of her mind. She could out her, but Sarah figured that would be just as good as outing herself. There was no way Parker would keep her secret if Sarah pointed her out to Ziven. For the moment, she'd keep that information in a back pocket. There was a whole different storm awaiting her on that front and the knowledge put a pit in Sarah's stomach.

"Seems like I've got my work cut out for me then," Ziven said, "If anyone else starts to get out for sorts, keep me informed. I just hope my pocketbook can keep up."

The connection dropped, and Sarah was left sitting at her desk in silence. Without the drone to hover about, the quiet was unnerving. She really needed to find where that thing went. Grumbling burbled from her stomach to remind her of how long it had been since she'd last had food. Already, she could hear Yasmin lecturing her about it. A meal could be a good distraction. All the pieces were in place, and all that was left for Sarah to do was wait and hope Ziven pulled through.

Sarah left her room and wandered through the corridors until she found the mess hall. Others, it would seem, had a similar idea. The hall was an open space with gray-paneled walls, large overhead lights, and simple plastic tables set up at its center. A single counter with kiosks for vending stims, food, and beverages lined the far wall. Lucas hovered around one of the kiosks in his dark pilot's uniform, sharp collar pointed neatly beneath his chin, with the puzzled look of a hard choice painting his features. He wasn't who grabbed Sarah's attention, however, as Parker and Yasmin sat at one of the tables deep in conversation. Yasmin with her leather jacket on had her back to Sarah while Parker glanced at her over the doctor's shoulder. She winked as Sarah walked in which caused Yasmin to turn. Yasmin smiled, waved, then let an unreadable expression take over as she glanced at the shirt Sarah was still wearing. Parker pulled her attention back by tapping on her forearm.

"Anyway," Parker said, "as I was saying."

"Something about a stim?" Yasmin asked. "What did you cook up?"

"I think you'll love it," Parker said. "It'll taste better than that standard issue garbage. Here, try one."

As Sarah walked past them toward the kiosks, she witnessed Parker pull a small food bar out of a container. It looked like the usual nutrient stim given to spacers, but there were bits of something else floating within its brown material. Yasmin took it with no small amount of hesitation before nibbling off a corner. Her face lit up, and she consumed the rest in mere seconds.

"You aren't lying," she said around mouthfuls of the stuff, "this is amazing. Better make more of these, a lot more."

"I can show you the process. Come on, I'll show you the lab." Parker stood and grabbed Yasmin by the arm. She practically dragged the doctor to her feet, and the two started toward the door. Sarah wasn't sure how to feel as she watched the two disappear round the corner. Her thoughts were interrupted by Lucas's voice.

"I've flown freighters through asteroid belts, piloted fighter jets across the surface of nearly every type of planet you can think of," he said while running a hand through his golden hair, "nearly been shot down twice. And yet, I can't for the life of me think of anything more terrifying than picking between flavors of iced coffee. It's rationed, you know. I thought about getting one of each, but out of all the expenditures Ziven decided to make, he cut corners on iced java. Limited to one per ID chip. Not per day, mind you, but for the whole trip. Who does that?"

Sarah couldn't help but laugh. Of all the things to be concerned with during this trip, flavored coffee was not something she would have ever imagined. What's worse, was someone had to make that decision when getting the ship ready. Actual resources went into making the call to ration a sugary beverage. She had no way to tell if the pilot was joking or not. She barely knew him. Come to think of it, this was the first time the two had even spoken to each other. The absurdity of it all made it even funnier to her. His mouth turned up to a boyish grin. There was an innocence to it she didn't like. Chances were, Sarah would get him killed before this was all over. She'd get them all killed if she had any guesses as to what she was about to walk them into. At best, they'd end up like Kyllen. The thought sobered her mood considerably.

"Which are your top two?" She asked.

Lucas pondered for a moment before pointing to vanilla swirl and something called velvet deluxe. Both looked so full of sugar it made Sarah's stomach revolt just thinking about it. Before he had a chance to say more on the matter, Breckett interrupted over comms. He sounded angrier than usual.

"Listen up," he said, "I know many of us want to go home after what just happened, but the mission isn't over. We have co-ordinates of a potential drop point for the missing crew. I've nev-er heard of Dwemyri taking slaves, even Skren, but the matter is worth investigating. Extra payments are being added to your ac-counts as we speak. Our target is a bigger jump. Our chief engineer has figured out a way for the Villimath to make it in one jump, but we'll need to make a quick pitstop to bring on extra fuel. Even with this pitstop we'll get there faster than traditional methods. Plus, it means some time for planet leave for those who need it. Success or not, this will be the last part of our mission before we return to the Ifrit. Get yourselves ready."

The comms went silent, and Sarah and Lucas exchanged a look. Whatever Ziven had done, it had pulled the right strings. She reached past Lucas and pushed the button for vanilla swirl. It chimed as the machine registered her ID and docked her own ration. Before it finished vending, Sarah was already on her way toward the door.

"Wait," Lucas said, but hesitated when Sarah looked over her shoulder. "You didn't have to, but thanks."

"Sounds like you're going to need it," Sarah said, and started toward the engine room.

CHAPTER 21
- KALLIK -

1

Wind swept through Kallik's hair as he sprinted through the ravine, feet spraying small pebbles which splashed into the stream beside him. The violet-hued cliff faces above him blurred past, however, the daylight sky with its visible cosmos above drifted by at a much slower pace despite his breakneck speed. He could hear Nathfnitu's laughter behind him as she trailed in pursuit. She had shown him a trick with his abilities that he would have never learned on his own. If he focused on his own feet, his own body, he could imagine them being lighter and more powerful. His frame, small as it was, could now muster the strength to outrun the best sprinters in the galaxy. He had been warned, however, not to overdo it. While he could create strength with his powers, his body's endurance would always remain the same. If he pushed too hard, he could break himself without realizing it. The pain would come much too late in warning, and by then he would already be on death's door. He tried to keep this in mind as he leapt over a stone as though he were a god. When he thought he was supposed to land, however, he froze midair. Nathfnitu chortled from somewhere behind.

"Caught you, little devil," she said. Kallik hovered back over the rock, and was rotated to face his pursuer. Her gray silks and blue carapace shimmered in the daylight with her black hair glistening over one shoulder. With a righteous grin smeared across her otherwise pretty face, she brought Kallik close enough to tap a black, sharpened fingernail against Kallik's broken antler while folding her other arms beneath her breasts. There was a scent to her that Kallik had not noticed before, probably due to the fact that he was afraid for his life. Now, with them seemingly on the same side, he picked up the faint aroma of moss and wet stone permeating from her skin. It wasn't a bad smell, quite the opposite, but not the one he expected from someone looking as feminine as Nathfnitu. All of the women and girls Kallik had met before had smelt of either perfume or body odor. Nothing like this.

"Now show me," she said, and her grin deepened, "how does the little demon escape his snare?"

Kallik snapped back to reality, or unreality as it were, and tried to focus on this next task in his training. They had been doing this for several days. Each time Kallik was synced with her, Nathfnitu would put him through various exercises in the use of his powers, and expect him to try and escape her using what he'd learned. If he couldn't escape, he was expected to fight. It was all part of a larger goal. The two of them were giving the scientists what they wanted while Kallik was gaining much needed training in secret. Soon, he'd use his training to break the alien free, and let her wreak havoc upon the unsuspecting laboratory. Kallik gritted his teeth, and concentrated. The stones beneath her were floating. They *were* floating. He fixed the image in his mind. Tiny pebbles would snap at her legs and inner thighs at a velocity strong enough to sting, but not break skin. He wanted to get loose, not hurt his tutor. Kallik's scalp began to burn and itch, and the feeling of nettles scraped across his skin. The effect did not quite garner the reaction he sought. Rather than being a distraction, Nathfnitu laughed at the tiny rocks bouncing off her legs.

"Try again," she said.

Kallik slapped her. His arms had been left free, and he swung full force with an open hand. The sudden contact stung his palm, and rang out with a loud clap. Nathfnitu's head jerked to the side, and Kallik was released. Thinking he had gone too far, Kallik bolted. He used his new speed to leap ten meters before taking off at a dead sprint. There was no escaping an angered Nathfnitu, to his dismay, and she was on him in an instant. Not even bothering to use her powers, she used his own momentum against him. Slamming a hand into the back of Kallik's neck, she drove him down to the dirt. He slid a few meters face first, good antler digging up dirt as he went. Groaning, Kallik rolled over onto his back to see a looming, four-armed alien filled with malice standing over him. He threw out a defensive hand, closed his eyes, and started to apologize, but her anger gave way to laughter. Smacking his hand aside, Nathfnitu used her powers to lift Kallik to his feet. She used her hands to brush the dirt off one shoulder before setting him down gently.

"The look on your face," she said, and brushed Kallik's other shoulder. The skin of her cheek, normally a deep gray with a violet hue, had turned a throbbing red. "I should commend you. It was a clever move; one I'll be more careful of in the future. Who knew I would learn a lesson as well. But, I fear your mind is at its limit for the day. I must send you back."

"I don't understand why," Kallik said, "I've not used too much of my power. I can keep going, I swear."

"Simply being in this place is a tax on your mind, little devil," she said, "this is a reality of my own creation, and every second you come here as an outsider takes a toll. No more arguments. Just make sure your scientists send you back. It's almost time, I think."

Nathfnitu did not give Kallik the chance to speak again. She floated his body within a centimeter of her own, and wrapped a hand around his mouth. He hated this part. Sending him back meant killing him. At least she had grown gentler about it after their agreement, and the two of them seemed to be growing closer each time he visited her. Another of her hands crept up to rest on the back of his skull. She filled his vision with a warm smile, and twisted his head with a sharp crack.

Kallik awoke in the inset seat at the center of the alien ship. The ribbed ceiling above him was lit clearly with blue lights shining across its surface. All the scientists were abuzz, calling out different readings and giving each other congratulatory comments. Lightheadedness washed over him, a far shot better than what he felt when these experiments started. Though nausea still threatened his stomach. He hadn't puked in a long time, and he took that as a win. His powers were still at the tips of his fingers. The scientists had yet to replace his inhibitor. If Kallik concentrated enough, he could do it now. He could set the entire plan into motion, and be done with this place once and for all. However, his friends had yet to be filled in on this plan, and he wasn't sure how they would get through unscathed. Kallik needed to create a second part of the plan to ensure his friends escaped as well as himself. The idea of leaving someone behind was a concept too cruel to consider. Even Morkus had a right to his freedom from this pit.

Karaska appeared above him, cat ears twitching with excitement, and hopped down into the inset. The Suttack patted Kallik's head before snapping the inhibitor back in place. Straps were undone, the patches removed, and the wires around Kallik's head were pulled free. Kallik stretched his neck, and flexed his newly-freed hands. The woman with the wrinkled forehead and the dark hair lingered nearby. Karaska noticed her as well, and seemed annoyed by it.

"What is it, Doctor Foster?" He asked. "I told you to take the day off."

Doctor Foster looked over her shoulder toward someone else. The room fell dead silent as both Karaska and Kallik realized who it was. Dark cloak swooshing about his broad frame, and blue light glinting off the edge of his white mask, Vigamere stalked through the door. Sabastian waddled close behind with a satisfied grin plastered across his wide face. He nipped at the Butcher's heels like a newly adopted pup, bald head gleaming. Kallik's heart sank into the pit of his stomach at the sight of him. Laying reclined in his seat, he could not see Nathfnitu from here, but he wished he could. He wanted nothing more than to set her free the very instant Vigamere walked through the door. It was a hope too far gone with his inhibitor already in place. Kallik wasn't even sure if Nathfnitu could kill the Butcher. He wasn't sure if *anyone* could.

"What is the meaning of this?" Karaska said. Standing in this pit, he hardly reached the height of the Butcher's ankles. "I sent you away until further notice, and as far as I'm aware that notice has yet to be sent."

"Your little inquiry is on her way," Vigamere said, "Not alone, I'm afraid. It appears she's bringing some highly trained friends. Your time is running short, doctor."

"Friends?" Karaska asked. "Kill him then. It's not a difficult solution to arrive at."

"I have a different idea, doctor," Vigamere said. He drew his sword, and Karaska flinched. "Your dream of outgrowing Xaranor is dead. You've failed, Karaska, and I think it's time for new leadership. We ramp up testing on all subjects, vipers included, and wait for Sarah's little team of mercenaries to arrive. I don't want them to miss out on the fun."

2

Anna kept a hand on Kallik's shoulder as they rode the tram back to the lab proper. He didn't look up. He was afraid to. Already tears threatened the corners of his eyes, and to see the look of pity Anna would have for him would push Kallik over the edge. The Butcher changed everything. In one fell swoop all of his clever scheming had been laid to ruin. Freedom was a pipedream, and Kallik should have known that from the start. Vigamere had promised him something before having Anna escort him out. The Butcher had proclaimed Kallik's new punishment before the entire team of scientists. Kallik was to sit back and watch as one by one Vigamere burned his friends out in testing. His methods were to start tomorrow, and they were to start with Leo. The poor guy was already on the edge of cracking.

"Try not to stew," Anna said. "I know Aillon has been planning something in secret. There's a chance he'll move up those plans to protect you kids. I know that's all he really wants in the end."

"Aillon's a coward," Kallik spat. The sadness in his stomach boiled and churned into rage at the mention of Aillon's name. He was a so-called Master Conduit. He should have stood up to Vigamere when he had the chance. This could have all been avoided if Aillon had done something about it. Anna's grip tightened on Kallik's shoulder, and her tone turned disapproving.

"Cowardice and intelligence are often confused," she said. "He waits for the right moment, but I assure you he has your best interests in mind."

"You're just defending him because you sleep with him," Kallik said, his hatred burning hotter. "You're in love with him, but that's your own fault."

Anna let go of his shoulder and slapped him across the cheek. Kallik recoiled more out of shock than pain, and pressed a hand to the side of his face. He stared daggers at the blonde-haired woman, and made himself large. Seeing the danger in his stance, Anna took a step back. Her own anger was replaced by fear.

"That was a very adult thing for you to say," Anna said, "and honestly quite hurtful."

"Children don't have their brains dissected," Kallik said, "children don't have to toil away in a white room until their minds are tested to the limits. Children don't have to watch their friends be slaughtered like cattle before their very eyes. Tell me more about what's an adult thing to say."

"You're right," Anna said, and lowered her eyes to the floor, "and I'm sorry. What you go through is horrid beyond comparison. Please understand, Kallik, Aillon and myself are not beyond pain as well. Both of us are here because we have to be. You see, me and Aillon were wed once. Back in the sands of a Xaranor temple, we said our vows. We even had a child, a baby boy named Tavish. A deceitful creature named Sondra took him from us. Now my dear Tavish is stuck in a cage somewhere deep within the lower levels of this lab. Karaska uses the promise of his safety to keep the two of us in line."

The anger drained from Kallik, and he slumped. He'd seen those cages first hand. His own family was trapped in one of them. He leaned against the wall of the tram and crossed his arms. Aillon had been a convenient outlet for his anger, a controllable one that did not carry the weight of fear behind it like the Butcher or Karaska. However, it was a misguided one. Neither of them made eye contact, and neither of them spoke again until the tram reached the lab. Before the doors could open, Anna spoke to the floor.

"You remind Aillon of him," she said, "that's not your fault, but you do. He'll want to talk to you when you can. Take care, Kallik."

The doors opened, and she left without saying another word. Kallik watched her walk down the hallway, and turn a corner before the rec area. Aillon would be on his list of people to talk to, but at the moment Kallik needed to see his friends. Leo was on the top of the list. An idea was starting to form, and he wanted to pass it by Leo while he still had the opportunity. It may be the last chance they got.

3

The five of them, Xoriah, Leo, Toby, Rekkeh, and Kallik all crammed into the plastic cube at the top of the jungle gym. With all of them in here together, they were almost sitting on each other's laps. Xoriah was pushed up against Kallik shoulder-to-shoulder with their thighs rubbing up against one another. Focusing on the peril of their situation was all Kallik could do to keep himself from turning a beat red. She had worn a floral perfume today, and it was making his head spin. Curse his sensitive nose. Fixing his attention on Leo, who was looking much better than he had before, with color returning to cheeks that weren't nearly as gaunt, he let them in on the full situation. They already knew about his deal with Karaska, it was impossible not to, and they had seen the Butcher return to head directly for the alien ship. What they didn't know was Vigamere's intent. When Kallik filled them in, a stillness fell over the group.

"So, we're dead," Toby said, "Leo for sure is dead. Then I'm dead. Then Xoriah is *definitely* dead. Rekkeh's gonna die. At least Morkus is dead, and all the other kids that give us funny looks. They're dead too."

Leo smacked the red-headed boy on the shoulder. Toby started to protest, but Leo said, "You have a plan, don't you?"

"Starting to," Kallik said. He looked at each of them in turn, watching dour faces turn hopeful. He turned his neck to look at Xoriah, realized how close her face was to his, and snapped his head back to the center. There was no avoiding turning red after that. "I've been working on a plan on my own for a long time. I know this sounds crazy, but I managed to befriend the alien in the tank." A look of awe spread across the room, and Toby's face split into a stupid grin with more than a hint of lude implication. Ignoring it, Kallik pushed on. "I'm going to set her free. I don't know what she's capable of, but she intends to kill everyone in the labs, including Karaska. The problem is that I'm not sure I trust her enough not to harm you guys. She's agreed to let me free, but that's as far as her assurances have gone."

"If you're friends with her, won't it be as simple as asking?" Xoriah asked. "If she's strong enough to pull that off, then all we would have to do is stay out of her way."

"I should have asked," Kallik said, "but we've run out of time. I kept dragging my feet thinking I needed more time to get stronger, but Vigamere stormed in and ruined everything."

"So, what's plan B?" Leo asked. He smiled at Kallik, and nudged his knee with a fist. "I know how clever you can be. You've got something already, don't you."

Kallik swelled with the compliment, and nodded. "We've got one final chance to do this. Leo, you're going to be tested until you break, but maybe if Nathfnitu - sorry, that's the alien's name - maybe if she knows you're working to help, she'll go easy and keep you alive. You can buy time to explain the situation to her, then have her send you out."

"Have her kill me," Leo said.

"Yeah, sorry," Kallik said, "But, once you're out, the scientists won't put the inhibitor back on. They intend to keep testing you. That gives you a chance in between sessions to break the door off Nathfnitu's tube."

"Then she's free," Xoriah said, "then we're free."

"We'll need a distraction," Leo said. Kallik gave him a confused look. Freeing Nathfnitu was all they needed to do. If what she could do within the other reality was any indication, she had far more power than anyone in this lab. She'd make the business a cake walk.

"You don't understand," Leo said, "we don't know how

long she's been in cryo for. I don't know about you guys, but if I wake up from so much as a nap, I feel lost and confused for a few minutes, minimum. I can't imagine how disoriented the alien will feel. There's a dozen Skren on that ship at least, so if she doesn't get the chance to do her thing because of a bit of sleep in her eyes, we're all screwed."

"How do you suppose we do that?" Toby asked. "Moon them? We're not exactly tough enough to cause the Skren to come running. And, if we somehow *do* get them to come to the labs, they'll just stick us like pigs."

"I could set them free," Rekkeh said. It was the first time she'd spoken since Kallik arrived back in the rec area, and she was busy fiddling with a strand of wiry brown hair. "I'll set them all free."

"I'll be your distraction," a voice interrupted. They all turned to see Morkus blocking off the entry to the cube. Kallik's mouth hung open, Toby shrunk away, and both Rekkeh and Xoriah froze still. Leo started to stand, but Morkus waved him off with a thick hand.

"We hate each other, I get it," Morkus said. He dropped his gaze to the floor, and picked at a fingernail in an attempt to hide his eyes. His next words sounded choked. "They killed Mari. I'll crush em for that. I'll crush all of em."

Kallik discovered another thing he had completely misunderstood. Mauricia and Morkus must have been closer than he thought. Perhaps much closer. All he had seen out of Morkus was bully, but beneath the hateful exterior there was something much deeper. All of them were afraid, and none of them knew when their last day would be. Each of them handled that fear differently, bullies included. Kallik wasn't sure he'd ever forgive Morkus for his cruelty, but he could at least understand him.

"You're in," Kallik said, and Morkus's head shot up. Sure enough, tears glinted at the corners of his eyes. "What kind of distraction did you have in mind?"

A smile crept across his broad face, and Morkus tapped the inhibitor stuck behind his left ear. "I know which orderlies carry the keys to this."

4

Kallik was now familiar enough with the hallways to navigate them on his own. He ran their new plan through his head over and over again as he made his way toward Aillon's office. Master Aillon was the only part of this plan that was unaccounted for, and he had no idea what to expect. His perception of people was growing more and more muddled with each new interaction. Kallik wondered how his father managed to deal with so many different people, and he often did it all at once. Maybe Aillon would have a way to get his father and cousin out of the cages below. Reaching the master's door, he rounded the corner and stopped. Kallik wasn't sure what he was seeing.

Master Aillon lounged back in the chair behind his desk with his legs kicked up on its surface. His usual tidy black uniform was crumpled and unbuttoned. A large shard of some sort of black stone was stabbed into the desk's top next to his feet. Before him, a black cloak with a large collar of black feathers floated in a circle in midair. At the sight of Kallik, the cloak dropped, and Aillon yanked the stone from the desk to shove it in a coat pocket. Straightening himself and his suit coat, Aillon stood while clearing his throat. He put on a fake smile to address Kallik.

"Kallik," he said, "I wondered when I might see you again. With everything that's been going on, hard to say when the old kitty cat would let me resume lessons. What can I help you with?"

Kallik said nothing. Instead, he wandered over to where the cloak was pooled in a heap on the floor. Kneeling down, he picked it up to feel the material. The feathers were soft, the cloak heavy. All of it was as black a material Kallik had ever seen. Next, he looked at the deep gouge left behind on the desk.

"What is this stuff?" He asked.

The smile slipped away, and Aillon looked around his room for some sort of answer. Finding nothing, he sighed and said, "relics from a life long gone."

"We're leaving," Kallik said. He decided to be forward about it, and not put off what he needed to say any longer. "I have a plan, and you can't stop it."

Kallik looked for some sort of protest from Aillon, but the man only nodded. He removed the black stone from his pocket, and set it on the desk. He looked at it like a dying man might a carrion bird. A mix of fear and hatred intermingled to form a tight frown. Without breaking his eyes away from the stone, he said, "I should have acted while I had the chance. I should have wreaked havoc upon this lab as soon as Vigamere was sent away. I thought I had more time."

"But your son-"

"Is dead," Aillon interrupted, "and it's time I acknowledged it. I've been lying to myself for too long. Karaska had him turned into one of those mutants years ago, but I kept telling myself otherwise. *Not my boy, that was someone else's boy.* What a fool I've been. This plan of yours, you'll need someone to fly a ship, and it would be a dangerous assumption to think a group of kids can fly a ship off world."

"You're going to help?" Kallik asked.

Aillon picked up the black shard, and turned it over in his hands. "I'm going to do much more than that.

5

- Rekkeh -

No one listened to her. No one *ever* listened to her. Even Kallik, one of her own kin, refused to acknowledge her contributions. Rekkeh crawled through the vents toward her favorite part of the lab. She could hear all of their voices, their beautiful voices, calling her name. *They* needed her. *They* would listen. Her pets, her children, her friends, all of them would listen to what the great Rekkeh had to say. She would rescue them, and in turn, they would rescue her. All of her peers would thank her then. They would crawl back to her feet and kiss her toes. They would apologize and beg to be forgiven for ignoring her. Of course, Rekkeh would forgive Kallik but the others were a coin toss. Leo and Toby perhaps, but Xoriah was out of the question. Her perfect hair needed to be ripped out of her perfect head. The way she touched Kallik infuriated her. Xoriah could spend some quality time with her *real* friends.

Rekkeh smiled to herself as she descended a ladder. It was the last ladder before she reached the correct floor. Crawling into the adjoining vent, she made her way to the opening which looked down into her favorite room. It's where the scientist took all of her best creations and locked them up in cages. Before pulling away the cover, she glanced at the other vent. That one opened up to the cells with the unturned. She held no interest in them. Kallik did, but when they were all free that was his problem to worry about. Taking out the piece of rope she had brought with her, a simple chain of stolen shirts tied together, she fastened it to a pair of bolts protruding from the ceiling of the vent. Testing her weight on it, she then lowered herself into the dark chamber below.

Her friends howled at her arrival, and rattled their cages. There were rows upon rows of them. Not all of them were her creations, in fact, a good number of them were the works of others. However, those others had done what Mauricia had done and gotten killed. Now, she was the only one strong enough to make new friends. That was okay with Rekkeh. She'd take care of all of them, especially Mauricia's. Rekkeh was jealous of her work. Her creations were so large, so imposing. One day, Rekkeh would do even better. She stepped in front of a cage that was filled with the dead girl's work. At first glance, they looked like normal people, but they were floating with their heads and limbs sagging toward the floor. One of them rushed the cage, and out of the dark toward Rekkeh's light. She stood her ground, unflinching and unconcerned. The truth of their floating became apparent. Black stocks sprouted from their backs to form long, spindling spider legs that folded out over their bodies to hold them aloft. This one stamped one of these legs in frustration. Rekkeh pressed a hand against the glass that was placed between each bar.

"You don't have to be angry anymore," she said. "I'm going to let you out. All of you. I have the code. I watched the doctor type it once, and I remembered it."

Something in the far corner of the room caught her eye. At the edge of her light, she noticed the silhouette of a larger cage, much larger. It hadn't been there the last time she came down here.

Working her way around another group of cages, each filled with similar creations, Rekkeh held her light up to the glass. The cage towered above her like a small house, and she wanted to know what it contained. Something stirred in reaction to her light. A sound like a thousand moans echoed in her head as a hundred tiny eyes squinted at her light. The creature was massive, it was beautiful, and Rekkeh was going to set it free.

CHAPTER 22
- SARAH -

1

Sarah decided to change into her blue Kara Corp coveralls before heading down to the engine room, and she was glad for it. Thusi seemed as though she wanted to get in as much work as she could before they were allowed some leave time. The docking process, which was normally as simple as watching a few monitors to be sure nothing went wrong with the engine, turned into a self-imposed nightmare. The two of them replaced valves, swapped out the drive core - a process so nail biting that Sarah never wished to be part of it again - purged the coolant lines, and finally set the engine through an idle sequence to meet port codes. By the time they were done, Sarah was sweating through her coveralls and panting. Only once Breckett had given them the clear signal indicating the Villimath had docked successfully did either of them rest easy. Sarah intended to leave right after to get cleaned up, but Thusi stopped her. The chief engineer revealed a small box she had left in one of the maintenance shafts.

"A moment, Sarah, if you would," Thusi said. It was odd for Thusi to be about anything more than work, so Sarah nodded in compliance. Part of her was curious while the other part was concerned. Thusi took a seat on the floor, and set the box next to her. Opening the lid, she removed a thermos along with a pair of cups and a package of sealed food.

"This may be our last chance to enjoy ourselves like this," she said, "and it's a tradition for us Dari to have a ceremonial meal on our last flight. This may not be our last, but I fear once we arrive at our destination, we won't get the chance for this. Please, sit."

Sarah sat crossed legged on the floor across from Thusi, and was handed one of the cups. Steam wafted from the thermos as Thusi poured dark liquid for each of them. Sarah was careful not to drink it until she understood the ritual. It smelled sweet. Thusi held her cup out in front of her, one hand on the handle, the other beneath it, so Sarah did the same. Thusi closed her eyes, and took in a sharp breath. Sarah mirrored the action the best she could, cracking an eyelid to watch for what came next. The cup was placed against the forehead followed by another inhalation. The last step was to set the cup on the floor, and swirl the dark liquid with a claw. Sarah lacked the benefit of long claws, or even long enough nails to mimic the action, so she had to grit her teeth as she swirled the drink with her pinky. Thusi smiled at her and the two of them sipped their beverages. It was, indeed, sweet. The drink tasted more sugar than anything else, but there was an herbal aftertaste that tickled the back of Sarah's throat.

"This brother of yours," Thusi said, "he's worth all of this?"

"He is," Sarah said, "though I haven't seen him for many cycles. Someone might say he deserves what he got, but he's still family."

"Family is a strange concept to Dwemyri," Thusi said. "We selectively breed, you know. All of the clans do it for the bettering of our species. Makes the idea of family a bit laughable when your partner is picked and your child is born for a predetermined purpose. Only once we've reached ninety cycles in age are we allowed to venture out on our own."

"So, do you even know your family?"

"Of course," Thusi said, "I know them like I know anyone else. I have a son, in fact,"

"So, your son is how old then?" Sarah asked. "Sorry, I don't think I fully understand the Dwemyri life cycle."

"Fifty-seven," Thusi said, "and no need to apologize. It is always better to admit flaws in the pursuit of correcting them than to remain willfully ignorant. The Dwemyri lifespan varies from clan to clan, but most don't make it past one hundred sixty."

"Ninety of those are spent doing what your clan dictates? Seems like a big ask."

"And humans are different?" Thusi asked. "You spend most of your lives toiling away at useless endeavors for somebody else's benefit, not even the greater good of your societies. Only once you've lost all use are you released from your master's clutches. Some of you don't even get that benefit. You work until you die."

"You aren't wrong," Sarah said. "Hector always tried to change that for us. He had these grand schemes to make us an insane number of credits so we'd never have to worry again."

"But, now you're here," Thusi said.

Sarah nodded, and drained the rest of her drink. Thusi did the same, and took hold of Sarah's hand before she had the chance to get up. She wasn't sure if this was part of the ceremony or not, so Sarah sat patiently waiting. Thusi patted the top of her hand, and offered another smile.

"When we save this brother of yours," she said, "if he causes you any more trouble, I'm shoving him out the nearest airlock. I've never worked with a human as competent as you, and you deserve better."

She gripped Thusi's hand and smiled back. The chief engineer drove her hard, but she meant well. Of all the crew on the Villimath, she'd miss Thusi the most when this was done. The two of them let go of each other, and Thusi made a shooing motion with her hands.

"Go now," she said, "I'll get this cleaned up. Go get some needed leave time. And, keep your mind off the Groal boy. He'll pull through. I've seen his kind survive much worse."

Sarah hesitated at first, but knew better than to argue with her. Thusi was as stubborn as she was hard working, and once she set her mind to something there was no shifting her off of it. Thanking her again, Sarah made her way to her cabin to clean up.

2

Sarah wrapped her cardigan around her as she exited

the docks. The hem swayed with the chilled breeze as she exited through the port's registration booth and got a full view of the city Breckett had called Banvahiri. Being the only city on the planet Inriea apart from small villages and farm communities, Banvahiri was a big deal in this part of space. It was winter on this side of the planet and small flecks of snow drifted lazy paths through the sky to melt once they hit the pavement. The city itself was comprised of a mass of skyscrapers all built around a single megastructure. This megastructure took the shape of a towering pyramid taller than anything around it. Banvahiri wasn't as large as some of the cities Sarah had seen in her youth, but it was the prettiest. All of the buildings twinkled with gold accents, and the pyramid itself was made of white stone. A long bridge stretched out from the port gates to the city proper, and beneath it was a frozen lake. According to Breckett, Banvahiri resided just outside the edge of CRG territory and thus abided by their laws. He said they were a bit strict on different aspects when compared to the HFS, and each of the crew needed to be careful. Prison sentences weren't much different than death sentences in the Coalition, and convictions were handed out liberally with little in the way of due process.

Steady crowds of strangers flowed to and from the bridge, bumping shoulders and meandering toward their destinations. Sarah started to fall in line when a hand grabbed her elbow to stop her. She'd been so lost in thought, the sudden contact startled her. Whipping around thinking it was some kind of small-time thief, Sarah came face to face with Lexi Biles. Her golden hair was worked into a wide braid, and pulled over one shoulder. She had gone full bore on her makeup today with contour and a gradient eye shadow that was black toward the inner eye but transitioned to a sparkling teal closer to the eyebrow. Her lips were coated dark with a single white stripe painted down the center of her bottom lip. That, paired with her black overcoat with its high collar and teal leggings running down into heeled boots made her look immaculate.

"Sarah, wait up," she said. "Wanna grab a drink or something? I feel like you're the only person on the ship I haven't gotten to know properly."

"No Lucas today?" Sarah asked. "I thought the two of you were joined at the hip."

"Only during the evening hours," she said and winked, "but no, he got reeled into hanging out with Breckett and Parker."

"That can only spell trouble," Sarah said. "What about Yasmin?"

In truth, Sarah had thought about asking Yasmin to join her as well, but something had made her hesitate. The two of them were growing closer, and that frightened her. Better that she didn't. Yasmin had her own troubles to deal with.

"Do you want to grab a drink, or not?" Lexi asked. Engines screamed overhead drawing Sarah's attention. Two hovercrafts sped through the overcast sky toward the bustling city, and Sarah watched them until they disappeared into a hole on the front of the pyramid.

"I know nothing about this place," Sarah said, "but if you think you can find a good spot, then yeah, let's get a drink."

"I'm as clueless as you, but that's part of the fun I think," Lexi said. She smiled, showing a perfect set of teeth, and grabbed Sarah's hand from beneath her cardigan. Together the two of them hurried over the bridge and into the city proper. Skyscrapers towered overhead, cars buzzed through the streets and flew above, and crowds all jostled one another for space on the sidewalks. No matter where they were in the city, however, Sarah could always see the pyramid looming above all. The view from it was never blocked by another building no matter which street they found themselves on. From time-to-time Lexi would stop to peer into a storefront of a bar or shop, but would shake her head and drag Sarah along further. It seemed she had a particular aesthetic in mind, but Sarah wasn't about to get in the way of that. Instead, she enjoyed the sights and helped point out potentials.

Sarah couldn't shake the itch of being watched. She kept glancing over her shoulder periodically, but never caught a glimpse of anyone who might be following. She wrote it off as her own paranoia of being in an open city again, and tried to move on. Something was beginning to feel odd about the pyramid as well. The crowds dwindled the closer they got to it. From here, Sarah could see the city opened up to a massive garden which encircled the pyramid. It was luscious and green despite the cold, but still no one occupied its stone paths. Apart from the two cars she saw earlier, there was no traffic near the upper parts of the structure either.

"This looks like a good spot," Lexi said, interrupting Sarah's thought. Lexi pointed down a set of narrow stairs set into the side of a building. It almost looked like an alleyway save for a bright neon sign flashing pink with the word "Drinks" scrawled next to an arrow pointing down. Lexi liked the dive crowd it seemed. If it got Sarah away from watchful eyes and out from under the looming pyramid, then she was fine with it. Sarah nodded, and the two of them went in.

The place was dark with the only lights being ambient glow bulbs placed under the bar top and set in the corner. Cigarette smoke filled the air, and stung Sarah's eyes as the two of them found a place to sit. A small stage sat in the far corner lit up by a ring of pink lights, and atop it was a sleek, black piano. A beautiful woman sat at its bench with her white dress cascading over the bench's side like a fabric waterfall. Narrow hands worked at ivory keys, and her flawless black hair bobbed in time as she sang a mournful tune. Her husky voice was enough to quiet the din of the bar. Next to her an equally beautiful man leaned against the piano, and sang in harmony during the chorus. Sleek black hair, trimmed beard, and blue eyes which were emphasized by dark eyeshadow, he tapped his thigh with a white-gloved hand in beat. His red suit was a shocking contrast to the woman's white, and the two were a magnificent sight to behold.

Lexi brought them to a small table near the edge of the stage so the two of them could get a better view of the musicians. A waiter in a dark suit greeted them as they sat, a white towel thrown over one arm. He poured each of them a glass of water before addressing them in hushed tones.

"Here for the ceremony?" He asked as he poured.

"Just passing through," Sarah said. "What ceremony?"

"Inriea is being initiated," the waiter said.

"Wait, what?" Lexi asked, a bit too loud so she asked again more quietly. "What?"

"It seems the Coalition finally gave the High Priestess an offer she couldn't turn down," the waiter said, "you came just in time for the ceremony. Starts in about an hour."

"I bet the Federation isn't happy about that," Lexi said. The waiter just shrugged, and handed them a couple drink menus.

"I'm confused," Sarah said, "the way Breckett spoke, I thought they already were part of the Coalition."

"Nope," Lexi said, "Inriea follows the CRG laws, but only as a formality to keep things civil between Inriea and the powers that be. Otherwise, this planet has been resolute in being neutral. This system technically falls within the lines of the Neutral Zone, but only just. So, for them to accept being officially initiated as CRG breaks *so* many treaties signed after the war. There's going to be a lot of saber-rattling by the politicians after this."

"I guess it's a good thing we're Vultures," Sarah said, "no need to be part of any of it."

"Exactly," Lexi said. "I'm not getting dragged into a war."

Sarah ordered a strange sounding drink, something called the Starkiller, but it had rum and lots of pineapple which sounded good to her. Lexi ordered something on the rocks, but Sarah missed the details due to the rising crescendo of the music. He took their orders and left. Looking around like she was up to something, Lexi pulled a small box from beneath her coat and raised it to her dark lips. She pulled a stick out with her teeth, and Sarah realized it was a cigarette - a classic one with real tobacco and no filter. Sarah's face must have said it all as Lexi gave her a sheepish grin before lighting up. She inhaled deep, holding the smoke in her lungs a few moments before exhaling it all out through her nose with a heavy sigh. White smoke billowed from her nose in streams, and Lexi closed her eyes, basking in the moment.

"Don't tell Lucas," she said. "I've been holding off on this for ages. Thought I was going to crack on the Villimath."

"Not a word," Sarah said, "but how have you hidden it this far? Haven't you been together a while?"

"Only a cycle," Lexi said, "and hiding it hasn't been easy. Like you said, Lucas likes to be attached at the hip. So clingy sometimes."

"Think it would bother him?"

"I know it would," Lexi said, "he has such an innocent set of morals. But, it's part of what I like about him. It's cute. What about you, got yourself a man?"

"No," Sarah said, and sipped her water. "I had a partner, but she didn't work out."

"She," Lexi said, and reconsidered Sarah with an odd look. "Sorry, I didn't mean to assume."

"No offense taken," Sarah said. "To be honest with you, I'm not even sure what I like at this point."

"Been there," Lexi said, and pulled another drag from her cigarette, "during my academy days I took an entire cycle to figure it out. Let myself go on a huge binger. Girls, guys, everything in between, nothing was off limits. Even had a few Groal now and then. It's true what they say about them, you know. Huge-"

'Your drinks," the waiter said. Lexi laughed as he set their beverages down. Hers was hardly out of the waiter's hand before she snatched it up and took a gulp. Sarah was a bit more patient with her own, and let the waiter put a coaster down in front of her before placing the drink. He folded his hands and waited to see if there was anything else they needed, but Lexi waved him off.

"If I find a cycle to spare," Sarah said with a laugh, "maybe I'll have to do the same."

"It's how I met Lucas, actually," Lexi said. "I'd known him before, but I'd never *known* him if you catch my drift. He was a nice change of pace between the incels and the narcissists. I knew I could settle with him almost as soon as we started dating."

"Sounds nice," Sarah said.

"It really is."

Their conversation trailed off, and the two of them contented themselves with sipping their drinks and watching the stage. Sarah's drink was an assault of sugar, pineapple, rum, coconut, and something else she couldn't decipher. Bourbon perhaps, but Sarah wasn't up to speed on her alcohols and the room was too dark to read the menu properly. She was enjoying it, and that's all that mattered. She had a gut feeling it would be the last moment of peace she'd get for quite some time.

3

Sarah and Lexi found themselves back on the streets. The cold air wasn't as cold as it had been with her drink warming her belly. The streets were more crowded this time around, and people jostled one another on their way toward the pyramid. The two of them exchanged a glance, and decided to follow the general crowd to see where they were going. They filtered out at the edge of the gardens, with everyone being careful not to enter the grounds. Sarah could see why as there were ceremonial guards positioned every ten meters or so ready to prevent the crowd from taking a single step into the greenspace. They wore large plates of gold armor covered by blue tabards, and each of them carried a polearm with a rifle slung at their sides. Sarah stretched up on her tiptoes to try and see over the crowds, many others doing the same. Toward the far end of the garden away from the pyramid, a large procession of people was starting to walk. They were all dressed in red robes and sashes, and they carried large banners that fluttered with the wind. Upon the banners was a massive orb of red upon a field of black. Lexi tapped on her elbow, so Sarah drew herself back.

"It's been fun, but I think I'm going to head back," she said, "don't get lost, yeah?"

Sarah debated going back with her, but she wanted to see this play out. She said her goodbyes, and went back to craning her neck to watch. In the center of the procession a large drum was carried between two robed figures. They slammed the leather face with each new step. The procession would take a step forward, pause to slam the drum, a man would scream some unintelligible chant, and they'd repeat. If they intended to do this all the way to the pyramid's entrance, it was going to be quite the long event. Some of the faces around her were giving the group a hateful stare. Now that she noticed it, the entire crowd seemed to be growing more hostile to the newcomers. The guards sensed it too. They poised up, ready to take action in defense of the procession.

Sarah took it as a good sign to leave. Getting caught in the middle of some sort of political upheaval was far from her best interests. Lexi must have sensed it on her way out and feared for

Sarah's sense of self preservation. As Sarah turned to push through the crowd, Lexi was there to grab her by the arm.

"On second thought," Lexi said, though she had to shout to be heard over the growing noise, "I think it's time for you to leave too. I'd feel guilty if you got caught up in this."

4

Back aboard the Villimath, the two of them closed the airlock behind them and exchanged a look. They were panting by the time they got back having almost run through the city streets to get out of the crowds. The place was growing scary. A message sprang up in Sarah's feed. It was from Breckett. Lexi must have gotten it too as she looked at her wrist.

"Time to go," is all it said.

Lexi shot Sarah an apologetic look before hurrying down the corridor, opposite the direction Sarah needed to go. Sarah looked at her cardigan and thought about what Thusi might have her do this time around. They were supposedly about to put this ship through something never done before. If that were the case, she was going to need to change. She hurried her own way and back toward the crew quarters. She found herself no longer needing to use the colored lines on the wall despite the size of the ship, a small ounce of pride shooting through her chest. The good feeling died when she found Yasmin waiting for her outside of her door.

The doctor was seated, back leaning on Sarah's door with her elbows propped up on her knees. A spherical object was tucked under her legs. She wore a troubled look that was only accentuated by the black leggings and leather jacket. The look deepened as Sarah approached, and Yasmin pushed herself to her feet. She picked up the sphere, and Sarah realized it was her drone.

"What are you doing?" Sarah asked.

"I wanted to talk to you, but it wasn't urgent," Yasmin said, "so I guess I thought I'd just wait around."

It was a weird answer when she could have just sent a message. The thought must have been plain on Sarah's face because Yasmin stammered and backtracked. She waved a hand and pointed to the drone.

"He's doing better, if that's what you're concerned about," Yasmin said, "He's going to make it. That's not why I came. Honestly, I have no idea what I'm doing. I, um, for some reason I thought if I just left it here you'd think someone had done this intentionally. Or, if I just left a message then you'd think *I'd* done it for some reason. Point is, I found the little guy in the cargo hold. I think its power cell is dead. I thought it meant a lot to you for some reason, so I wanted to make sure to give it to you in person."

Sarah could tell there was something more, words trapped behind Yasmin's lips ensnared by second thoughts and self-doubt. A better person would have done something more. A better person would have made Yasmin feel at ease. Then, perhaps, she'd say whatever it was she was holding back. Sarah was so caught off guard by the situation, she didn't know what to say or what to do. Instead, she stood there like an idiot while Yasmin struggled, a struggle which felt out of place for the usually solid Yasmin. The sudden shift in demeanor put Sarah on her back foot.

"Thanks," was all Sarah was able to get out.

Yasmin nodded, and set the drone back down in front of Sarah's door. Her expression had changed by the time she straightened. Impassive, stolid, an unreadable blank slate hung in front of her eyes. Sarah knew it was a mask, but she let the doctor keep it. She wasn't sure she wanted the truth of what lurked in the depths. She couldn't afford the distraction. Not now.

"Come see me if you have issues with that scar," Yasmin said, "or if you need another session in the tank. I'll let you get back to your work. I have a feeling we'll be jumping soon."

She strode past Sarah without making eye contact. Sarah waited for the sounds of her footsteps to disappear before daring to move herself. She wasn't sure if what she'd just witnessed was her fault, or something else entirely. How she handled it certainly could have been better. Stooping over to pick up the drone, Sarah rolled it over in her hands. Eryn's power cell was fine. That meant the internal motors must have burnt out from overuse. These things weren't built to last longer than a few hours. She brought it inside her room and set it on the desk. She kept glancing at it as she changed. Kyllen had put a lot of work into making that thing work. Stupid kid. Sarah's breath caught, and her heart rate began to pick up. He should have stayed home with his grandmother. The back of her neck and tops of her ears felt hot. Could have been something great if he'd only set himself to it. Anger swelled, and before she knew what she was doing Sarah whipped the drone across the room where it smashed against the far wall. Bits of glass, metal and fiber scattered across the space in a loud bang.

Time stopped as Sarah's mind caught up with what she had done. Her first instinct was to listen over her shoulder to make sure no one was going to come running. She didn't want to have to explain. Her next was regret. She could have fixed the drone. Replacing its motors would have been simple enough, but its current state placed it beyond repair. Not wanting to look at what she'd done, Sarah zipped up her coveralls and slipped out into the corridor. She took a moment to find her composer and started her way toward the engine room.

PART 3

INTERLUDE

Everett scrubbed one dry hand with the other as he paced up and down the narrow corridor. The passageways of the Cloud-burst were a far tale from the vast open walkways of his beloved library. What's worse, he was usually the one to cause the waiting. With the exception of the master, Everett waited for no one. To be told to wait outside until called for was an insult he wasn't prepared to handle. His digital ledger swung near his waist from a chain that was looped over one shoulder. He stopped his pacing to note the insult in his logs, then set himself back to his path. They were getting close to their destination, and he had so many notes he needed to pour over with the captain before they got there. Every detail needed to be correct from first contact with this AI followed by its subsequent disappearance to the accumulation of these coordinates they now pursued. They had already gone over them once, yes, but a third and fourth time must be required to ensure legitimacy. However, the captain was on the bridge, and the bridge had been closed off. So, Everett paced.

"Jump complete," an automated voice said over the comms. Everett gave a start. He hadn't even realized the ship had initiated a jump sequence. The Cloudburst and its captain lived up the reputation. The light above the door of the bridge switched from red to green, and Everett wasted no time. He told himself not to falter as he crossed over the horrid catwalk with the dozen or more crew members working at terminals several meters below. The captain stood at the far end of the catwalk before numerous holo-displays with one hand scratching his chin. The female morak'casai hovered near his shoulder which confused Everett. She had been dismissed upon the arrival of the twins as their shadow was said to be enough. However, she decided to stay for some inexplicable reason. No matter, her presence made little difference to Everett. She turned her white mask only slightly as he approached, but Everett was wise enough to know she had him in full view. A single twitch from her would spell his death should she deem it necessary.

He held up his ledger to prove that he intended no harm, but she made no notion to either confirm or deny his presence. Likewise, the captain too remained disinterested in Everett's existence. He simply stood there with his hand on his chin, and considered the information being read out on the displays before him. Everett tried to wait patiently, but several moments dragged by, and still the captain said nothing. Everett attempted a different approach and cleared his throat.

"What is it, ledger?" The captain asked without turning around.

"Before we reach our destination, I was hoping-"

"We are *at* our destination," the captain said, "have been for the last hour. The jump you felt was to put us in the shadow of the moon."

"Last hour? I didn't feel us jump," Everett said.

"Then you are welcome," the captain said.

"Why the shadow of the moon?" Everett asked. "If we've reached the laboratory, should we not be getting ready to storm it?"

"Your friends are on standby in the hangar," the captain said, "but for now, we wait. Another ship jumped in nearby, and I want to be sure it hasn't spotted us."

"A separatist ship?"

"No," the captain said, "something else. There's no registration on the ship, but a name came through our scan. They call it the Villimath."

"Maybe they're mercenaries working for the separatists," Everett offered. He had forgotten his ledger entirely and was now caught up in the interest of the moment. "Or perhaps they purged the ship's ID to get through security sweeps."

"I don't think so," the captain said. "They seem as interested in the planet as we do. I think we'll wait and watch their next move."

"Captain," a voice yelled from below, "our scanners managed to pick up an audio feed from the lab on the planet."

"Put it through," the captain said.

An audio wavelength appeared on one of the holo-feeds. At first glance, it looked like any other wavelength, but Everett noticed the chaos in it. The wave spiked to a peak, and very rarely came back down. The captain waved a hand over it causing it to play. What they heard made Everett's blood run cold. Playing over the bridge's comm was what he could only describe as pure pandemonium.

CHAPTER 23
- KALLIK -

1

Kallik never heard from Master Aillon again. He never got the chance. The man stormed out of the classroom after their confrontation, hellbent on making a difference, and disappeared down the hallway. Kallik had intended to follow him, but shouting from the opposite direction caught his attention. It was his name. Someone was screaming his name. Kallik hurried back down the hall toward the commotion, and ended up back in the recreational area. What he walked into was a pair of the other kids taking turns kicking a hunched over Leo. Xoriah was screaming Kallik's name as the younger pair of siblings drove their feet into Leo's side. Kallik's friend was curled up in the fetal potion trying to ward off each kick to his ribs with his arms. The male sibling took a break from kicking Leo to shove Xoriah to the ground. His sister laughed, and stalked over to start kicking her as well. A few other kids watched from afar, but Toby and Morkus were nowhere to be seen.

One nudged the other as they noticed Kallik enter, and they both stopped. They exchanged a silent glance before making their way in his direction, one heading to either side of Kallik. The boy clenched and unclenched his fists as he circled, while the girl set her jaw and cracked her knuckles.

"We're all going to die because of you," the boy said.

"It's all your fault," the girl said.

"Toby told let it slip," the boy said, "told us how the

Butcher's gonna do us in one by one while you watch. We're gonna break your bones first."

Kallik stepped back and bumped into someone. He looked over his shoulder to find Morkus towering above him with Toby in tow. At first, the siblings grinned thinking Morkus would help them. Something on his expression must have given it away, however, as once the much larger boy cracked his own knuckles the siblings' expressions turned to that of fear. Morkus put a hand on Kallik's shoulder and moved him gently to one side.

"You've got a bigger fight to be ready for," Morkus said, "and I think I came just in time to start our little distraction. I'll be starting things up with these two."

For a moment, Kallik was confused. They didn't need a distraction until Vigamere came to start the testing. That was when the man himself came strolling down the far hall, and Kallik understood what Morkus meant by "just in time." A bloodied Karaska limped behind with the aid of a smug looking Sabastian. Doctor Foster with the wrinkled forehead followed close behind the group keeping a wary eye on the Butcher's back. The two siblings turned to see what Morkus was staring at, and shrank away at the sight. All the onlookers started to vanish in a vain hope they wouldn't be noticed. Xoriah got to her feet and looked from Leo to Kallik, then back to Leo. Tears threatened the corners of her eyes, but her expression solidified to that of determination. She turned to Kallik and offered him a stern nod. Kallik tried to give her a reassuring smile, but it wouldn't come, so he resorted to nodding back. Ready or not, it was time to set their plan into motion.

2

Vigamere dragged Kallik and Leo with a hand on the back of their necks. Sabastian prodded Kallik with his baton every time they slowed down, and the two scientists closed off the rear. Leo grinned at Kallik as they stepped into the tram, blood dripping from a broken lip. It had been a gift from the two siblings, one Kallik hoped Morkus returned in kind. At least Leo looked healthier than he had before. His chestnut hair was messy but well taken care of, and his cheeks weren't so gaunt. Kallik was starting to believe they had a chance at pulling this off. If anyone had the strength, it was the boy he looked at now. The tram lurched into motion. Kallik would have fallen if it weren't for Vigamere's grip. His fingernails dug into the sides of this neck, and he was certain the man had broken skin. Kallik gritted his teeth and imagined the Butcher being ripped apart by Nathfnitu's powers. She could do it. She *would* do it. Her failing was out of the realm of possibilities. Leo would tear open the cryotube, and she'd wreak havoc upon the unsuspecting lab.

The group reached the ship, and the Skren leered as Vigamere escorted them to the testing area. Once in the oval chamber, the Butcher let go of Leo and gestured for the scientists to begin strapping him in. Sabastian dragged Leo by the arm, and tossed him into the pit where Karaska started to apply the cybernetics and wiring. The Suttack reached into his pocket, and pulled out a small fob. This was it. Once that fob reached Leo's head, his friend would be free. Leo needed to go into Nathfnitu's world just one time to explain the situation. Then this nightmare would be over. A different kind of nightmare would take shape, a nightmare for the Butcher and Karaska and all of their goons. Morkus better have a good distraction.

3

Morkus waited until the Butcher was long out of sight, and then waited a few moments more. He could be patient when something was this important. He locked his eyes on the two siblings who looked from each other back to him. They were too afraid to go anywhere which suited Morkus's plans just fine. All the other kids had made themselves scarce which was also fine. Except for the pretty blonde-haired girl, she hovered near his shoulder like she was unsure of what to do. She might cause a problem if she decided to get in the way. Always the peacekeeper, that one. She had agreed to Morkus being part of the plan, however, so she might prove to be helpful instead. Toby should be here any time now with the exact orderly he needed. He'd be spouting off some nonsense about Morkus being a bully to the other kids, and he'd send the orderly running. Well, it was nonsense now, but by the time the orderly arrived it would be the truth. He cracked his knuckles and rolled his shoulders. It was good to limber up before a beating. The two siblings in front of him never were the smart ones. If they were, they'd have hightailed it out along with the other kids. Now, they got to play a small part in something much bigger. Good for them being useful for once.

Morkus lurched forward without warning, and slammed his fist into the brother. He crumpled to the floor with little resistance. Pity as Morkus hoped the boy would put up a better fight. They needed this to be a convincing distraction, and the boy had been all barks and bared teeth just a moment ago. No matter. Morkus twisted and pounded his other fist into the sister's chest. He accidentally hit her breast, and the girl howled with pain as she stumbled back. The girl fell back into the small library area, and tripped over a plastic tote filled with books before falling to the ground. He hadn't meant to hit her there, quite the opposite. It was part of the reason Morkus held a strict rule against hitting girls. Not so strict a rule today, but now he reaffirmed it for the future. Today was special. There was something in the air Morkus couldn't explain. Excitement and tension vibrated throughout, and a strange sense of finality lingered like an odor one couldn't quite place.

Morkus stepped over the brother who was still curled up on the floor. He spared a glance for the blonde girl, wondering if she was going to try and stop him. She crossed her arms over her chest, and nodded. She knew the importance of what he was doing. That was good. He rolled the boy over onto his back, and hit him in the stomach once more. The boy cried out with pain, and held up a hand for Morkus to stop. Morkus didn't. He punched his stomach twice, and then a third time until a voice called out from the hallway.

"Knock it off," Master Aillon said. Morkus stopped himself mid punch to look up and find the red-haired man looking vastly different than he had before. Instead of the black uniform, he was enveloped by a black cloak. Dark feathers encircled the collar. Accompanying him was another redhead, Toby. The stupid boy must have betrayed them to bring Aillon. The orderly he needed was there too, so maybe Aillon was an accident. She stood at Aillon's side with her short blonde hair tied back. Anna, Morkus thought her name was. Accident or no, their plan was shot with Aillon here.

"Your plan was clever," Aillon said, "but not needed."

Toby looked as ashamed as he should. Morkus was going to hit him next if he got the chance. Then, what Master Aillon said hit him. The red-haired man exchanged a glance with Anna before nodding. The orderly strode over to Xoriah with fob in hand. In one swift motion, she removed the inhibitor and dropped it on the floor. Xoriah glared at it with anger, and stomped on it. The device cracked beneath her heel. Toby smiled at her, and revealed the spot behind his own ear. His too had been removed. Anna was hesitant to approach Morkus, and she glanced down to the boy Morkus still stood over. She glanced at his sister next who was lying on the floor nursing her head.

"We'll need him," Toby said. That was a surprise. Of all the people to cover for him, Toby would have been the last he expected. Morkus removed himself from over top of the boy to stand in front of Anna. She sighed, and swiped the fob against his head. The small white disk dropped to the floor with a clatter. He too crushed it with his heel. He could feel his powers within reach. The whole world could shift at his slightest thought. His mouth worked into a smile as he realized the potential of his new freedom.

"What's going on here?" Another orderly asked from down the hall. He was a short man with dark hair and a beard. Flanking either side of him were armored Skren. Each of their hands hovered near their hips where curved swords hung. The orderly was going to hit the ceiling at high speed. Morkus believed it to be true, and he saw in his mind's eye. His powers responded, and man flew head first into the light above with a shrill cry of startlement. The armored Skren collided into each other at the same time. That wasn't his work, and Morkus noticed Xoriah concentrating on the pair. She was just as excited as himself to be free.

There was definitely something in the air. Today was going to be a good day. Now all they needed was for Leo and the antlered boy to do their part. The Butcher was going to be the real test. Morkus hoped he got to try out that test himself. He had a score to settle with the masked man. For Mari's sake, he was going to kill Vigamere.

4

Kallik watched as Leo convulsed and snapped out of the trance. He slumped over in his seat as he tried to gain his bearings. Kallik wanted to rush to him, but Vigamere's hand rested on his shoulder preventing him from going anywhere. Leo convulsed again, this time gagging. Karaska flinched back like he was afraid of being puked on. Only once he saw the coast was clear did he bother to check Leo's vitals. It looked grim, and Kallik was growing more and more afraid for his friend. Leo wasn't opening his eyes. He needed to open his eyes to break Nathfnitu free. Now was going to be their best chance to do so, but Leo looked broken. The boy sagged in his seat. His eyes fluttered and his mouth worked for air, but Leo looked incapable of doing much else. Was it really that bad for him? Had Nathfnitu given him a chance to speak, or had she killed him on the spot? Kallik's hopes were drying up. Despair clutched his chest as the doctor began to remove the straps.

"What are you doing?" Vigamere asked. The doctor ignored him, and continued to undo the straps. "He's going another round."

"He can't," Karaska said, "the boy is as good as dead. Another session would cause his body to hemorrhage in the chair. Then we'd really have a mess to clean."

"That's the point," Vigamere said. He let go of Kallik, and started to walk over to the pit. Karaska let go of Leo, and stood to face the oncoming Butcher. What neither of them noticed was the smile that crept across Leo's lips. Hope returned as Kallik realized the full brilliance of this friend's deceit, and Kallik realized a major flaw in his previous plan. Leo couldn't see the cryotube if he was lying in the chair, but if he could stand then the world was his.

Leo cracked open an eye as the doctor and the Butcher started to argue. Another piece of beauty occurred in the form of Sabastian. The man had been standing near the door, but he now waddled toward the two arguing men. He looked paler even in the dim light, and wiped sweat from his bald head. He tapped Vigamere on the shoulder. At first, the Butcher ignored him, but after being tapped again he turned to look at what Sabastian was pointing at. The vile orderly pointed to a message displayed on his wrist, and Vigamere cursed loud enough for the whole chamber to hear. He pointed at a pair Skren guards.

"We aren't done, Karaska," he said. "I'm going to deal with your Master Aillon, and then I'll be back to settle this. You better have the boy strapped in when I return."

He stalked out of the room with Sabastian and the Skren in tow. The chamber fell silent for a long moment with the scientists unsure of what to do next. Karaska looked around the room to find all eyes were on him. Leo seized the opportunity. He bolted to his feet, and got a good view of the cryotube. Concentrating, Leo started to work his powers. Karaska tried to interrupt, but Kallik was not about to let him. Now freed, Kallik rushed the Suttack doctor and leapt upon him. He tackled Karaska to the floor of the pit and pounded the feline face with his fists. The doctor tried to ward off the blows, but Kallik was too ferocious. Blood slicked his hands, and he wasn't sure if it was from his knuckles or from the doctor's face. Probably both, but he didn't care. Someone's hands tried to pull him away, but he fought those off too. The only thing that made him stop was the glorious sound of shattering glass.

Kallik relented, and all went still. Even Karaska paused in trying to defend himself. Pushing himself off the doctor, Kallik stood to get a better view of what Leo had done. The boy stood with a proud grin, but had to lean on the side of the pit's wall for support. One of his eyes was closed, and blood ran in a small rivulet from one nostril. The cryotube on the far side of the chamber was shattered. The door was bent and twisted on the floor, and all of the blue cryo fluids had poured out. Nathfnitu was curled up at the bottom of the open tube, coughing and spluttering as she tried to suck in air. No one dared move as she caught her breath. Nathfnitu uncurled herself, and looked at each of her hands as though they were foreign to her. She flexed each one before grabbing the edges of the cryotube to pull herself to her feet. Wobbling slightly, she held onto the edge of the tube as she took in her surroundings. Her eyes locked with Kallik's and she smiled. The sharp teeth frightened the scientists around her as they took a step back.

Karaska pulled himself out of the pit, and approached Nathfnitu slowly. He held out both of his hands to show he meant no harm. Kallik held his breath as he watched the doctor draw close to her. All of their bets would either pay off or fall short at this moment. If the doctor managed to calm her or coax her in any way, all of them were done for. Nathfnitu watched him with a curious expression. Karaska opened his mouth to speak, but his head twisted at a sharp angle with a loud snap. It continued to twist until it was pulled free of his body. A fountain of blood spurted from his stump as his corpse fell to the ground. His head continued to float with Nathfnitu staring at it. Doctor Foster shrieked. Nathfnitu flung the head at her, and all things descended into madness.

5

- Toby -

Toby watched in awe as the others made dealing with the enemy a simple task. Their group had grown large at this point. Room by room, Master Aillon had led them through the labs to free the other kids and deal with the orderlies and Skren. He felt bad for just watching, but the others were so much stronger. Toby felt as though he could barely lift a stone with his powers, let alone throw a man across the room. He wasn't like Morkus or Xoriah who worked together in tandem to smash their enemies against the laboratory walls. He wasn't like Master Aillon who could toss an entire group of Skren through the air without blinking. The man was amazing. Toby wasn't even like little Aaron who tossed a chair into one of the guards who had almost stabbed Anna, or Sullah who put one of the orderlies in some sort of deep trance. Toby was just Toby. Part of him wanted to be jealous, but the other part was too caught up in how amazing his friends were.

They were several rooms into their liberation, but none of them had spotted Rekkeh. That was strange to him as the little Groal girl was part of their original planning. She almost never left Kallik on his own and to find her missing was unsettling. Had something happened to her while the rest of them were caught up in fighting the bad guys? She'd turn up soon. Toby was sure of it. Their party, which had started off as five and had grown to twelve, rounded a corner of the office section of the laboratory. Toby had never seen this part of the labs, and everything was new to him. While the hallways were identical to what he'd seen before, the rooms were all filled with computer terminals, data slates, and equipment he had no idea of what their purpose was. Most of these were empty except for the occasional scientist. Toby expected the same from the next room, but hung back toward the center of the group just to be on the safe side. The door to this room was already open, and when Aillon poked his head in he held up a hand for everyone to stop. Whatever it was had Master Aillon frightened. The orderly named Anna, the one Toby had a difficult time not staring at, covered her mouth with a hand. One of the other kids peeked in and screamed. Both Morkus and Xoriah looked stunned. What could be that bad as to cause these reactions? Toby thought of a way to make light of the situation, but caught a whiff of a foul odor like rotting meat. He had to know. Pushing his way through the group, he worked his way to stand next to Xoriah. Blood coated every surface and dripped down the side of the desk. Atop it was what used to be a person. Now all that was left was shredded chunks of flesh. Standing over the gore was a creature spawned from the deepest of Toby's nightmares.

Thick spider legs sprouted from the back of a nude man. They held him aloft as he bit into a chunk of meat that he held between clawed hands. His mouth was too wide for any human with narrow mandibles helping shovel bits of shredded flesh into his maw. The creature seemed content with ignoring the group as it fed. Toby wanted to puke. His stomach churned, and his mouth salivated in response. He tried to hold it back by taking deep breaths. Master Aillon stepped out of his own shock, and took control of the situation.

"Close your eyes," Master Aillon said to the group, but Toby couldn't look away. He noticed others felt the same as they watched Master Aillon lift the creature into the air, and rip it apart limb from limb like a sadistic child pulling legs from an insect. The creature fell to the floor in pieces without so much as a scream of pain. Aillon shuffled the kids away from the room, and shut the door so they could no longer see.

"Someone let them out," Aillon said. His face had gone white making his red hair even more shocking. "Change of plan, we're taking everyone we've got and heading to the surface. I'll come back down to look for stragglers. Come now, everyone to the elevator."

Anna started to protest, but she was cut off by the sound of rattling metal. All around them thudding and scuttling echoed through the walls. It sounded like the vents were about to shake apart. A sharp clang from down the hall caused all of them to turn. The cover of a vent had been thrown aside, and from the vent shaft emerged long, spindly legs. They latched onto the sides of the walls, and pulled the body of another creature out into the open. Another started to follow, and more vent covers began to be pushed open.

"Everyone stay close," Master Aillon said, "we'll have to take a different route, but I know the way. Hurry."

They all started to jog down the hallway, the sight behind them growing more and more grim as creatures pulled themselves out of the vents. Several of the spider-legged men jumped out of the adjoining room, and tried to take a few of the kids on the outside edges of the group. Aillon was there in a flash and ripped them to pieces with his powers. As long as their teacher was here, Toby knew they would make it through this.

Aillon said something to Morkus as they ran, and the bigger boy fell to the back to cover their rear. He exercised his powers liberally to do as Aillon had done and rip apart the creatures that got too close. How many of these creatures were there? The white halls were filled with them now, and no matter where they turned the bulls in the group were forced to fight through them. White walls became red as they fought down one hall and into the next.

The creatures shambled toward them in droves, all trying to get a taste of their flesh. Another corner, and Toby recognized where they were now. Aillon's classroom wasn't far from here which meant the elevator was close.

All of them were growing tired, and the bulls in their group were starting to show the fatigue of their powers. Morkus's nose was bleeding, and Xoriah squinted each time she sent a spider-legged monster flying off down the hall. Toby wished he could help, but his powers were so limited. During his testing, he had barely been able to move the metal ball. What good was he against nightmares. One of the siblings Morkus had beaten fell to his knees, and Morkus had to help him to his feet. Toby told himself that if they could make it to the elevator, they would be safe. A noise like bending steal caused Toby to turn around, and his world erupted into chaos.

The door to his left exploded outward into the hallway, directly into the center of their group. More creatures stormed through the newly formed gap, but these were different. These were larger. Instead of spider legs, their own limbs had hardened to black carapace and narrowed to dagger tips. One of the bulls, a taller boy with black hair, stood up to the creatures to try and ward them off with his powers. They tore through him like paper. Stow is what Toby thought his name was. Everyone started running at once. Master Aillon tried to direct the chaos in the right direction, but it was no use. Toby tried running toward the red-haired man, but was knocked over by a couple of girls running in the opposite direction. Face to the floor, Toby could only hear the monsters chasing after, and the screams of his friends. Toby pushed himself to his feet and bolted, not daring to look back. He ducked under the swipe of a claw, and swerved out of the way of a spider leg. Darting around the corner, Toby found the adjoining hallway to be empty. Thinking it a streak of luck, he sprinted down it and away from the massacre he thought he heard.

6

- Aillon -

Aillon watched in horror as the boy before him was ripped in two. The claw tore through his torso in a flash, spraying those closest to him with his blood. The others started to all run in different directions. This was a disaster. He should cut his losses, grab Anna, and get out while they still could. He wouldn't do that, *couldn't* do that. Not now. He'd stood idly by and let these kids suffer for too long all in a vain hope that his own son was alive. He knew better. Aillon was going to put a stop to this. He reached into his pocket for the spike, and wrapped his fingers around the dark stone. Power flowed through it, and he could feel his scalp begin to heat up with its energy. His mind raced with commands. The creatures before him were being ripped to shreds. The children would stop moving, and float over to him. A barricade would be made of scrap, desks, and corpses. His eyes burned with the sheer pressure of his powers as each of things began to take shape. All around the group, monsters exploded as their bodies were ripped limb from limb. The running children were frozen in place before they were lifted up and toward himself. Body parts, desks, and pieces of door levitated from the hallway and nearby rooms to create a barricade between their group and the rest of the hall. The passageway behind them lead to the elevator, so he left that side open.

Everything calmed to a stillness as the kids settled down before him and Anna. All was quiet for now, but Aillon knew there would be more of those things heading this way. He needed to do a quick headcount before marching everyone to the elevator. It was the only way to the surface and once there, they could barricade the door and take a ship off this planet. He pointed a finger at each of the kids while counting in his head. It was a grizzly scene. Each child was covered to some degree by layers of blood. All of their eyes were wide with shock and fear. Nine. There were only nine of the kids left. The first one died in front of him, but the other two he was unsure of. Glancing around he saw the other corpse. It was the young girl, Leah he thought her name was, one of the siblings he had walked in on Morkus beating before this all started. Her brother was standing next to Anna, but his eyes were fixed on his sister's corpse. Who was the third? He looked around for another body before realizing who wasn't there. Toby was missing.

"Did Toby fall?" Aillon asked the group. "Did someone see him?"

"He ran," Morkus said, "I saw him do it. Tried to grab him, but he was too quick. Went down that hall."

Morkus pointed past the barricade where another hallway joined this one. Aillon scrubbed a hand through his crimson-dyed hair. If they made it through this, he was going to treat himself to a new color. Anna liked the red, but she could deal with a new color if she had to. A large part of him wanted to leave the boy to his fate. He was never extraordinarily talented which was why he had lived so long. The doctors rarely bothered to test him. With the viper's creations loose throughout the labs, there was no telling how long poor Toby would survive. Aillon made up his mind. He grabbed Anna's hand and pulled her in for a kiss. He kept it quick, merely brushing his lips against hers. It was still enough to smear a fine coat of blood across her mouth, and Aillon wondered what his own face must look like. All the showers in the universe wouldn't be enough to clean this group.

"The elevator is just through there," he said and pointed down the hall. "Make sure all the kids make it, then escort them up to the surface. Get a ship ready, and wait there for me."

Anna nodded. She understood. There was no need to explain himself to her, and they both knew what was at stake. She started to guide the kids down the hallway, but Morkus lingered. His fists were clenched, and his jaw set. Aillon wondered if the boy wanted to help him or hurt him. Anna noticed and grabbed the larger boy's arm. He resisted at first, but started to move at Anna's urgings. Before he turned to go, he spoke.

"I regret a lot of what I did," Morkus said, "been thinking about it a lot now that everything's gone to hell. Make sure you bring him back."

"I will," Aillon said. The boy nodded, and left with Anna.

Once they were out of sight, Aillon used his powers to make a hole in the barricade large enough for him to squeeze through. He slipped past it, and closed it again once he was through. He started down the hallway Morkus had pointed out, utilizing this brief moment of peace. Compared to where they had been through, this part of the lab appeared to be untouched. He poked his head in through a few doors, and called out Toby's name as he walked. He rounded another corner and found himself in the part of the labs that housed the kid's bedrooms. Aillon couldn't remember which one was Toby's, but that seemed like a good place to start. The lab was eerily quiet, and all he could hear was his footsteps and the sound of his own breath. There was a rumble from somewhere deep within the lab, and the lights flickered. Taking that as a bad sign, Aillon hurried his search.

"Master Aillon?" Toby called out. His head poked out from a room further down the hall. Letting out a sigh of relief, Aillon ran down the hall to his room. The boy smiled as Aillon stopped in front of his door, but looked on the verge of crying. He leapt out from the doorway and wrapped his arms around Aillon's midsection in a hug.

"I thought the monsters got you," he said. "I thought all of you were dead."

Taken aback by the sudden contact, Aillon wasn't sure what to do. He needed to get the boy out of here, but Toby wouldn't let go. Resorting to patting the boy on the head, Aillon pushed Toby back and made sure the hallway was still clear. Another rumble shook the floor. The lights went dark. Toby whimpered. Aillon blocked Toby's door with his body to be on the safe side while he squinted into the dark. The floor lurched and it felt as if the entire lab might shake apart. The clattering of vent covers hitting the floor echoed down the hall. The light's flickered for a brief moment, and Aillon thought he saw the silhouette of a little girl standing at the end of the hall. Was there another child trapped down here? It was too dark to see anything now. The lights flickered again and, sure enough, a little girl was making her way toward him. He thought he recognized her, but not as one of his students. She was a viper if he recalled, the little Groal girl.

Flicker

Behind her were countless of the viper's creations with

spider legs holding them high enough for misshapen heads to brush the ceiling. They weren't interested in her. It all started to click. Aillon felt behind him to ensure Toby was still there. He pushed the boy back into the room.

"My poor, poor Toby," Aillon said. Skittering legs sounded all around him though he could not see them. Ignoring Toby's protests, Aillon slammed the door shut using his powers, and sealed it. He hoped the boy would be safe. He hoped someone would come for him. The best Aillon could do now was keep these things away for as long as he could.

Flicker

Legs and maws lunged for him from the dark. Aillon pressed his back against Toby's door, and unleashed his powers. Clenching onto the spike until his hand bled, Aillon gave it everything he had.

CHAPTER 24
- MORKUS -

1

Morkus kept the kids in front of him running while Anna guided them toward the elevator. He'd never gone up the elevator since his first arrival here, only down. What came next was going to be foreign. He'd heard others talk about it, namely Xoriah due to her good behavior, and he remembered there being a second elevator after this one to get to the surface. Between was some sort of garden. A shame the only time he'd get to see it was through a trail of blood.

A boy in front of him tripped. It was the sibling he'd punched earlier. Covered in his sister's blood, the boy seemed lost for any sort of hope. He lagged and fell behind the others until only Morkus was at his back. The light's flickered, the floor shook, and the boy fell to his knees. The whole lab seemed to be falling apart. Morkus wrapped his arms around the boy's back and hauled him to his feet. No words were said, and the boy refused to look up from the floor. He was as good as broken. A mere day ago, Morkus would have dropped the boy and left him to his fate. Not today. Morkus wouldn't let anyone else fall behind.

He could see the elevator doors just ahead. If the boy lacked the strength to get there, he could borrow some of Morkus's. He had plenty to spare. Morkus imaged the boy was half his current weight, *knew* he was. The boy could be lifted, and he could run like the rest of them. The lab rumbled again. His powers answered with a tingle in his scalp. The boy stood firm, and Morkus helped him run.

Reaching the elevator, Anna ushered all of the kids through the still opening doors. There was no time to waste as the lights flickered. If the power cut, all of them would be stuck down here. Morkus carried the boy through while Anna did another head count. With all of them inside, the elevator left little room to breathe. The doors slid shut with a ding, and the elevator lurched into motion. Air thick with body heat and the stench of blood, Morkus had a hard time keeping himself from gagging. He never thought himself to be afraid of tight spaces, but the walls felt so close here. The air was choking him, shoving thick particles of sweat and blood down his throat to drown his lungs. An unconscious hand massaged his neck in a poor attempt to find some sort of comfort.

The labs rattle again, and scared whimpers echoed throughout. Morkus put on a brave face, but he'd be lying to say he wasn't afraid. A sharp pain lanced through his mind. It was a hurt so incredible it nearly blinded him. Tears welled up in the corners of his eyes, and Morkus had to grit his teeth to keep from screaming. He clutched at his temples and keeled over. The pain only got worse to where he thought his head might explode. Tears streamed down his cheeks but in an instant, the pain was gone like it were never there to begin with.

Morkus blinked. Something was off. The heat of his peers was gone along with the stench. The elevator floor he had been staring at was gone, replaced by some sort of dark stone. He stood and cleared his eyes to find himself alone. Darkness tempered only by the dim light of the moon surrounded him. There was a chill to the air, and a shiver ran down his spine. Faint motes of glittering dust danced in the moonlight all around him. Morkus looked up and nearly leapt out of his skin. Above loomed statues larger than skyscrapers all lined up in a row as if forming a path to follow. Four-armed and narrow-featured, their figures reminded him of the alien in the tank. Each of them glowered down at him with what he could only describe as disapproval. His eyes followed the line until the dust grew too thick to see through.

"Help!" A voice called out from the dust. It sounded

weak, strained, as if the simple effort of crying out was a task too great. The voice called out again and a pang of familiarity tickled the back of Morkus's mind. Where had he heard that voice before?

"Please help," the voice was hardly more than a whimper now.

"Mother?" He asked. It had to be. There was no mistaking it now.

Silence was his reply, and a deep fear clawed at the depths of his belly. What if she was hurt? It had been so long since they last saw each other. How long had he been trapped in that lab? He sprinted forward into the dark and through the dust. While he couldn't see, he could still hear the direction his mother was calling from. A silhouette formed in front of him. It was frail but in a way that announced a gentle nature. While he couldn't make out the details, Morkus would recognize that build anywhere.

"Mother!" He cried. He rushed to the form and embraced it. His arms wrapped around his mother's shoulders in the best hug he could muster. Her familiar scent filled his nostrils, and Morkus breathed deep. She returned the hug with thin arms and a nurturing touch. The chill seemed to disappear under that grasp.

The wind picked up and droplets of rain began to dampen Morkus's hair. The sprinkle turned into a downfall, and soon the rain began to wash away the dust. Still, his mother hugged him, and Morkus clung to her like he'd never let go. As the dust cleared a form began to take shape before him. It was colossal in size, and Morkus wasn't sure how he had missed it before. As the shape grew more visible, his blood ran cold.

At first, Morkus couldn't comprehend what he was looking at. But as his mind caught up to his senses, he was too stunned to even scream. Its foundation was a writhing mass of gray-scaled tentacles slithering, coiling, and amassing upward into the shape of a human torso. Where a stomach should have been, however, was a fang-filled maw gaping and gasping for air. Black shoulders stretched out into disproportionally long arms which transitioned into spindly hands. Resting atop these shoulders was a bulbous head with a single eye taking up its entirety. The gargantuan orb with its violet iris blinked as it observed Morkus. Floating above it was a halo made of flesh, pinkish and all too human. Hundreds of smaller eyes were embedded in its surface as it hovered and spun above the creature's head. No, Morkus realized this was not a creature but a god.

He tried to pull away from his mother and warn her, but she wouldn't let go. He struggled to break free, but to no avail. He loved his mother, but they needed to leave. Twisting his head to get a better view of her, his fear grew into unpolluted terror. The shape clinging to him was but a crude semblance of his mom. Gray scales covered the back of her featureless head, and what he had thought to be arms were thin tendrils. His eyes traced the tendrils back to the writhing mass of the god's base. He'd been tricked.

Morkus was hoisted into the air. Higher he went, and higher still until he was brought before the colossal eye. With a pupil the size of a car, the god peered through Morkus's very soul. He could feel its gaze strip him apart layer by layer, calculating his sins and weighing each of his choices like a coin on a scale. A voice rumbled deep inside his skull. It sounded like a thousand voices deeper than thunder all speaking in unison.

"Unwise to steal from a god," it said. A sharp pain flared in his head where the implant was embedded in his brain.

"No," Morkus said, "I didn't – It wasn't my choice!"

"It matters not," the god said, "I will do as I have always done with arrogant lifeforms."

The toothy maw below Morkus chattered with contempt, and Morkus strained against the god's hold. More pain erupted in his skull, and Morkus cried out. It hurt so bad he couldn't breathe. He screamed with what little air he had left in his lungs, and his world shifted once more.

2

Morkus was back on the elevator. It's cramped, stifling air corrupted by blood-stench and sweat assaulted him all at once. He was not the only one to have a vision it would seem. All around him the other kids came out of shock as reality dawned on them once more. The poor boy he had dragged in here was huddled up in the corner and whispering to himself. A look of terror was etched into Anna's face. Her once fine features were marred by age lines and wrinkles. The elevator slowed to a stop, and the doors slid open. No one seemed to notice. Each of them stood there in silent confusion. Morkus looked toward the only vipers left in their group. They shook their heads to indicate the visions weren't their doing.

"We need to keep moving," Anna said. At last, she broke out of her trance and started to hurry them along. One by one, the kids shook themselves back to the present and filed out of the elevator. The garden beyond was as elegant as the others had made it sound. Vibrant flowers and rich greens overran every centimeter. Narrow walkways of paving stones wound their way throughout like a maze. The lights were more natural here rather than the colorless white from the labs below.

Xoriah held out her hand to brush the plants as they walked by, and Morkus found himself doing the same. The sudden change in atmosphere was almost enough to make him forget what they had just been through. The blood drying on his clothes was a rude reminder. It stiffened and stuck to his skin as it coagulated. Whispering continued from the boy he had saved. It was incoherent babble as far as Morkus was concerned, but it did little to ease the ever-growing tension. Just a bit further and they'd all be on their way to the surface.

The lights flickered and the sound of clanging metal echoed somewhere off to the left. Morkus flinched. That was not a sound he wanted to hear. Death followed that sound. Wordlessly, the group picked up the pace. The others knew what that sound meant as well. The only one to speak was the boy with his continued whispering. This time, Morkus managed to catch a few words.

"Triangle," he said, "triangle with a gemstone. She's not going to save you, Kallik. She's not going to save anyone."

The boy wasn't a viper, so why had he cracked like this? It was driving Morkus nuts. What had the god shown him? Morkus shuddered at the thought of that thing. No one should have to witness such a horror. He could still hear the chittering of its teeth, the feel of the thing that was not his mother.

"Mommy?" A child's voice cut in, and everyone in the group froze. Anna strode to the back of the group, a deepening look of concern growing on her features. She almost looked as if she might cry. She peered through the greenery, scanning for the source of the voice.

"Mommy?" It said again. Another sound accompanied it this time. The sound of something wet being dragged across the floor grew closer.

"Tavish?" Anna called out. "Is that you?"

Morkus exchanged a look with Xoriah. Something was wrong, very wrong. Anna didn't see it. She was too caught up in searching for the voice. They needed to keep moving. Morkus started pushing some of the other kids along, and Xoriah joined in the effort. The other elevator was within sight. Anna stayed where she was, searching. Once the kids were moving again, Xoriah went back for Anna and grabbed her arm. The orderly didn't budge. There was a wild look in her eyes that worried him.

"Xoriah, we need to go," he said. "The elevator is right there."

"We can't leave her," Xoriah said.

"Xoriah," Morkus warned.

It was too late. Greenery parted and a figure emerged. The smell was worse than the sight which was saying something. Hunched over and dragging a sack of flesh which had once been an arm, the child pushed his way through the plant life to approach Anna. His entire body was covered in cysts and pustules, and not a single hair coated his naked skin. The boy smiled at Anna through mutated lips, and tears flowed freely down the orderly's cheeks.

Morkus should have used his powers. The thought never crossed his mind. It all happened so fast, and exhaustion had sunken its teeth in. Anna opened her arms for an embrace, and the child pounced faster than Morkus thought possible. Xoriah was tossed aside by the force of it. The creature that had once been Tavish wrapped all of its good limbs around its mother and trapped her in a vice. Its mouth opened into a fanged maw and bit down into Anna's neck. She didn't make a sound as the blood shot from her open veins. The sack of flesh clinging to its shoulder began to hiss as air rushed out of its open wounds.

Morkus sprinted over to Xoriah and dragged her back across the stones with what little strength he had left. Any later and they would have both been dead as the hissing stopped, and Tavish exploded. Gore and bones flew in all directions like shrapnel. He looked to where Anna should be laying but all that remained was a mangled corpse, unrecognizable as even human. The sound of skittering stalks echoes somewhere else in the garden. It was time to leave.

3

Xoriah grabbed Morkus by the back of the shirt and hauled the two of them to their feet. Together, they bolted for the elevator and began ushering the other kids inside. Morkus cursed the boy's whispering as he shoved the last of them in before stepping through the doors himself. Several of the creatures with spider legs holding them aloft burst into view. They noticed the kids as the elevator door started to slide shut, and they stormed their way in a mad dash to catch up.

Xoriah was on top of it in a heartbeat. The first had its limbs ripped from its back to stumble limp on the floor. The other two were smashed together at high velocity. Morkus turned to thank her as the door shut, but paused. The girl spluttered in a coughing fit, her hand coming away with fresh blood. They were all burning through their powers at a rapid pace. No wonder why Master Aillon had once spoken so highly of a device called a limiter.

With the door secured, the elevator began its ascent. Low rumbles from the elevator's rails sent Morkus's nerves to the edge. The tightening walls and growing odors made the neck of his shirt feel all too tight. Clenching and unclenching his fists gave him a bit of a distraction, but it wasn't enough. Something was about to break. He could feel it in his gut. A soft hand touched his shoulder, and he gave a start.

"You're doing well," Xoriah said. "Kallik would be proud of you."

Morkus let the compliment hang between them. He didn't need her approval. Well, he did, but he wasn't about to let it show. He took a deep breath and studied the door. This elevator was going up for what seemed an eternity. There were no numbers above the door to indicate how far it had climbed or how much further was left. Xoriah's comment made him think about the boy with the antlers, Kallik. He hated him before; wasn't sure he didn't hate him now. He did his part, though, him and Leo both. He found himself hoping the pair survived. Vigamere could be alive as well. Morkus hoped he was. Killing that man himself would be a pleasure beyond comparison. He still owed that death to Mari. She should've been here. Morkus would have traded the lives of all of these kids just for another minute with her. He could almost remember what she smelled like. Another whiff of blood corrected that.

One last clench of his fists and the elevator stopped. The doors slid apart, and cold air blasted through the opening. Morkus had to squint and throw a hand above his eyes to see. Others did the same, some turning their heads entirely. They had made it to the surface. They were free.

4

Never in his life did Morkus think he would be happy to see snow, yet here he was worshipping its existence. The landing platform stood a hundred meters above the surface of a frozen ocean. He peered out over the simple slab of concrete and steel to observe the frozen wasteland. There were entire mountains of solid ice, but Morkus knew beneath the surface pockets of unfrozen water ran. A shout of excitement drew his attention back to his friends.

Only two ships remained on the platform. They were simple transports, little more than oblong rectangles with wings. The first had been locked and inaccessible. The second had been what caused the commotion. Xoriah had gotten the loading ramp open and the other kids were clamoring to get inside and out of the cold. All except one. The whispering kid stood on the very edge of the platform and stared out over the endless sheet of ice. Maybe it was time to apologize and learn the kid's name. Afterall, the boy had just lost his sister. He strode over to the boy to do just that. Heights were never his strong suit, so Morkus had to be careful not to get too close. The boy's toes kissed the very edge. Morkus wondered how he wasn't suffering from vertigo.

"We'll make it through this," Morkus said, "I'll keep you safe. Before long we'll be up in the stars and on our way home. Maybe we go in the ship for a bit of warmth?"

The boy didn't answer. Wide eyes remained fixated on the horizon. Morkus followed his gaze to the peak of a mountain. It stood above the others like a blue dagger. His mouth continued to move with his whispered tones. Morkus stepped closer to try and hear what was being said.

"Mercury sulfide, brilliant red like blood," the boy said. "So much blood. Kallik thinks she'll save us. Xoriah will believe it too. Lies, all of it lies. Yes, so many lies. She relishes in her name. You've seen it too. I know you have. She'll do it. You know she'll do it. Yes, yes, she will. She escapes here and the galaxy will burn. She'll unleash it, you know. Then she'll find the one thing that can put the fires out, and she'll kill it. Killing is all she knows. It's in her name."

Morkus grabbed the boy's shoulder and tried to shift him away from the edge. The boy's eyes snapped to attention and drilled holes into Morkus's own. He was breathing heavy, panting. Cold wind had nipped his cheeks into a bright red, and tears streamed down his face.

"It's in her name, Morkus!" The boy shouted.

Startled, Morkus let go and stepped back. Fear threatened to hold his speech, but Morkus managed to squeeze out a final question. "Who?"

The boy blinked. His mouth contorted into a horrid smile made worse by the thick smear of blood across his face. Morkus couldn't move. He knew what was about to happen, and still he froze.

"All of us will bleed," the boy said, and he stepped out over the edge.

CHAPTER 25
- SARAH -

1

The engines of the dropship hummed as it descended to the planet. Breckett had the particle shields down so Sarah and Yasmin could look through the thick windows on either side. Below was an endless wasteland of snow interrupted only by a long mountain range comprised of jagged ice. Their approach needed to be steady and low in order to land safely on the facility's solo landing pad. Sarah shifted in her armor and switched her attention to Yasmin. The doctor sat across from Sarah and hummed softly to herself.

"Vermillion," Sarah said. Yasmin stopped humming and straightened in her seat. Though shrouded by a thick helmet, Sarah knew a look of confusion was waiting behind the gray plate.

"That's my name," Sarah continued. "It's Sarah Vermillion. If I make it back, I'll tell you everything, yeah?"

A long moment of silence stretched out between the two. They hadn't spoken since their last interaction outside of Sarah's cabin, and an awkwardness still loomed between them. The mentioned *if* also worsened an already heightened anxiety spreading across the crew. The audio the Villimath's sensors had picked up had them all on edge.

"Promise?" Yasmin asked.

"Promise."

Yasmin nodded and the conversation died. The sound of the engines picked up as Breckett pushed the ship to a higher altitude. They crested one of the highest mountains, an icy shard that reminded Sarah of a blue dagger. Parker's voice cut in through the comms.

"Remember the facility runs several hundred meters deep," she said. "Scans show there are multiple levels to it beneath the surface. There's also another structure nearby partially embedded in the ice and fully submerged. Something is off about that one though. The material looks all wrong."

"Confirmed," Breckett said, "if the crew we're looking for is down there, we'll find them."

"Scared?" Yasmin asked. She was looking at the leg Sarah didn't know she was bouncing.

"Yes." Sarah clipped the word in an attempt to kill that line of conversation before it started. It didn't work.

"Same," Yasmin said, "we have no idea what we are walking into. Never bodes well."

Sarah remained quiet. She knew very well the kind of hell they were walking into. From the screams and the skittering and the other horrible noise they had picked up, there was no mistaking what awaited Sarah. It was a familiar kind of hell. It scared her, true, but what Sarah was really afraid of was something else entirely. A tinge of excitement lingered somewhere in her mind, and that worried her above all else.

2

Two other ships were present as they landed, and Breckett had to fly with care as there was little room left. Sarah watched through the window as he landed it snuggly between them. The captain was out of the cockpit and down the aisle before the engines were even done powering down. Sarah pulled free of her straps and followed him toward the ramp. Before lowering it, Breckett pointed at the rack of Golden Boys.

"We need you on this one, doc," he said. "You have training, and there's no way we're pulling this off with just two."

Yasmin hesitated at first, glanced at Sarah, then nodded. Pulling herself free of her seat, she went over to the rack to be the

first to grab a rifle. She checked it over with a no-nonsense expertise before slinging the strap over one shoulder. She grabbed the
other two and handed them off. Sarah slid a magazine into her
own and ensured the second chamber was loaded up with breacher
shells. Breckett waited for a thumbs up from both of them before
opening the ramp.

Sarah was first out. She led with her rifle checking either
side to make sure the landing was clear. A word from Breckett sent
her toward one of the other ships. They needed to find out if they
were operational. If they were, they could use them to transport
more survivors should the need arise. The last thing they wanted to do was make multiple trips. She hurried over to the one on
her left while Breckett and Yasmin went toward the right. Both
were plain looking, no more exciting than a simple freighter. She
reached the access panel and pushed the command to open the
ramp. Hydraulics hissed as the ramp slowly lowered to the ground.
What awaited her was something she did not expect. Children,
eight of them by her count, all stood huddled together in the far
corner. They all wore the same white uniform, or used to be white,
as they looked as though they had bathed in blood. It was an eerie
sight that put Sarah's hackles up and her finger on the trigger.

"Kids," she said, "we've got kids here."

The largest of them, a brutish boy with dark hair and wide
shoulders, stepped forward to confront her. Several expressions
slid across his face in rapid succession and Sarah had a hard time
understanding what she was looking at. First it was fear, then hatred, then something along the lines of confusion.

"You're not one of them" the boy said, "you aren't Skren
either. Just who exactly are you?"

By the time the words were out of his mouth, Breckett
and Yasmin arrived. A gasp sounded from Yasmin, and she pulled
her helmet off. Her look of concern must have put the kids at ease
because the larger boy backed down a couple steps, his shoulders
slumping. Yasmin set her rifle and helmet down to pull a pack out
from behind her waist. Sarah could see it was filled to the brim
with medical supplies.

"We're looking for someone," Sarah said. "A lot of people

have gone missing, and we're trying to bring them home. Are you part of that group?"

"All of us were taken," one of the girls said. Her golden hair was stained and matted with blood, but she spoke with confidence. "We managed to escape, but there are more of us down below. I fear some of our families are there too."

"New plan," Breckett said, "Yasmin, you get these kids back to the Villimath and make sure they get treated. Sarah, looks like it's just you and me after all."

A few of the kids exchanged excited glances, and Yasmin was within their midst in a flash. She had bandages, sanitizers and any number of other things out on the floor before Breckett could say another word. She dabbed faces, checked cuts, and flashed a light in several of the children's eyes. The larger boy stepped forward once again, this time determination was locked into his features.

"You're going down below?" He asked. "You're going to save more people?"

"We're going to try," Sarah said.

"Then I'm going with," he said. "Someone has to show you the way."

3

The boy's name turned out to be Morkus; Sarah learned that as the three of them waited in the elevator. He stood between herself and Breckett, sweat beginning to bead on a bloodied forehead. She couldn't tell if it was his blood or someone else's. He was brave to go back down. She didn't know what all he had faced, but by the way he clenched and unclenched his fists, the way his wide eyes rolled in his skull to look back and forth between Breckett and herself, the way Sarah could tell his breathing was forced and controlled, it was obvious only death waited for them down here.

"Ever seen a monster?" Morkus asked. His question wasn't directed at either of them. Rather, his wide eyes glared at the doors in front of him as if he wished he could do anything to keep them from opening. Breckett remained silent, instead choosing to double check his Golden Boy was ready for immediate action.

"I have," Sarah said. Morkus's eyes rolled to stare up at her helmet. She tried not to flinch away from the intensity of his gaze, the whites visible on all sides while his pupils were dilated to the extremes.

"Not like these, you haven't," he said. He didn't elaborate. The boy turned back to the front of the elevator and clasped his hands in front of him. Sarah noted one of his thumbs rubbed the other in a comforting gesture. If Carlisle Station offered any sort of clue, she could only imagine what must be running through his mind. At least this time she had something larger than a pistol. Double checking her pouches, she also reminded herself she had more than a single clip of ammunition. What she wouldn't do to have her sledgehammer with her now. A quick glance at the display in her helmet told her everything she needed to know about the weapon secure in her arms – fully loaded and syncing perfectly with her suit. The elevator started to grind to a halt, and Morkus took a sharp breath. He decided to make one last comment before the doors slid open.

"If you see a man in a white mask," he said, "don't shoot him."

Sarah knew who Morkus was talking about, but she kept that information to herself. Breckett still didn't know the real reason they were here in the first place. Better to keep it that way. Some secrets were best taken with you to the grave. Breckett gave her a nod as the elevator dinged, and he pointed his Golden Boy toward the entrance. The doors opened and Sarah found herself in a familiar hell.

4

The world was a blur of white muzzle flashes and red spray. The doors were barely open before the creatures made their move. These were different than what Sarah had seen on Carlisle Station but just as awful. Mutated people with massive spider legs bursting from their backs rushed the elevator with open maws. Mandibles clicked and claws chittered as they climbed over each other in a rushed dash toward their next meal. Hesitation wasn't an option. Breckett and Sarah both opened fired at the first sign of movement. Her reticle blinked red to indicate a lock, and Sarah pulled the trigger. One after the next, the pair ripped into their attackers until little else moved.

The boy hardly blinked as the last round was fired, and the last corpse fell in a heap atop the others. Sarah counted eleven of the creatures all heaped around the same area. Behind the mound of corpses was a garden. Memories of the hydroponics lab threatened Sarah's calm. She could see Sondra's fanged mouth curling into a wicked smile as his centipede body chased her through row after row. She fought back the memories by focusing her attention on finding the next threat. With the armor covering her body, the Golden Boy pressed to her shoulder, and with Breckett by her side, Sarah felt nearly invincible. She'd be bringing her brother home today wherever that home might be.

A stillness settled. Green leaves and full-spectrum flowers gave no hint of motion beyond. Stone paths wound through the garden while strange looking bushes reached up to brush the white ceiling. Breckett was the first to step out. Morkus trailed on his heel seeming to not notice the pile of bodies just outside the door. Her helmet filtered out any smells, but Sarah could imagine the stench. The kid didn't even wrinkle his nose. Shock must still have its claws digging deep into his mind. Stepping over a spider leg, Sarah tried not to jump as it twitched one last time.

The three of them stalked through the garden, Morkus pointing out which path led to the other elevator. The little display inside Sarah's helmet darted from plant to plant scanning for potential threats before moving on to the next. There was an odd sense of security knowing her helmet would find something before she would. She let the scanner do its job while they walked and put her own attention on the boy. He couldn't be older than thirteen. None of those kids were. What's more, they all wore the same uniform. There was little white left untouched by blood, but it was clear they were some sort of patients here. What was going on in this facility? Yasmin's voice over comms interrupted her thoughts.

"I've got the kids loaded up in the dropship," she said,

"about to bring them back to the Villimath. They're claiming to be conduits, though I'm not sure what that means. The blonde girl floated a rock with her brain, so I'm not sure this is a facility we want to stick around for too long. Just a thought, but be careful."

"That true?" Sarah asked. She was asking the boy and realized he wasn't connected to their comms channel. "It's true you're a conduit?"

Without breaking pace, Morkus nodded. Breckett stopped which forced all of them to. Lowering his rifle, the captain glared through his helmet even though he knew the kid couldn't see his face. Morkus wasn't intimidated. Instead, he stood taller and squared his shoulders.

"Not by choice," he said. "They dragged us down here and put things in our heads. Ran terrible experiments on us until we cracked. Know what cracked means?"

"Yes," Sarah said, "but we need to keep moving."

"Hold on a second," Breckett said, "how the hell do you know any of this?"

Sarah never got the chance to answer. Another voice interrupted their conversation. This one, lower and filled with malice, had Morkus frantic. Once he realized it was coming from the overhead speakers, his shoulders slumped. Sarah recognized the voice as well. It belonged to the man on the data-chip. This man took her brother.

"Sarah Vermillion," he said, "so pleasant of you to finally stop by. I'd apologize for the mess, but I've come to the realization that you may be just the solution I need."

"Where's my brother?" Sarah asked. She could feel Breckett's glare, but she ignored it. There was no hiding it now. Her hope of keeping the truth in the shadows shriveled up as soon as this alleged morak'casai spoke. She couldn't afford to play dumb when Hector was so close to being within her grasp.

"I'll tell you what," the man said, "clear a path to me, help me clean up our little mess, and maybe I'll tell you. Afterall, I feel like I owe you for taking care of my Kade problems. Karaska wanted to dissect you, you know. I, on the other hand, feel like we'd make a great partnership. Communications room on the third floor. Do your best to not die on the way here."

The speakers went silent, and Sarah was left standing with a glaring Breckett and a confused Morkus. Breckett had his rifle lowered but his finger twitched near the trigger hinting at a dangerous intent. Morkus was picking up on the tension and took a couple steps back until he brushed up against the greenery.

"And I thought Ziven was the one keeping dangerous secrets," Breckett said. "Mind telling me what's actually going on? Need I remind you that people died to get us here."

"I just want my brother back," Sarah said. "I'll tell you everything after. You can do whatever you want once you know."

Morkus stepped forward with clenched fists. "Are you actually going to help him? The Butcher, I mean, I thought you were here to save us."

"If you're talking about the man on the speakers," Sarah said, "no. I'm not going to help him, I'm going to kill him. But I need info about Hector first."

"Down below," Morkus said. A confidence returned to his posture, and he relaxed after Sarah's answer. "If your brother is still alive, he'd be in a cell down below. Mari told me all about that place. I can show you."

"Tell me one thing," Breckett said, "what is all of this to you?"

"Closure," Sarah said. "I don't expect you to understand, but I could really use your help."

"Your cut goes to Vaughn's family," Breckett said, "if we make it out of here, that is."

"Deal," Sarah said.

Breckett's finger eased away from the trigger and the air of tension subsided. He tilted his neck first one way then the other as if limbering up, and he rolled his shoulders with a crack. Morkus caught on and started to crack his knuckles. The two of them looked a part of a pair.

"Let's pay this Butcher a visit," Breckett said. The doors to the next elevator parted.

5

As the trio stood in the elevator as it descended, a chill spiderwebbed its way from Sarah's heart. Despite the temperature control units in her suit, nothing could stop the onsetting cold from sending goosebumps across her flesh. It ripped away the confidence she'd been clinging to earlier and replaced it with a deep sense of dread. Something horrible was about to happen; she could feel it. Perhaps Breckett would turn on her sooner rather than later. Looking at the captain gave no telltale signs of his betrayal, but the man was clever. If he was going to strike, he'd do it without warning. The boy as well set her nerves on edge. His wide, unblinking eyes glared straight ahead at the door in front of them. Perhaps he would crack. Perhaps he already had, and it was only a matter of time before he killed both her and Breckett. She'd seen firsthand what a viper could do once unleashed, but had no idea what a bull might look like. It was then Sarah realized they'd just sent an entire dropship of these kids to the Villimath. They all might already be doomed.

"How do I know you haven't already cracked?" Sarah asked. Morkus didn't even glance in her direction as he replied.

"You'd be dead," he said. "They don't put limiters on us here. Makes us stronger, but burns through us far more quickly. If anyone was going to crack here, they'd already have done it by now."

The comment made for little reassurance in Sarah's opinion, but she let the matter rest. It did nothing to warm the chill. The body they stepped over a few moments ago to get to this elevator could have something to do with it. Morkus gave the corpse a strange look as they passed by but said nothing. Whoever the person had been was little more than a pile of gore beyond recognition. Once again, Sarah found herself thankful her suit was a self-contained environment that blocked outside smells.

The elevator slowed to a stop, and the doors slid open. Sarah and Breckett raised their rifles to point them down a long hallway. Light flickered across white walls and identical gray doors, and Sarah noticed the floor was black with a texture like sandpaper. The hallway curved to the left making it impossible to see what awaited them.

No one dared moved. The stillness stretched on for minutes while they waited for any sign of an attack. A few times Sarah swore she heard the sounds of scuttling claws, but nothing ever came. Just as Sarah was about to think the coast was clear, a cry of terror echoed from down the hallway. It was a shrill voice calling out for help. A look from Breckett sent both of them storming down the hallway. What greeted them made Sarah stop in her tracks.

Once spotless white walls were now soaked and splattered with scarlet and crimson while some areas were dried to dark burgundy and brown. A barricade of mutilated corpses and debris blocked the passage forward. Sarah wasn't sure what she found worse, the barricade or the lack of reaction from Morkus. The boy simply stood there and waited for her and Breckett to make a move. The voice was calling out from the other side. The lights flickered and the voice's next words came out in a whimper.

"Please," the voice said, "please. I can hear someone there. Please don't go. I just want out. Let me out of this place."

With a wave of Breckett's hand, he and Sarah set aside their Golden Boys and began pulling apart the barricade. She tried not to think about what she was grabbing and setting aside, but it grew more difficult as her suit's gauntlets grew slick with blood. Dropping a severed arm to the floor, they managed to clear a small hole to peak through. A bald man poked his pudgy face into the newly created hole to stare at them. His panicked eyes considered both of them in a brief moment of confusion.

"Who the hell are you two?" He asked. "Wait, doesn't matter. Just get me out of here."

A loud thud echoed from somewhere down the corridor. The man pulled his face out of the hole to glance behind him. Whatever he saw put him into a panic. Pressing his face back into the hole, he peered into Sarah's helmet and mouthed the word *please*.

Sarah and Breckett redoubled their efforts while Morkus stood back and watched. More thudding echoed and this time it grew nearer to the barricade. The man's whimpering grew more frantic. Sarah cleared a whole large enough for him to push his head and arm through but that was all. He kept whispering *please, please*, but the two of them could only work so fast. Working from his own end apparently never crossed the man's mind. Fear did horrible things to a person. Sarah was about to point that out when a spear-like claw erupted from the man's mouth. A grotesque gargling burbled from a mouth spread far wider than humanly possible, the edges of his mouth torn at the corners. Sarah's head was close enough that the claw's tip scraped the side of her helmet.

Breckett fumbled back for his Golden Boy, but all Sarah could do was watch in stunned horror. The man's head was pulled away from the hole, and a new face peered through. Three misshapen, yellow eyes glared through at Sarah's helmet. They were sunken deep into a bloated head covered by festering lesions and puckered tumors. It smiled at Sarah with a mouth that nearly split the head in two. The teeth were all too white, all too perfect, for such a mutated visage.

Before Breckett could return with his rifle, the monster had already pulled away from the hole to sink its perfect teeth into its victim's shoulder. White teeth turned red as it chewed, and Sarah got a full view of its figure. Lopsided and hunched over, it had one clawed hand still with the bald man stuck to it while the other was a decrepit human hand. It used that one to hold down the corpse as if it might try and get up to flee.

Morkus snuck up behind Sarah and peeked through the hole. Breckett stood impatiently behind the two of them with his Golden Boy at the ready. He was right. The two of them needed to move so Breckett could get rid of the creature, but something about the boy's expression held Sarah in place. His forehead was wrinkled in concentration and, for the first time since Sarah had met the kid, his eyes were narrowed to slits.

"Good bye, Sabastian," Morkus said. The creature was launched to the ceiling by an unseen force where it smashed into the light above. The white light shattered with a pop plunging the surrounding area in shadow before the creature was slammed back to the ground. Again, it was hurled into the ceiling to be smashed against the floor. The corpse of the man clung to the claw, flying with the creature as it was hammered against the two surfaces. Over and over again this happened until both bodies were little more than pulp. Breckett drew close to peer through the hole.

"Could've used your help moving the barricade," he said, "that man might have lived."

"He deserved it," Morkus said. He wiped a bloody nose with the back of his hand. "Besides, don't know how much I've got left. Wanna keep whatever I do got for the Butcher."

Breckett only nodded and went back to taking down the barricade. All three of them pitched in this time until there was a gap large enough for them to squeeze through. Sarah grabbed her rifle, and one by one they shuffled to the other side. Once through Morkus tapped Sarah on the shoulder to grab her attention. Apparently, the boy thought she was in charge. He pointed down an adjoining hallway that curved around another corner.

"Some of my friends ran down that way," he said with an expectant look, "hope they lived."

"I guess we better go find out," Sarah said with a nod to Breckett. He nodded back and double checked his munitions. A set of bloody footprints trailed down that direction. Combined with what they had just witnessed, the sight put Sarah's hopes next to zero. They could humor the boy, however, at least this once.

CHAPTER 26
- KALLIK -

1

All around him scientists, orderlies, and Skren warriors toppled to the ground. Some clutched their heads in agony while others simply fell limp. Kallik looked on in horror as Doctor Foster babbled wordless chants in a violent madness until she bit down. Her tongue was still halfway out of her mouth, and the woman bit right through it. Instead of stopping, Foster chewed through the rest of it. The severed muscle flopped to the ground while the doctor began to choke on her own blood. Nathfnitu stalked toward him, naked, angry, and with a hungry look gleaming in her black eyes. Kallik was still shivering from the vision he'd just scene, the god-like entity that had addressed him. He glanced over to Leo for support, but his friend was curled up into a ball on the floor. The only two left standing were himself and this vengeful alien they had just unleashed. Her mouth didn't move but her voice reverberated inside his skull.

"Hello little devil," she said, "I see you held up your end of the bargain."

"What was that?" Kallik asked. "What did you do? What did I just see?"

"A warning," she said, "something your people don't deserve, but something I gave them anyway. It's what happened to my own kin when we got too greedy, too curious."

She stopped in front of the still gurgling Foster. The dying woman was lifted into the air and rotated as her lab coat was peeled away. Nathfnitu plucked the coat out of the air and wrapped it around her body. She had to tear holes in the sides to make room for her extra set of arms. It was only then when Kallik realized something deeply disturbing. Through his entire captivity he'd been taught people could be one thing or another. Bulls and vipers, that's what existed. An individual could be one or the other, but never both. This creature before him was doing something an entire species could not. All of her threats held new weight, and Kallik worried he'd made the wrong choice by setting her free. He looked over to Leo. His friend still wasn't moving. Maybe they all needed to die down here, especially if they were risking the ire of an ancient god by using their abilities.

Kallik stooped over his friend and tried to shake him awake. Leo wouldn't move. He felt for a heartbeat. It was there, slow and faint, but at least it was beating. Kallik checked to make sure he was breathing by placing his hand beneath Leo's nose. Soft breaths brushed against his skin, and Kallik let out a sigh of relief.

"Help him," Kallik said, "we need to get him up so we can get out of here."

Nathfnitu ignored him. Stepping over another incapacitated scientist, she strode over to one of the control panels near the far side of the chamber. Kallik had to strain his neck over the lip of the inset to see what she was doing. All of the implements and computers the scientists had put there were blasted away by her powers. Kallik threw a hand over his face to shield his eyes as bits of broken materials flew in all directions. She began pushing buttons and fiddling with controls. Meanwhile, a pair of Skren spears levitated up from the floor. They flew around the room to pause for just a brief moment above someone before lancing down to finish them off. Kallik placed himself over Leo out of instinct as the other remaining survivors were slaughtered without a second thought. Nathfnitu hadn't even looked up from her work as the stench of blood quickly filled the chamber. No spear came for Leo, but Kallik dared not move. The spears sank into their last victims where they remained unmoving.

"Come," she said at last, her voice a sudden shock in Kallik's mind, "there's something I must show you."

She left the range of controls to hop down into the inset. Kallik put up a defensive posture over Leo, but she only glanced at him before turning to look for something else. She slid a long-nailed hand along the stoney texture of the pit until her fingers came to stop on a small patch of uneven texture. Placing her palm against it, the stone made a sound like a click. The floor beneath them began to rumble and shift, and Kallik started to realize this pit was actually a lift. He dragged Leo away from the wall as the floor lowered them into the dark.

2

A silent blackness surrounded them as the lift touched the bottom. The floor above them was little more than a pale blue ellipse which offered none of its light to the floor below. Kallik strained his eyes to see anything at all, but it was of no use. He held his hand out in front of him, and he couldn't even see that. The darkness was quiet enough to hear his own heartbeat pounding in his chest. He could hear the soft breaths of Leo next to his feet along with the shifting movements of Nathfnitu. The silence was broken by the sound of snapping twigs. No, that wasn't quite right. It almost sounded like the popping joints of an old man who had been sitting for far too long.

A light bloomed in front of them causing Kallik to wince. After taking a moment to let his eyes adjusts, he gasped at what now stood before him. The figure was similar to Nathfnitu but it was gaunt and skeletal. Black and gray eyes were sunken so far into its skull, Kallik had a difficult time seeing if they actually existed. Its skin was withered and just barely clung to the bone. A dark carapace made of the same stone-like material as the ship covered a majority of its body making the creature resemble some sort of insect. It held a glowing yellow orb above its head as it considered the newcomers. Several moments passed before it spoke. Its voice rasped out in a hoarse whisper, and the creature spoke in a language that sounded like nothing Kallik had ever heard. A dialect filled with grating mumbles and sharp clicks; the sounds added to the insectoid semblance.

Nathfnitu tilted her head as she listened to the creature. Once it was done, she pointed to Leo and spoke in the same language. While they were speaking, Kallik noticed something over the creature's shoulder. Behind was a monolithic structure of black tubes and glittering stone. It was difficult to make out as just the edges of the structure were visible in the light. The conversation ended which snapped Kallik's attention back to the pair. The creature nodded at Nathfnitu before shambling toward Kallik and Leo. Its joints cracked with each movement, and each jerking motion reminded Kallik of a marionette being strung along by some hidden puppeteer. It caused the light in its hand to shake in uncontrolled rhythms. It shoved Kallik out of the way to stoop over Leo. Kallik shouted in protest, but was ignored as the creature scooped Leo up with its other three arms. He'd fight if he had to. Kallik stepped forward to make that clear, but Leo spoke at last.

"Wait, Kall," he said. One eye was cracked open to just a slit, but a faint grin played across his lips. "It was my turn to cut a deal."

3

Leo had always been the cleverest of them. For a brief moment, Kallik thought he had outdone his friend. Here Leo had proved him wrong. Kallik's chin wanted to sink into the floor as he followed the two aliens deeper into the dark. The shambling one carried Leo gentler than Kallik would have expected despite its lumbering gait. Nathfnitu strolled next to him with an eagerness about her that concerned Kallik. Concern for his friend lingered deep in his chest. The trade Leo had offered hurt Kallik more than anything. His concern grew deeper as he looked up.

The monolithic structure Kallik had caught a glimpse of earlier now towered above them. It looked like a black asteroid suspended in countless cables, wires, and tubes. The black rock shimmered with faint luminosity, and he could *feel* the presence of the rock in his mind. A metal box stood upright at the base of the structure, and Kallik couldn't shake the idea that it resembled a coffin. Wires and straps hung loose at its side and a glass chamber filled with dark liquid was attached to its side. More chambers rested beneath the filled one, but those remained empty.

"All this time," Nathfnitu said in his mind, "your doctors and scientists tried to make my ship run again. They thought they had it figured out with their little experiments. Funny, when the secret was right beneath their very feet. They knew conduit powers were what fueled it, but they had no idea what they were actually feeding. If they'd only found out where our powers were being directed."

"What is that thing?" Kallik asked, but he felt as though he already knew.

She pointed to the suspended meteor as if Kallik might have missed it. "That stone is the exact material of the little thing embedded in your head. With it, this galaxy is as good as mine."

Kallik rubbed the spot behind his ear. The inhibiter was still firmly in place so he had to be careful about how much pressure he applied. Triggering its security protocol was the last thing he wanted to do. The last thing she said registered, and Kallik did a double take.

"You mean to go through with it then?" He asked," you mean to watch it all burn?"

Nathfnitu tapped a fingernail against her chin like she was pondering the question. Her shoulders slumped, and she waved the thoughts away. She said something to the shambling creature, and it began strapping Leo into the metal box. He was far shorter than its intended use, and Leo looked even more a child as his head hardly scraped the midway point.

"No," she said at last, "I don't think I will. A pleasant dream, but I think I'll leave it as such. A quiet life sounds much better. Someplace I can mourn my people. Besides, I'd only draw *its* attention again. No galaxy is ready for that, and I don't think I'd survive it a second time."

Kallik thought about the entity from the vision and a shudder ran through his body. His fear was replaced by hope, however, when he realized what she was saying. She was going to leave and let the galaxy be. That could mean she'd let him, his family, and all of his friends go as well. Except for Leo, that is. The ship needed a spark, and that spark was a conduit. It would feed off of the conduit's mind, and now Kallik understood why. The massive stone gleamed above him, an ominous hunger lurking beneath its surface.

The creature grabbed a narrow tube with a syringe poking from one end, its other end ran into the bottom of the glass chamber, and stuck the tip into Leo's arm. His friend barely flinched. In an instant, the dark liquid began to pump into Leo's arm. Nathfnitu explained the liquid would keep him alive as long as Leo remained integrated with the ship. A black crown was lowered onto Leo's head. Two needles on either side of it sank into his scalp. They were thin enough so that no blood was drawn to the surface. Leo's one hand was left unstrapped for the time, and he used the opportunity to grit his teeth and give Kallik a thumbs up.

Kallik fought back tears as Leo accepted his fate. It was his fault. If Kallik had been better at bargaining, all of his friends would have been able to get out of this. Instead, Kallik only thought of his own safety. Now his friend paid the price.

"He won't be in pain," Nathfnitu said as if reading his thoughts, "the stone will keep his mind in an alternate reality similar to the one you met me in. It's a better life than some can hope for."

Kallik didn't answer. He watched as Leo slowly closed his eyes once more. His hand fell, and the creature strapped it down inside the box. A low hum emanated from the stone above and the entire ship began to creak and groan in response. It felt as though the ship itself was a living creature waking up from a long slumber. Perhaps it was. Lights began to spring to life and the massive chamber was illuminated with an ethereal glow. The dark stone formed shapes like bone structures where the walls arched up to the ceiling like a giant's ribcage and gargantuan pillars resembled femurs. It made the tubes and wires holding the meteor in place look like veins, and the meteor a heart.

"I suppose it's time I held up my end of the bargain," Nathfnitu said, "after all, I've got some time to kill while my ship melts free of this icy prison."

CHAPTER 27
- SARAH -

1

Sarah checked for a pulse, though she knew there was little point. Amongst the carnage of desecrated bodies and mangled corpses was a lone man leaned up against a door. There was no white left to be seen on these walls. His shock of red hair was matted down by clumps of dried blood, and his tattered cloak was something Sarah was all too familiar with. Ruined or not, there was no mistaking the feathered collar and black material. The man's eyes were still open but the whites had turned a deep crimson and tears of blood ran down his cheeks. Likewise, more blood dripped from his ears and the corners of his mouth.

"He cracked," Morkus said, "he should have brought me with."

"You knew him?" Sarah asked. Breckett stood nearby, and even though he pretended to be focused on his watch, Sarah knew the man was listening intently.

"Master Aillon," Morkus said, "don't remember his first name though. He taught us bulls how to use our powers. Looks like he's got something in his hands."

Sarah looked down to where Aillon's hand was clutched by his side. A sliver of black rock was clutched between bloodied fingers. She had to pry his hand open to grab it and once free, she held it up to the light. It was a long, dagger-like shard of pure black stone. It shimmered with a faint gleam as she turned it in her hand.

"Recognize this?" Sarah asked.

Morkus squinted at it for a few moments but shook his head. He glanced up at the door Aillon was leaning against, and pointed at it. "Recognize that, though. That's Toby's door. That's who Aillon went running after."

Catching his meaning, Sarah shoved the stone into a belt pouch and dragged Aillon's corpse away from the door to make room. To her chagrin, the door had been slammed shut and the walls around it crumpled enough to make it impossible to open without cutting tools. Cutting tools were something they hadn't brought with them. She glanced at Morkus who was already on top of it. His eyes narrowed and a small bead of blood dribbled from his nose. The sound of straining metal groaned then popped as the door slid to the side. A young boy flung up his hand and started screaming at them from the back corner of the room.

"I'll kill you!" He yelled. "Not a step closer!"

"Toby," Morkus said as he stepped into the boy's view, "we've come back for you, doofus."

Toby, red-headed with a face full of freckles, broke out into tears at the sight of Morkus. The tears turned into sobs once he noticed Aillon's body. He hugged himself and shook as the tears rolled down his cheeks. To Sarah's surprise, Breckett was there in an instant. His helmet was off, his rifle leaned against the bed, and his black eyes with golden irises held a softness to them Sarah had not seen before.

"Close your eyes," he said, "we're going to get you out of here."

"You let her in," Toby said.

"Who did we let in?" Breckett asked. He glanced around the room for a clue, but Morkus only shrugged.

"The door was shut," Toby said between sobs, "it was keeping her out. Now it's open, and now she's going to come back."

A sound like a little girl's laughter echoed from down the hall. Sarah had grown to hate that sound. The lights flickered and made a high-pitched whine. She pulled her rifle around, leaned out of the door, and pointed the barrel down the hall. Nothing was there. Both Morkus and Breckett were giving her a strange look, but Sarah paid them no heed.

"That won't help," Toby said, "Rekkeh is going to get us."

The whine of the lights grew to a loud hum. It was enough to make the two boys clamp their ears with their hands, and force Breckett to put his helmet back on. The lights cut, and all at once the atmosphere turned deathly quiet. That was a bad sign. It meant the power was down which meant no elevators. If they wanted any hope of getting everyone out, they were going to have to bring the power back online. More laughter interrupted her thoughts.

"More guests to play with," a little girl's voice said from the dark, "my friends will be so happy."

2

Sarah's helmet switched to its perceptive mode where it used various sensors to create a basic image of what lurked in the dark. Walls and objects were outlined using blue silhouettes while living things were outlined in green. It made details next to impossible to make out, but it outlined general shapes with perfection. Sarah blinked at the green silhouette standing toward the end of the hall. Her reticle was locked on and blinking red, but Sarah held off from pulling the trigger. It was the shape of a child with arms crossed and held tilted.

Everything in her body screamed for Sarah to pull the trigger, but she forced herself to a calm. She wasn't about to murder a kid on instinct. Keeping her rifle trained down the corridor, Sarah flipped on her helmet light to get a full view of what she was aiming at. The beam of light pierced the dark and fell upon a little Groal girl with wiry brown hair. Her antlers weren't much more than horns protruding from her forehead. Compared to the other children Sarah had encountered, this girl's white uniform was soiled but not by blood. The white was dust covered, but otherwise left untouched.

The girl was smiling. It was not a welcoming smile or a *thank you so much for rescuing me* smile, but rather a smile that spoke of a manic hunger. Her tilted head added to the effect, and Sarah noticed other shapes start to move behind the girl. The reticle jumped from newcomer to newcomer and blinked red each time. Breckett came to stand behind Sarah and kept his rifle at the ready.

"I was never as strong as the others," the girl said, "I could only ever focus on one person at a time."

At first, Sarah was confused. Between her words and the dark shapes beginning to stir behind the girl, she thought now as a good time to start shooting. Breckett's rifle clattering to floor made her realize what was going on. Sarah looked up to see the man clutching his head between frantic hands. He muttered something over comms before tearing his helmet free. Tossing it away, Breckett dropped his hands to his side with a new found calm. With Sarah's light pointed at him, his golden irises glowed like a predator in the dark. His hand twitched by his side and a knife appeared in his grip. Black and gold eyes regarded Sarah with boiling hatred. It was the only warning she had as the blade came plunging down.

Sarah didn't have the time to react. She didn't have to. Before the strike could land, Breckett was thrown against the far wall by an unseen force. Morkus stumbled out of the room and raised a hand toward Breckett. The captain lifted into the air and was launched at the little girl. She cackled with delight as she ducked and disappeared into the dark. Sarah raised her Golden Boy and began to fire at the creatures now swarming Breckett's fallen body. She could still save him.

Careless of her aim, Sarah fired again and again until the magazine ran dry. She swapped it out for another but still the creatures clawed for Breckett. He fought them off the best he could, flailing the knife in wild and violent swings, but it wasn't enough. Toby grabbed Sarah's arm and tried to pull her away.

"We need to go," Morkus said, "or they'll turn on us next. Too many of them to fight."

Breckett sank his blade into one of the spider-creature's skulls where it got stuck. He managed to give Sarah one last look of regret before a claw took him through the boot. He let out a gasp of pain and let go of his knife. Sarah fired several more rounds but it was too late. Breckett was dragged into the swarm and vanished under a mass of flesh and claws.

Sarah slung her rifle over her shoulder, grabbed the two boys, and sprinted back down the direction they had come from. Toby whined as she pulled him by the arm, but Morkus managed to keep pace without complaint. They barreled past the macabre barricade and kept pushing on until they reached the elevator doors. Sarah knew the power was out, but she had to at least try. Maybe if they were lucky the elevators ran on a different circuit that still had juice.

In one fluid motion, Sarah unslung her rifle, slammed her hand against the elevator access panel, and turned around to face any oncoming threats. Her head lamp reflected off white surfaces and empty corridor. She listened and breathed trying to ignore the sound of her own pounding heart. Nothing. There were no sounds of scuttling monsters nor the chime of an opening elevator door. She tried again. Still nothing.

Desperate, Sarah tried the comms. Maybe someone on the Villimath could help devise a plan. That hope shriveled up and died as the connection was greeted by static. She was alone down here. No Breckett, no Jax, just her and a responsibility to save two boys with conduit abilities. Not to mention she still had a morak'casai to contend with in order to save her brother. She spoke to the boys behind her while keeping her rifle aimed down the hall.

"I suppose neither of you happen to know where the generators are," she said, "or can at least point me in the right direction."

"Down," Toby said. "Been there once. All the way at the bottom floor."

"Of course it is," Sarah said. "This elevator goes down to that floor?"

"It *did*," Toby said.

"One of you get it open."

Morkus rolled his shoulders and wiped his nose on an already grimy sleave before giving Sarah a curt nod. He put his hands to either temple as if his head were hurting and squinted. The doors rumbled a bit before giving way, and they only slid apart wide enough to let them through. The boy needed rest. Sarah could tell he was at his limit. That ruled out her initial idea. She had hoped the boy had enough strength to at least lower the elevator to get to the generators. She'd have to do things the hard way.

She ushered the boys in and once through, had Morkus close the doors behind them. Each of them absorbed the moment of quiet the closed doors brought them. Morkus slumped into the corner, Toby leaned against the far wall while hugging himself, and Sarah took a moment to take a deep breath. She leaned her rifle against the wall, and pulled her helmet off. The wide headlamp was the only source of light to go by so Sarah kept the helmet close to hand.

Inspecting the floor, Sarah pulled up a pair of the grated panels to reveal an emergency door beneath. She pushed a button that popped up a hatch lever, and Sarah tugged on it until the hatch snapped loose. Open air rushed through the new opening as she stared down the black pit.

"How far down does that go?" She asked more to herself than the two boys.

"Long ways," Toby said. "There are maintenance shafts connected to the vents, but that's where all those monsters came from. Plus, you'd just get lost down there."

"Helpful," Sarah muttered, and the boy shrugged. She put her helmet back on and shined the light down the shaft. The darkness went on forever. Anything could be lurking in that blackness. Centipedes and sharp-toothed smiles threatened her imagination, but Sarah concentrated on the doors to the other levels. She thought she could see the last one and started to count the number of doors between here and there. The display in her helmet gave her readouts of how far each door was until she reached the final one. Eighty meters was the readout displayed in her helmet. While most other doors were closed, the last two looked like they had been torn open. Their frames were bent, and the doors hung at odd angles. The little number blinked at Sarah, and she wished it had not. It was going to be a long climb.

3

Sarah turned to the boys and pulled out her sidearm. She

turned it in her hand to hold its grip out toward Morkus. He took it carefully with both hands, fingers cautious to avoid the trigger. The boy acted like it was a coiled snake he was holding. She showed him the safety, the magazine release, and gave him an extra magazine as a precaution. Morkus took it with just as much confusion as he had the gun.

"I can tell your abilities are taking a toll," Sarah said, "if you have to defend yourself, better to use this. Hopefully it doesn't come to that."

Before she could second guess her entire plan, Sarah grabbed her rifle, turned on the magnetism of her boots and gauntlets, and readied herself over the opening. Using her body's momentum, she grabbed onto the lip of the opening and swung herself down and out toward the elevator shaft's wall. She let go and slapped her magnetized limbs against the wall with a silent prayer. She stuck with a loud thud. The sound reverberated all the way down the pit. If anything was down here, she just rang the dinner bell. Gritting her teeth, Sarah tried not to think about it as she started the long descent.

Long moments stretched by with only the thud of the magnets detaching and reattaching to the walls and the sound of her own breath filling her helmet to keep her company. Sarah climbed until she reached the first destroyed set of doors. Lowering herself into the open corridor, she turned off her suit's magnets for the moment. If anything, she could use a chance to catch her breath and let her muscles ease up. What her light revealed was the aftermath of a catastrophic storm of gore and debris. Bodies of mutated creatures littered the area, some of them still alive and twitching. All around grates and vents were open, some with bodies still hanging halfway out.

Sarah raised her rifle and debated on whether or not she should stay or continue on her way down the shaft. She only had one floor left to reach the generators. Someone groaned from under a pile of corpses. Shining her light on the source, a man's upper half was poking out from under the desecrated body of a spider creature. His hand was reaching toward Sarah, but he winced once the light shone upon him. His balding head and pale skin were smeared with crimson. Sarah noted a missing finger on his out-stretched hand. His clothing was different than the others she'd encountered. They were finer, made of silk.

"Help us," he groaned, "please."

Keeping her rifle ready and pointed forward, Sarah made her way over to him. Once again thanking her helmet for blocking out the smell, she kneeled next to the man to get a better view. His lower half was still buried beneath other corpses, but his upper body appeared to be unharmed with the exception of the missing finger. The bodies on top of him and around looked as though they had trampled each other in a mad dash to get to the vents. There was only one way to get him out, and she'd have to set aside her rifle to do it. Another groan from the man solidified her decision.

Setting her weapon to one side, Sarah began to drag bodies off the pile one-by-one. The man groaned more as the bodies shifted. If he wasn't quiet, they'd risk gaining unwanted attention if anything alive was left lurking in the dark. She tried to speed up the process to compensate. She grabbed one of the mutated spider creatures by the dark leg stalks protruding from its back and began to pull it to one side. It sprang to life, twisting in her hands, and its human arms and legs wrapped around her body to lock her in place. The tips of the spider legs stabbed and lashed at her armor trying to find a week point to pierce. Sarah tumbled to the ground in a poor attempt to break free of its grip. With arms pinned to her side, Sarah rolled but the maneuver helped little. The creature clung tight and opened a fang filled maw that split its head from ear to ear. The jaws slammed shut around her helmet. Her head-lamp illuminated the inside of its mouth with its bloated tongue flailing across her visor.

Sarah managed to lurch to her knees. All she could see was the inside of the monster's mouth, but she had a general sense of where the wall was. The glass of her visor began to crack; the digital display flickered and died. Panic set in. One of the claws found the soft mesh between the joints of her suit and searing pain lanced through her leg. Launching herself to her feet, hands still pinned to her side, Sarah sprinted toward the wall. She slammed into it with a sickening crunch of creature's cracking bones. It wouldn't let go. Pulling her head back, she smashed against the wall again and again until she felt the creature's skull begin to give. Its teeth snapped and her visor became a thick smear of red, but a final headbutt broke the vice. Limbs loosened and the creature slid down to plop on the floor.

Sarah stepped away from the wall on shaking legs. Shooting pain through the back of her knee caused her to nearly fall a second time, but she managed to keep her balance. She ripped her helmet off and instant regret assaulted her senses in the form of a putrid stench. Rotten meat and festering bile clung to the air thick enough to taste. It was too much too quick. Sarah gagged out of reflex and had to fight to keep her stomach from heaving. Without her helmet the world was thrown into darkness and all that was left was the smell. She could hear something dragging itself across the floor.

There had to be another light. She patted the pouches lining her suit's belt and felt around the plates of armor for something she might have missed. The sounds of dragging grew closer, and Sarah tried to back away. The wall behind held her in place. She dropped to one knee; the pain now too great to stand on both feet. She couldn't be certain in the dark, but she had a strong feeling she had an open wound bleeding freely down the back of her leg. Sarah grabbed the only weapon she had left, the dagger that had almost killed Kyllen, and prepared herself for whatever came for her in the dark.

4

Snickering and child's laughter danced in the blackness like a ghostly tune. They carried a secret with them only Sarah knew. The song promised death. Hers, of course, but the death of others as well. Always the death was her doing, and the laughter grew joyous at the realization. Sondra's toothy smile loomed above an apparition of her childhood self. Despite the dark they glowed as if the blackness belonged to them and them alone. Sondra's centipede body coiled around the child's body, both of them laughing as its legs cut deep into young Sarah's skin.

A light cut through the darkness evaporating the visions and the dread. Sarah flinched as it shone across her face and into her eyes. The voice of an old man rasped and the light shook with faint tremors.

"You aren't one of them," the man said. It wasn't a question. "You saved me, and for that I'm grateful, but I need to know who you are why you're here."

Sarah held up a hand to try and shield her eyes from the harsh beam. Through it she could see the faint outlines of her rifle and the hunched over man who carried it. Rather than answer, she loosened her grip on the dagger and took the opportunity to check her leg. Sure enough, the mesh was ripped open at the back of the knee and an angry wound bled through. She wasn't sure how deep it was, but it felt bad, really bad.

"Answer me," the old man said, and he shook the gun at her.

"Sarah," she said, "and I came here looking for someone."

"To free them?" The old man asked.

"Yeah," Sarah said, "to free them."

"Only a few of us left," he said, "but maybe if you survive that wound you can find a way to get us out of here."

Sarah nodded at him, and put the dagger away. Dizziness was starting to creep its way into her head. She fumbled about her pouches for a med kit. Her suit only came with a couple, so as she ripped the package open and spread the salve across the open wound, she hoped this would be the only time she'd need it. The second one was larger and intended for more serious wounds such as loss of limb. A gut feeling told her that despite her hopes, she was going to need it before the day was out. The pain killers in the salve worked immediately and the blood began to congeal even as she fastened the bandage patch over it. Yasmin would scream at her haphazard work, but it would have to do. By the time she got out of this mess she was going to be nothing more than a bundle of scars and pent-up trauma. Steadying herself, Sarah pushed off one knee to stand. She had to favor the left leg, but she could stand.

"You said there were others," she said, "take me to them."

"There were," the man said, "might be dead now. Been a

bit since I got trapped under those bodies. I can take you to where I last met them at least."

Keeping the rifle, he started down the hallway at a pace far too slow given their current circumstances. Sarah followed him until they reached an open door. Pointing the light, the man revealed a room filled with cages. Many were ripped open with nothing but blood left behind to indicate they had been occupied. One, however, was crowded with a group of people all huddled together in the dark. Sarah noticed him immediately.

"Hector!" She cried. She couldn't stop herself from calling out, and flinched at the volume of her own voice. Hopefully there were no mutants around to hear. She snatched the rifle from the old man's grasp before he could react and bolted over to the cage.

Her brother was surrounded by four others, two of them burly looking Groal with dark hair, an older man with gray hair and white stubble, and lastly a young woman with blonde hair streaked black by dye. Grime covered each of them from head to toe, and Sarah could smell they hadn't been bathed since their arrival. All of them looked at Sarah with wide and confused eyes. Hector's expression cut worse than her wound. He searched her face for some sort of recognition but came up short.

"It's me," Sarah said, "it's your sister."

"Sarah?" Hector's eyes lit up, and the grin Sarah remembered spread across his lips.

"What's important," the old man said from behind her, "is that she's here to get us out. I hope you brought a team with you."

"What about my boy?" One of the Groal asked. He was the larger of the two with a beard large enough to swallow his face. "Did you rescue my boy?"

"We found a group of kids on the surface," Sarah said, "but the only Groal I noticed was a little girl who was... less than welcoming."

His expression sank and the other Groal started to console him. She looked around at the others. Their confused looks were being replaced by hopeful ones. Her heart sank for the big man. Toby hadn't been with the others up top, so perhaps that meant others had run off on their own as well. She could save these people. She knew she could. Sarah had to for her sake as much as any. Too many died because of her already.

"I'll find him," she said, "I have to get the power going first, but once I do, I'll make sure your kid makes it to the surface."

Determination solidified in the Groal's features, and he glared at her before nodding. The Groal next to him cracked his knuckles, and even Hector appeared to have a new found resolve.

"How can we help?" The Groal asked.

5

Sarah found herself climbing down the elevator shaft once more. She wished she could have left the Golden Boy with the survivors, with her brother, but she knew that choice would be a grave mistake. She was going to need every weapon she could find moving forward if she wanted to survive this horror house and bring everyone out of here with her. They had settled with hiding everyone in the same cage with a pair of swords they had salvaged off some dead Dwemyri. They would have taken the armor too, but the Dwemyri body structure made it impossible for the armaments to fit. Once she got the elevator back into operation, Sarah could get everyone back to the surface then continue her search. Hopefully Yasmin would be on her way back to fly another group of survivors back to the Villimath. First, the power.

Sarah's boots clanked against metal grating after she dropped herself onto the next floor. The magnets powered down, and she found herself standing on a suspended catwalk rather than a solid floor. All around her was a vast chamber of open air. Small motes of fuzz floated throughout and glowed a faint teal. It was enough light to see by, but only just. Knifing upward from the dark were massive cylinders. Those had to be the generators. All were dark and noiseless. Sarah hoped one would be enough to get things moving again. Any more, and she risked losing time she didn't have. At least, for the moment, it appeared she was the only one down here.

Risking a glance over the railing, the depths of the chamber went on forever. Not even the motes of glowing dust traveled down that far. They floated above the walkways and congregated near the generators. Sarah felt a tickle as one landed on the top of her scalp. She brushed it off gently and made her way toward the closest generator. A small ladder ran up the side which indicated to Sarah that whatever access panels existed resided on the top. There were no guardrails on the ladder. If she slipped and missed the catwalk, she'd plunge who knew how far into the darkness below. She tried not to think about that as she climbed. Cresting the top, Sarah pulled herself over the small lip of the edge. The top of the massive cylinder was indented in a series of steps until it reached the center.

Sarah let out a sigh of relief upon seeing what waited at the bottom of the inset. A node of protruding machine work stood behind a glass case. It was not dissimilar to what she had dealt with on Carlisle Station if not a bit outdated. Descending into the bottom, she propped her rifle up so as to point the light where she needed. The dim glow wasn't nearly enough to work by. Sarah pulled open the case and began to examine what she was dealing with. It was another stroke of luck with a simple solution staring her in the face. All of the generators were interlinked and one of them had been damaged badly enough to cause a surge. The others shut down to prevent catastrophic failure, and simply needed to be reset. First, she'd need to identify which one was causing the issues and prevent it from resetting.

Sarah retrieved her rifle and climbed back up to the edge of the generator. Panning her light over the other cylinders made it clear which one was the trouble maker. At the far side of the chamber, the top half of the generator looked mangled and warped. It almost looked as though something had tried to chew on it. The sudden feeling of being watched wrapped around Sarah like a wet blanket. She shivered, but turned herself back to her work. Whatever had done it wasn't here. Heading back toward the center, she set to work disengaging the generator's network and running it through a reset cycle. In a matter of moments, the generator was humming and teal light glowed from a ring around its edge. Sarah let out a satisfied sigh and closed up the glass case. A noise shuffled behind her.

"We liked the dark." The voice was the whisper of a hundred people speaking in unison. The breath carried a cadaverous stench. Sarah turned to witness a monstrosity beyond the scopes of her imagination. Like a gargantuan spider made of flesh, hundreds of human faces sprouted from a pale pink thorax. Long legs ended in massive human hands and instead of mandibles, the spider had the wide mouth of a human with needle sharp teeth. A bloated abdomen sagged over the side of the generator and inflated and deflated like it were breathing. The soft sounds of sizzling flesh reached her ears, and Sarah noticed the glowing motes burning the monster's flesh where they touched.

"Mother warned us of this one," one of the faces whispered, "we should tell her its down here."

"Mother is preoccupied with the other one," another of the faces said, "I say we eat it. We are *so* starving."

Sarah didn't give it the chance to decide. In one fluid motion, the rifle was to her shoulder and firing round after round into every face she could hit. Countless voices screeched out in a cacophony of agony. It flailed as one of its faces exploded on impact, and a massive leg swung to smash into her side. It sent her sailing across the dark pit to collide with the side of a catwalk. Her stomach caught the edge of the metal grating causing her to nearly fold in two over the walkway. She clutched on, digging her fingers through the holes while her feet dangled over a pit of pitch black. Her rifle was nowhere to be seen.

"Kill it, kill it!" The voices screamed. "Eat her now!"

The spider leapt from the generator to land above her. Its body spanned across several rows of the walkways with its too-human like hands wrapping around the entirety of the metal grates. One of its free hands coiled its long fingers around Sarah's body and ripped her grip free. Sarah tore the dagger free from her hip and stabbed into the hand repeatedly before the hand could bring her to the monster's mouth. Another screech pierced her ears, and the creature let go. Sarah dropped, falling flat on her back against the catwalk. The air was knocked out of her lungs, and she gasped. She rolled to her feet just in time as a giant fist slammed into the walkway in the exact spot she had just been. The catwalk's supports buckled under the force and the section collapsed.

Sarah clung to the grating once more as section of walkway dangled by a single strip of metal railing. Above, the muzzle of her rifle poked over the edge of the still-intact section of walkway. If she could only reach it. Another massive hand reached for her, and Sarah slashed with the dagger. Flesh parted, and the blade sank deep through muscle and bone alike.

The spider fought through the pain, however, and snatched her up with the dagger still embedded deep in one knuckle. While her left hand was pinned to her side in the monster's vice grip, Sarah managed to keep her right arm free. The arm began to lift her up to a widening mouth, but Sarah managed to snag the rifle on the way up. The angle made it difficult, and Sarah was forced to grab it by the barrel. The Golden Boy's size made turning the weapon the right way around difficult with one arm.

"Eat her," one of the faces said. "Chew her bones, swallow her blood."

The mouth grew close. Needled teeth loomed large above and below. Her hand fumbled on the edge of the stock. She almost had the grip. Warm breath and moist spittle greeted her helmetless head with the odor of a fresh sepulcher. Sarah got her hand around the grip, her finger on the trigger, and she switched the rifle to breacher rounds. She held it the best she could with one hand and fired straight into the spider's gaping maw. A wet scream shrieked from the monster's mouth as all five shells were unloaded in rapid succession. All it cost was Sarah's wrist. Vibration and force wracked the narrow joint, but Sarah held tight until the chamber was empty. A horrid whoosh of air blew across her face in response; one last gasp being part of its final death throes.

All went limp. Sarah's only saving grace was the hand that clutched her remained tight around her torso as the arm fell over the side of the walkway. She hung suspended in the air, trapped by the bloodied hand, and the rest of the monster was draped over several walkways like a deflated balloon. In the same regard that she swung from the monster's hand her rifle swung from hers. It dangled over the dark, its weight sending shockwaves of pain through a wrist that felt broken.

      She should just let it go. There was no making it out of this. The painkillers were wearing off, and the wound in her leg bled anew. The iron grip around her chest made it hard to breathe, and each breath only grew more difficult. Sarah had done what she needed to. The boys had the elevator now. They could get her brother out. Who knew, maybe they'd even find that Groal's son. Not her though. She was tired, so very tired. The rifle slid from her grip and fell into the abyss. It was all the permission the universe needed. The monstrous hand loosened, and Sarah began to slide. An inner voice screamed at her to grab on, to cling to life, but she didn't want to. Peace loomed in the dark below, and it called to her. Sarah let herself fall.

CHAPTER 28
- KALLIK -

1

Kallik hoped this would be the last time he ever had to ride in the confining pod that carried him from the alien ship to the hateful labs. He could feel Nathfnitu's impatience more than he could see it, but he'd be lying if he claimed he didn't feel the same. Whatever awaited them at the other end of this tram had no idea what was coming. Kallik hoped Morkus's distraction had worked. He hoped his friends had managed to stay out of the crossfire and stay safe. The Butcher was still out there somewhere. It all came down to this.

"Where will you go?" Kallik asked. It was more to break the awkward silence than it was to satiate his curiosity, but only by a small degree.

She didn't answer. A glare was her only response, and it spoke louder than any words could have. It told him *what a stupid question to ask*. He let it drop. There were other things to worry about even if he didn't want to think about them. What if Vig-amere had won? What if all his friends had been killed in their attempt? Their deaths would be his fault. Afterall, it was *his* plan that brought them to this point.

The tram slowed to a stop and the sound of water being expelled from the gaps met his ears. Kallik took in a sharp breath as the doors opened. Whatever he had been expecting, it wasn't what awaited him. Mutilated corpses littered every surface from the entrance of the tram all the way down the hall toward the play area. Some were orderlies, some Dwemyri, and some were kids he recognized. Many, however, were the horrific creatures Rekkeh had shown him from the labs below.

She had actually done it. Kallik brushed aside the comments she made as simple thoughts, the intrusive kind you often had when daydreaming about your enemies getting what they deserved. He never imagined, even for an instant, that she would follow through on her words. Corpses painted the scene of the error of his ignorance. Even Nathfnitu was caught off guard. Her expression spoke of confusion and shock.

"Are you sure you wouldn't rather come with me?" She asked. "Looks like everyone here is gone."

Kallik shook his head. "I know these people. None of them are my friends. They're still out there somewhere. Same with my dad and cousin. They're still alive. I know they are."

"If you insist," she said, "but my presence doesn't guarantee your safety."

"But it's better than not," Kallik said, "help me find them."

Nathfnitu shrugged but conceded the point. Kallik steeled himself for what was to come. His hopes laughed at him from the darker corners of his mind. They taunted him, told him everyone he knew was dead. Hugging himself, Kallik pushed the thoughts away. They were alive. Together, the pair stepped out of the tram and into the chaos.

2

It was a stillness after a storm. Whatever had happened here was finished. Kallik and Nathfnitu stepped through the carnage and peaked over bodies like carrion birds after a battle. What they looked for, however, was not a meal but faces Kallik would recognize as his friends. Each new corpse that wore a stranger's face added a stoke to the flame of Kallik's hope. They passed through the play area with the same results. He recognized a few of the orderlies, but no one he knew showed up. Maybe all of them had already gotten out. They could be waiting for him on the surface. He'd have to explain to them why Leo wasn't with him. It would hurt, but they'd understand. Everyone knew how Leo was, how brave he could be in the face of such horrors. Kallik needed some of that bravery now.

They were just about to leave the rec area when the lights flickered and died. All was plunged into an impenetrable darkness. Kallik could see nothing, even his own hand in front of his face, but he could still feel Nathfnitu's presence nearby. He tried to head towards her, feeling his way and careful not to trip on a corpse. If anyone could navigate the dark it would be her.

Gunshots rattled in the distance followed by some shouting and more shots. Kallik froze. Since first arriving here he had no recollection of seeing a single firearm. Not even the Dwemyri guards carried projectile weapons. Either the orderlies had a cache of them hidden away, or someone else was down here.

All at once the darkness disappeared and was replaced by a world of grayscale. Every detail of the environment around him was crisp and more focused than he remembered. When he looked at his hand, the background stayed in focus. His peripherals were as clear as what was in front of him. It was almost too much for his mind to process. Blinking did nothing to make the effect go away.

"You're seeing the world that I see," Nathfnitu said. "It may be overwhelming at first, but you'll adjust."

"You can't see colors?"

"Not in the dark."

Another shot rattled his senses. It was louder than before, but everything was. His own breathing sounded like screams compared to his own senses and his father said Groal's were far more acute than a human's. If a human were to endure this, Kallik thought they might explode from overstimulation. Nathfnitu was already heading in the direction of the gunfire, so Kallik tried to shake off the feelings of being overwhelmed and follow. The smells were by far the worst. His nose was already sensitive. Now every smell was strong enough to carry a flavor. Ignoring the twists in his stomach was going to prove difficult.

The noises led them to the kid's living quarters. What they found was the aftermath of another storm. More corpses, more blood, and more silence were all that was left by the time they arrived. Kallik froze over one of the bodies. They stood near Toby's room; the door had been ripped away by force. He couldn't break his eyes away from Master Aillon's pale face. He had been so angry at the man, and now he was gone. Nathfnitu was busy examining a large rifle that had been left behind in Toby's room. She didn't touch it, instead rotating it around in the air to peek at each detail.

"You knew him?" She asked without looking away from the gun. At least with her speaking in his head rather than vocally, her voice wasn't cracking his eardrums like every other sound thus far.

"I did," Kallik said while keeping his own voice to a whisper. "He kept a lot of us out of trouble. Tried to, at least."

"We should keep moving," she said, "whatever did this may come back for seconds."

"Couldn't you deal with them?"

"I could," she said, "but being awake after such a long slumber is making me tired. Mistakes happen. You could still die."

"Alright, you've made your point," Kallik said, "let's head to the surface. Maybe the others already made it out."

3

Kallik hadn't considered the elevator being out of commission. With the power out, the elevator was a lifeless set of doors blocking his way to freedom. If he knew his way around the vents, he could take that path to find his family. Getting back out was a different story. Kallik was already almost too large to get through. His father would never make it. Not with those things crawling around in them. How they contorted their bodies to squeeze through the narrow shafts was beyond him. His joints hurt just thinking about it.

Nathfnitu approached the doors and tapped on them with a long fingernail. She had a strange look on her face like she was considering what to do with an uninvited guest. She tapped her chin with another hand, two more resting on her hips.

"Last chance to change your mind," she said, "I could always drop you off somewhere along the way."

"Open it," Kallik said.

She shrugged and at the same time the door screeched open. Morkus and Toby were huddled in the back corner, the larger boy with something in his hands pointed toward the door. The sound of a gun cracked. Morkus and Toby were thrown against the back wall by an invisible force, and Kallik blinked. Hovering several centimeters away from his nose was the bullet Morkus had fired. It vibrated as if it still wanted to rush forward. The vibrations stopped, and the bullet dropped to the floor. Kallik glanced from the bullet back to Morkus.

"You just tried to shoot me," he said.

"Kal?" Toby asked. "Is that you?"

Oh. Kallik realized the two were blind and scared. He could smell the sweat of their fear. He glanced at Nathfnitu who had a dark streak of blood running from a nostril. She had known what was about to happen. She dropped the two boys to their feet, and they tested the floor with caution. Morkus tried to peer into the dark and see who had opened the door while Toby tried to shrink further into the corner.

"Projectiles that fast are still a challenge," she said in his head and wiped away the blood.

"It's me," Kallik said, "I'm glad you two are still alive."

A hundred words started pouring from Toby's mouth in an instant, none of them Kallik could understand. Morkus interrupted and started to speak more tangibly. He spoke of everything that had happened since Kallik's departure. The monsters, Aillon, and the newcomers were all covered. Two strangers had come to rescue them, now only one remained and Rekkeh was the one to blame for all of it. Only a few of them were left alive. The other woman who had come to save them had climbed below to get the power back up so they could all get out. Kallik recounted his part, and told them about Leo. Neither of them took the news well, but Toby in particular deflated.

"How are you able to navigate in this dark?" Morkus said. "I'm afraid to so much as move in here. There's a hole in the floor that woman opened, so be careful if you step in."

"Oh, right," Kallik said. "Nath, can you do for them what you did for me?"

The two boy's gasps were answer enough. Morkus and Toby stared at each other in awe then at the alien. Toby was busy gaping when Morkus turned to Kallik.

"What about the Butcher?" He asked. "Any news on him? He spoke over the speakers, but has been absent since all of this started."

"I'm right here," a voice said, and blade erupted from Nathfnitu's stomach.

4

They never heard him coming. The man was a ghost when he wanted to be. Wide eyed and panicked, Nathfnitu clutched at the sword sticking out of her belly. A white mask marred by a black scar appeared over her shoulder. Kallik could almost feel the smile lurking behind the it.

"No one wants to listen to my instructions," Vigamere said. "Fine then, I'll just burn this whole place to the ground and start over."

The boys were too stunned to move. The Butcher ripped the blade free of Nathfnitu's abdomen and pushed her forward. She stumbled and slipped, just as startled as Kallik, and fell feet first through the hole in the elevator floor. Toby stumbled forward and stuck his head through the hole after her. His face looked strained, and Kallik noticed he could still see in the dark despite Nathfnitu's absence.

Morkus roared a deep bellied scream that rocked Kallik to the core. He flung Vigamere down the hall but not before the man managed to throw his sword. It spun toward Morkus as the Butcher was thrown back. Luckily it sank into the metal wall behind Morkus rather than the boy's head. Vigamere rolled to his feet and darted forward in the blink of an eye. That was how they did it, Kallik realized. *Speed*. Kallik tried to throw him back, but the man was too quick to imagine him in one spot. Morkus realized it too, and raised the gun. Too late. Vigamere got to Kallik first. He slammed a fist into Kallik's side, doubling him over, and used him as shield to prevent Morkus from shooting.

The Butcher thrust Kallik forward and ran the two of them all the way into the elevator to collide with Morkus. The two boys crumpled together, and Vigamere used the opportunity to pull the blade free of the wall. Toby was still concentrating on the hole as Vigamere drove the blade down toward the back of the red-haired boy's head. It stopped a centimeter short of his neck. Vigamere's heavy breathing intensified as he pressed harder, but to no avail. Nathfnitu's hand reached up from the hole and grabbed the edge of the floor. Vigamere was thrown upward to slam into the ceiling. The sword went tumbling away, and Kallik used the chance to throw the man back into the hallway.

Morkus pushed Kallik off of him and ran out into the hallway after Vigamere. Kallik followed suit leaving Toby and Nathfnitu to take care of themselves. The Butcher was already on his feet and reaching for his sword. It was only a couple paces away. If he wanted it so bad, he could have it. Vigamere was stumbling on a broken leg and Kallik imagined the blade flying point first into his chest. He concentrated on the sword, his scalp growing hot and prickly. It rattled on the floor then flew. Despite the broken leg, Vigamere moved with impossible speed. He twisted to the side with snake-like reflexes and let the sword fly past him. He snatched it out of the air with a deft hand, but what he wasn't ready for was the charging Morkus.

The larger boy slammed into Vigamere at full speed and the two fell in a heap. The Butcher brought his blade to bear, but Morkus still held the gun. In one fell swoop, Morkus pushed the muzzle to Vigamere's masked face and pulled the trigger. The white mask exploded with a loud bang and a spray of red. Morkus wasn't finished, however, and he pulled the trigger again and again until the gun was empty. Kallik could hear the faint clicks as Morkus continued to pull the trigger after the magazine was spent.

Behind them, Nathfnitu had pulled herself back up into the elevator and was seated against the back wall. Toby looked at a loss for what to do. Dark blood pooled around her too fast to be stopped. Toby's wide eyes considered Kallik, pleading for some sort of help. Kallik didn't know how to treat wounds, especially one that bad.

"She might know what to do," Toby said and nodded at the hole in the elevator floor. "If we could get to her. Maybe I can float you down?"

It was worth a shot. None of them knew what they were doing, and the only person that seemed to was on the bottom floor. As if summoned, the lights flickered back to life and the elevator chimed with a soft ding. Toby's face lit up with newfound hope.

"Morkus," Kallik called back. The boy still straddled Vigamere's corpse with the pistol pressed against the man's mess of a face. "We're going."

CHAPTER 29
- SARAH -

1

Where Sarah expected to feel the rush of air followed by the inevitable sudden stop that would usher her soul into whatever afterlife awaited, or lack thereof, she was instead suspended in a frozen state. The massive hand around her still fell telling her that she wasn't imagining things. Heart beats pounded in her ears telling her she wasn't already dead and was in the process of feeling her soul leave her body. No, something else was at play here. That something else became apparent when she started rising into the air. The dark abyss calling out her promised peace shrank from Sarah's grasp as she was lifted to the safety of the walkway. She was dropped unceremoniously to the metal grating on her knees. Three boys with success plastered across their faces looked down at her. She recognized the two. The dark-haired Morkus looked proud, the red-headed Toby wore a shit-eating grin, but the third boy was a stranger to her. He had one horn protruding from the side of his forehead and the broken stub of another on the other side. Sarah nodded to the largest of the three of them.

"Thanks, Morkus," she said. She bit back the anger she felt at being saved. Peace would have to come later, it would seem.

"It wasn't me," Morkus said. The pride in his eyes grew, and he shoved a finger into Toby's side. "It was this one."

Sarah was beginning to understand the expressions now. Toby had just done something they all thought him incapable of. She gave the boy a pat on the shoulder as she got to her feet. Pain burned on the back of her knee, and the wrist *had* to be broken. Most of the patch held, but blood did leak around the edges. At least she wasn't about to pass out from blood loss. She had to lean on a rail to keep herself steady, however.

"That was amazing!" Toby said. "The way you handled that thing was insane. You missed your chance though."

"Did I now?" Sarah asked, a brow creeping further up her forehead.

"Sure did," Toby said, "you should have dropped a spicy one-liner when you had the chance. You should have said something like *chew on these*, oh, or like *swallow this*."

"I'll remember that for next time," she said.

The new boy nudged Toby to get him to be quiet. A spark of recognition bloomed. Something about the kid's facial features reminded her of the Groal above. Sarah only smiled and gave Toby another pat on the shoulder. With their insistence that she keep on living, there was more she had to do to get them all out of here. She gave the blackness below a final glance.

"We need you to help someone," Toby said, "she's in the elevator."

Sarah held back a groan. She had barely gotten out of the last situation. What was waiting for her in the elevator? Keeping her dismay to herself, Sarah nodded and limped toward the open doors. Nothing could have prepared her for a four-armed woman bleeding through an open hole in her stomach. Yasmin might have known what to do, but not Sarah. She barely knew human physiology let alone that of an alien species she'd never encountered before. What even was this woman? The boys were all looking at her with hopeful expressions. Right, she was the adult here and was expected to be in control of the situation like only adults could be.

She took a deep breath and pulled out her last med kit. This one was made for severed limbs not open holes, but maybe it would do the trick until they found a better solution. Sarah kneeled over her with the kit and the alien glared at her with apprehension through eyes squinted by pain. Tearing open the pack, Sarah spread the salve over the open wound. She forced the alien to lean forward to apply more to her back. There was no telling if the chemical composition would even work with her blood, but this was the only option they had. The blood sizzled as the wound was chemically cauterized, and the alien hissed with pain.

One of the boys muttered something about their sight fading, and Sarah looked back at them. Toby was holding a hand out in front of his face and waving it back and forth. The Groal boy looked worried.

"Ship," the alien hissed through gritted teeth. "Get me... to ship..."

She struggled with the words as though she were sounding them out for the first time. Sarah had no idea what she was talking about. There weren't any other ships she could have used to get here.

"I can show you the way," Kallik said. "It's on the other side of the labs above."

Sarah chewed her bottom lip. They were this close to getting out. The alien's breaths were turning ragged. She didn't have much time left regardless of what they did, and her brother was on the floor just above them waiting for Sarah's return.

"If I do this," Sarah said, "then there is something you've got to do for me. Besides, I have a feeling there is someone you're going to want to meet."

2

Sarah was right. Tears streamed down the big man's cheeks, and Kallik – the name the boy had given her on the way up – echoed his father's sobs. The other Groal rested a hand on each of their shoulders as they all embraced. The elevator was cramped with all of them packed in. At least she had closed the hole in the floor. Her brother watched her with silent disbelief while she did everything she could to keep the alien stable. The elevator hummed as it rose, and Sarah cursed it for not moving fast enough. The external bleeding had stopped, but Sarah knew little about the kind of damage that had occurred internally.

The elevator slowed to a stop and the doors opened to a corridor that had grown all too familiar. At least the lights were back on. Sarah hoisted the alien, or Nath as the boys called her, to her feet the best she could, given Sarah's own leg was injured. Kallik broke away from his family to stand by her side. His father dabbed away tears and adorned a look of stoicism. Hector just looked confused. She'd travelled all the way across the galaxy and the asshole hadn't even thanked her yet. In fact, he hadn't spoken more than two words since she'd gotten here.

Morkus stepped between her and her brother to hold something out. It was the pistol, she realized, though it was covered in a significant amount of blood. Sarah looked from it to him with a questioning look.

"Sorry," he said with a shrug, "tried to wipe it off, but my shirt didn't quite do the trick. Also, it's empty. Sorry again."

His shirt was bloodier than the gun. All of them were. Instead of taking it, Sarah pulled a pair of fresh magazines from her belt. She gestured for him to take it, so he did. Toby might have unlocked some sort of latent abilities, but Morkus still seemed on the edge of passing out. They weren't out of the woods yet, and Sarah wanted Hector safe regardless of how thankless he was.

With a bit of help from Kallik, Sarah ended up crouching down to carry Nath piggyback. The woman was still conscious but unable to walk by herself. Luckily, the small, motorized joints in Sarah's armor helped with the added weight. The three of them got out of the elevator. An awkward silence clung between the two groups, but Morkus put an end to it by pushing the elevator button. The door slid closed, and that was that. Only one way remained open. Sarah just hoped this Rekkeh kid didn't show back up to resume her little house of horrors.

3

Sarah stooped down to examine the man's corpse. A pity she hadn't been the one to make it, but the man was dead, and that's what mattered most. There was nothing left of his ruined head. Morkus had fired every shot he had into his skull at point blank. Another pity. She would have liked to see his face. This was no time to linger on such thoughts. She picked up his sword –

lighter than she anticipated – and shoved it through a loop on her belt before she continued down the corridor to follow Kallik.

The world was unnervingly quiet. It felt as though even the walls, blood soaked as they were, held their breath as they passed. Sarah kept looking for the little girl, but there was no sign of her. Only corpses and ghosts remained down here. And Breckett. Poor soul. Someone else was going to have to take care of his plants, though his body was nowhere to be found.

They passed through an area that looked like a kids' play place. Jungle gyms and bookshelves held a different feeling to them when they were soaked in blood. Sarah tried not to look at it as they walked by. The bodies littering every meter did little to help. They stopped before a set of open doors – a tram, Sarah realized – and Kallik was hesitant to step in. The windows of the small pod were open to reveal a view of the deep ocean.

"I think I've grown to hate these things," Sarah said.

Kallik snorted a short laugh and said, "me too."

They stepped in together and Sarah took a moment to set Nath down while Kallik got the tram moving. She was still breathing. That was a good sign. Her eyes were open and watching Sarah's every move. One thing for certain was this alien was tough. Any human would have been dead by now, med kit or no. They made the rest of the trip in silence. The only sound was the water outside the pod.

They reached the ship and Sarah found herself too tired to be awestruck. As much as a cycle ago, Sarah would have been shaken by the strange architecture and alien design. Now, she strolled through the wide corridors with their ribbed ceilings and an alien clinging to her back like it were any other day. Even the bloodbath on the bridge did little to shift her mood.

Nath pointed over Sarah's shoulder toward an inset in the middle of the room. Kallik helped get her down and the pair of them set her down in one of the seats. The alien's nail struck a small groove in the seat next to her and a series of strange instruments sprouted from the floor in the form of thin skeletal arms.

"Leave," she hissed. Kallik started to protest, but she repeated the word. A deep rumbling sent a tremor through the ship and the unmistakable sound of engines fired up.

"Agreed," Sarah said, and grabbed Kallik by the wrist with her good hand. "It's time we made our own exit."

They were barely out of the inset before the floor and seats began to sink into a dark hole. Kallik's eyes regarded the sight with a haunted, solemn expression. He knew what was down there. Sarah could ask him about it later. Something told her this Nath wasn't going to wait for them to get off the ship before she initiated her launch sequences.

They were back in the pod in short order with the sound of the engines boiling the water around the ship. Even though it was insulated, this thing couldn't move fast enough. The lab itself might be in jeopardy if Nath put enough boost into those thrusters. The size of that ship was cruiser class, even larger than the Villimath.

They docked at the labs, and Sarah's fears were confirmed. The floor beneath them started to rumble and creaking metal echoed somewhere in the distance. She grabbed Kallik by the wrist and limped as fast as she could through the corridors. Bestial howls bellowed from the air vents. The creatures knew they were in danger as well. All the more reason to pick up the pace. Sarah loped to a sprint regardless of the wound that started to reopen. To her relief, Kallik was able to keep pace without being dragged along.

They reached the elevator and were greeted by another tremor. This one almost shook them off their feet. Sarah pushed the button over and over again until the doors finally slid open. She all but shoved Kallik through before pushing the button for the garden floor.

"What about Rekkeh?" Kallik asked. "Part of me still wants to believe she could be brought back."

"Fuck her," Sarah said. It slipped out as she jammed her thumb into the garden button one more time. She knew it was immature, and she knew the kid deserved a better answer. For the moment, however, Sarah didn't care. Kallik went silent and instead of apologizing, Sarah checked her wound. It bled freely and the throbbing in her wrist was only growing worse. She could hear it crack and snag as she rotated it around.

The elevator shook but continued its ascent. She would have rather died at the hands of that monster than get stuck in an elevator while the facility crumbled down around her. It never came to that. The elevator dinged, and the doors opened to lush greenery. She didn't waste a second. Sarah shoved Kallik out the door and the boy took off at a sprint. She took off after him, ignoring the pain of her knee.

The ground shook, and the sound of tearing metal resounded from somewhere deep within the facility. If this next elevator was even a second too slow, both of them would be dead. Kallik had the doors open and was inside the next elevator before Sarah caught up. She leapt inside and slammed her hand against the button for the landing pad. The doors slid closed, and their small coffin rumbled into motion.

"I think I hate elevators as much as I hate trams," Sarah said. It was more to break up the tension than anything else. Another tremor rocked the facility and Sarah had to lean against the wall to keep from falling over.

"It's the waiting," Kallik said. "There's nothing you can do but sit and wait for the horribleness of outside to find its way in."

"It is, isn't it," Sarah said, "and once it's in, you're trapped with it."

Kallik wiped his eyes, and Sarah realized the boy was crying. That was probably her fault too. She needed to be composed, controlled, and exerting a sense of security. Not throwing this boy through a sense of unadulterated panic. He'd been through more than she could imagine down in that facility, and now he worried he'd never see the sunlight again. Sarah stepped closer to him and rested a hand on his shoulder.

"If I know anything," she said, "is for some reason this universe wants me alive. As long as you stick close, we'll make it out."

Sarah tried not to think about the times that made the comment a lie, and she put on a brave face. *She* had lived, yes, but the only other person to get out of a situation like this with her was Jax. At least Jax got to leave on her own terms. Her words appeared to help a small degree, however, and that's what mattered. She tightened her grip on him as the elevator shook again. They both let out an audible sigh of relief when it slowed to a stop and the doors opened to reveal the surface of the icy planet.

Kallik's family was waiting just outside the elevator, huddled together to combat the cold winds. To her relief, the others had already gotten one of the other ships up and running. That still left a looming question. What had happened to Yasmin? She was supposed to come back after dropping off the first round of kids. Sarah never heard back from the Villimath either. The sound of cracking ice told her there was time to worry about those questions once they were airborne.

The four of them rushed over to the ship's open bay door and slammed it shut behind them. A quick glance at the cockpit confirmed Sarah's sneaking suspicion. Her brother sat in the pilot's seat with hands already on the controls. They were in the air before the door was sealed.

4

Morkus helped Sarah climb to her feet. Toby and the other survivors were already strapped into their seats and Kallik's family was in the process of doing the same. The larger boy tried to usher Sarah into her own, but she paused to look out the window. Below, all around the landing pad sheets of ice cracked and burst open. Visible parts of the facility swayed and began to crumble apart as a monolithic ship began to break through the surface. It looked like the spine of some sort of titan bursting from the ice. As it emerged, the full scale of its black hull became visible. Its entire mass resembled a skeletal sea creature from the depths of the hells themselves. Long fins of pale sinew jutted from the ship's bottom supported by long fingers of black bone.

A shockwave burst from the ship's rear thrusters and Sarah could see the force ripple through the air toward their small transport. That was all the motivation she needed. Sarah threw herself into her seat and strapped herself in as fast as she could. Morkus followed suit, and none too soon. The shockwave washed over their ship and sent it careening on its side. Hector fought the controls to pull the ship back into a balanced flight. His face scrunched and he gritted his teeth, and for a moment Sarah thought they were goners. The ship pitched left and dropped a dozen meters or more, but Hector brought it back. Metal wings groaned under the pressure, but they remained in one piece as her brother sent them soaring upward into orbit. He turned back to everyone strapped into their seats.

"Hold tight!" He yelled over the roar of the engines and the ear-bursting blasts coming from the other ship's thrusters. "That ship is starting its jump sequence!"

"This close to the planet?" Sarah called back. A grin spread across her brother's face. It was the exact smile she remembered from her childhood, the one he always used right before they were about to do something incredibly stupid.

"Don't worry little sis," he yelled, "I'll get us out of this."

He turned back to face forward in his seat and pushed the little transport's engines to their limits. Sarah glanced out the window and saw another shockwave jetting out as the alien vessel pivoted to face orbit. She couldn't believe it. Nath was about to use a jump drive not only within the planet's gravity, but within its very atmosphere. She should have let the alien die.

Hector altered their trajectory to match the direction of the shockwave, putting the stern to face the other ship. He was going to use its force to propel them into orbit. Clever if it didn't get them killed. Sarah held her breath as the shockwave hit. The little ship rattled and rumbled as it was forced into speeds faster than it was built for. The g-force being applied to the cabin was more than the ship's dampening tech could mitigate causing immense pressure to force her into her seat and the edges of her peripheral vision to shrink. Sarah squeezed the muscles in her lower body to keep the blood circulating upward. In mere moments they were launched through the outer atmosphere and into open space. The pressure subsided and Hector slowed the ship to a more manageable speed.

"That your ship heralding us?" Hector asked.

"The Villimath?"

"The very one."

"It is," Sarah said. She let out a long sigh of relief upon knowing it was still up here. Why, then, hadn't they responded to her, and why hadn't Yasmin returned? At least now she was sure to get answers. She relaxed in her seat as Hector brought them in and was surprised to find herself having to fight off sleep.

5

Sarah's answers came as soon as they entered the hangar. They no sooner landed and got the hangar bay doors closed than a group of strangers in dark uniforms surrounded their ship. Hector showed her the camera feed of the group that waited just outside the ship's door, and her stomach dropped. A tall man with gray hair pulled into a topknot stood before a group of individuals Sarah wished to never encounter for the rest of her miserable life. Next to him, clad in violet robes and dangling gold jewelry, was a tall creature that looked humanoid save for its feline head. Sarah knew it to be a Suttack, though she'd never seen a live one before. Behind those two were what really stressed her out. Identical twins with crimson hair shaved on one side stood behind the man in the dark uniform. The unmistakable black cloaks with billowing black feathers around the collar made the pair stand out from anyone else in the room. Behind them a pair of individuals in dark robes that stopped at the ankle waited like deadly shadows. Perfect white masks adorned their faces and stared straight ahead.

They had the kids behind them, Sarah noticed. They were still in their soiled white outfits, and each of them looked worried. Sarah glanced back at the boys still seated in the cabin. Did they know something about this? If it weren't for the kids standing there, she'd have Hector open the bay doors and space the whole lot of them.

"I'll talk to them," Sarah said, "if anything happens, I want you to get as many of the kids as you can and run. Take them across the galaxy if you have to."

Hector looked dumbfounded, but he nodded. She hadn't noticed them sneak up, exhaustion worked its way into every part of her body, but the three boys were standing in the doorway between the cockpit and the cabin. All three glared at the camera feed with grim expressions.

"We're with you," Kallik said. "Whatever happens, we won't let another experiment like below take place."

"I'm not going back," Morkus said, "I'll die first."

"None of you are going back," Sarah said. "Let me take care of this."

Sarah pushed past the three boys and made her way to the door. She lowered the exit ramp to the waiting crowd and paused. The older man with the graying topknot straightened his posture and folded his hands before him. Everyone around him tensed. The children behind the group glanced from the man back to Sarah. She took in a deep breath and limped down the ramp toward her fate.

CHAPTER 30
- KALLIK -

1

Kallik watched as Sarah descended the ramp. Morkus stood on one side of him, Toby the other, and the three of them stared at her back as she limped toward the crowd. A hand grabbed his wrist and Kallik turned to find his father standing behind him. His large form towered over Kallik, and a wave of comfort washed over him knowing his father was safe. Him and Amic and even old Harold had made it through. Kallik did not want to think about all the others that hadn't. His father stooped over to whisper in Kallik's ear.

"That woman saved us," he said. "She strode through the fire and dragged us out by the antlers. To let her stand alone in this would be an insult to our family name. Come, boy, let us show her what our gratitude can mean."

Amic was standing close by, and he grinned at Kallik with a wink. He tapped is good antler and Kallik realized they now shared something in common. Kallik now only bore a single antler and it grew on the same side as his cousin's. He felt the antler with his thumb and it dawned on him what his cousin was hinting at. It had grown longer since that fateful day, and the beginnings of his first tine were sprouting. It was little more than a nub on the side of the main beam, but it was something. His father was smiling now too.

Kallik looked back toward the open door. Sarah had reached the end of the ramp and stopped before the man with the topknot. Everything around them fell silent, not even the air daring to move. Kallik would dare, and so would his father and Amic. They'd face the storm for the woman who'd brought them back together. The three of them started down the ramp together, and Kallik noted Morkus and Toby followed.

Sarah glanced back at them, a brief look of surprise flashing across her face, but she said nothing. Her eyes locked onto someone else Kallik hadn't noticed. The tall man with the long hair and too-large coat had joined them as well. Hector, if Kallik remembered his name, and the two were siblings? He couldn't remember. He knew the man had been part of his dad's crew before all of this. So many things had happened in such a short span, the details were swirling out of control in Kallik's head.

Sarah wiped her nose with a bloodied gauntlet before turning back to the crowd. It was a subconscious gesture, one that Kallik guessed she didn't realize only added to the filth already encrusted on her smooth features. It just now occurred to him how pretty the woman was, grime and all.

"Sarah Vermillion," the man with the topknot said. His voice was loud and carried throughout the hangar. "Or should I be calling you Sarah Renza? Regardless, all of this must be a shock to you, but you may rest easy now."

He paused for a moment as the Suttack by his side glanced at a data-slate and whispered something in the man's ear. The Suttack was too close in appearance to Karaska for Kallik's comfort. He glared at that one with the fiercest look he could muster. Kallik's abilities were at the edge of his fingertips just asking to be grabbed, to be used, to be thrown at this creature with all of his might. The man nodded with a satisfied smirk. It was then Kallik notice Xoriah standing in the crowd at the front of the other kids. Their eyes met, and she smiled at him. She appeared to be nervous, but not afraid. In fact, all of the other kids looked ready to face whatever came. The newcomers in this hangar had no idea the danger they had just put themselves between. Kallik smiled back for more reasons than one.

"I think I'm ready for some answers," Sarah said, "and I think you best give those answers and be on your way. I'm not exactly known as a safe haven for your kind."

"Quite the contrary," the man said, "Xaranor lauds your achievements. Perhaps I may introduce myself. My name is Commander Orian Malkus of the Cloudburst. The people and things you've dealt with down there and on Carlisle Station were not but separatists who wanted little more than the death of our organization."

"More of the same," Sarah said. Her hand hovered near her hip. Kallik knew a dagger was stowed away in a sheath unseen from the front. There was also the matter of the sword she had tucked in her belt. Kallik readied his thoughts to strike. He'd start with the Suttack. "I won't let these kids go back to being experiments. I won't let anyone else be hurt."

"Then we're in agreement," Orian said. "Perhaps you should hear me out before jumping to rash conclusions. The practices of these separatists sicken Xaranor to its core. Conduits are a delicate matter, a secretive one. It's not one made for children."

A skeletal man, one more skin and bone than flesh, jotted notes at a frantic pace in a massive ledger. He glanced from person to person, noting every detail and word. His brown robes clung to a frail frame, and the man looked like he could keel over at any moment.

"What you've done," Orian continued, "is singlehandedly removed a deep thorn in Xaranor's side. It took us many cycles to gain clues of their whereabouts."

"Then you're welcome," Sarah said, her hand still hovering near her side, "but I get the feeling you still want something."

"Indeed," Orian said. "Our leaders will want you to come back with me for questions. They'll be wanting to meet you in person. Do this willingly and in return, all of these poor souls will be put before our best surgeons. They'll undo the horrors Karaska committed, and send them on their way."

"And if I refuse?" Sarah asked.

"You'll still be taken in," Orian said, "but things will be far less pleasant."

Sarah looked around at everyone in the hangar. She glanced up to the walkways where there were people watching from above, and her eyes lingered on a strange woman with color-shifting eyes. She looked at the kids huddled behind the masked figures. Each of them looked ready to fight their way through this. She turned to look at the group behind her. His father straightened, puffed out his chest, and clenched his fists. Amic did the same. In the end, her eyes landed on Kallik. Her blue-green eyes regarded him cooly. Nodding at her, he fixed a vision of the Suttack in his mind. He'd fling that creature all the way to the ceiling of this place and let the artificial gravity do its work. What she said next surprised him.

"So be it," she said. "I'll go, but I want guarantees. These kids get patched up, and you do everything you can to get them back with their families."

"I can guarantee we'll try," Orian said. Sarah nodded, and he continued. "So, that settles it then. I'll be returning to the Cloudburst, but I'll leave behind a small retinue to ensure you make it to the correct coordinates. I hope your navigators know what they are doing."

2

Orian left once everyone cleared from the hangar. He made a final comment about having to track a ship, and Kallik could guess which ship he was referring to. Kallik just hoped Nath was as far away from this place as physically possible. Orian had left behind a single conduit and a single masked individual which he later found out were called morak'casai. Whatever that meant. For the time being, Kallik mulled over what the future might hold for them while he chewed on a protein cube. The round table in the center of the mess hall accommodated himself along with his father and cousin. The dull gray panels and utilitarian design of the counters and food vendors didn't exactly excite Kallik, but were at least a welcome change to the stark white he had learned to dread from the planet below. All of them sat in silence as they ate, too focused on their food to be bothered by anything else. His father looked to have lost more than a few kilograms especially around the stomach.

After their confrontation in the hangar, Sarah had been all but dragged away by the ship's doctor, and Kallik hadn't seen her since. He hoped she was doing okay. The other kids were allowed to wander as they chose, but not before a Dwemyri named Thusi gave them a tour of the whole ship. Toby's dad and Xoriah's mother were among the survivors Sarah brought back, and they joined the kids on the tour. Kallik, however, wanted nothing more than to sit and eat with his family. Their meal was interrupted by a woman's voice over the ship's comms.

"Vosk family?" The voice asked, "we have a communication request from someone for you."

"Put them through," Kallik's father said.

A hologram appeared above the table. The blue light shimmered and flickered from time to time, but it displayed a solid image of someone Kallik hadn't seen in a very long time. The round belly and broad shoulders of his uncle caused him to resemble his father a lot more than he remembered. Upon seeing the three of them, uncle Ziven's face lit up with joy.

"She did it," he said, "that little beggar actually pulled it off. I'm glad to see you alive, brother. You too, Kallik, you've grown so much since we last spoke. Amic treating you well?"

"All of us are fine," his father said. "If by beggar you mean Sarah, then yes. She's the sole reason we got out."

"I do," Ziven said, "came to my door begging to be let on to my little rescue mission. Anyway, that's beside the point. I just finished speaking with her, and what's this Xaranor business about? She says you won't be coming home for some time yet."

"Nothing to concern yourself over," his father said. "Our captors did something to Kallik here, and there are some doctors that said they'd fix him up. We'll be home before you know it."

"Good, good," Ziven said, "don't take too long. I'm wanting to put together a celebration for your return. Make sure Sarah knows she's invited. In fact, I think the whole crew of the Villimath should be welcomed. Those of them left, anyway."

A strange look crossed his father, one that was contemplative and mournful. He exchanged a look with Amic who pulled up a data-slate and began scrolling through profiles on people.

"How many died to rescue us?" Kallik's father asked.

"One confirmed dead, one severely wounded, another MIA," Ziven said, "but each of them knew the risks when they signed up, and I'm sure they'd do it all over again if they had the chance."

"Almost every member of my crew died," father said. "Just the three of us and old Harold made it out."

A long silence stretched. None of them knew what to say. The conversation made Kallik think of the others lost in the fray. Aillon, Anna, Leo, and all the other kids and their families were gone. No one would be around to mourn them either.

"Maybe we can put together a memorial," Kallik offered, "for all of them. I can help include the ones no one knew. The other kids would help, I'm sure."

"That's a wonderful idea, Kallik," his father said.

"I can work out some details," Ziven said, "maybe integrate it with the celebration. Anyway, I just wanted to hear from you guys in person. I hate to disconnect, but I've got some preparations to get ready. Hurry back, please."

The hologram disappeared and left the three to their meal. Kallik's father rubbed his back with a massive hand and offered a small smile, but the three of them went back to eating in silence.

3

It was Kallik's turn to wander the Villimath and explore. Amic and his father had found the room they were to share and decided to settle down for the evening. It was announced that the ship would jump to its first set of coordinates in a little over an hour. From there, the journey would take three weeks of continuous jumps to reach their target destination. He might as well start to familiarize himself with the ship.

Lines of numerous colors steaked across the gray-paneled walls to direct people toward specific locations. Kallik discovered they didn't account for everything the ship had to offer, however. They pointed to the essentials, yes, but some rooms and cabins went unmarked. Kallik was paying attention to the lines and not where he was going when he bumped into someone as he turned the corner.

It was a tall woman with red hair and a white lab coat. Kallik turned to apologize, but caught her eyes. It was the woman Sarah was glaring at in the hangar. Her irises shifted from a deep violet to a vibrant green, then to an angry orange. Those eyes regarded Kallik like a bird observing a strange rodent that it wasn't sure if it wanted to eat or leave alone. In a blink, the woman shifted her posture to be more welcoming and adorned a pleasant smile.

"You came in with Sarah," she said, "I don't think I caught your name."

Something about the woman's scent put Kallik on edge. Everything about her body language spoke of a relaxed invitation, but Kallik still found something about her he didn't like. If he'd learned anything over the last events is that his gut was a good thing to take advice from.

"I never gave it," he said. He offered little more and glared at her with an apprehensive eye.

"What's with the reproach?" She asked. "Just wanting to get to know you and your friends, is all. No need to put up walls."

"Kallik?" Xoriah called out from down the corridor. "Where've you been?"

"So, Kallik is it?" The woman asked. "I'll be keeping a keen eye on you little Kallik. You haven't seen our mutual friend, have you?"

"Nope," Kallik said and hurried toward his friend. He could feel the woman's eyes on his back, and he did everything he could not to run.

"Who was that?" Xoriah asked as he got close.

"No idea," Kallik said, "but I don't like her."

"Well, if it makes you feel any better," she said, "I found something really cool to show you."

Kallik returned her smile and gestured for her to lead the way. All thoughts of the strange woman fled as the two of them hurried down the corridors. They were joined by Morkus somewhere along the way. The larger boy strode beside them in silence, but his presence was not unwelcome. Despite how they first met,

Morkus was one of them now. Kallik realized he'd miss him once they went their own ways. When that would be was a whole different question.

Xoriah led them up a narrow ladder. She said there was an elevator as well, but all of them agreed they'd prefer a ladder over an elevator for the foreseeable future. They were on the top deck of the Villimath, and soon they were led through a long corridor and into a massive chamber.

Confused, Kallik looked around. Nothing appeared to be special about this room, so why had Xoriah led them here. Blank, gray walls surrounded the circular room and a few leather chairs littered the center. Otherwise, the room was empty. Morkus must be in on the joke because he looked just as excited as Xoriah. She laughed at Kallik's confusion and closed the door behind them. She walked to the other side of the chamber and pushed a button on the far wall. Then, Kallik understood.

A low rumble echoed throughout. Above, the gray walls parted and peeled away to reveal a spectacular view of the cosmos. Once finished, it felt as though the three of them were standing on the outside of the ship. Before he realized what he was doing, Kallik plopped himself down into one of the leather seats and reclined back as far as he could. He could hear Morkus do the same. Xoriah, however, squeezed in next to him in the same chair. His face blushed to the deepest red he'd ever felt, and Kallik hoped she couldn't see it in the dark.

"No Toby?" Kallik blurted out. Stupid, he should just be enjoying the moment.

"Hasn't left his dad's side since they got here," Morkus said, "can't say I blame him."

Kallik tried to steady his breathing as he felt Xoriah's warmth pressed against his side. Only a loser would get flustered like this, but here he was struggling to form a coherent thought. He thought about Toby and Toby's father, about Xoriah being reunited with her mother, and about his own family. Their plight was over, but it felt like there was so much more left to do. He couldn't help but think something much bigger waited for them just around the corner. If only he had the foresight to be able to tell if it were good or bad. He remembered the vision Nath had forced them all to see and shuddered. Xoriah must have taken that as a sign he was cold because she snuggled closer.

"What do you think happens next?" He asked the room.

"I'm not sure," Xoriah said, "but whatever it is, I'm sure it will be beautiful."

EPILOGUE

Jax hummed a familiar tune as she swayed to the rhythm of her own mind. She danced in the little open space the Sheet Skimmer's cockpit offered. Sarah watched from the dark corridor beyond – wrapped in the black cloak with its feathered mantle – and she wore a faint smile on her lips. It was a hungry smile, a seductive smile. The illusion wanted more than a dance, but a dance was all Jax had time for. Unless... no, more important things were about to happen.

The shadows surrounding Sarah laughed at Jax's hesitant choice. They knew what they both wanted. They taunted her in their growled whispers. Jax turned from the corridor to face the wall of the cockpit. There, her newest friend waited.

Percy's face extruded from a pustule of flesh clinging to the cockpit wall. He smiled when he realized Jax was about to give him attention. The face of this mother, Rooth, slumbered just below his. Altogether, the skin covered boil resembled some sort of insect hive stuck to the wall, only it was made of human tissue.

"They'll be coming soon," Percy said, "then we'll all be free."

Jax gave his cheek a pat and checked the monitor to determine the truth of his words. Indeed, the ship that had heralded them was only a few minutes out. She'd best be ready. Jax checked the pistol was still in her pocket and ensured all of the supplies she had left were tucked away in her bag. There would be no need of an enviro-suit as she'd given the approaching ship permission to attach directly to the Sheet Skimmer's airlock. It was about to be the last she'd ever see of this ship, and Jax was glad of it.

The confirmation code chirped through the terminal, and Jax couldn't keep back a giggle. It was a ship alright, a big one, one large enough to get her back to the neutral zone where she belonged. She'd get back to Sarah, the *real* Sarah. Maybe then the illusions would go away.

Sarah laughed at her as if reading her thoughts. It occurred to Jax that this Sarah *could* read her thoughts. She stepped out of the corridor and into the cockpit, leaving the whispering shadows behind. Sarah wrapped her hands around Jax's waist and pulled her close, sliding her fingers under the hem of Jax's pants. Percy laughed and stared while Rooth began to snore.

"We aren't going anywhere, sweet," Sarah said.

Jax pulled away and double checked the monitor. It was time. Avoiding eye contact, she pushed past Sarah and into the corridor beyond. The shadows dispersed around her, but Jax knew they'd be back. They always came back.

She stopped in front of the airlock and waited. Through the windows she could see the other ship prepping its docking maneuvers. She was almost giddy with excitement. How long had she waited? A week? Two? It didn't matter. It was all about to change. A loud thud echoed through the bulkhead as the clamps sealed the two ships together. The doors hissed and slid open. Beyond waited a brightly lit corridor of white and silver metal, a far cry from the dinge she'd grown used to. The entrance to the other ship opened, and a figure began to march down the boarding tube. Each step reverberated with a metal clang as the figure's mechanical legs stomped down the walkway. Jax had to do a double take when she recognized who the legs were carrying. As the figure grew closer a single name slipped from between her parted lips.

"Throx?"

Note from the Author

Here we are. Once more I find myself wrapping up another novel. How it's been quite some time. Over two years have passed since the first run of Carlisle Station. Short, in the grand scheme of things, and as you read this - if you read this - only a matter of days might have gone by between finishing the first and second book. But, to me, it feels as though a lifetime's worth of events have slipped through that passage of time. I republished Carlisle Station under my own name, then republished it again under my own brand. Changed the cover thrice, explored the options of printing privately, switched back to Amazon, second guessed every life choice I've ever made, published anyway. The woes of self-publishing are as endless as they are unforgiving.

As I sit here in the small corner of my small home on the edge of a small town in the middle of nowhere, I can't help but reminisce about all that's transpired between finishing Carlisle Station and finishing A Fear of Kronos. Cathartic in some ways, to finish this novel. It almost didn't happen. More experienced authors like to claim the second book is always the most difficult to pull off. I never believed them, but I should have. I scrapped four separate manuscripts before deciding to reoutline and replot the entire thing. After the second time, there was honest consideration in tossing the series as a whole and moving on to writing smaller one-offs. The opinions and urgings of a couple individuals prevented me from doing just that. Apologies for the wait on this one.

Here's to hoping book three is a smoother ride. I can only imagine what feeling will come with sending out the last novel to this series. That goes to say there's one more book, at least, as far as Sarah is concerned. As I stated in my last note, Sarah will have a trilogy, but Starlight's Eternity Saga may have future titles including more series a few single novels on occasion. There will be break before that, however. A long one as multiple ideas, more contemporary concepts though still horror, are rattling around and demanding to be put to the page. They'll have to be patient enough for one more book. I only hope the next time I pen one of these notes will be sooner than two years from now. As always, thanks for reading.

Acknowledgements

Once again, it takes a crew of people, and an endless amount of support to create a novel. Again, I'd like to start by thanking LaDonna for taking on the task of editing the hack-job I call prose. I promise you the third book will be better yet. I can't promise the article situation will improve. Apologies again. I'd like to next thank the cover artist Indiana Maria Acosta Hernandez aka Indicreates. Your artwork continues to amaze me. Thank you to John Provenzano for taking on production of the audiobook. As with Carlisle Station, I look forward to hearing it. And now I arrive to the last group I'd like to thank, my readers and supporters. Without you, this book would not have happened. No, seriously, the manuscript for this novel would have been left in the drawer never to see the light of day again if it weren't for a few key individuals regularly asking me for updates. You know who you are. Again, to all of you, thank you.

As a special thanks, the following pages are a sneak preview of what's to come in book three. While as of writing this, the novel is far from any form of completeness, I hope it can serve as a wonderful taste of what's to come.

Enjoy.

PREVIEW

Smoke curled from the end of Quince Cane's cigarette. It twisted and plumed and spread across the ceiling of the confined pilot's cabin, the ship's air filtration not quite robust enough to clear it out faster than it spread. It clung to the air like a haze, clouding the monitors surrounding the pilot's chair in a half-moon arch whose blue lights cut through the smog in sharp beams. Quince himself leaned back in the pilot's seat, feat propped up on one of the panels, cigarette hanging loose between his lips. It was early, too early to be awake, but something was making him uneasy. Something strange had awoken him, and caused him to crawl down from the loft to make a pot of coffee and light a smoke. Ned hated his smoking habits, but Ned was asleep. Besides, he'd closed the cabin door to keep the smoke contained.

Removing his cigarette with one hand, he sipped coffee from a mug he held in the other. Though worn, he could still feel the *Universe's Greatest Dad* still carved into the ceramic. Even while taking a sip, Quince kept his eyes glued to one of the monitors. The camera feed from one of his scouting drones projected live updates. He'd stopped the drone from getting too close to his target, instead having it hold in place where it was. It caused the image on his screen to look like a painting, like a portrait of a dull ship hanging in the empty void of nothingness. The closest star was far enough away that little light played across the other ship's hull, making it seem more a shadow than anything real. Something about the image made his stomach uneasy.

He could feel the heat of the cigarette getting close to his fingers, so Quince tapped the ashes into his mug and dropped the butt in with a hiss. The coffee had grown cold anyway. One of the monitors to his left beeped to indicate someone was trying to connect via a long-distance communication satellite. As he reached to answer, however, the cabin door slid open, and an angry Ned stormed through. Quince glanced over the back of the pilot's seat to see the man's broad shoulders and round belly bounce as he coughed and muttered about the smoke.

"I told you not to smoke on my ship," Ned said. The man's scraggly beard reminded Quince that he needed to shave. His own graying stubble was starting to itch something fierce, but a part of him thought it complimented his undercut.

"Our ship," Quince corrected.

"I acquired it," Ned said.

"Stole it," Quince corrected again and took a sip of his coffee. Realizing his mistake, he winced but kept the coffee at hand.

"The previous owner abandoned it," Ned said, "just left it right there for the taking. With all its unpaid docking fees, I was just doing those poor dock workers a favor."

"And I'm sure you had nothing to do with the silly name, either." Quince said.

"I think Bill is quite the majestic name for a ship, no?" Ned paused, noticing for the first time what was up on the monitor. He forgot the smoke and the conversation both, and leaned over the pilot's seat to get a better look. "That our target?"

"It is," Quince said. He sank back into the seat and stared at the image some more. It was a perfect match of the report. Dwemyri made, sophisticated tech engineered from recycled parts, it held no registered name through either the HFS or the CRG. Its only identifying mark being a white triangle painted on one side.

"Well?" Ned asked. "What are we waiting for? Let's get this show moving. Old Ned here's got some bills to pay."

"Hold up," Quince said. "Something about this feels wrong. I think we leave this one be, yeah? Pick up something else."

"Quince," Ned said and patted Quince's shoulder, "we

spent all our credits getting here. There *is* no something else. Besides, what if my ex-wife shows up and steals all the loot? Hate the thought of that."

"Ned," Quince said. He took on the tone of a patient parent lecturing their toddler. "We're on the outer edge of the Neutral Zone, skirting the very edge of uncharted space."

"What's your point?" Ned asked.

"The odds of your ex-wife and her crew making it aaalll the way out here at the same time as us is next to impossible."

"Next to," Ned said, "but the odds are still there."

Another beep sounded from a different monitor. Quince looked up to see a proximity sensor sounding off as another ship jumped into nearby space. His gut told him there was no need to run a scan on the registration, but he did so nonetheless. Sure enough, an ID pinged marking the ship as the Brass Pony, the captain being a woman named Miranda Bay. Ned's ex-wife was on course to intercept the derelict ship. The big man's meaty hand clapped Quince's shoulder as they both realized who it was, and Quince started powering up the engines.

"Where's Frisco at?" Quince asked as the ship rumbled to life.

"Powered him down for the night," Ned said, "think he's broken. Kept asking if I wanted tea before bed."

"Get him ready," Quince said, "we're going to need to be quick with this."

Ned turned to do just that, but stopped. "Say," he started, "there weren't any survivors on that ship, were there?"

"Vital scans showed two," Quince said. "One Dwemyri, one human. Why do you ask?"

"My ex gets to them first," Ned said, "they won't be survivors for long."

Quince glanced at the visual feed once more. The smoke was clearing and so was his head. Ned was right. If Miranda got to that ship first, disaster would follow them all the way back to the Ifrit. Setting down his coffee cup, he put both hands on the control sticks. The bad feeling in his stomach refused to go away, however. Just what exactly were they getting themselves into?

About the Author

Colton lives, works and writes from Iowa in the Midwestern United States. He's worked mostly in the field of digital media marketing and graphic design, however, writing has always been his passion.

Colton has decided to pursue his passions and make the shift into taking writing seriously and push his talents as far as he can. Whether he has one reader, one hundred readers, or thousands of readers, Colton intends to write stories he's passionate about until he can no longer physically do so.